# Raffles
# of the Albany

BARRY PEROWNE

# Raffles
# of the Albany

FOOTPRINTS OF A FAMOUS
GENTLEMAN CROOK IN THE TIMES
OF A GREAT DETECTIVE

'Lives of great men all remind us
We can make our own sublime
And, departing, leave behind us
Footprints on the sands of Crime.'
—Longfellow, as misquoted by Raffles.

ST. MARTIN'S PRESS   NEW YORK

Though certain real characters from history have been introduced in these stories, all the episodes described are fictitious.

**Library of Congress Cataloging in Publication Data**
Perowne, Barry.
   Raffles of the Albany.
   I. Title.
PZ3.P426Rafm3 [PR6031.E54] 823'.9'12 76-28049
ISBN 312-66220-3

To
Otto Penzler, Crime Encyclopædist

In respectful memory of the Gentleman
Crook's creator, E. W. HORNUNG, and
his Great Brother-in-Law, the Real-Life
Original of Raffles' fictional contemporary,
the World's Most Renowned Investigator.

Grateful acknowledgment is made to the following magazines for permission to reprint the stories in this volume:

*Ellery Queen's Mystery Magazine* for: 'The *Victory* Match' (originally titled 'Enigma Of The Admiral's Hat'); 'John L. Sullivan Obliges' (originally titled 'The Raffles Bombshell'); 'Tusitala and the Money-Belt' (originally titled 'Raffles and the Money-Belt'); 'Carriages for Buckingham Palace' (originally titled 'Raffles and the Midnight Hansom'); 'Dinah Raffles and Oscar Wilde' (originally titled 'Raffles and the Bridge of Sighs'); 'The Baffling of Oom Paul' (originally titled 'The Raffles Special'); 'Raffles and the Automobile Gang' (originally titled 'The Raffles Hunt'); 'The *Baskerville* Match' (originally titled 'Raffles on the Trail of the Hound').

*Saint Magazine* for: 'Adventure of the Dancing Girls' (originally titled 'Raffles and the Innocents'); 'Cocaine and the Thief with Trembling Hands' (originally titled 'Raffles and the Showman's Safe'); 'Stealing the Venetian Horses' (originally titled 'Raffles and the Long Golfers').

# CONTENTS

# 1    THE *VICTORY* MATCH

'Moral or otherwise, Bunny,' said Raffles. 'it's a fact of life that possession is nine points of the law.'

His remark was prompted by a correspondence that had been going on for months in *The Times* about some ancient bas-reliefs, the Thracian Marbles, unearthed by an archaeologist on a field expedition and presented by him to the British Museum.

'That savant's probably hoping,' I said, 'to be awarded a peerage by the Queen.'

'Talking of whom,' said Raffles, 'this royal occasion we're on our way to should be a pretty good week, with luck.'

Immaculate in a summer suit, a pearl in his cravat, his dark hair crisp, his keen face tanned, he tossed aside the newspaper and offered me a Sullivan from his cigarette-case.

The train in which we were speeding through the sun-basking countryside was bound for Portsmouth, which Her Majesty, making one of her now rare public appearances, was visiting for the purpose of declaring Navy Week open.

Among the official functions and sporting events arranged for the week was a three-day cricket match between the Royal Navy and a Gentlemen-of-England team captained, for the first time, by A. J. Raffles.

At Portsmouth Town station we found our host, the skipper of the Navy team, Lieutenant-Commander Braithwaite, in dazzling white naval uniform, waiting to greet us off the train.

'You and Bunny Manders here, Raffles, are the first of the Gentlemen blokes to arrive,' said Braithwaite, as we followed a porter carrying our valises and Raffles' cricket-bag to a waiting four-wheeler. 'The Navy Week opening ceremony went off very well this morning. You'll get a chance to see the Queen after lunch. She's due to board the royal yacht at two o'clock, at Portsmouth Hard, and proceed to Osborne House on the Isle of Wight, just across the water. To see her pass by, I'd hoped to get you fellows on board *Victory*—'

'Nelson's old flagship,' I said, 'at the Battle of Trafalgar?'

'Yes, indeed,' said Braithwaite, as our open cab jingled through streets ablaze in the sunshine with flags and pictures of the Queen. 'There's a public outcry from time to time for *Victory*'s preservation, so the old flagship's been given a coat of paint in honour of the Queen's visit and towed to an anchorage on the Gosport side of the harbour. But only invited bigwigs are allowed on board *Victory* today—including a bunch of millionaires.'

'Millionaires?' said Raffles, with quickened interest.

'The international social set,' Braithwaite explained. 'Commodore Vanderbilt, the Duke of Westminster, the Prince of Monaco, Mr. Leonard Jerome of New York with his beautiful daughter Jennie and her husband, Lord Randolph Churchill. All that crowd, real swells! They've come over in parties for the day from their private steam-yachts which are at Cowes for the Regatta.'

Cowes Regatta! Raffles and I exchanged a rueful look. We had clean forgotten the most brilliant event of the summer social season. At Cowes some lucrative adventure might have come our way. Instead, Raffles had tied himself up in a three-day cricket match on just the wrong side of the water. What irony!

'By courtesy of the Admiralty,' Braithwaite was saying, 'Portsmouth's been loaned, in honour of the Queen's visit, a national treasure—the hat and the bloodstained knee-breeches, nankeen waistcoat and swallowtail blue coat with epaulettes which Nelson was wearing when he fell, mortally wounded, in the very hour of his triumph at Trafalgar. From tomorrow *Victory*'ll be open for the public to view Nelson's uniform, on display in the wardroom, but today only those invited bigwigs are on board. Still, I can get you on to a Navy tug to see the Queen pass by presently in the royal yacht.'

After lunch at a grand old waterfront inn, The Lord Nelson, where our Navy hosts had arranged billets for the visiting cricket team with myself as supernumerary, my cricket not being up to Gentlemen standard, Braithwaite conducted Raffles and me aboard the tug *Gosport Jezebel*. And as she steamed out sturdily from her berth, the great harbour, backed by the Portsdown Hill forts built to repel the Grand Army of Napoleon, presented a memorable sight in the sun-glare, being crowded with craft

2

of every description, all laden with sightseers, many of them waving Union Jacks.

Besides Raffles and myself, there were a few other favoured civilians on board *Jezebel*, and as I leaned with Raffles and Braithwaite against the tug's throbbing rail, a cloud of strong shag-tobacco smoke drifted my way from the pipe of some man who had come up behind us.

'There she is, Watson,' I heard a voice say—'the old *Victory*, as taut and trim as on the day Nelson sailed her, at the head of the fleet, into the blood and thunder of Trafalgar.'

'A study in scarlet, that day,' a second voice said.

'Yes, indeed. Look, Watson, there's a vacant space at the rail along there. Let's claim it.'

Braithwaite, seeing Raffles and me glance round at the two frock-coated, silk-hatted men as they strolled away along the deck, the taller, burlier man tossing pipe-smoke over his shoulder, told us who they were.

'The shorter chap,' said Braithwaite, 'is a Mr. James Watson, Secretary of the Portsmouth Literary and Scientific Society. The big fellow with him is a Dr. A. Conan Doyle, in medical practice in Southsea. Not many people have heard of him, but mark my words—he'll be a Man Who Counts, one of these days. I say, though, by Jove, look at the rank and fashion on the old *Victory*.'

Our tug had hove-to as near as was permitted to Nelson's flagship, around which circling whaleboats rowed by sailors preserved a space of water clear of the jostling sightseeing craft.

The bowsprit chains of the fine old ship-of-the-line shone like silver. Her masts, yards and intricate rigging towered to the blue sky. Her oaken hull was freshly tarred. Through her open gunports, framed in fresh white paint, her guns looked ready to rumble out with a lion's roar from their muzzles.

On her decks, her distinguished visitors stood about in groups, conversing. Elegant ladies twirled their parasols languidly. Jewels sparkled. The top hats and gold watch-chains of the millionaires glistened in the hot sunshine.

'So near, Bunny,' Raffles murmured to me—'yet so far!'

Braithwaite explained to us that some of the unfamiliar naval uniforms visible on board *Victory* were those of Captains from American, Greek, German and other foreign warships which, on

3

courtesy visits for Navy Week, were lying at anchor off the Isle of Wight.

Suddenly the report of cannon clapped across the harbour.

'First minute-gun of the royal salute,' said Braithwaite. 'The Queen's yacht is putting out.'

The guns of the saluting battery at Haslar Point continued to fire at one-minute intervals through the storm of cheering as the august vessel flying the scarlet-and-gold of the Royal Standard steamed into view through the multitude of small craft that made way for her stately progress.

Up the rigging of *Victory*, as the royal yacht approached, raced bare-footed sailors in the uniform of Nelson's time, the two topmost men running out to either tip of the mainmast yard, to stand rigidly at attention there, dizzily aloft, as the whole team formed in the rigging a gigantic V—alike for *Victory* and for the royal widow whose tiny figure, in black shawl and jet-beaded bonnet, stood in regal solitude, well apart from her clustered ladies-in-waiting, on the deck of her yacht steaming slowly by.

As the Queen passed and, to the continued firing of the minute-guns, the royal yacht began to recede towards the harbour-mouth, a wild cry reached my ears. Looking up quickly, I was just in time to see the sailor balanced on the larboard tip of *Victory*'s mainmast-yard sway giddily and, falling, turn helplessly in the air and strike the water with a glittering splash.

Instantly, the *Jezebel*'s bridge-telegraph bell clanged, the tug throbbed to life, and I hardly heard the cheering, further off, or the continuing reports of the saluting battery's guns as, with a dozen other assorted craft, sightseers and Navy whaleboats, we surged to the rescue.

One of the Navy whaleboats beat us to it. As our tug slowed alongside, I saw sailors in the whaleboat heaving the fallen man in, drenched and apparently unconscious, over their gunwale. They stretched him on the floorboards and, at a barked order from their midshipman coxswain, bent to their oars and, leaving a dozen flung lifebelts and a confusion of would-be rescue craft bobbing on the water, pulled around under the chains of *Victory*'s great bowsprit and passed from my view.

It was smartly done.

Even before the last report of the saluting cannons marked

the passing of the Queen's yacht out of the harbour-mouth, the incident was over.

Yet, if rumour was to be believed, something else had happened on board H.M.S. *Victory.*

From what source the rumour emanated I had no idea, but by the time we disembarked from the tug *Jezebel* at Portsmouth Hard the excited crowd there was abuzz with a story that a Marine sentry guarding Nelson's uniform in *Victory*'s wardroom had been found chloroformed shortly after the Queen had passed —and that, with the exception of the hat, Horatio Nelson's uniform, stained at Trafalgar with his lifeblood, had disappeared.

'Impossible!' Braithwaite kept saying, as he, Raffles and I elbowed our way through the crowd besieging some waiting cabs. 'Nelson's uniform stolen? It just *can't* be true!'

A whiff of smoke from the pipe of Dr. Conan Doyle, who, with Mr. Watson, was just ahead of us, making for the cabs, floated back to me.

'*Can* it be true?' I heard Mr. Watson ask.

'The mention of the hat, Watson,' replied his companion, 'has a circumstantial ring. Yes, I think this rumour *could* have some factual basis.'

'In which case, does any point occur to you to which particular attention should be devoted?'

'The hat, Watson—the enigma of the Admiral's hat.'

'But people are saying the hat was *not* taken!'

'That is the enigma, Watson.'

People pushed between us at that moment, and I lost sight of the two men.

Raffles and I dined, that night, at the Royal Naval Barracks. The rest of the Gentlemen cricket team had arrived during the day and all of us were dinner guests of the Navy team in a vast room from the walls of which gilt-framed portraits of bygone admirals, of Mr. Samuel Pepys, sometime Secretary of the Navy, and of Horatio Nelson himself, wearing what was in all probability the very uniform which now had been stolen from his old flagship, gazed down on us.

The *Victory* crime was indeed a fact. At dinner, the talk was of nothing else, and I gathered that the rating who had fallen from the yardarm was an Able-Seaman John Hayter. His fall was said to have been due to sunstroke and he was now in

5

Haslar Naval Hospital with concussion and a dislocated shoulder. As for the Marine sentry, apparently he had been chloroformed from behind and could state only that his assailant had been a man of great strength.

'What about the distinguished guests, Braithwaite?' Raffles asked.

'They had to be regarded, of course, as above suspicion,' said Braithwaite. 'They've all dispersed now.'

'The millionaires gone back to their steam-yachts at Cowes?' said Raffles. 'H'm! Has the Navy called in the Hampshire Constabulary?'

'Naturally. Police reinforcements are pouring in from all over.'

'Including the Isle of Wight?'

'Yes, indeed,' said Braithwaite. 'Except for the Queen's bobbies, guarding her at Osborne House, not many police will be left, over in the island.'

'Steward,' Raffles said, a thoughtful look in his grey eyes, 'I'll trouble you for a little more of that wine.'

As we were leaving the Barracks, Braithwaite handed Raffles a book with a coloured cover.

'It's a yarn called *A Study In Scarlet*, published not long ago,' said Braithwaite. 'That doctor chap, Conan Doyle, who was on the *Jezebel* this afternoon, wrote it—in his spare time, as he doesn't get many patients.'

'This'll give me something to read in bed tonight,' Raffles said, pocketing the book in his red-lined evening cape. 'See you in the morning, Braithwaite—ten-thirty on the cricket ground.'

Out of curiosity, I borrowed *A Study In Scarlet* from Raffles next morning. He told me he had skimmed through it in bed. Not being a player myself, I commandeered a deck-chair on the pavilion terrace at the cricket ground and sat in the sunshine, reading the book, while the game went on.

A remarkable individual turned out to be by far the most important character in the yarn. A private investigator of crime, who claimed to have methods of his own, he held my interest. Even when Raffles went in to bat, second wicket down, I read on with increasing absorption—until a sudden collective groan from the spectators who, mostly in Navy whites, ringed the boundary, made me look up.

Out at the wicket, on the great, green expanse of flawless turf, Raffles had thrown down his bat. He was unwinding the tape of his right hand batting-glove. As he pulled it off, I saw blood dripping from his fingers.

'Bad luck, Raffles,' I heard Braithwaite call, as Raffles wrapped his handkerchief round his hand. 'Will it put you out of the match?'

'I'm afraid so,' Raffles replied, and he headed for the pavilion. 'Kicking ball, Bunny,' he told me, as he came up the steps. 'Split my forefinger open. It'll need a stitch or two, by the look of it. I'll get changed and join you.'

I had an uneasy suspicion about the mishap, and when he rejoined me I accused him of having invited the damage.

'Not entirely, Bunny,' he said, as we left the ground. 'I intended to get out of the match, but that ball came at me very fast and I mistimed it more than I'd planned. A mere bruised wrist would have served my purpose. Still, no matter—I'm out of the game. It's only a friendly, and you and I have fish to fry at Cowes Regatta—goldfish!'

He gave me a wicked look.

A hansom was passing. He hailed it and, as the horse jingled to a standstill, asked the cabbie, 'D'you know the address of a Dr. Doyle?'

'Yes, sir—Number One, Bush Villas, Elm Grove, Southsea.'

'No, Raffles,' I said. 'Not *that* doctor!'

'Why not?' said Raffles, surprised.

'I can't say exactly. This book of his—I just feel, somehow—'

'Pure fiction, Bunny—hobby of a doctor who doesn't get many patients, so he'll probably be glad of a fee. Come on, hop in!'

Bush Villas, in residential, tree-shaded Elm Grove, proved to be a terrace of four houses, tall and dignified, with lace-curtained windows and bathbricked front steps.

Raffles gave the bellpull of Number One a tug with his undamaged hand.

The polished brass nameplate on the area railings had a newish look, as though the doctor had not been long in practice. And in fact, when he in person opened the door to us, he looked to be, though himself tall and dignified, with a bushy brown moustache, no more than about thirty, half-a-dozen or so years Raffles' senior.

Powerfully built, frock-coated, a watch-chain looped across his white waistcoat, the doctor seemed to take us in at a single glance of his keen blue eyes.

7

'One of the Gentlemen cricketers had a knock on the hand, eh?' he said. 'Come in.'

'That was a quick diagnosis,' said Raffles, as we entered.

'Navy *v.* Gentlemen is the Match of the Week,' said Dr. Doyle, leading the way into a small surgery off the rather sparsely furnished hall. 'You're not in uniform, so you're not Navy. You're wearing a Zingari Club cravat, so you *are* a cricketer.'

'Hence,' said Raffles, with a smile, 'one of the Gents? I see. Doctor, my name's Raffles. This is my friend Manders.'

'Well, let's have a look at that hand, Mr. Raffles.'

'A study in scarlet,' said Raffles, unwinding the gory handkerchief.

'From that remark,' said Dr. Doyle, 'I gather you're one of the multitude of a dozen or so who've read my little shocker. H'm! Who did this to your finger—the Navy's fast bowler? He always leaves a trail of blood. Incidentally,' the doctor went on, as, having given Raffles' finger a jab of local anaesthetic, he threaded a needle with surgical gut, 'didn't I see you gentlemen on the tug *Jezebel* yesterday?'

'We were there,' said Raffles, as the doctor worked on his finger. 'What would your detective character make of this theft from H.M.S. *Victory*?'

'I fancy he'd be interested in the minute-guns, Mr. Raffles.'

'The guns?' said Raffles, surprised.

'Everything,' said Dr. Doyle, 'tends to indicate that the crime was the carefully planned work of a number of persons. They can have prearranged to co-ordinate their respective actions by means of the cannon reports.'

'What a novel use of the royal salute!' Raffles exclaimed.

'The crime presents several features of interest to an inquiring mind.' The doctor completed the stitching of Raffles' finger, bandaged it, slid a kid-leather black finger-stall over it. 'There you are then, Mr. Raffles.'

'Thank you, Dr. Doyle. What fee do I owe you?'

'You won't be able to play,' said the doctor, 'but I take it you'll be at the cricket ground? Very well. We'll see about a fee when I have another look at that finger and take the stitches out. Drop in here towards the end of the week.'

The genial doctor ushered us out, and the door of Number One, Bush Villas, Elm Grove, closed on us.

That afternoon found us, not at the cricket ground, but over

8

in the nearby Isle of Wight, reconnoitring the magnificent steam-yachts gathered at Cowes—among them, Commodore Vanderbilt's; the Duke of Westminster's, with Mr. Leonard Jerome and Lord and Lady Randolph Churchill in his party; the S/Y *Achilleion*, property of the Greek merchant-shipping millionaire Mr. Aristotle Andiakis; and a graceful vessel flying the candy-striped burgee of the famous yachtsman and ichthyologist, Prince Albert of Monaco.

'Excellent, Bunny,' said Raffles, as the little puffing-billy train carried us away through the lingering summer twilight to Ryde, where we would board the paddle-steamer ferry back to Clarence Pier, Southsea. 'Tomorrow, as skipper of the Gentlemen team, I shall have to put in an appearance at the cricket match for a few hours. While I'm there, you can look around for some togs we shall need.'

'Togs?' I said. 'What kind of togs?'

'Nautical togs,' said Raffles—'so that, in the evening, we can return, dressed as longshoremen, to Cowes. We'll then make our move as opportunity offers. There's a small fortune in sparklers to be picked up in the ladies' cabins of any one of those millionaire yachts.'

Next morning, while Raffles was at the cricket ground, I hunted Portsmouth for a sailors' secondhand slopshop, and found one in the old Portsea area, birthplace of Charles Dickens when his Mr. Micawberish father had been a civilian clerk employed by the Navy.

I bought a couple of blue jerseys and well-worn longshoremen type caps.

Just as I was about to leave the slopshop, where a dissolute parrot squawked salty insults at me from a cage among the junk, I saw Dr. Doyle and Mr. Watson.

They were on the other side of the narrow street, looking in at the window of a foreign-looking little restaurant—the Corfu Restaurant, according to the name on the window, from which lobsters on a bed of seaweed gazed with stalked eyes and waved languid antennae.

'You can get good shellfish across the street,' said the slopshop man, seeing the direction of my gaze as I hesitated, watching Dr. Doyle and Mr. Watson go into the restaurant. 'It's run by a Mrs. Miranda Hayter, widder of a Royal Navy gunner-rating.'

'It's far too early for lunch,' I said—which was in fact so

9

true that, as I slunk out of the slopshop with my brown-paper parcel, I could not help wondering what Dr. Doyle and Mr. Watson were doing in the restaurant across the way.

Suddenly I remembered something. I at once hailed a cab, jingled off to the Lord Nelson Inn, locked the parcel into the valise in my room there, then continued to the cricket ground.

I found Raffles watching the game from a deckchair on the pavilion terrace. I told him I had just seen Dr. Doyle and Mr. Watson.

'The name of the woman who runs the restaurant is Hayter,' I said. 'Raffles, the name of the sailor who fell from *Victory*'s yardarm is Able-Seaman Hayter!'

'Well done, Bunny,' Raffles said. 'This is interesting news. Dr. Doyle must have stumbled on to something to do with the *Victory* crime. He's probably following it up. And the major part of the County Constabulary's fully preoccupied with the same crime. Nothing could suit us better! As opportunists, you and I've never had such a chance as this. Over in the Isle of Wight tonight, we'll be on an easy wicket—and something good is bound to turn up for us.'

Yet, somehow, I could not shake off a feeling of uneasiness when, dressed as jerseyed longshoremen, we slouched, hands in pockets, off the little puffing-billy island train at Cowes Station that evening.

The small town, all yacht-building yards, sail lofts, rope-walks and ship's chandlery stores, was *en fête* for the Regatta.

We sauntered around the harbour, where the beautiful racing-yachts, their masts a forest of bare poles, lay moored against the harbour-wall, while the millionaires' yachts, lying at their anchors, were a scene of animation. Under Japanese lanterns pendent from the deck-awnings, jewelled ladies and plutocrats in evening dress were dining to the squeak and sob of violins played by hireling musicians. Much further out, in the Channel, twinkled the lights of warships, British and visiting ironclads at anchor.

Throngs of sailors, liberty men, many of them from the foreign warships, were roistering in and out of the water-front taverns.

'We haven't a chance, Raffles,' I said. 'There are too many people on those millionaire steam-yachts.'

He gripped my arm. 'Bunny, there's a boat putting ashore from the S/Y *Achilleion*—and there's a carriage pulling up on the wharf along there and a crowd of sailors gathering round it. Let's see what's going on.'

We added ourselves to the throng around the open carriage and saw at once why it had attracted attention. The top-hatted driver and groom on the box wore the royal livery; on the glossy doors of the carriage were the initials V.R. surmounted by a crown.

'The Queen sending a carriage to take somebody to Osborne House?' Raffles murmured. 'Bunny, it's highly unusual for Her Majesty to receive a visitor at her summer residence.'

Alongside the sea-weedy, water-lapped steps of the harbour wall, the S/Y *Achilleion*'s boat drew in. Oars were shipped and willing hands held the boat steady for a tall man of striking appearance to step out. His face leather-dark, aquiline, with a square-cut iron-grey beard and a monocle, he wore full evening dress and a scarlet-lined cape, the azure ribbon of some foreign Order of Chivalry slanting across his shirtfront.

'Mr. Aristotle Andiakis,' Raffles murmured to me.

With the demeanour of a king, the merchant-shipping million-aire came up the steps and, the royal groom holding open the door for him, mounted into the carriage. Closing the door, the groom climbed back up to the box, to sit stiffly there with folded arms as the coachman touched up the two noble black horses with his whip and the royal carriage clattered off along the wharf.

The boat's crew from S/Y *Achilleion* tied up their boat and, like the sailors who had gathered around, repaired to the nearest tavern.

'Bunny,' said Raffles, 'I told you something good was bound to turn up for us. Look at the *Achilleion* out there. Very few lights on board. Mr. Andiakis evidently has no party of guests. The owner and most of the crew are now ashore. There'll only be an anchor watch on the yacht. Now's our chance! Let's borrow a dinghy. There are dozens moored around the harbour wall.'

From a lampless section of the harbour we commandeered a dinghy. The oars were lying in it. I put them in the rowlocks and, with Raffles piloting me in such a way as enabled us to avoid the lights reflected on the water, I pulled out towards the S/Y *Achilleion*.

From the Greek yacht, as we neared it, sounded a sudden sharp report.

'It's all right,' Raffles whispered. 'Just a champagne cork. There are two or three men on the yacht's bridge. They seem to be drinking toasts. Pull on your right oar a bit. Now—both oars together—gently—to bring us under the yacht's counter.'

As the jut of the counter loomed shadowy over us, Raffles leaped up, making the dinghy rock, and got a two-handed grip on the yacht's deck-coaming. He pulled himself up, vanished soundlessly on board.

Letting the oars trail in the rowlocks, I checked the dinghy against the yacht's rudder. And here, in the deep shadow cast by the S/Y *Achilleion*'s counter, the sultry thumping of my heart measured out my vigil.

It seemed interminable. Reflected ribbons of light trembled on the harbour water. Music, voices, laughter reached me faintly from the other millionaire steam-yachts. Sweat stung my eyes, salted my lips. My throat grew parched.

What in God's name was Raffles doing? I strained my ears. No sound from *Achilleion*. Raffles had been gone too long. I cursed him. I wished I had never met him. I swore he would never again lure me into such a situation as this. I would see him in hell first.

And there suddenly he was—not in hell, but a dark-jerseyed figure dangling from the yacht's deck-coaming. I brought the dinghy under him. He dropped into its sternsheets almost without sound.

'Shove off, Bunny,' he whispered. 'The quicker we're away from here, the better!'

I asked no questions. I dipped my oars cautiously, cursing the slight creak of the rowlocks as I pulled away from the *Achilleion*'s stern. All seemed quiet on the yacht, but I sensed from Raffles' tone that things had not worked out to his liking.

We tied up the dinghy where we had found it. In the distance, a train whistled.

'Puffing Billy coming in from Ryde,' said Raffles. 'It'll start back in a few minutes—and we'll be on it!'

We were on the wooden platform of the station when the diminutive locomotive came steaming into view.

'What happened, Raffles?' I said, as the train approached.

'Most of the cabins seemed unused, Bunny. But I found Mr. Andiakis's day cabin—furnished as a study, luxurious. There was a small safe in it—combination-lock—fairly simple. I got it open—'

12

He broke off, gripped my arm, jerked me into the tiny waiting-room.

'Look who's getting off the train, Bunny!'

I peered out through the grimy glass of the waiting-room window. Stepping from a compartment of the now stationary train were Dr. Conan Doyle, pipe in mouth, and Mr. Watson. Frock-coated and silk-hatted, the two men strode with an intent, purposeful air out of the station.

'What on earth,' I whispered, 'brings *them* to Cowes?'

'It can only be one thing, Bunny—the contents of Mr. Aristotle Andiakis's safe. Dr. Doyle's got on the trail somehow.'

'The trail of what?'

'Horatio Nelson's bloodstained uniform, Bunny—in the safe on the S/Y *Achilleion!*'

I felt stunned as we boarded the train. We had a compartment to ourselves. Raffles offered me a Sullivan from his cigarette-case. Never had I seen him so tense.

'What did you do?' I said, as the train clattered along through the starlit meadows towards Ryde and the ferry-steamers.

'I shut the safe,' Raffles said grimly, 're-set the combination, wiped off everything I'd touched, and got off that yacht. The *Victory* crime's set all England by the ears, Bunny. You and I want nothing whatever to do with it.'

'My God, no!'

'As skipper of the Gentlemen team,' Raffles said, 'I shall have to be at the cricket ground when the match ends, then we'll get out of Portsmouth without delay, and follow *Victory* crime developments like everybody else—in the newspapers!'

In the newspapers next morning, when we seized them at breakfast in the panelled dining-room of the Lord Nelson Inn, there was not one word about the *Victory* crime. The sudden, total silence on the subject, when previously the papers had been full of it, seemed strange, unnatural, somehow sinister.

The cricket match finished just after five o'clock that afternoon, the Navy winning by six wickets. Raffles, telling Braithwaite we had an engagement in London, got us out of the usual post-match carouse at the Naval Barracks, and we went straight to the Lord Nelson and packed our valises.

I carried mine into Raffles' room, added it to his valise and cricket-bag. Ready for the inn bumpkin to carry down, they were on the fourposter bed in which Nelson himself had probably spent many a night.

Raffles, immaculate in a light tweed suit, a pearl in his cravat, was standing in the window-bay with its wide-open diamond-paned casements. Smoking a cigarette, he was gazing out thoughtfully over Portsmouth harbour.

'Look at the old *Victory*, Bunny,' he said, as I joined him at the window—'lying peacefully at her anchor out there. I wonder just what's going on—behind that tranquil scene?'

'Let's go,' I said. 'I'll ring for the bumpkin.'

Almost as I spoke, hoofs clinked on cobbles, harness jingled, wheels ground. A hansom pulled up, below. Two frock-coated, silk-hatted men stepped out—Dr. Doyle and Mr. James Watson. They entered the inn.

We looked at each other.

'Can't be anything to do with us,' said Raffles.

But my throat had gone dry. We waited tensely.

A firm knock sounded on the door. The latch lifted. The door creaked open. Dr. Doyle stood looking at us.

He came in. He seemed bigger than ever, formidable, under the low, beamed ceiling. He was followed by Mr. Watson.

'Just leaving?' Dr. Doyle said, glancing at our luggage on the bed. 'Mr. Raffles, there's a bill outstanding.'

'Doctor,' said Raffles, and I sensed and shared his relief as he glanced at his finger-stalled hand, 'I'm so sorry. I'd clean forgotten this. How much do I owe you?'

'That depends. Watson, make sure that door's quite closed.'

His blue eyes intent on Raffles, the Elm Grove doctor took pipe and tobacco-pouch from his pocket.

'Mr. Raffles,' he said, loading the pipe, 'let's discuss the *Victory* crime. First, the enigma of the Admiral's hat. Why was it not taken? Reflection suggested to me that the stiff, glazed hat was not amenable, as were the other garments, to being tightly rolled-up for concealment in some receptacle—a receptacle that would have to be very quickly spirited off *Victory*, since a minute search of the ship would have been in progress even before the distinguished guests left her. Perforce, those guests had to be regarded as above suspicion. They were neither questioned nor searched. Yet, even had one of them been guilty, in what receptacle could the uniform have been concealed?'

'One of the distinguished ladies' reticules?' Raffles suggested.

14

'Not big enough. However, Mr. Raffles, recall the scene of the fallen sailor's rescue. When we saw him pulled into the whaleboat, a number of objects were floating on the water—objects flung from *Victory* and from several sightseeing craft, including the tug *Jezebel*. I refer to lifebelts.'

The doctor, lighting his pipe, puffed smoke from under his bushy moustache, his steady eyes on Raffles.

'I came to the conclusion,' Dr. Doyle went on, 'that Nelson's bloodstained uniform left his old flagship inside one of her own lifebelts—prepared beforehand by cutting out part of the cork, thus hollowing the lifebelt, then plugging the orifice with part of the cut-out cork and roughly stitching back the canvas cover. If the prepared lifebelt were then placed among those in *Victory*'s wardroom lockers, all the man who chloroformed the Marine sentry would have then to do would be to slash the stitches of the canvas, pull out the cork plug, thrust the tightly-rolled uniform into the orifice, replace the cork plug. Meantime, every eye on board *Victory*—except his own—was watching the Queen pass. *But*—for that lifebelt to be thrown overboard by the Marine's assailant, certainly a member of *Victory*'s crew, somebody had to fall, spectacularly, into the water.'

'Able-Seaman John Hayter,' said Mr. Watson.

'Quite so, Watson. And the agile Seaman Hayter and his crewmate confederate co-ordinated their respective actions by means of the minute-guns of the royal salute—while other confederates, in one of the sightseeing small craft, watched for their fellow-conspirator, the chloroformer, to throw the relevant lifebelt, so that they could retrieve and make off with it in the confusion of the rescue.'

'Quite simple, really,' said Mr. Watson.

'When analysed, Watson, and explained,' said Dr. Doyle, with a hint of asperity. But his gaze remained steadily on Raffles. 'Inquiry at the Navy Records Office provided me with the home address of Seaman Hayter, who proved to be a Portsmouth-born man, like many sailors. Mr. Watson and I visited that address, a small restaurant owned by Hayter's mother—a woman from the Greek island of Corfu. From 1815 until 1863, Corfu was under British jurisdiction, and Hayter's mother, a Corfu girl, married a British sailor, Hayter's late father. Their Portsmouth-born son, Able-Seaman Hayter, was brought up—due to the mother—with loyalties divided between Britain, land of his father, and Greece, the land of his mother. But these are simple people.'

Dr. Doyle puffed thoughtfully at his pipe.

'Could Seaman Hayter, a certainly physical type, have conceived and co-ordinated the *Victory* crime? Improbable. Could his crew-mate confederate, no doubt a man of the same type, have done so? Improbable. No, Mr. Raffles, those men were *paid* by somebody. Whose was the *mind* behind the *Victory* crime?'

Raffles and I knew. But we neither moved nor spoke.

'Our local newspaper, the *Portsmouth & Southsea Chronicle*,' said Dr. Doyle, 'published a list of the distinguished persons invited to be present on board *Victory* on the opening day of Navy Week. The newspaper published a second list—those distinguished guests who actually *were* on board the old flagship on that day. Comparing the lists, I noted that, of the yacht-owning visitors at Cowes, who had all received invitations to *Victory*, only one had not availed himself of the invitation.'

'Mr. Aristotle Andiakis,' said Mr. Watson, 'of the S/Y *Achilleion*.'

'Precisely, Watson. Mr. Andiakis. A powerful mind. A Greek mind. A man, moreover, with seamen at his disposal—the crew of the *Achilleion*—to pose as sightseers and, in some hired boat, manoeuvre into a convenient position to pick up the lifebelt flung for them from *Victory*.'

Dr. Doyle tamped down the tobacco in his pipe.

'Why was Mr. Andiakis not on board *Victory*? Was it from fear of personal involvement in the crime he possibly had planned? I wondered. I noted an absence of violence in the crime. Seaman Hayter's dislocated shoulder was unforeseeable. The Marine sentry was not brutally blackjacked, as would have been quicker and easier. He was harmlessly chloroformed. Was Mr. Andiakis, then, if his was in fact the mind that planned the crime, a man of some nicety of scruple?—sufficient nicety, perhaps, to decline to be a guest on board a ship he planned to rob? To you, personally, Mr. Raffles—would such a scruple be comprehensible?'

The question appalled me. It foreshadowed serious trouble.

'Yes, Dr. Doyle,' Raffles answered quietly, 'it would.'

'But if Mr. Aristotle Andiakis,' said the Elm Grove doctor, 'were a man of scruple, what possible motive could he have

16

for so drastic a deed as the illicit acquisition of a historic treasure of the British nation?'

'I can't imagine,' said Raffles. 'Unless—' He stopped suddenly.

'Something has occurred to you?' Dr. Doyle asked.

'The Thracian Marbles,' said Raffles.

'Ah! You read *The Times*. So do I, Mr. Raffles. And when I recalled a long-standing wrangle in its correspondence columns about the moral right of the British Museum to possess those ancient bas-reliefs commemorating a battle as important in Greek history as is the battle of Trafalgar in British history, I felt sure of my ground.'

'Dr. Doyle,' said Mr. Watson, 'immediately invited me to accompany him to the Isle of Wight.'

'To Cowes, Watson—yes. Millionaires! Millionaires were all around us there. But some things,' said Dr. Conan Doyle, 'cannot be bought with minted money. We found Mr. Andiakis absent from his yacht. He was being granted the extremely unusual privilege of being received in audience by the Queen at Osborne House. Mr. Watson and I were invited on board the yacht to await Mr. Andiakis's return. On his arrival, I immediately accused him of being in possession of the uniform in which Horatio Nelson died at Trafalgar.'

In this room, in this ancient waterfront inn, there was for a moment no sound.

'Realising,' Dr. Doyle said, then, 'that I had found him out, Mr. Andiakis confided to me—under seal of secrecy—the outcome of his audience with Her Majesty. Mr. Raffles, the Nelson uniform is in due course to be returned to the Admiralty. In due course, in exchange, the Thracian Marbles will be restored to Greece, the land of their origin. By command of Her Majesty, no explanation will ever be given. But, as to this—a danger exists.'

My heart thumped slow, heavy, stifling. I could not breathe.

'Mr. Raffles,' said the Southsea doctor, 'Mr. Andiakis's possession of the Nelson uniform became known—last night—to an intruder. The safe on the S/Y *Achilleion* was opened.'

I stared at the polished boards of the floor. Raffles, at my side, was still as a statue.

'I asked Mr. Andiakis,' Dr. Doyle said, 'if Mr. Watson and I might see the uniform. You've read, you told me, my small shocker, *A Study In Scarlet*. Nelson's blood is not scarlet. Time

17

has blackened those honoured stains. But I noticed a faint red smear on Nelson's swallowtail blue epauletted coat. Blood, Mr. Raffles. Mr. Andiakis assured me that, when he set the combination of the safe just before leaving for his audience with the Queen, that faint blemish of fresh red blood had not been on the coat.'

'Dr. Doyle,' said Mr. Watson, 'thereupon máde a close examination of the safe's exterior—'

'And found on the carpet before it, Watson, something that led me to the conclusion that the intruder had been wearing a fingerstall.'

Blue as an arctic iceberg, Dr. Doyle's eyes were fixed on Raffles.

'For greater tactile sensitivity in the manipulation of that relatively simple combination-lock,' Dr. Doyle said, 'the intruder took off his fingerstall. For greater sensitivity still, he removed from the finger, probably with his teeth, two surgical stitches and, with his tongue, flicked them from his mouth. I have them —together with my bill, Mr. Raffles—in this envelope.'

So—it had come. Raffles had made his first, his fatal mistake. He was exposed. We were finished. I could not swallow the great lump in my throat. I stared at the floor.

'Seaman Hayter,' Dr. Doyle said, 'and his crew-mate confederate will not be charged before an Admiralty Court-Martial. They are no longer ratings in the Royal Navy. They've been bought out by Mr. Andiakis and will be employed in his merchant-shipping fleet. Further—because a ban of silence has been imposed on every facet of the *Victory* crime, the intruder last night on S/Y *Achilleion* cannot be charged at Winchester Assizes. Mr. Raffles, I don't know why you left the Nelson uniform where you found it. Perhaps the devil looks after his own. You remain free to catch your train. But I—I, personally —have a bill to present. I shall hold it pending. If ever, traceable to you or your crony Manders, there comes to my ears any mention of what you know about Mr. Andiakis, I shall seek you out, Mr. A. J. Raffles, and infallibly present my bill—at a price a great deal higher than you will care to pay.'

The doctor of Bush Villas, Elm Grove, knocked ashes from his pipe-bowl into a tray on the dressing-table.

'To each,' his strong voice said, 'his own. To every nation, the mystery of its own soul, which is born of its past. Our Queen grows old. Her heart has known sorrow, but in that heart is the pride of kings. And the man who stood before her last night in Osborne House is a king among men—a self-made aristocrat, an Odysseus of our own century. He was confident of the lady to whom he spoke, and he knew how to present his case to her. He quoted to her four lines from one of her favourite poets, Lord Macaulay:

> For how can man die better
> Than facing fearful odds
> For the ashes of his fathers
> And the temples of his gods.

And that great Greek gentleman, Mr. Aristotle Andiakis, told me that that little, ageing, indomitable widow looked long at him. Then she turned to her Private Secretary and said, "In this matter of the Thracian Marbles, convey to Ten Downing Street this, Our Royal Command: *Let right be done.*" '

Staring blindly at the floor, I heard the door of the room open.

'Come, Watson.'

The door-latch clicked shut.

Neither Raffles nor I moved.

Outside, hoofs clopped and harness jingled as the hansom departed. Through the open casements, the breeze from the sea blew in cool and salty upon us. Thinly over Portsmouth Harbour floated the bugle notes of the day's end call, 'Retreat'. The report of the sunset gun clapped across the water. From the masthead of H.M.S. *Victory*, as on all the Queen's ships at their anchors, the flag of her realm fluttered down.

I heard Raffles draw in his breath slowly, deeply.

'From now on, Bunny,' he said, 'the shadow of an unsettled bill hangs over us.'

'In account,' I muttered, 'with Dr. A. Conan Doyle.'

'Or in account,' Raffles said, in a strange tone, 'with the other name he uses for himself—in the pages of that book.'

On the four-poster bed, with our valises and Raffles' cricket-bag, lay *A Study In Scarlet*.

# 2    JOHN L. SULLIVAN
OBLIGES

It so happened that Raffles was batting when the open carriage
with the four portly gentlemen in it entered Lord's Cricket
Ground, St. John's Wood, London.

Around the stands, brilliant with the hues of parasols, blazers
and boaters in the sunshine, rustled a sibilance of whispers, and
from my seat on the pavilion terrace I heard some chatterbox
young woman behind me ask who the newcomers were.

'Surely, Daisy,' a man's voice answered, 'you recognise the
bland gentleman with the beard and the white Homburg hat?'

'Oh, of course—it's His Royal Highness! Who's that big,
exciting-looking man sitting beside him?'

'That's John L. Sullivan, the great prize-fighter from Boston.'

'Heavens, fancy the heir to the throne going about with prize-
fighters!'

'He's no ordinary bruiser, Daisy. There's only one John L.
Sullivan. He's in London on a visit and is being lionised socially.
H.R.H. is very taken with him. I expect he's brought Mr. Sullivan
to see something of our summer game. Americans don't play it,
you know.'

'How contrary of them,' said Daisy.

Meanwhile, the carriage, with its top-hatted coachman and
groom on the box and its two fine horses arching their proud
necks against the bearing-reins, pulled up in an advantageous
position just to the right of the pavilion terrace.

'There seem to be a lot of policemen about, all of a sudden,' I
heard Daisy say.

'When royalty appears, bobbies pop up out of manholes and
materialise from behind trees in an almost magical way. A lot
of thought must go into it,' said Daisy's escort. 'Oh, good shot!
Well hit, sir!'

Raffles had struck a ball from Lockwood, the world's most
hostile fast bowler, firmly to the boundary.

20

'H.R.H. is saying something to Mr. Sullivan,' remarked Daisy.

'He's probably explaining the co-ordination of wrist and foot necessary to the execution of the classical off-drive, Daisy.'

'Oh, look, they're lighting cigars,' said Daisy. 'How Mr. Sullivan's diamond ring sparkles, and that diamond stickpin in his cravat!'

'My dear, I beg you—refrain from staring at the royal carriage. It's not done, you know.'

'Those poor horses,' said Daisy. 'Why don't the coachmen put nosebags on them to munch in?'

'With royalty in the carriage, I think nosebags would be rather *infra dig*. In any case, H.R.H. probably doesn't intend to stay long—just till the tea interval, I expect, at four o'clock. Now, really, Daisy—do please pay some attention to the game.'

It was, in fact, at a fascinating stage. Raffles had scored 73, so there was a good chance of his reaching his hundred by teatime. The sun blazed down. Except for the sound of bat meeting ball, and an occasional ripple of hand clapping, a hush increasingly tense brooded over the ground as the hands of the pavilion clock crept towards the hour of four.

Suddenly, just as the burly Lockwood was making his run up to the wicket to launch one of his thunderbolts at Raffles, a scream pierced the silence, causing Lockwood to miss his stride and almost trip over his own feet. Recovering himself, he glared off to his left, towards the stand on the opposite side from the royal carriage.

'Oh!' gasped Daisy, behind me. 'Whatever's happening?'

From a swirling among the spectators in the stand over there, a lithe, lightly-built figure broke free, vaulted the low rail, ran out on to the turf. The interloper wore white flannel trousers and a Cambridge-blue blazer. I glimpsed dark glasses under the floppy brim of a grey flannel hat. But it was the globular object in the interloper's hand which wrenched from the crowd a concerted gasp of horror.

'Oh, my God!' muttered a man sitting beside me. 'Another damned nihilist!'

From the globular object, considerably larger than a cricket ball, dangled a length of fuse which, as the bizarre intruder hurled the object overarm high through the air towards the middle of the wicket, trailed a thin feather of smoke.

The bomb landed midway between the two batsmen. The

21

thrower came running on towards H.R.H.'s carriage. Bobbies raced out to intercept. Seeing them coming, the bomb-thrower whipped off the floppy hat and dark glasses. Long hair, of a honey colour in the sunshine, rippled down over her shapely shoulders as, flinging up her hands, she cried out, 'Your Royal Highness—We, the Women—'

Her further words were lost to me, for the bobbies were on her. Crowd and cricketers alike were struck to immobility—all except one. Raffles, his bat raised, was running to the bomb, which lay with its fuse smoking and spluttering on the turf.

'Leave it, Raffles!' I was on my feet, shouting at him, in panic. 'Don't touch it! Stand back!'

But he slammed down his bat on the fuse. It was undoubtedly quick-match, for it still spluttered fiercely. Raffles threw aside his bat, snatched up the bomb with one batting-gloved hand, jerked the fuse right out of it with the other.

Dropping the little that remained of the fuse, Raffles trod it out with his nailed cricket boot and, seeing a bobby approaching at the double, lobbed the now harmless bomb to him as casually as if it had been a cricket ball.

'Well done, that man!' a voice cried—as a collective sigh of relief went up from the crowd.

Bobbies hustled the bomb-thrower, quite a young woman, smartly away to some lurking Black Maria.

'What was the wretched girl shouting about?' I heard Daisy ask. 'It sounded like "We the Women of England"—and something about concubinage. What's concubinage?'

'It's a form of—uh—domestic arrangement—more or less. By Jove, though, Daisy, that was quick thinking by Raffles—a jolly good show. Hark at the people clapping him!'

'There's a gentleman from H.R.H.'s carriage gone to speak to him,' said Daisy. 'Oh, look—the gentleman—'

'The Equerry, Daisy.'

'Well, whoever he is, he's taking Mr. Raffles to meet H.R.H.'

'In the circumstances, Daisy, congratulations are in order—though, of course, Raffles may merely have been thinking that he didn't want a hole blown in the turf before he'd scored his hundred.'

This remark nettled me.

'Sir,' I said, turning to look the speaker in the eye, 'as a personal friend of A. J. Raffles, I resent that observation. No

22

such selfish thought would have entered his head. His action was instinctive—and typical of him.'

'I beg your pardon,' Daisy's escort said, with a flush. 'I confess the remark was ill-considered. I gladly withdraw it. Uh—come, Daisy dear, I think perhaps we'd better go to tea now.'

The couple sidled off, the fellow shamefaced, his chatterbox companion looking back at me curiously.

I glanced across at the royal carriage. Raffles, standing beside it, still wearing his batting-pads, doffed his cap as H.R.H. shook hands with him and introduced him to John L. Sullivan.

Knowing Raffles as I did, I knew that he would not fail to note, as he shook the great pugilist by the hand, Mr. Sullivan's diamond ring and stickpin; but I also knew that, their meeting being under royal auspices, Mr. Sullivan's belongings would remain perfectly safe from Raffles' attentions.

The man who had been sitting beside me now addressed me.

'Sir,' he said, 'did I hear you say that you're a personal friend of A. J. Raffles?'

'I am indeed, sir.'

'In that case, I'd deeply appreciate it if you would introduce me to him. I see that H.R.H.'s carriage is departing and the Tea Interval is now upon us. If you could arrange for me to meet Mr. Raffles during the interval, I should be most grateful. I have a proposal to make to him.'

Though he had been sitting beside me all afternoon, I had not until now taken much note of the man. Impeccably dressed in a grey frock-coat and grey topper, he was tall and thin, with a sallow, haughty face and a ribboned monocle.

'A proposal?' I said cautiously.

'I am Lord Pollexfen, of the Pollexfen Press. Sir, just listen to this crowd!'

As umpires and players were coming to the pavilion, which Raffles already had entered by a side door, the crowd in the stands was chanting, to rhythmic handclaps, 'We—want—A. J. Raffles! We—want—A. J. Raffles!'

'You are hearing, sir,' Lord Pollexfen informed me, 'the Voice of Britain. Within an hour, newsboys will be crying on the London streets the name of A. J. Raffles—a man already thrice capped for England, and well known as representative of all that's finest in British sporting life. Tomorrow he will be the subject of laudatory editorials in every newspaper in these islands. For some time I've been seeking a name for a project I have in mind. Sir, I have found that name.'

His monocle glittered compellingly at me.

'The iron is hot,' said Lord Pollexfen. 'Will you please tell your friend Mr. Raffles that I should like to discuss with him immediately the launching of a magazine—a monthly magazine of the highest class—a magazine, edited by himself, to be called *A. J. Raffles' Magazine Of Sport*.'

To cricketers the world over, the Long Room at Lord's is little short of a shrine. And it was in this historic chamber, with the sun shining in mellowly through open windows on to panelled walls bearing priceless relics dating from the beaver-hatted forefathers of the game, that the foundations of *Raffles' Magazine* were laid.

He himself, still in flannels, blazer and muffler, his keen face tanned, his dark hair crisp, determined my own role in the project.

'I'd like to point out, Lord Pollexfen,' he said, 'that my friend Manders here is himself no mean journalist. While I'm prepared to figure as editor of the proposed magazine, my sporting engagements occupy most of my time. I should need the routine conduct of the magazine, under my general guidance as regards policy, to be in able hands—and there could be no abler Assistant Editor than my friend Manders.' He offered me a Sullivan from his cigarette-case. 'What d'you think, Bunny? Could you spare the time from your more exacting literary preoccupations?'

'I shall be happy,' I said, taking my cue from his slight wink, 'to co-operate.'

At this, Lord Pollexfen expressed his pleasure, and he proceeded to suggest that a royalty on sales would be appropriate for Raffles, and for my own services an emolument in the nature of a salary. Though delicately enough phrased, the actual sums proposed by the Press baron were nothing to write home hysterically about, but Raffles accepted them with casual inconsequence.

When the peer had gone off to arrange about office space and staff for us in the Pollexfen Press building in Covent Garden, I told Raffles that I felt we might have driven a harder bargain.

'Why strain at sprats, Bunny,' he said, 'when there may be mackerel in the offing?'

'You have some idea, Raffles?'

24

'That depends, Bunny.'

'On what?'

'On the girl who threw the bomb. You heard what she was shouting about. It may have possibilities.' His grey eyes danced. 'She'll be up in front of the beak at Marlborough Street to-morrow. We'll be there.'

Actually, we arrived a little late, but the bobby at the court-room door was a follower of first-class cricket and, recognising A. J. Raffles, let us slip in unobtrusively to the rear of the public benches.

In addition to her honey-coloured hair, the accused in the dock proved to have other attractions. Though she had spent the night in a cell, she evidently had been allowed to receive more appropriate attire in which to appear before the Justices than the trousers and blazer she had worn at Lord's. From a man sitting next to us on the back bench, we learned that the lady bombadier's name was Mirabel Renny. And certainly she was a fine figure of young womanhood standing there, with a proud bearing and defiant expression, in the dock.

Apparently, inquiries had been made by the Court's official Nosey Parkers into the girl's background, for the beak was holding forth at her like a Dutch uncle.

It seemed that she was the only girl in a family of five large, athletic brothers. In these circumstances, the beak told her, a young female must naturally expect to occupy a subordinate place in the affections of her father.

'However,' continued the magistrate, 'pernicious literature anent the social and political status of the female sex has recently been filtering into this country from the United States. Some of this stuff, penned by such notorious agitators as Miss Susan B. Anthony, chanced to fall into your hands. Inflamed by it, you forsook the shelter of your parental roof and came irresponsibly to London. Here you lodged at a Ladies' Hostel in Fulham, where you appear to have fallen in with some elder persons of your sex who likewise have been emotionally disturbed by these fallacious American doctrines.'

The girl in the dock opened her mouth as though to voice some hot rebuttal. But the magistrate was continuing.

'In a foolish attempt to woo your father's affections by rivalling your brothers' athletic prowess, you appear to have abandoned yourself to pastimes for which Nature did not intend you.

Taking advantage of your hoydenish proclivities, the elder persons at the Ladies' Hostel appear to have prevailed upon you to be the instrument of yesterday's lamentable demonstration at Lord's Cricket—'

'I protest!' cried a woman in a conspicuously plain hat, springing to her feet among the public benches. 'If Your Honour pleases—'

'Madam,' barked the magistrate, 'be seated this instant, or I shall have you moved directly into a place of restraint.'

The woman in the plain hat subsided, muttering rebelliously.

Silence restored after the momentary sensation, the magistrate continued his admonition to the defendant, whose hands, lightly suntanned, clenched hard on the rail of the dock.

'I accept the probability,' the magistrate told her, 'that any actual damage to the turf at Lord's would be incompatible with your so-called sporting inclinations, however unbecoming these may be to your womanhood. Indeed, as Inspector Harrigan has stated in evidence, the bomb-casing could not possibly have been fragmented by the detonation of its contents, consisting as these did merely of small fireworks—so-called squibs or farthing bangers.'

This was news to Raffles and myself, and we exchanged a surprised glance.

'Had the case been otherwise,' the magistrate told the girl, looking hard at her, 'you would have rued this day. However, as you are a first offender and your bombshell was designed only as a means of attracting attention to illusory female grievances, I shall exercise leniency on this occasion. Don't ever let me see you before me again. The fine for disturbing the Lord's peace—that is to say, the peace at Lord's—will be five guineas, with a guinea costs. Next case!'

'Come on, Bunny,' said Raffles.

To my astonishment, he sought out the functionary who collected fines, and he paid the girl's fine for her. As he returned his wallet to his pocket, Miss Mirabel Renny, accompanied by the elder lady in the severely plain hat, came to the desk—and the functionary, indicating Raffles, told the ladies that the fine had been paid.

Though Raffles now was immaculate in morning dress, a pearl in his cravat, the girl recognised him immediately.

'Why, you're the man who was batting at Lord's when I—'

26

She broke off. Her magnificent eyes flashed. 'How dare you,' she said, 'presume to pay my fine?'

'Miss Renny,' said her companion in the practical hat, icily, 'has friends. She stands in no need of charity from *men*!'

'No charity is involved,' said Raffles. 'The amount, Miss Renny, will be deducted from your first month's salary.'

'Salary?' she exclaimed. 'What d'you mean? What are you talking about?'

'The post of contributing editor on a sports magazine now in the fruitful planning stage,' said Raffles. 'Your taste for outdoor pastimes would fit you admirably for the post—and if, with the opportunity it provides for the dissemination of opinion, it should happen to appeal to you, Miss Renny—'

No doubt about it! Mirabel Renny jumped at the job. And as the next few weeks proved, Raffles could not have made a happier choice of young sportswoman to help in carrying out the editorial policy on which he had decided.

He expounded his policy to Mirabel and me before he went off to join cricketing house parties at some of the stately homes of the country.

'Sport,' Raffles explained to us, 'is in the British blood—which biologically, as far as I know, is no different in women from what it is in men. So we want to make *Raffles' Magazine* a well-balanced periodical which'll equitably represent the interests and views of those of both sexes who have a taste for vigorous outdoor pastimes.'

Mirabel's enthusiasm knew no bounds. She threw herself heart and soul into executing the role Raffles assigned to her. She was a dynamo of activity.

Our office in the imposing building of the Pollexfen Press looked out on Covent Garden vegetable and flower market, a sunny, colourful scene.

Despite Raffles' absence, his guiding editorial hand was manifest in the marvellous articles which, thanks to his wide circle of acquaintances, were coming in, for merely token fees, from some of the greatest names in the world of sport.

What with this and with Mirabel's aptitude and energy, my own task in putting together our first issue was by no means onerous.

Notwithstanding her advanced views, Mirabel was enchanting to look at in the trim skirt and crisp shirtwaist she wore to the

27

office, and I often suggested that I take her to lunch—upstairs, where ladies were admitted—at Simpson's Tavern & Divan, in the Strand.

But she was too much enamoured of her work to leave it.

'You go ahead, Mr. Manders,' she invariably said. 'I shall just have a sandwich and a cigarette at my desk.'

She made out that she smoked habitually, but this was just a gesture of emancipation, as I had noticed that cigarettes made her cough and fan the smoke away with a set of galley proofs.

So I would leave her to hold the fort, and I would go to my club in Adelphi Terrace for lunch, and a few rubbers of cards with Phil May, Tom Browne, Ralph Hodgson, Jerome K. Jerome, breezy Robert Barr, or such other hard-working artists and literary men as happened to be there. And, tearing myself away, usually a bit out of pocket, I would drop back to the office at about four o'clock for a last supervisory look round before returning to my Mount Street flat to take a nap and dress for dinner and whatever theatre happened to have sent first-night complimentary tickets to the office.

All in all, it was not a bad life, the editorial life.

I sent a card to Raffles at Woodstock, where he was a guest of the Duke of Marlborough for Blenheim Palace Cricket Week, to let him know when the foundry proof, the final proof of our first issue fully made-up, was due from the printers, the McWhirter Printing & Engraving Company, in Long Acre.

He turned up, looking tanned and fit, the same morning as the proof arrived. He was delighted with it.

'A great job, Bunny,' he said. 'You and Mirabel have done wonders. Our first issue's a corker. It'll open a new era in sporting journalism.'

There was a knock on the door. Lord Pollexfen strode in.

'Ah, good morning, Raffles,' he said. 'Morning, Manders. Mr. McWhirter, the Master Printer, tells me he's delivered your foundry proof. I'd like a look at it before deciding how many thousands of copies to venture on as a printing order.'

Raffles handed him the proof, and I offered him sherry and a biscuit, which Raffles and I were taking as a mid-morning bracer. The peer shook his head, pushed his silk hat to the back of it and, still standing, screwed his monocle into his eye to examine the proof.

'A splendid *Contents* page, gentlemen,' he said. 'You're to be

congratulated. Such names! John L. Sullivan on *Boxing*—James
Braid on *The Ideal Caddy*—Tod Sloan, pioneer of the short
stirrup, on *How I Won The Kentucky Derby*—Prince Ranjitsinjhi, the distinguished cricketer, on his other favourite sport,
*Tiger-shooting From Elephants.* Excellent! Outstanding! The
man-in-the-street will lap this up!'

'We owe those great names to our editor's wide circle of
personal friends,' I said, indicating Raffles, who was sitting on
the edge of my desk, swinging a leg idly.

The Press baron beamed at him. 'I foresaw this, of course,
when I was inspired to approach you, Raffles. *I* knew what I
was doing. I have a reputation for it.' He turned the pages. His
smile faded. 'What's this? What are these interpolated effusions
by *women*?'

'Those are articles,' Raffles said, 'obtained by our Contributing
Editor from various eminent ladies with active tastes.'

'But good God, man! John L. Sullivan's article on the manly
sport followed by some female whining about the exclusion of
her sex from witnessing the bouts staged at the National Sporting
Club? Raffles, this is monstrously out of place!'

'I'm grieved to hear you say that, Pollexfen,' said Raffles.

'And here again—James Braid's golf article immediately
followed by some wretched woman advocating a "different kind
of garment" to be socially accepted as a first step to eradicating
the insult to her sex implicit in their being obliged to drive off
segregated tees. What bilge from the zenana is this? What's the
idiotic woman blathering about— a *"different kind of garment"*?'

'It's shown there in the illustrations,' explained Raffles. 'One
illustration depicts the hampering effect on the golf swing of
ankle-length skirt and petticoats in windy weather. The con-
trasting illustration demonstrates the physical and mental freedom provided by the adoption of a garment, a form of functional,
all-purpose knickerbocker, especially designed by our own contributing editor.'

'This unseemly illustration,' shouted the peer, 'seems to have
been posed for by that young woman in the adjoining office.
I've seen her before somewhere. Isn't she the one who threw the
bomb at Lord's?'

'Indeed yes,' said Raffles—'Miss Mirabel Renny, our contributing editor.'

Lord Pollexfen hurled the proof down on my desk.

'I will *not* publish, under the Pollexfen Press colophon, a magazine polluted through and through with this scandalously corrupting stuff. It's entirely contrary to our policy here, which is to keep women demure, wholesome and industrious in the station—the hearth and home—for which Nature intended them. Raffles, this has ruined my day. I'm deeply disappointed. This issue will have to be re-made, omitting the offensive material. And call that young woman in. I shall dismiss her instantly.'

'I'm sorry, Pollexfen,' Raffles said evenly. '*I* engaged Miss Renny. As a matter of principle, I will neither dismiss her nor alter one word of this first issue of my magazine.'

'Then, by God, you must look elsewhere for a publisher!'

'In that case, Manders and I will publish *Raffles' Magazine* from our own resources—shall we not, Bunny?'

'Absolutely, Raffles,' I said—wondering uneasily what resources he was talking about, as we both were overdrawn at the bank.

'I categorically warn you,' said the Press baron, glaring haughtily through his monocle. 'A. J. Raffles is not the only name to conjure with in the sporting life of these islands. I shall seek an alternative name for the banner of my sports magazine—and use the powerful financial resources of the Pollexfen Press empire to crush any amateurish attempt at a rival publication.'

'That is your privilege,' Raffles said courteously.

'I also decline,' barked the peer, 'to be responsible for expenses incurred to date, including McWhirter's bill—and I hereby give notice that I require vacant possession of this office accommodation by six p.m. today.'

He stalked out, slamming the door.

'Excelsior,' said Raffles. His grey eyes danced. 'In heraldic terms, Bunny, there goes a male rampant, mounted on a prejudice, in a field ensanguined. Of course, this was inevitable.'

'You expected it?' I said, astonished.

'I counted on it, Bunny.' He offered me a cigarette from his case. 'Well, now—first things first. We're without premises. We're overdrawn at the bank, but the manager's keen on cricket and a good friend. He won't mind our using the bank as an accommodation address. Got a pencil handy? Take down this announcement.'

Smoking thoughtfully, he paced to and fro.

' "Due," ' he dictated, ' "to the refusal of the original publisher to permit the expression of feminine opinion, and therefore withdrawing financial support, prospective contributors to *A. J. Raffles' Magazine*, which hopes to publish soon under less prejudiced auspices, are notified that unsolicited contributions should be submitted to The Editor, *Raffles' Magazine*, care of County & Confidential Bank, Berkeley Square, London, accompanied by a stamped, self-addressed envelope for return if unsuitable." That's the conventional wording, I think, Bunny?'

'In effect, yes.'

'Good. Run it in the Personal columns of the leading newspapers till further notice. Now, another thing, Bunny. As eligible bachelors—or, at least, so regarded by a credulous society—we both get plenty of invitations to dine out—'

'You in the best houses,' I said, 'myself in the second best.'

'Comparisons are invidious,' said Raffles. 'Accept all the invitations you get. I shall do the same. And we owe no duty to Pollexfen, so there's no need to make it a secret, in mixed company, that we've parted from him, and the reason for it, and are trying to get the magazine out by our own unaided financial efforts. Now, let's call Mirabel in and see if she's prepared to stand by us in this crisis.'

One flash from Mirabel's eyes, when she heard the reason why we now found ourselves batting on a sticky wicket, made it plain where she stood. So, for better or worse, I rented a sparsely furnished little office for us over a moth-eaten theatrical costumier's shop behind Drury Lane Theatre.

Money being tight, I was glad enough to dine out frequently, and it seemed to me, when I recounted our trouble with Lord Pollexfen, that the guffaws of the men at the dinner table were offensively raucous, but that some of the ladies looked at me sympathetically as they withdrew to the drawing-room and whatever ladies talk about there, and left us men to our port.

My leg was pulled unmercifully by some of these hearties, but my real worry was the Master Printer, Mr. McWhirter. We were in a galling position. We had a fine magazine made up and ready for a print run, but there was not a hope, now that Lord Pollexfen had washed his hands of us, that a single copy would roll off the presses of canny Mr. McWhirter until his bill for services to date was paid.

'H'm,' said Raffles, when I reported to him my fruitless

attempts to melt the dour heart of the Master Printer. 'Bunny, we shall have to call on somebody.'

'Who, for instance?'

'I have in mind,' said Raffles, 'a certain barrister of my acquaintance—Sir Humphrey Cullimore, Q.C. He's a bullying brute who makes at least fifty thousand a year reducing men to jelly in the witness-box and women to tears.'

'Then what's the use of calling on a man like that?'

'His wife has a valuable necklace, Bunny.'

My heart lurched. 'Oh, dear God!' I said.

The Cullimore mansion was in Eaton Square, and Raffles, masked, shinned up one of the porch pillars to pay his call, by way of the window of the master bedroom, at two a.m. on a warm, dark night. I myself lurked on the other side of the street, ready to reel out, in evening-dress and silk hat, and, enacting the role of a gentleman who had dined, confuse with maudlin inquiries and garbled expostulations the bobby on the beat if he should make an inopportune appearance.

Fortunately, he did not show up at all—and when Raffles rejoined me, removing his mask, he told me he had the necklace-case safe in his pocket.

Ivor Kern, the fence we did business with, a young-old man with a perpetual, cynical half-smile, had an antique shop in King's Road, not far off. Under the hissing gas-jets in Kern's cluttered sitting-room over the shop, I watched with admiration the masterly skill with which Raffles picked the lock of the necklace-case. By my half-hunter, it took him sixty seconds flat. Then he threw back the lid.

The case was empty.

It was a severe blow to me, and no less so to Raffles. But Kern's smirk widened.

'"Emmeline Cullimore,"' he said, reading the name embossed on the blue leather of the necklace-case. 'Well, as it happens, *I* can tell you where that necklace is. It's about thirty paces from here—just across the street, in fact—in the very secure safe of a pawnbroker friend of mine.'

'How d'you know?' Raffles said grimly.

'Because jewellery offered to him in pledge,' Kern said, 'he usually brings over to me for an expert valuation before making an advance. A lady visited him yesterday morning with a neck-lace she wanted to pledge. She wore a veil and gave her name as Mrs. Doris Stevens, but he recognised her because he's often seen her, as she lives nearby, in Eaton Square. She was Lady Cullimore. I valued the necklace at two thousand and seventy pounds. He's a conservative, ten per cent type of pawnbroker, so he let her have two hundred and seven pounds on the pledge.'

Raffles took it philosophically. 'We shall have to think again, Bunny,' he said, as our hansom dropped me off at my Mount Street flat before taking Raffles on round to his rooms in The Albany, just off Piccadilly.

In view of the fiasco, I was rather surprised by his buoyant spirits when he showed up at the office next morning.

'I have news for you, Bunny,' he said, as he helped himself to the office sherry and a biscuit. 'I dropped in at the bank on my way here. Yesterday afternoon, just before closing-time, a veiled lady made a deposit to the credit of *A. J. Raffles'* *Magazine*. She signed the paying-in slip in the name of Doris Stevens. It was a cash deposit, in five-pound notes, with two sovereigns, of exactly two hundred and seven pounds.'

'Good God!' I exclaimed. 'What d'you make of this, Raffles?'

'Who can read a woman's mind, Bunny?' he said, with a shrug. He took out his wallet. 'I cashed a cheque for a hundred quid for incidental expenses—to keep our announcement running in the Personal columns, and to pay Mirabel's salary, with a little ready money for ourselves.'

Actually, we did not need much, as we were dining out so frequently, but I accepted my share, and was glad of it. But the McWhirter problem remained. He was badgering for his bill to be paid, and obviously it was quite useless to offer him, on account, the mere £107 remaining to our magazine's credit and expect him to print thousands and thousands of copies of our first issue on the strength of it.

I pointed this out to Raffles one morning a week or so after the curious incident of the veiled lady.

He nodded regretfully. 'There it is, Bunny—I'm afraid we're stymied. The only thing we can do is see if we can make our peace with Lord Pollexfen. It's no use sitting here hoping something will turn up. Come on, let's face the facts—and go and take our medicine.'

Significantly, we were kept waiting for some time in the ante-chamber of the Pollexfen Press building before we were admitted to Lord Pollexfen's sanctum, which was almost as large as the Long Room at Lord's.

Without rising from his desk, which was as big as a billiard table, or inviting us to be seated, he screwed his monocle into his eye.

'Well?' he snapped.

'I hear rumours in Fleet Street,' Raffles said, 'that you're going ahead with your plans for a sports magazine.'

'I informed you of my intention of doing so. I've found a suitable name for its bannerhead. When I say I will do a thing, Raffles, I *do* it. That is my reputation.'

'An admirable one,' Raffles admitted. 'As for Manders here and myself—frankly, Pollexfen, we've run into certain difficulties —McWhirter and one thing and another. We've found the business side of producing a magazine a considerable encroachment on our time and—to make no bones about it—on our personal resources.'

'I categorically warned you,' the peer said coldly. 'Publishing is not for amateurs. Fleet Street is paved with their tombstones. If you're now here to seek a return to our former relationship, I'm not interested. You're too late. My alternative plans are afoot. Now, if that's all—'

'You expressed some interest,' Raffles said quickly, 'in the literary material prepared for me, as a personal favour, by— among others—Mr. John L. Sullivan—Prince Ranjitsinjhi—'

The peer's hand, about to slap down on the bell on his desk, hesitated.

'I could, I think,' Raffles said, 'persuade those gentlemen, as an act of friendship to myself, to allow the transfer of their material to your own magazine, if you— Oh, the devil! Look here, Pollexfen—Manders and I are out of our depth in publishing. This magazine of mine is running away with more money than we can afford. If you'd care to consider acquiring its literary and art assets for a reasonable sum—'

'What d'you call a reasonable sum?'

'Well, if you'd care to take over McWhirter's bill to date,' Raffles said, 'and—we'd like to get back a crumb or two of what we've so misguidedly spent. If we decide we're in too deep and *must* go on with the magazine, I could, of course, go to the City for finance—I have friends there. But—'

'But publishing inconveniences your hedonistic way of life,'

34

Lord Pollexfen said, with a haughty sneer.

Raffles shrugged. 'I don't know what little we have left of what we put into the magazine's bank account, Pollexfen, but if you'd care to pay a sum equal to the current balance, such as it is, you can take over the magazine's literary and art assets, and all the work done so far on the preparation of the first and subsequent projected issues—the whole thing, in fact, lock, stock and barrel—and Manders and I'll be free of it,' he added, with a gesture of weary disgust.

The Press baron hesitated. But he knew our present balance could not possibly be greater than the amount of McWhirter's bill, or—with McWhirter threatening to sue—we should certainly have paid it.

'Very well,' said the peer, with the abrupt decision for which he was famous. 'I'll accept your offer, Raffles. Naturally, I shall require your bank manager to vouch for the amount currently standing to your magazine's credit.'

'Manders and I'll have a word with the manager,' said Raffles, 'and report back to you, Pollexfen.'

My spirits rose. I saw Raffles' game. When we returned, having pretended to consult our bank manager, we could name our balance as a reasonable sum.

But Lord Pollexfen said, 'Nothing of the kind.' He struck a chirp from the bell of his desk. The door of his sanctum opened. 'Call my brougham,' ordered the peer. 'Raffles, where's your bank?'

'In Berkeley Square.'

'Then let us go there and settle this matter.'

I was disgusted. The peer's implied refusal to accept Raffles' word for the amount of our magazine's current balance was tantamount to an insult. As we rode in Pollexfen's brougham to Berkeley Square, I was writhing inwardly at the thought of our imminent humiliation.

'This is Lord Pollexfen, of the Pollexfen Press,' Raffles told our bank manager, when we were shown into his office. 'Lord Pollexfen is acquiring the literary and art assets and all extant copyrights—except only in the title—of *Raffles' Magazine*, in consideration of a sum equal to the amount of the present balance in the magazine's account. Correct, Pollexfen?'

'That is the agreement,' said the peer coldly.

'I can tell you the balance in a trice,' said the bank manager, opening a large ledger.

I could have told him in less than a trice. Our balance was £107.

'At the conclusion of yesterday's business,' said the manager cordially, 'the sum standing to the credit of *A. J. Raffles'* *Magazine of Sport* was precisely seven thousand five hundred pounds, sixteen shillings and—'

My knees went weak. The room spun round me. There seemed to be a long, long silence. It was broken at last by an angry scratching sound. This was made by Lord Pollexfen's pen. He was writing a cheque. He threw it on the manager's desk.

Stalking to the door, he turned, lean and tall, frock-coated and silk-hatted, his monocle icily glittering.

'The name of A. J. Raffles,' he said, 'will never again be mentioned in any periodical published by the Pollexfen Press.'

The door slammed.

A few minutes later, as Raffles and I were leaving the bank, I noticed a heavily veiled lady at the counter. Raffles gripped my arm, checking me. The lady pushed a sheaf of banknotes across the mahogany to the attentive cashier.

'To be placed,' said the mysteriously veiled lady, in a voice so furtive and conspiratorial as scarcely to be audible, 'to the credit of *A. J. Raffles' Magazine.*'

We walked on out into the sunshine of Berkeley Square.

That night, we took Mirabel Renny and a friend of hers called Margaret, just such another fine, forthright type of girl as Mirabel herself, to dine at the palatial Holborn Restaurant.

'I'm afraid, Mirabel,' Raffles said, as the wine waiter brought champagne bottles in a silver ice-bucket to our table, 'that you won't be entirely pleased by the reason for this dinner. Perhaps we'd better admit the truth right away. The fact is, we've sold the magazine.'

'*Sold* it?' said Mirabel, incredulous.

'For seven thousand five hundred pounds,' Raffles said. 'To Lord Pollexfen.'

'To *him*?' Mirabel was deeply shocked. 'But—that means—'

'It means you're sacked, I'm sorry to say,' Raffles admitted. 'So this cheque I'm handing you is—in lieu of notice.'

Mirabel's fine eyes flashed. '*Men!*' she said. 'I might have known this would happen, Margaret. The moment things get difficult, men think only of themselves. They're selfish, through and—' Something about the cheque caught her attention. She looked at it more closely. 'This cheque,' she said, 'this cheque—it's a cheque for *seven-thousand-six-hundred pounds*!'

'Bunny and I owed the magazine account a hundred,' said Raffles, 'so we repaid it—being honest men. I've already apologised to Bunny for clean forgetting to tell him that I've kept in close touch with the bank regarding the day-to-day state of the magazine's finances.'

'Apology accepted,' I said.

'Naturally,' said Raffles, 'Bunny shares equally with me the seven thousand five hundred from Pollexfen—which has nothing whatever to do with this cheque, Mirabel. This money came in, some by post, some by personal deposit, from other sources. What marital injustices or male brutalities may explain this money out of the blue, I just don't know. But you need have no hesitation in using it, Mirabel, to start a magazine of your own, to further the cause you have at heart. This money came entirely from women—unknown women in this country, Mirabel—that their voice, at last, may be heard in the land.'

She gazed at him. She blinked. Sudden tears sparkled in her eyes. They were the tears of sheer happiness at the dazzling future now opening before her. But Raffles, embarrassed by them, quickly unwired a champagne bottle. The cork popped.

'We must admit,' he said, as he poured the bubbly fizzing into our glasses, 'that we owe much to Mr. John L. Sullivan, Prince Ranjitsinjhi, and those other great names who provided priceless literary material. But let's drink now, above all, to those anonymous others, that veiled legion of nameless ones who so hopefully submitted,' said A. J. Raffles, raising his glass, '*unsolicited contributions.*'

# TUSITALA AND THE MONEY-BELT

'Ah-hah there, my dear fellows! So you've noticed her, too. Enchanting, is she not?'

At the intrusive voice, Raffles and I turned from our rapt contemplation of a nubile maiden who, sun-gold in her state of nature and arcadian innocence, was roaming through a field of wheat, twining poppies idly in her hair.

Tophatted like ourselves, gentlemen with catalogues sauntered by in cultured converse with ladies flourishing lorgnettes, for it was Private View Day at the Summer Exhibition of the Royal Academy, Burlington House, Piccadilly.

Twinkling his eyes at us over half-lensed glasses was the Secretary of a club to which we belonged. With him was a tall, bronzed, handsome man with a grey moustache.

'Mr. William Haggard, a fellow Club member of ours,' said the Secretary, effecting introductions. 'You may have read a book which his brother, Rider of that ilk, published not long ago—*King Solomon's Mines*.'

'Who hasn't?' said Raffles, with a smile.

'Haggard here is on leave from Samoa,' said the Secretary, 'where he's the British representative on the Land Commission. I'm glad we've run into you chaps, as there's a matter I'd like to take up with you. Have you chanced to notice the letters which another fellow Club member of ours, Robert Louis Stevenson, is now publishing, with great effect, in *The Times* newspaper here and also in an American periodical called, I understand, *McClure's*?'

We had to admit that, though we both were well acquainted with the works of Mr. Stevenson, we had never met him personally, and the letters in question had escaped our attention.

'For some years now,' said the Secretary, 'Stevenson's made his home in Samoa—for health reasons, don't you know. And by Jove, my dear fellows, these letters he's sending from his home there, Vailima, are real scorchers. They make a vehement attack on the United States, Germany and Great Britain—the three Powers signatory to the recent Berlin Convention, which purports to have settled the Samoan Problem, eh, Haggard?'

'A problem, principally,' Mr. Haggard told us, 'of the rival claims of two Chiefs to the Paramount Chieftaincy. The people of Samoa, like the people of Stevenson's own country, Scotland, are a warrior people, a people of clans. Their history, like that of Scotland, is a history of clan warfare.'

'Massacre of Glencoe sort of thing,' said the Secretary.

Mr. Haggard nodded. 'Yes, blood has too often run red in the palm forests. And husbandry's been neglected because of clan conflict—with the result that foreigners have come in and, as happened in Scotland, bought up for next to nothing much of the land that had belonged for centuries to Samoan families. The foreigners are mostly British, American and German planters. So the three great Powers offered to arbitrate between the claims of the rival Chiefs.'

'Hence the Berlin Convention,' said the Secretary, 'where the diplomats decided in favour of the Chief who's more amenable to their influence. Right, Haggard?'

'I'm afraid so,' said Mr. Haggard. 'The Convention arranged for the setting up of an Island Council, composed of the British and American Consuls and the German Consul, Baron Senfft Von Pilsach, under the Chairmanship of a neutral Swedish gentleman, a Mr. Cedarcrantz, to "advise" and "guide" the chosen Chief.'

'And what happened,' said Raffles, interested, 'to the other Chief?'

'Ah! Chief Mataafa,' said Mr. Haggard—'a wise and able man. I'm sorry to say he's not even been given a voice on the Island Council.'

'Fishy, is it not?' said the Secretary. 'It could lead to a fresh outbreak of conflict between the factions—'

'And if that happens,' said Raffles, 'it'll give the three Powers an excuse to intervene, on the grounds of protecting their planters, and collar the swag—I mean, annex Samoa—for division among themselves?'

'Precisely what R.L.S. suspects,' exclaimed the Secretary, 'and what his letters from Vailima are trying to stir up decent public opinion in England, Germany and the United States to prevent!'

'In fairness,' said Mr. Haggard, 'one must admit that the

39

Convention set up a Land Commission with three members—one American, one German, one British—to study ways and means of restoring some of the plantation properties to the Samoans themselves.'

'Window-dressing!' said the Secretary. 'You told me yourself, Haggard, that your recommendations, as a member of the Land Commission, are being consistently pigeon-holed. And certainly R.L.S.'s letters to *The Times* are stirring up a hornet's nest in Whitehall, to say nothing of Washington and the Wilhelmstrasse. Which brings me, my dear Raffles and Manders, to the matter I'd like to take up with you—'

'I'm afraid,' Raffles said, 'that Manders and I don't go in much for politics, do we, Bunny?'

'Absolutely not, Raffles,' I agreed.

'This has nothing to do with politics,' said the Secretary. 'It's purely a Club matter. We of the Committee have been putting our heads together, and we feel that the Club should have a portrait of R.L.S. So we propose to commission the artist whose fresh young talent is so evident in his *Poppy Girl* here, which you were admiring, to go out to Samoa and paint a portrait of our absent member in the exotic surroundings of his house, Vailima.'

'Excellent idea,' said Raffles, and I concurred with enthusiasm.

'Splendid,' said the Secretary. 'I'm empowered to take up a subscription to finance the project. May I put you down, then, for—shall we say, my dear fellows—fifty guineas apiece?'

My enthusiasm diminished. Fifty guineas! Both Raffles and I were overdrawn at the bank. But Raffles produced his chequebook with a casual air and, painful though it was to me, I could hardly do less than follow his example.

'Fresh English faces,' Mr. Haggard remarked, as we shook hands with him on parting, 'are always a welcome sight to us exiles in Samoa. If ever you should find yourselves at loose ends in the Pacific, you must look me up and be my guests between the monthly steamers.'

'The Pacific, I fear,' said Raffles, 'is a bit beyond our horizon.'

'Absolutely,' I agreed.

Yet, such are the chances of life, the early sunshine of a beautiful morning many months later found us standing at a liner's boat-deck rail, with Raffles studying through binoculars three faint smudges of smoke which, widely separated, blemished the illimitable blue of the Pacific sea and sky.

'Warships,' he said. 'Take a look, Bunny.'

He handed me the binoculars, which belonged to the liner's Purser, who was standing at the rail with us and had drawn our attention to the smokes. Focusing the binoculars on them I saw that they were indeed made by warships, which were steaming along slowly with guns jutting from their turrets, sailors moving around on their decks, flags fluttering from their jackstaffs.

'The Stars and Stripes,' I said, 'the Imperial German eagle, and the British white ensign.'

'Light cruisers,' said the Purser—'patrolling, hull down, off Samoa.'

'The long arms,' Raffles said thoughtfully, 'of the Three Big W's—Whitehall, Washington, and the Wilhelmstrasse.'

His dark hair crisp, he was wearing white flannels and an I Zingari Cricket Club blazer. His keen face was deeply tanned by the fierce sunshine of antipodean cricket grounds, for, not long after our meeting with Mr. Haggard, Raffles had been selected for an All-England team to tour Australia. Thanks to some cajolery of our bank manager, we had raised enough money for me to accompany the team and provide moral support.

Out of sheer curiosity about the proposed portrait of Robert Louis Stevenson in which we had a hundred-guinea vested interest, we had decided, at the conclusion of the cricket tour, to return to England *via* San Francisco, stopping off on the way at Samoa to visit Mr. Haggard.

'D'you happen to know, Purser,' Raffles said, offering us a Sullivan apiece from his cigarette-case, 'if Mr. R. L. Stevenson is still living in Samoa?'

I felt a thrill of excitement as Raffles asked the question, for we had been long out of touch with British and American newspapers, and anything might have happened to a lone man, in a remote corner of the world, who was making himself a nuisance to the Three Big W's.

'We'll be raising Upolu Head any minute now,' said the Purser, 'and I can point out Mr. Stevenson's house to you, but I don't know if he's still living there. Mr. Manders, I'll trouble you for the binoculars.'

Taking them back from me, he focused them on a distant sailing-vessel.

'Schooner,' he said—'the notorious Tattooed Man's. No mistaking that blackguard.'

'Blackguard?' I said, intrigued, being one myself, in an amateur kind of way.

'He's well-known all over the Pacific, Mr. Manders,' said the Purser, passing the binoculars on to Raffles. 'Calls himself an island trader, but if there's any dirty work going on—opium-smuggling, spying, pearl-poaching—he's usually mixed up in it somewhere. God alone knows what his nationality is, but he keeps himself well in with the island folk, picks up a lot of inside information.'

'He's a work of art, Bunny,' Raffles said, passing me the binoculars.

I focused them on the schooner. Heeled over a little, with a bone in her teeth, she had a litter of green stuff on deck. A giant of a man stood at the wheel. He wore only tattered duck trousers and a brass-studded leather belt equipped with pockets. He was indeed a work of art, for intricate tattoo designs writhed all over his muscular torso, shark-mouthed visage, hairless head.

'He's on his way out to those cruisers,' said the Purser. 'He'll peddle that green stuff to their crews—yams, breadfruit, fresh coconuts. And you can bet your life he's got the latest scuttle-butt on the shore situation, for their Captains, that'll stuff some of their dollars, deutschmarks, and pounds sterling into that money-belt of his.'

'Money-belt?' said Raffles.

I glanced at him furtively. Our funds were low, and travelling came expensive. But Raffles' grey eyes were unfathomable.

The schooner bore away to starboard, and I forgot the Tattooed Man as the Purser pointed out to us a headland, grown over with palm forest, rising steeply out of the sea.

'Upolu Head,' said the Purser. 'You can just see Vailima, up there.'

I glimpsed the gable end of a house high up among the dense foliage—the house, solitary and enigmatic under the heat-shimmer, of the lone man who challenged with his pen the guns of the Three Big W's.

Was he still there?

I swallowed with a dry throat as the sudden booming of the liner's siren awoke deep echoes in the island hills.

'The portrait of R.L.S.?' said William Haggard, as, in the light from a pendent hurricane lantern, we sat at dinner that night on the screened verandah of his secluded bungalow on the outskirts of the little Samoan capital, Apia. 'Yes, I was about to mention that matter.'

'The portrait exists?' Raffles asked.

'Certainly,' said our host. 'The young artist arrived, spent a couple of weeks up at Vailima, and has done a fine job. He's gone on now to Tahiti. There's some beachcombing French artist there called Gauguin whom he's keen to meet, for some reason. Anyway, he's left the Stevenson portrait up at Vailima, as I told him you chaps were coming and would deliver it to the Club for him. I thought you wouldn't mind?'

'Good heavens, no,' said Raffles. 'We'll be delighted.'

'We'll ride up to Vailima next week, then, and collect it. R.L.S. is alone up there just now, except for his old mother. His American wife, Fanny Vandegrift Stevenson, and her son and daughter, Lloyd and Belle—R.L.S.'s stepchildren—have gone to Sydney for some dental treatment that's a bit beyond our island resources.'

Raffles mentioned the lurking cruisers we had seen, and our host nodded.

'Stevenson's friend, Chief Mataafa, who was passed over by the Berlin Convention, has a problem. Four hot-headed young village chiefs of his made a warlike demonstration on his behalf the other day. The Island Council advised the Paramount Chief to have them jailed. Mr. Cedarcrantz, the neutral Swedish gentleman who's Chairman of the Council, wisely protested at this, but the three Consuls on the Council pay little attention to him.'

'The usual fate of neutral chairmen,' said Raffles—'however wise.'

'The result, of course,' said Haggard, 'is that Chief Mataafa is having difficulty in restraining his other hot-heads. I'm afraid trouble's brewing. Hence those cruisers.'

He rose.

'If you'll excuse me,' he said, 'I've some paper work to finish. It'll merely be pigeon-holed in Whitehall, of course. All the same, it must go on the liner when it leaves tomorrow. Make yourselves at home.'

It was such a lovely night, however, fragrant and tranquil under a sky splendid with stars, that Raffles and I were lured out for a post-prandial stroll around.

'Washington, Whitehall and the Wilhelmstrasse,' I remarked, as we sauntered with our cigarettes under the palm fronds, 'seem as remote as—'

'Shh!' said Raffles. 'Listen!'

We paused, listening—and I became aware of a faint crooning sound. To find out where it was coming from, we walked along a footpath that meandered, starlit, through the palm trees, and the crooning became gradually identifiable as that of male voices intoning, in slow harmony, a song of profound melancholy.

Abruptly, the trees ended. Across a narrow, starlit space, the wall of a building loomed up before us. The building stood on squat brick pillars, like Haggard's bungalow, but was bigger, with glassless, unlighted windows, very small, about twelve feet above ground.

'Barred windows, Bunny,' Raffles murmured. 'Cells. This must be the side of the jailhouse—with those four prisoners in it that Haggard mentioned.'

Under the fringing trees, we stood listening to the slow, rhythmic, deep-toned lament of the imprisoned village subchiefs in the darkness of their cells.

'White Shadows in the South Seas,' Raffles muttered—and suddenly gripped my arm, whispering, 'See who's here!'

Soundless, a man was stealing along in the narrow space between the trees and the jailhouse wall. Barefoot, huge in the star-glimmer, his torso, face and scalp writhed over by tattooing, he held in one hand what looked to me like a large reel of the kind used for big-game fishing.

He passed quite close to us and vanished around to what evidently was the back of the jailhouse. Hugging the tree-shadow, we followed, to see what he was up to, but when the back of the jailhouse came into view, there was no sign of the man there. The crooning of the prisoners continued—and suddenly, from among the trees to our right, sounded a screech so strident and weird that my hair stood up at it.

'Jungle fowl disturbed,' Raffles whispered. 'The fellow must

44

have gone into the trees there. Come on!'

Cautiously, we prospected around for quite a while in the gloom and glimmer under the fronds, but it was in vain. We had lost our man.

'*And* his brass-studded money-belt,' Raffles said wryly. 'We missed our chance, Bunny. We should have collared him the moment we saw him. We'll say nothing of this to our host. Samoan politics are no business of ours. But if we get a second chance at that belt—*that's* our business!'

In the darkness of the jailhouse, the prisoners crooned on.

The way to Vailima was by a rough bridle-path that serpentined upward through dense and sweltering rain forest. William Haggard provided us with horses and, as the three of us rode them, mostly at a walk, up the frond-shadowed, narrow track, he told us that Stevenson had an old white horse called Harry, but seldom rode down to Apia on it—even to get a haircut.

'R.L.S. is no longer the velvet-jacketed, aesthetic young Scot,' Haggard told us, 'who wrote the exquisite *Prince Otto*, then took London by storm with *Jekyll. And Hyde*. Those days are gone. He's spent years now as a sea gypsy roaming the Pacific in chartered schooners—the *Casco*, the *Equator*—writing on every subject under the sun and searching for a home in a climate he can survive in.'

'And he's found his home here?' Raffles said.

'Yes—at last,' said Haggard. 'An old house—Vailima—that he's planning to enlarge. He's come a long way, R.L.S. He's still only just turned forty, and he's nearly that many books to show for it. He owes a lot to the comradeship and care of his American wife.'

' "Steel true, blade straight," ' I quoted, ' "the Great Artificer made my mate—" '

'Right, Manders,' Haggard said. 'That's what R.L.S. wrote in a poem to Fanny Vandegrift Stevenson. She collaborated in one of his books, you know—*The Dynamiter*, a sequel to his *New Arabian Nights*. It's a pity you won't meet Fanny, as she's—'

He broke off sharply—for, as we rounded a bend in the steep bridle-path, there burst upon us a sight of such ferocity that our horses shied, snorting, at it.

It was a gigantic grimace, a painted visage dangling from a coconut-fibre rope slung between trees and squarely barring our way.

'Mataafa's war totem,' said Haggard, as we quieted our horses and edged them past the dangling monstrosity. 'It's a warning to all and sundry that Tusitala's house, Vailima, is under the protection of Chief Mataafa.'

Here, in this sweltering rain forest, some lines of Stevenson's came with a haunting new reality to my memory: *'There fell a war in a woody place, In a kingdom by the sea—'* And between the trees I glimpsed for a moment the gleam of the wide Pacific.

'Tusitala's house, Haggard?' Raffles said.

'The Samoans' name for R.L.S.,' Haggard told us. 'Tusitala, Teller of Tales. He's composed one specially for them— *The Bottle Imp*, the first original tale ever actually written down in the Samoan language. As a matter of fact, we may find some of Mataafa's people at Vailima. They can't hear their friend, Tusitala, read his tale to them often enough.'

But when we reached Vailima, there was nobody to be seen. The burning hush of noon quelled the old house and held it silent. Steep steps led up to a palm-thatched verandah. Here at the foot of the steps, as we dismounted from our horses, I became aware, in the stillness, of the rippling of some small waterfall unseen among the trees crowding close around the small clearing, and a thin piping sound, as of a musical instrument, was faintly audible to me.

'A flageolet,' Haggard said. 'R.L.S. likes to play on it, says it helps him write verses—his "penny whistles", as he calls them.'

From the tawny shade of the verandah, a woman's voice called, 'Good day to ye, Mr. Haggard. Hitch your horses to the steps rail, they'll be seen to.' The voice rose, calling, 'Poë Amailé! Go tell Mr. Stevenson that Mr. Haggard's here wi' two friends.'

Hitching our horses, Raffles and I followed Haggard up the steps to the verandah, where he introduced us to R.L.S.'s mother, who bore a marked resemblance to our monarch, the Widow at Windsor.

'Ye'll forgive me if I bide in my chair,' said the old lady, sparing Raffles and myself a hand, in turn, from her crochet-work. ''Tis a grand chair, this—what my daughter-in-law Fanny

46

calls a patent American rocker. She had it sent all the way from San Francisco for me. She's impetuous wi' her siller, is Fanny.' The old lady gave us a keen look. 'Ye'll be the Club gentlemen, nae doot, come for Louis's portrait?'

'We're very much looking forward to seeing it, Mrs. Stevenson,' said Raffles, making no mention, of course, of our hundred-guinea vested interest in it.

'Aye, 'tis nae a bad portrait,' said Mrs. Stevenson—adding, as the faint sound of the flageolet fell silent, 'There noo, Louis hae done wi' his piping. He'll be wi' ye in a wee while. Mr. Haggard, show your friends the portrait. 'Tis within, on Fanny's harmonium. Ye ken the way.'

We followed Haggard through a bead-curtained doorway from the verandah into a sparsely furnished living-room. Framed pictures of spray-swept lighthouses were on the walls, with a large, yellowing lithograph portrait of the stern, side-whiskered old Scottish engineer, R.L.S.'s late father, who had designed and superintended the building of those lighthouses on the stormy coasts of Mull and Skye and the remote Hebrides.

In marked contrast was the portrait of R.L.S. Propped on top of a small harmonium against one wall, the freshly painted canvas, tacked to a stretcher, portrayed a man lankly, painfully thin, with the fine dark eyes and longish hair of a gypsy. In an open-necked shirt, white trousers tucked into mosquito-boots, he stood in tropical sunshine, rolling a cigarette, against the vivid green background of the palm forest.

The bead curtain rattled. We turned from the portrait to the man.

'Ah, Louis,' said Haggard. 'Here are Raffles and Manders, the Club's envoys.'

'The Club's honoured me,' said R.L.S., shaking hands with us. He gestured with a half-rolled cigarette at the portrait. 'If any disagreeable member says "Stevenson's gone off a lot," shoot him for me.'

'Both barrels,' Raffles assured him.

R.L.S. smiled. 'William, what's new, down in Apia?'

'Baron and Baroness Von Pilsach are giving a Ball next week,' said Haggard, 'at the German Consulate. I've received an invitation for myself and my house guests, Raffles and Manders. And—you, Louis?'

'Not I, William! Not the meddlesome Scot! My bombardment of the British and American press, with my long-range pea-shooter, is getting results. Two whole sacks of mail came in for me on the liner. Ten per cent imperialistic abuse—but, for the rest, pledges of support from decent public opinion.'

'That's good, Louis.'

'Give us just a little more time, William, and sundry bald-headed diplomats will be compelled to revise their Berlin Convention arrangements, and we shall get on the Island Council a strong voice that speaks for *Samoa* and the *Samoans*—the voice of Chief Mataafa.'

'His four village chiefs are still in the jailhouse, Louis.'

'Pray God, then,' said R.L.S., 'that Mataafa can keep his other hot-heads in check, or—with cruisers in the offing—we know what to expect. But no politics now! Raffles, Manders, you're fresh from London. I hunger for news of gaslight, theatres, Thames-side fogs and hansom-cabs.'

He had indeed the exile's lust for talk, and at luncheon on the verandah, where we were waited on by a barefoot Samoan youth in a *lava-lava*, our conversation covered a multitude of subjects.

We sat long over our claret, and when Haggard, Raffles and I rode off at last, Raffles carrying the portrait of R.L.S., the brief tropic dusk had brought out the sparkle of early stars over the palm forest, and there followed us for a little way, down the bridle-path from Vailima, the lonely note of the flageolet.

'The German Consulate, Mr. Manders, is quite the handsomest in Apia,' said Mrs. Pumphrey-Yeats.

It was the night of the Von Pilsach Ball, and I was waltzing with Mrs. Pumphrey-Yeats, a planter's lady, somewhat fulsome of figure, to the strains of a Marine band from the cruiser *Kronprinz Eugen.*

'The coloured lanterns in the trees out there, if only they weren't *palm* trees,' continued Mrs. Pumphrey-Yeats, as I piloted her around the floor, 'would remind one of the enchanting beer gardens of the Unter-den-Linden. Are you familiar with them, Mr. Manders?'

'Alas, no, Mrs. Pumphrey-Yeats.'

'Ah, well—how *gay* we all are here tonight, Mr. Manders! Baron and Baroness Senfft Von Pilsach are quite the arbiters

48

of our planter society, don't you know. You are seeing us at our best. Everybody who's by way of being *any*body in Samoa is here, of course. And it's so pleasant to see fresh English faces, such as your own and that of your friend Mr. Raffles.'

'It's kind of you to say so, Mrs. Pumphrey-Yeats.'

'I see that Mr. Raffles is treading the light fantastic with the Baroness. Dear Gardi Von Pilsach, how well she carries herself, all things considered. And Baron Senfft! A Potsdam moustache, I always think, lends so much distinction to a man—given the right kind of face.'

'Indeed yes, Mrs. Pumphrey-Yeats.'

'Tell me, Mr. Manders, have you met our more prominent residents? The United States Consul? A demon poker-player, they tell me. And our own British Consul, with that delightful manner of his? An Old Etonian, don't you know. And poor, dear Mr. Cedarcrantz, Chairman of the Island Council? He's that large, flaxen-haired Swedish gentleman with the *wilfully* neutral expression.'

'Yes, I've had the pleasure, Mrs. Pumphrey-Yeats.'

'Oh, look! See who's arriving, Mr. Manders! Lo and behold, the Navies are in our midst!'

I saw that an influx had occurred, into the ballroom, of bronzed, handsome Naval officers—German, American and British—in white uniforms splendid with gold braid and medals.

'It's an open secret, of course,' said Mrs. Pumphrey-Yeats, 'that cruisers are lurking in the vicinity—*much* to the reassurance of us planter folk, with Chief Mataafa's followers threatening to cut off our heads just because four of his malcontents are rightly held in the jailhouse. So wretchedly unreasonable, the Samoans, but never mind—I expect arrangements will soon be made for them to *belong* to us, don't you, Mr. Manders?'

Before I could reply, the concluding chord of the waltz sounded, and clapping broke out.

'How hot it is tonight!' said Mrs. Pumphrey-Yeats, as I escorted her from the floor. 'I must fan myself vigorously before I make myself agreeable to these stalwart mariners. They've been cruising around Samoa for so long, waiting for something to their purpose to happen, that the poor boys will need feminine help to find their land legs, don't you think?'

'Undoubtedly,' I assured her. 'Thank you for the waltz, Mrs. Pumphrey-Yeats.'

Mopping beads of relief from my brow with my handkerchief, I turned from her, to find Raffles at my side.

'I've danced with her, too, Bunny,' he said. 'She's a type the sun never sets on. Come on, you need a drink—there's a buffet in the ante-room.'

We were having a drink at the buffet when Mr. Haggard joined us. He looked troubled.

'A police runner just came in,' he said, 'and spoke to Mr. Cedarcrantz. I caught a word or two—something about Chief Mataafa's people demonstrating at the jailhouse. Cedarcrantz beckoned to the three Consuls. They've gone into Von Pilsach's sanctum, taking the three cruiser Captains with them. I don't like the look of it. The Island Council's gone into session.'

Two other men joined us just then, and Haggard introduced us, saying that we would be leaving on the liner for San Francisco, taking the portrait of R.L.S.

'It really is a pity,' Haggard added, 'that there'll hardly be time, Raffles, for you and Manders to meet R.L.S.'s American wife, Fanny. She'll be coming in with Lloyd and Belle from Sydney in the liner you leave on.'

'Fanny Vandegrift Stevenson,' Raffles murmured.

Something in his tone made me glance at him, and I saw in his grey eyes a glint that, knowing him as I did, gave me a tingle of foreboding.

He said nothing more, but, as the conversation became general, he touched me on the arm and jerked his head, almost imperceptibly, towards the exit.

The band was playing again in the ballroom as we strolled out unobtrusively into the Consulate gardens, where the coloured lanterns glowed among the palm fronds.

'What's on your mind, Raffles?' I said uneasily.

'Fanny Vandegrift Stevenson, Bunny—and it's just possible that she's put an idea in my head.'

The lilt of the music faded behind us as we left the Consulate gardens. We walked quickly along the road, dusty, palm-fringed, deserted. The lamps of bungalows glimmered among the trees.

Soon a confused shouting of angry voices became audible. I saw a flare of torches ahead. The front of the jailhouse came in sight. A crowd seethed before it, in the tossing light of blazing palm-knots.

I caught a glimpse of brandished, bizarre totems such as the one we had seen on the bridle-path to Vailima. On the jailhouse verandah, reached by a steep flight of steps, four Samoan policemen, white-uniformed, with white topees and drawn truncheons, stood facing the crowd.

On the steps, a grey-haired Samoan of magnificent stature stood with upflung arms, evidently trying to silence the crowd and make himself heard.

Raffles checked. 'Bunny, that's undoubtedly Chief Mataafa, trying to control his people. Come on, quick—round the back!'

We dodged off to the left, skirted around through the trees, gained the back of the jailhouse. The tumult of the crowd at the front sounded like breakers on a reef, but at the back here all was still.

'That night we saw the Tattooed Man, Bunny,' Raffles said. 'What was he up to with that fishing-reel? And how did he manage to vanish so damned suddenly?'

'He went into the trees,' I said. 'We heard a bird screech.'

'Suppose it was something else that disturbed that bird, Bunny? Suppose *this* is where the Tattooed Man vanished to so suddenly.'

In evening-dress as he was, Raffles dropped on all-fours, crawled in between the squat brick pillars that supported the jailhouse. Mystified, I followed. Weeds grew here. They brushed my face. I did not know whether there were snakes in Samoa, but the thought of putting my hand on coils that suddenly writhed and lashed made my flesh creep.

From out front, the wavering glow of the torches reached in fitfully to us. But Raffles, crawling from pillar to pillar, was striking matches, peering at each pillar in turn. Suddenly he was still.

'Fanny Vandegrift,' he muttered, 'God bless you!' The match went out. 'Bunny, d'you remember the title of the book written by Robert Louis *and* Fanny Vandegrift Stevenson?'

'*The Dynamiter*,' I said.

'Look here,' said Raffles, and he struck another match.

'God almighty!' I breathed, appalled.

'A brick gouged out of the pillar here,' Raffles said, 'and dynamite packed in. Bunny, which of the representatives of the Three Big W's got tired of waiting for an incident to occur? Which of them bribed the Tattooed Man to *create* an incident, probably leaving it to his local knowledge how best to do it?'

My heart thumped. The uproar of the crowd outside continued.

'When we saw him prowling around here with that fishing-reel,' Raffles said, 'he was probably making his plans—deciding just how best to plant dynamite here. He probably heard us, and he laid low under here. And that infernal bird misled us. The chap's been back since and planted the dynamite. It must have been *wire* he had on that reel, Bunny—wire to unreel back, when he attached the blasting-cap, so that he could explode the dynamite from well out there among the trees. But there's no blasting-cap and wire attached yet, so he's not yet come back to complete his arrangements.'

'Why not?' I said, with a dry throat.

'Because they may not be needed, Bunny. He's set everything in readiness here, but he's probably had a hand in inciting Chief Mataafa's hot-heads into rushing the jail and releasing the prisoners. If that happens, there'll be no need to blow up the jailhouse with four sub-chiefs and several policemen in it. Rushing the jailhouse will create quite a serious enough incident to bring in the Marines of the Three Big W's—and ruin—' He broke off, gripped my arm. 'Listen!'

The crowd had fallen suddenly silent. Then a mutter of voices began—and swelled to a great, concerted shout: *'Tusitala!'*

'By God,' Raffles said, 'Stevenson's out there! Chief Mataafa must have sent word to him for help, and he's ridden down from Vailima.'

We crawled forward a little to get a worm's eye view of what was going on. In the swaying light of the torches out there, I could see the back of the steps leading down from the jailhouse verandah. And there he was, a gypsy-like figure, lank, long-haired, painfully thin, sitting astride a sway-backed old white horse.

R.L.S. began to speak. The crowd was motionless now, intent to hear his words. Only the torch-flares moved, flickering, and the shadows they cast. R.L.S. talked to the crowd in that voice which they had come to know well, often had walked miles to hear—the voice that on happier occasions had held them spellbound with the adventures of *The Bottle Imp*.

Tusitala, Teller of Tales, talked to the crowd, Chief Mataafa's people, and though I could hear his voice distinctly, I had no idea what he now was saying to that crowd out there, for he was talking to them—with hesitations, groping for elusive words —in their own tongue. And he held that crowd. He held them until he had said what he had to say. Then Chief Mataafa took over from him, speaking in a deep voice and pointing again and again at the man on the old white horse.

'They've done it, Bunny,' Raffles whispered. 'Between them, they've done it! You can *feel* the mood changing.'

A murmur ran through the crowd, then burst into a roar of acclamation: 'Mataafa! Tusitala!'

Palm-flares and totems swayed wildly as the crowd surged forward, surrounding and acclaiming their Chief by birthright and their Bard by adoption.

'The fever's broken,' said Raffles. 'There'll be no rushing the jailhouse now.'

We turned to crawl back—and met a stifled exclamation and, in the fitful light from the torches, the incredulous glare of the Tattooed Man, on all-fours scarcely a yard from us.

'Ah, good evening,' said Raffles. 'So you've decided your dynamite's going to be needed, after all, and you've come to attach the wire and blasting-cap?'

Baring his teeth at us with an animal snarl, the tattooed apparition began to crawl rapidly backward from us. But Raffles was at him. I flung myself into the fray. We thrashed around in a wild flurry of arms and legs. The man was all muscle. It was like trying to subdue a giant octopus.

'His belt, Bunny,' Raffles gasped, 'get his belt!'

He was trying to hold the man in a half-nelson. I managed to hook my fingers of both my hands under the dynamiter's money-belt. I yanked at it with all my strength. The buckle gave way so suddenly that my backward jerk brought my occiput into thundering impact with the pillar just behind me. Fireworks exploded before my eyes—and the next thing of which I was aware was that my tongue had swelled considerably, my face was cradled in weeds, and Raffles' voice was saying, 'Bunny! You all right?'

With an effort, I raised my face out of the weeds. Shadowy, Raffles was crouched on all-fours in front of me. My mouth seemed full of tongue as I managed to mutter, 'Where is he?'

'Gone,' said Raffles. 'I couldn't hold him—and had no desire to. He'll be streaking for his schooner now, and the quicker he gets the anchor up and heads for Fiji or somewhere, the better for all concerned. Come on, pull yourself together. Let's crawl out from under here, clean ourselves up at Haggard's bungalow, and get back to the Von Pilsach Ball.'

'What about the dynamite, Raffles?'

'We'll tell Haggard where it is, Bunny, and how, thanks to a hint from Fanny Vandegrift Stevenson, we thought of looking for it. Haggard can get it removed. But about this money-belt in our possession—not a word, Bunny! We're Englishmen.'

'What's that got to do with it?'

'Bunny—in the currency of which of the Three Big W's was the Tattooed Man bribed? In dollars? In deutschmarks? Or in —*pounds sterling*?'

'Oh, dear God!' I muttered.

'Exactly! The answer's probably in this belt. There's dynamite,' said Raffles—'*and* dynamite!'

On a foggy night nearly six months later, for we had chanced to touch lucky at a faro lay-out in California, so had taken our time in journeying across the United States, Raffles and I arrived back in London. I went with him to his set of rooms in The Albany for a drink before we parted.

In his living-room, with its saddlebag chairs and signed photographs of W. G. Grace, Archie McLaren, C. B. Fry and other famous cricketing friends, Raffles removed the wrappings from the portrait of R.L.S. and propped it up carefully on the well-filled bookcase.

'We'll deliver the portrait to the Club tomorrow, Bunny,' he said, as he poured a couple of whisky-and-sodas. 'It's good to know that Stevenson's succeeded in doing what he set out to do. As we saw in today's *Times*, in the train coming down from Liverpool, his masterly letters from Vailima have changed the situation in Samoa. Chief Mataafa is now a strong *Samoan* voice on the Island Council.'

'It's interesting to note,' I said, 'that Mataafa's people, in gratitude to R.L.S., have made that frightful bridle-path up to Vailima into a passable road for a horse-and-trap.'

'Yes,' Raffles said, unfolding *The Times* newspaper for another look at the report from Samoa. 'You know, I can't get over this speech he made to his Samoan friends at the Feast at Vailima on the completion of the road. I think he must have said *something* of the same kind to them, that night at the jail-house.'

Raffles read aloud, from the newspaper: ' "Chiefs! Samoans! When I saw you working on this road, my heart grew warm, for I thought I saw here something good for Samoa. Who is the true warrior? It is not the man who kills pigs and wounded men. It is the man who builds roads, plants food trees, gathers harvests. *That* is the true champion! And I say to you again— if you do not *use* your country, others will." '

'My God,' I said, 'how true that is!'

Raffles glanced at the portrait on the bookcase, then read on, ' "I have seen these things with my own eyes. I have seen them in Ireland, and I have seen them in the mountains of my own country—Scotland—and my heart was sad. For a time came to them, as it comes now to you, and they were not ready." '

'Go on, Raffles,' I said.

Raffles read on, ' "I love Samoa. I love the land and I love the people. I have chosen them to be my people, to live and die with, and Samoa to be my grave after I am dead. Chiefs! Samoans! The situation has changed. Much of your land is to be restored to you. And I say to you again that which is sure— if you do not *use* it, others will.... To this day, in Europe, there are whole areas that are marsh and bush. And it may be that, after struggling through a thicket, you will come out upon a road as firm and solid as the day it was built—perhaps fifteen hundred years ago—by the Romans. You will see men and women bearing their burdens along that even way. And they give thanks for that convenience, and say to each other that, as the Romans were the greatest of warriors, so also they were the best at building roads." '

'Go on,' I murmured.

' "Samoans! *Our* little road is not built to last for a thousand years—yet, in a sense, it is, for others will come after us to repair and perpetuate it. Samoans, Tusitala with his pen has worked for you, and you have shown, in return, that you are not too proud to work for gratitude. Tusitala thanks you from his heart. And my hope is that, long after you and I are mingled in the dust, your descendants will give thanks for the land they receive of their fathers, and will remember and be grateful to those who laboured for them today on the road to Vailima." '

Raffles laid down the newspaper. He picked up from the table the Tattooed Man's money-belt.

'Bunny, we agreed that we wouldn't examine the contents of this belt till we were back on British soil. And here, at last, we are.' Raffles looked at me strangely. 'Well?'

I hesitated. My palms felt clammy. I swallowed.

'Open it,' I said.

Raffles unstrapped the belt-pockets. He upturned the belt, shook it.

Sheafs of currency notes fell to the table and there slowly unfolded.

We stood gazing down at them.

The gaslight seemed to me to shine with a hectic, uncanny brilliance. Faintly, from fogbound Piccadilly, sounded the muffled bell of a passing hansom.

Raffles was the first of us to speak.

He said slowly, 'We should have foreseen this. We should have realised, Bunny, that whichever minion it was, whether of Whitehall, Washington, or the Wilhelmstrasse, who got impatient for an incident and paid this bribe to get one, he'd do it with money that—if anything went wrong—couldn't be traced back to him.'

Never, as an Englishman, whatever my failings of expensive tastes and fractured ethics, had I felt such a sense of relief.

'Of course,' Raffles said, 'there's food for thought in the fact that Captains of cruisers showing their flags in the Pacific are supplied, for coaling purposes and so on, with the currencies of all countries whose ports they're likely to visit. Still, there are other things in life than this, Bunny.'

He pushed the money aside, looked meditatively at the portrait on the bookcase, then handed me my glass and took up his own.

'Let's drink to him. Let's drink, Bunny, to a man who stands for those better things—on the far side of our horizon. Let's drink to Tusitala,' said A. J. Raffles, as we raised our glasses to the portrait—'before we take a look in *The Times* newspaper for the current exchange rate of the Japanese yen.'

# 4 ADVENTURE OF THE DANCING GIRLS

'Ah, Bunny,' said a familiar voice. 'Awake?'

A curious joggling sensation, accompanied by metallic clangings, had roused me from an uneasy sleep. As I ungummed my eyes, I realised that I was in a train. It was jolting over switch-points.

On the steamy windows of the compartment, wanly gaslit, was the legend *Fumeur Première Classe* spelt backwards.

'What time is it?' I mumbled.

In the corner seat facing mine, Raffles, his travelling tweeds immaculate, a pearl in his cravat, laid aside the book he was reading and consulted his gold half-hunter.

'It's three a.m.,' he said. 'We're just coming into Lyons.'

We were on our way to the so-called Riviera. H.R.H. the popular Heir to the Throne had been paying incognito visits to that coast and, smart Society emulating as always the royal example, there seemed possibilities of worthwhile pickings for us there.

As Raffles gave me a Sullivan from his cigarette-case, I glanced at the two men who shared our compartment. Facing each other, they were taking turns to shake poker-dice from a leather-cup on the raised service-flap of the door on their side.

'Damnation!' said one of the dice-players. 'One pip off a full 'ouse!'

He was English, a fat fellow, bald and flushed, a cigar-stub in his mouth and hammocks under his eyes. He had been in his seat when Raffles and I had boarded the train in Paris.

The other man, tall and gaunt, grey-haired and well groomed, had come along the platform a few minutes later. Evidently acquainted with each other, they had seemed surprised to meet again. They had joined company.

Now, from the look of the fat fellow, who wore a suit of emphatic checks and a coat with an astrakhan collar that seemed somehow to hint at the world of the Theatre, I judged that he had been recruiting his energies by frequent recourse to a large whisky-flask which stood on the service-flap.

The grey-haired man took his turn at shaking the dice in the cup.

'They're not running for you tonight, Mr. Wilton,' he said. 'But your luck will turn. These bouncing bones know neither fear nor favour. Now, let me see. We're throwing now, are we not, for the gentle Geraldine?'

'Never mind that,' said Wilton. 'Get on with it, Colonel, and I tell you straight, I wish I'd never left Shaftesbury Avenue.'

Couplings clanged as the train steamed ponderously to a standstill.

'Shall we get a breath of air, Bunny?' Raffles said. 'It'll help wake you up.'

The station platform being on our side, we were able to step out without discommoding the dice-players. Gaslamps burned blue-white in the clear, mild night.

'*Café! Café bien chaud!*' chanted a man trundling along the platform a trolley bearing cups and a big coffee-urn.

From the compartment we had just left, Wilton's voice was raised in bitter outcry, 'Fours! Strike me pink, 'ow d'you do it? Now you got Geraldine, pick o' the kitties!'

'What does he mean by that, Raffles?' I said. 'Is it some sort of slang term, like those used in the tombola?'

'No. Bunny. It's more interesting than that,' Raffles said. 'You were asleep quite a while, you know. Wilton's lost his bankroll. He's bust. And the fellow he calls "Colonel" brought up the subject of certain assets Wilton possesses. I gathered that the Colonel had vainly made Wilton an offer for those assets in Paris a couple of days ago. The Colonel suggested they play now for those assets. Wilton wouldn't do it at first, but after he'd had a few more drinks he decided his luck was *bound* to change. But so far it hasn't. He's already lost three of his assets, and we've just heard the fourth change hands.'

'What *are* Wilton's assets, Raffles?'

'Girls, Bunny.'

'*Girls?*'

'Eight of them, apparently,' Raffles said. 'They're in the compartment next to our own. Ah, there's one of them now!'

Astonished, I followed his glance. The blind of the compartment next to our own had gone up with a bang, the window
58

was being lowered. A girl with her fair hair in curlers leaned out and beckoned to the coffee chap.

'Oy!' she called. 'Eight cups, please.' She held up eight fingers. '*Huit!*'

'*A votre service, mademoiselle,*' said the coffee chap, trundling his trolley up at a trot under the girl's window.

Raffles moved forward. 'Allow me,' he said to the girl, 'to pass the cups up to you. Lend a hand, Bunny.'

I did so willingly, for, despite her hair being in curlers, the girl was very attractive.

'Yum-yum,' she said, 'doesn't the coffee smell good! We've been dying for it.' She passed the cups one by one into the compartment, saying, 'Becky, Sue, Rosemary—here you are.'

'Thanks, Gerry,' said a voice within the compartment.

'*Combien?*' Raffles asked the coffee chap—and paid him.

'Oh—well—that's very kind of you,' said the girl with her hair in curlers. 'Thank you. Excuse me if I pull down the blind—we look such a sight in here.'

With a charming smile, she raised the window, lowered the blind.

'Gerry,' Raffles said. 'So that must be Geraldine, "pick o' the kitties."'

'A girl like that—lost at poker dice?' I said. 'Nonsense, Raffles!'

'I'm afraid not, Bunny,' said Raffles, as we stood sipping a cup of coffee apiece ourselves. 'From what I gathered while you were asleep, the eight girls are a dancing troupe under Wilton's management. And now he seems to have gambled away their contracts.'

'At poker dice? Incredible, Raffles!'

'I thought it was amusing at first, Bunny—but now that we've had a glimpse of the girls, I'm not so sure. I thought they'd be experienced troupers, able to look out for themselves. But they seem very young, mere innocents abroad. And what does Wilton know about this Colonel fellow, who's certainly not English, to judge by his accent? As far as I've been able to make out, keeping my ears open while you had your eyes shut, the girls have been dancing at some *café-concert* place in Paris. It seems that the Colonel introduced himself to Wilton as a fellow impresario and offered to purchase the girls' contracts. Wilton turned him down, having plans to take the troupe to the Riviera.'

59

'So that's where they're bound for.'

'Yes, and I have a suspicion that the Colonel's seeming surprise at seeing Wilton on this train was bogus. He turned up by design, Bunny. For some reason, he badly wants to get control of those eight young women. He probably intended to make another bid, but Wilton's cooked his own goose with this poker dice business—aided by whisky. I—'

A hoot from the locomotive interrupted, and a cry rang along the platform: *'En voiture! En voiture, messieurs les voyageurs!'*

Back in the compartment, I saw that the two impresarios had discontinued their dicing for stakes that seemed to me to hint perilously at 'white slavery'. Wilton was handing over documents.

'There you are,' he said, with a disgruntled hiccup, 'you got the lot—contracts, identity documents, rail tickets to Nice, the lot! H.R.H. 'as made the Riviera a perishin' goldmine for a troupe of twinkle-toed English kitties. You'll be quids in, Colonel. I never 'ad such luck with the dice.'

'Come now,' said the Colonel, 'you lost half your troupe, but I've given you a good price for the contracts of the other half. No ill-will, Mr. Wilton.'

'Hand-picked, those kitties,' mumbled Wilton, unstoppering his flask—'fresh as a daisy, every one of 'em. Worst night's work I ever did in my life!'

At the next halt of the train, he transferred to the girls' compartment. What tale he told them I was able to judge from the gabble of glib assurances I heard the fat little fellow pouring forth to them later, in the dazzle of morning sunshine at Marseilles.

The Colonel had gone into the booking-hall, and Raffles had followed him unobtrusively to see what he did there.

Wilton was strolling up and down the platform with the girls, who looked charming now that they had taken their hair out of curlers, whereas Wilton in his astrakhan-collared overcoat and brown bowler looked flushed and shifty, his protuberant, frog-like eyes bloodshot.

'It's for your own good, kitties,' I heard him saying. 'It breaks my 'eart, but I couldn't stand in the way of your big chance. Not me, not Alf Wilton. I'm a babe in the woods on this 'ere Riviera, with the language problem an' all, but the Colonel's got the game taped. 'E can book you into the Casinos, see, where the

60

nobs go. 'E can do wonders for you. 'Ush now, 'ere 'e comes. Start right with 'im, kitties. Let 'im see big twinkling smiles!'

The girls' smiles, however, were somewhat reserved as the Colonel approached and was introduced by Wilton. Tall, impeccably frockcoated, the Colonel swept off his silk hat and bowed from the hips. I judged him to be an experienced squire of dames, well aware of those little attentions which young women appreciate, for he was followed by a railway porter wheeling a trolley on which were eight bouquets, besides champagne bottles and glasses and two large hampers which looked as if they contained a light but expensive collation.

While the Colonel was presenting a bouquet to each girl in turn, Raffles rejoined me.

'Bunny,' he murmured, 'he sent two telegrams. I was close enough behind him at the telegraph pigeonhole to get a glimpse of the addresses but not of the text. One was to somebody called Goubillon, at a Villa Françoise, in Nice. The other was to somebody called Miklos, at San Remo just across the Italian frontier.'

'What d'you make of it?' I asked.

'I don't know, Bunny, but I doubt if the fellow's an impresario. Anyway, these are naive young Englishwomen who may be getting out of their depth, so we'd better keep an eye on the situation.'

The Colonel joined the girls in their compartment, and as the train steamed out of the station, leaving Wilton alternately waving his handkerchief and mopping his bald head with it, I began to hear from the adjoining compartment the popping of champagne corks.

The heat of the sun increased as the train, sounding its falsetto hooter at intervals, wound among hills terraced with olive groves. Soon, close by on our right, appeared the sparkle of the sea, with beaches edged by date-palms, and the voices and happy laughter of the girls in the next compartment became increasingly audible and carefree.

'The Colonel's breaking the ice,' Raffles said dryly.

On arrival at Nice the girls, evidently now quite reconciled to being under new management, exhibited no trace of their initial reserve. In fact, it was a happy bevy of young English womanhood that the Colonel escorted on to one of a row of yellow-wheeled victorias with red-tasselled canopies waiting outside the station.

61

Porters loaded the party's luggage into a second victoria, the Colonel took his seat on the box of the first, beside the coachman, and the two vehicles moved off.

Raffles and I, with our valises, followed in a third victoria, instructing our jehu to maintain a discreet interval. Having seen the girls, he gave us a gallic wink, taking us to be mashers.

As our horse clip-clopped along pleasant, tree-shaded streets, we found ourselves leaving the more frequented quarters and going uphill into an area of elaborate villas, each embowered in extensive gardens.

The two carriages ahead turned to the left, into a by-road.

'Keep straight on!' Raffles called sharply, to our jehu—for, as we came level with the turning, it was evident that the by-road was a *cul-de-sac*, where the carriages we were following were turning in at a gateway.

Raffles now stopped our driver, told him to wait, and we walked back to the corner and along the by-road. From a gateway, the two carriages—now without passengers—came out.

'Villa Françoise,' Raffles said, as the carriages passed us, on their way back into town.

I saw that the name of the villa was woven in the wrought-iron of an arch over the gateway.

Suddenly Raffles gripped my arm. 'Bunny, we're in luck! Look at that noticeboard on the gate of the house just beyond Villa Françoise.'

The house indicated, the end house in the *cul-de-sac* and next door to Villa Françoise, had on its gate a noticeboard announcing: *To Let Furnished. Apply: Agence Leblanc. Rue Pastorelli.*

We exchanged a glance, then turned as one and walked back to our waiting victoria.

The house was called L'Hermitage. We rented it for a month, and, the agency undertaking to send us a certain Mademoiselle Hortense as a daily domestic, we moved in right away.

The place had been long neglected. The rambling gardens were a jungle of palmetto, prickly-pear, orange and lemon trees and rioting rose-briar, threaded by paths of crushed white seashell. Between our domain and the Villa Françoise next door was a belt of trees, a tall and tangled palisade of date-palms, cypress, pomegranate, fig, umbrella pine.

As we unpacked our valises. Mademoiselle Hortense arrived,

a sturdy little woman bearing a stringbag laden with vegetables, steaks and yard-long loaves with which to prepare dinner for us. Commending her happy forethought, Raffles inquired casually about the occupants of the Villa Françoise, next door.

'It belongs,' Hortense told us, 'to a foreign lady, a Madame Miklos. She's not often there, she travels much—a handsome lady but hard of feature, messieurs, if we are to be frank with each other. She has a caretaker at Villa Françoise—a Madame Goubillon—a soured, silent woman, messieurs. I speak as I find.'

'It does you credit,' Raffles said courteously.

'When Madame Miklos is in residence,' said Hortense, 'she often has a gentleman visitor—a monsieur of military appearance. As it happens, I saw him just ten minutes ago, going down into the town. If he'd called on Madame Miklos, he must have been disappointed, for I believe Madame's from home. *Excusez-moi, messieurs.*'

Hortense stumped off with her stringbag to the kitchen.

'To judge from the telegram the Colonel sent,' Raffles said, "Madame Miklos is at San Remo. The other telegram, addressed to Goubillon, was to the caretaker next door, probably to tell her to prepare to receive the girls. The Colonel and Madame Miklos are obviously hand-in-glove.'

'I don't like the look of it, Raffles,' I said. 'I think we've stumbled into a bad business here. Everything seems to indicate a white slavery gang at work—with the Villa Françoise, next door, a discreet staging-post from which the unfortunate young women are shipped out to Buenos Aires.'

'We need more data, Bunny,' said Raffles. 'Hortense says the Colonel's gone down to the town. I think I'll go down there and see if I can find out anything about him.'

It was very late when Raffles returned.

'I found him,' he said. 'He was coming out of a ladies' costumiers in the Place du Maréchal Masséna. From there he went to a hotel, booked a room, had a leisurely dinner. I heard him ask at the hotel desk for a morning call at eight o'clock with *café complet.* I shall be in the vicinity at that time, Bunny, to pick up his trail. You must keep a sharp eye on Villa Françoise, next door.'

Next morning, accordingly, found me prowling the wilderness of our grounds, trying to get a look through the tangled belt of trees and thickets into the grounds of the white slave gang's staging-post. Raffles was absent, Mademoiselle Hortense was shopping with her stringbag. Crickets seethed about me, butterflies danced in the quiver of heat and colour.

I had just paused to mop my streaming face when a shot rang out. I froze. A second shot followed almost instantly. I heard the cry of a girl.

My heart pounding, I forced my way through a choked growth of briar and cactus, got into the belt of trees. From here, bending and craning I was able to make out, across a wide, neglected garden, a verandah very much like her own.

The girl Geraldine stood on the verandah steps. She held a double-barrelled gun. She was shooting at clay-pigeons loosed by one of the other girls. In the instant I saw her, Geraldine flung the gun-butt to her shoulder and fired. I heard shot rattling in the treetops over my head. She fired the second barrel, on a lower trajectory, and I was unable to repress a shout of horror as what felt like a swarm of incensed bees assaulted my right arm. I clapped my left hand to it.

'Who's there?' cried Geraldine.

She stood for a second transfixed, then came running towards the belt of trees.

'Who is it?' she called, in panic. 'Did I shoot somebody?'

I started to back away as soundlessly as possible. But Geraldine, carrying her gun at the high port, thrust with it through the impeding foliage. She burst into view a yard from me. Her eyes opened wide. She was looking at my right arm. She went very white. I looked at my arm. I felt myself, too, go white. The sleeve of my blazer was drenched with blood.

I tried to be jaunty about it. 'It's nothing—just a bit of a peppering,' I said, but even to my own ears my amused laugh sounded far off and curiously enervated. 'If you'll excuse me—'

I made to bow and withdraw, but my knees seemed to be bending out sideways. The trees revolved. I was conscious of being surrounded by girls, upholding me. They supported me across the garden of Villa Françoise, up the verandah steps, through french windows, and guided me to a couch.

While some girls arranged cushions under my head and others put my feet up, Geraldine thrust the gun angrily on to a rack above a shelf bearing cartridge-boxes and half-a-dozen or so clay pigeons.

64

'Never again!' she said. She came to lean over me, looking into my eyes, and smoothing back my hair with her hand. 'Lie still,' she enjoined me. 'Madame Goubillon, the housekeeper, has gone for a doctor.'

By now, I was beginning to think that the mishap might pay dividends. It had got me inside the enigmatic Villa Françoise. The doctor came. Geraldine must have downed me with her choke barrel, for the Number Five shot in my arm were pretty well grouped. The doctor gouged out about a dozen of them, put a dressing on my arm, bound the dressing with adhesive tape.

The girls insisted that I stay for lunch. They wanted me to have it while lying down, but I felt strong enough to join them at table, where two French ladies also were present.

'They're sempstresses,' Geraldine told me. 'They're making new costumes for us. We're dancers, you know, and we've been taken over by a new manager. He has special plans for us. That's why we're at this villa, instead of a hotel. He wants to keep us in—what's that word the Indians use?'

'Purdah?' I suggested.

'In purdah, yes—away from the public eye,' said Geraldine, 'till our new costumes are ready. They're to be all alike, a lovely shade of fuschia, with picture hats, long gloves, parasols, everything to match. When we *do* show ourselves, he says, we shall make a sensation. To get people wondering and talking about us, the Colonel—that's our new manager—is going to take us on a trip along the coast to San Remo, in Italy, and back.'

My mind was racing. It was obvious that the girls believed this preposterous story they had been given. I judged that, once in Italy, they would not be returning. Their wardrobes were being replenished in order to impress the higher class of vice ring *entrepreneurs* when the girls arrived in the flesh market of Buenos Aires, having been shipped there from Genoa.

I asked Geraldine when they expected to be making their little excursion to San Remo.

'As soon as our new costumes are ready,' she told me. 'We're planning a sort of dress rehearsal tomorrow evening. You and your friend bought us coffee at Lyons, so would you and he care to take coffee with us here tomorrow evening—and tell us what you think of our new costumes?'

I jumped at the offer. I could not wait to tell Raffles about it.

65

As soon as I decently could, I returned to our own place. He was not yet back.

At midnight, he still had not shown up. I felt very uneasy, but, sitting up for him, I must have fallen into a troubled sleep, for the next thing I knew, it was daylight—and still no sign of Raffles.

There was nothing I could do except prowl to and fro on our side of the strip of trees and spy on any doings next door. All day the Villa Françoise basked, silent, in the heat—until, as twilight was beginning to close in again, a thud of hooves and jingle of harness told me of an arrival.

Peering through the thickets, I saw the girls running down their verandah steps to a delivery van. I heard their excited voices as bandboxes and hatboxes were unloaded from the van. The girls' costumes had arrived.

Behind me, as I crouched in the thickets, a voice said, 'What are you doing there, Bunny?'

I lurched round, in a fury of relief. 'Where the devil have you been?' I said.

'Most of last night,' said Raffles, 'I was crouched close to Mother Earth under the verandah of a villa at San Remo. I followed the Colonel there and I've followed him back again. He's now at his hotel in Nice, dining. I left him to it, as I know he'll be coming up to Villa Françoise tonight.'

'To attend a dress rehearsal?' I said. 'We're invited, too.'

I was gratified by his look of astonishment as I pushed back my sleeve to show him my arm, and explained how I had been winged.

'Bunny,' he said, 'what should I do without you? This invitation you've got for us fits in very well. We'll be there!'

At nine o'clock, the coffee hour suggested by Geraldine, I plucked the bellpull of the Villa Françoise. Raffles and I were in evening dress. The night was warm, the velvet sky dusted with stars. From the dark, overgrown grounds sounded the monotonous chirring of crickets. Geraldine herself opened the door to us. She looked enchanting in a gown of a fuchsia hue, her fair hair alluringly coiffed, her eyes bright with excitement.

'Is your new manager here?' Raffles asked.

'Not yet,' she said. 'We expect him later.'

She led us across a spacious hall to a room where a piano was being played. And there they were, one of them turning from the piano—the girls in their identical gowns of fuchsia. The Gaiety Theatre itself could not have presented a lovelier chorus of English young womanhood. That they had been gambled away at poker dice by a venal manager, had fallen into the hands of white slavers, and now were on the road to ultimate degradation—the notorious road to Buenos Aires—seemed to me almost incredible.

I wondered what Raffles' intentions were in the matter.

The excited girls served coffee to us. Conversation was animated. One thing led to another. Clarissa, the lovely brunette who played the piano, provided music for a little fashion show for us, the girls donning their long gloves and charming picture hats and twirling around for our admiration. The girls being dancers, and the floor polished parquet with rugs easily set aside, what followed was natural. I never had realised what a waltz could be until I spun round the big room with Geraldine in my embrace.

Suddenly the piano stopped. We all—including Raffles, partnering the auburn-haired Rosemary—looked towards the doorway.

The Colonel was standing there. He had a briefcase in his hand. He was white with rage.

'What,' he demanded, 'is the meaning of this?'

'If the ladies will excuse us,' Raffles said, 'and we can have a word with you in private, Colonel, I'll be happy to explain.'

The Colonel hesitated for a moment, looking searchingly at us, then said harshly, 'Come!'

We followed him across the hall into the room I had been in the day before. He slammed the door, turned to us.

'Now,' he said, tight-lipped. 'I saw you men on the train. Who are you? Who admitted you to this house?'

Raffles took a Sullivan from his cigarette-case.

'Colonel,' he said, 'I spent several uncomfortable hours last night under the verandah of a villa at San Remo—listening to a conversation between yourself and a Madame Miklos. It was very interesting. You acquired, at poker dice, the identity documents and contracts of the eight young Englishwomen in the other room here. I gather that you and your partner, Madame Miklos, operate a group of personable young women in the perpetration of a neat, ambitious swindle of your invention. You've done very well with it recently in the main Italian cities. You intended to operate your pretty puppets next in France. You went to Paris to prepare the ground. Madame Miklos was to have joined you with her group of harpies. But there had been complaints. The Italian police were becoming dangerous. She wrote to you that she was nervous about what might happen at the frontier when they tried to cross into France.'

Raffles lighted his cigarette. My heart thumped. The Colonel stood rigid.

'You wrote to Madame Miklos,' Raffles went on, 'to gather her party together at a certain villa at San Remo, and to dress her girls in a way that you carefully specified, with particular reference to large picture hats. You planned that, tomorrow, you would take the English girls in the other room here across to San Remo. Later tomorrow you would bring across the frontier into France, Colonel, *not* the English girls—no! Instead, you would bring—armed with the English girls' documents and contracts and dressed in identical fashion—Madame Miklos and her attractive harpies. Well, Colonel?'

'Who are you?' the Colonel said thickly.

'That's immaterial,' Raffles said. 'Colonel, if you'd pulled off your plan, these English girls would have been in a fix. Stranded in San Remo without documents of any kind, they'd have been picked up by the Italian police and accused of being the harpies about whom complaints have been made. The girls would have been jailed, and perhaps for a long time, before the British consular authorities could prove them innocent. Now, Colonel— what are you going to about this?'

The Colonel, close-set eyes glittering, gnawed at his grey moustache.

'No suggestion?' said Raffles. 'Then I'll *tell* you what you're going to do. You're going to hand over that money.'

'What money?'

'The money handed over to you by Madame Miklos—the fruit of your Italian operations,' Raffles said. 'Let's have a look at it, Colonel—the contents of that briefcase.'

Slowly, the Colonel unbuckled his briefcase, shook out on to the table a dozen slim sheaves of high denomination banknotes. His hand went to his jacket-pocket—and flashed out— and Raffles struck sidelong. A small revolver, a derringer, flew into the air—and Raffles, the best slip-fielder in English cricket, caught the weapon as it fell. But the Colonel, with a sweep of his

68

briefcase, smashed out the oil-lamp. Glass crashed, the room went black. I heard a rasp of curtain-rings, glimpsed a shadow dart out through the french windows, vault the verandah rail, vanish.

'Stampeded him, Bunny,' said Raffles. 'Good. I thought he'd do that when he lost his revolver—make a grab for the money, and run. But, from the feel of things, he's only got about two of the banknote packets, leaving the rest for—'

A shot was fired, out in the grounds—and, from all sides out there shouts sounded: *'Halte! Halte-là!'*

'Oh, dear God!' I said.

'Police,' said Raffles. 'They must have followed him up here —thrown a cordon round the grounds. That means the Italian police must have picked up Madame Miklos and her harpies, and set the Nice police to collar the Colonel and the money he was carrying. Listen!'

Somewhere out there, men were shouting at each other in urgent inquiry.

'The hounds sound baulked,' Raffles said. 'He must have got through the cordon. They'll be swarming into the house here any minute. Bunny, quick—peel that adhesive tape from your arm. Let me have it. Right. Now go to the girls, stop them panicking. Tell 'em anything. Keep 'em quiet!'

Though at a loss to divine his intentions, I did as he asked. As I stepped into the lighted hall, closing the door of the dark room behind me, Geraldine and the other girls came crowding into the hall.

'Don't be alarmed,' I told them. 'I'm afraid your new manager is a man of straw—wanted by the police. They're all around, out in the grounds, looking for him. They'll be coming into the house any minute, to ask questions, but there's no occasion,' I assured the girls, hoping they would not notice that my knees were knocking together, 'for the slightest alarm.'

The girls were bewildered. They plied me with questions. I answered them as best I could. I hardly knew what I was saying. Suddenly a heavy pounding sounded on the front door. It was flung open. A police officer with epaulettes surged in, followed by gendarmes with drawn truncheons.

'Did you get him, Officer?' asked a voice.

It was Raffles. He had come into the hall.

'Who are you two men?' demanded the police officer.

'Coffee guests,' said Raffles, 'of these young English ladies. We're their neighbours. The young ladies are *artistes-de-théâtre*. My friend and I had reason to be suspicious of their manager. We felt it our duty to demand to see his credentials. Instead of producing them, he produced a revolver. I now hand it to you, in evidence.'

'*Merci*, monsieur.'

'We wrested it from him, but he smashed out the lamp and took to his heels.'

'With a briefcase? He had a briefcase?' said the police officer eagerly.

'A briefcase?' said Raffles. 'Why, yes, I think he had—had he not, Bunny?'

'Such,' I faltered, 'was my impression.'

'I think he dropped it,' said Raffles, 'in the scuffle.'

'In that room there?' said the police officer—and, at Raffles' nod, took up one of the hall lamps, went into the room.

In a moment, he came out—carrying the briefcase. He shook out its contents on the hall table.

The blood surged in my head. There had been, originally, a dozen sheaves of banknotes in the briefcase. Raffles had said that the Colonel had snatched up and got away with not more than two. Yet there were now lying on the hall table, only five.

'This,' said the police officer, 'is only a small part of the money I had been given to understand the man was carrying in a briefcase.'

'Perhaps the fellow transferred some to his pockets?' Raffles suggested.

'That we shall know when we catch him,' said the police officer. 'Meantime, this house, and everybody in it, must be searched. *Mesdemoiselles*, a female person from the *Gendarmerie* will be here to attend to you shortly. You may wait in that room there.'

I dared not look at Raffles. Not for a minute did I think that the money unaccounted for would be found upon his person. Nor was it. But the search of the room where we had had the scuffle worried me. The police started their search with that room, and they were thorough. When they emerged from the room and started to search the hall, I knew that they had found nothing.

At last, all the searching was over. Geraldine and the other girls prepared fresh coffee for us.

'It was fortunate,' said the police officer, as he sipped his coffee, 'that you gentlemen concerned yourselves in the young ladies' interests. You will see soon enough, in the newspapers, what is at the root of this matter. For the moment, the man has escaped, and with a good deal of money—but we shall lay him by the heels before long, never fear.'

'We English visitors to your delightful Riviera,' Raffles said, 'have implicit confidence in the French police.'

'*Merci, monsieur! Trop gentil!*'

'All the same, Bunny,' said Raffles, as, the police having gone, and ourselves having recommended the girls to get a good night's rest, we walked back to our own place next door, 'it's to be hoped the police don't catch the Colonel till we're out of France. It might bring up the question of the money unaccounted for. All being well, we'll use part of the swag to make a theatrical investment in London—in exchange for these girls being given parts. One's only to dance with them to realise their natural gifts.'

'Personally,' I said, 'I was convinced they were on the road to Buenos Aires. But tell me, Raffles, how the devil is it that the police failed to find that missing money? Where *is* the swag?'

We were turning in at the gateway to our own shadowy grounds.

'It should be over here somewhere,' said Raffles, moving off to the left. 'It's a job for daylight, really, but— Ah, here's one instalment of it, I think!'

From the crushed white seashell of the path, he picked up a circular object. He handed it to me. It was a thin, greyish disc, about the size of a saucer. Like a saucer, it was concave. Pressed into the hollow side and held in place by a strip of adhesive tape was a thin sheaf of banknotes of high denomination.

'Good God!' I said. 'A clay pigeon!'

'There were five of them, Bunny. I noticed them when we went into that room with the Colonel. There were five of these discs on a rack with the cartridge-boxes. The projector was on the rack, too. With the police cordon surrounding the house, the only chance of getting away with some swag was to render it airborne. I depressed the spring of the projector, so like a crossbow in principle, to get long flight. If there had been any left for

71

the police to see, ideas might have occurred to them. As it was, I carefully broke the spring of the projector when it had served my purpose, and the useless object conveyed no significance to the searchers' alert minds. By the way, is your bandage staying in place, Bunny, without the adhesive tape?'

'I think so, Raffles.'

I spoke absently, as I looked, with fascination, from the disc in my hands to the belt of trees, an undulant rampart looming up darkly against the night sky.

I could see, in my mind's eye, those thin clay flying saucers skimming up, five of them in quick succession, from the french windows of that dark room in the Villa Françoise, and, soaring silently over the police cordon and the treetops, landing lightly in the wilderness of our rented grounds here.

'The disc in your hands,' Raffles said, 'is worth about five hundred pounds. The other four are each worth about the same. But leave them for now. We'll look for them at our leisure, in daylight.'

'Clay pigeons!' I said, marvelling.

'Birds of passage, Bunny, carrier pigeons homing unerringly, bearing momentous notes—banknotes!'

Crickets chirred around us, here in the shadowy garden, as Raffles offered me a cigarette from his case.

'Considering,' he said, 'the broad hint given to me by the availability of two useful things—the projector and your adhesive tape, Bunny—I think we can slightly revise the usual onomatopaeic rendering of pigeons' rhythmic but monotonous cooing.'

'Onomatopaeic rendering?' I said, mystified.

He crooned it for me. And I saw his wicked grin in the darkling as a corroborative echo came back from a woodpigeon roosting somewhere in the treetops.

'Take two *clues*, maybe,' it drowsily cooed.

# 5 COCAINE AND THE THIEF WITH TREMBLING HANDS

'I've heard a curious rumour,' said Ivor Kern, 'that might interest you, Raffles, with your knack of opening safes.'

'Your table talk, Ivor,' said Raffles, as we sat drinking Kern's whisky in the gaslit, cluttered living-room over his shambles of an antiques emporium in the King's Road, Chelsea, 'has occasionally proved fertile—eh, Bunny?'

'Admittedly, Raffles,' I said—though with certain mental reservations, for when Kern, the 'fence' we did business with, put us on the track of something lucrative, he did not scruple to sting us for what he called his 'introduction fee'.

'But safes, Ivor,' Raffles went on, 'can present problems. What I happen to know about safes I learned from a crooked old wizard of a Belgian locksmith. Compared with him, I'm just —at best—an amateur. I regard safes, in the main, as best left to professional cracksmen.'

'This fellow Warren Grapner, that I've heard the rumour about,' Kern said, with his cynical smile, 'is a pro—a brilliant one, pulled off a lot of good jobs. But he has a weakness. Cocaine! It did him in. He's an addict, sniffs the stuff when he works. It keys him up. But he struck a tartar of a safe at a stately mansion up near Matlock Spa. The effect of his dope wore off—'

'The Achilles heel of all addicts,' said Raffles—'the law of diminishing returns.'

'Result was,' said Kern, 'his hands began to tremble. He'd damned near got that safe open, but he couldn't finish. His hands were shaking like aspens, with the result that he knocked a plaster bust of Richard Wagner off the top of the safe, and the crash roused the whole house.'

'I've occasionally experienced that kind of *contretemps* myself,' Raffles said—'but in nightmares, fortunately.'

'Knock on wood,' I said, suiting the action to the word.

'Was this Grapner fellow nabbed, Ivor?' Raffles asked.

'He hadn't a chance, Raffles. His withdrawal symptoms,' Kern explained, 'had done him in. His wits were addled, his legs

73

were twitching, and his clever hands were trembling so badly that the peelers could hardly get the bracelets on him.'

'H'm,' said Raffles. 'A pitiful picture! An object lesson for us—eh, Bunny?'

'My God, yes,' I muttered, and my own hands were none too steady as I helped myself to Kern's whisky.

'Grapner came up in front of the local magistrate,' Kern went on, 'who remanded him for the Assizes. Grapner went down for five years. He was just recently released, and you'd have thought his experience would have put him off cocaine forever.'

'But he's at it again?' said Raffles.

'I hear he's sniffing the stuff with both nostrils,' said Kern, 'to make up for lost time. But the queer thing is this rumour that's come to my ears about him. It seems that that local magistrate—some old countrified J.P. called "Squire" Barribar—who remanded Warren Grapner for the Assizes is now in London looking high and low for him.'

I saw Raffles frown. 'Squire Barribar?' he said. 'Bunny, Squire Barribar—James Barribar, Esquire, J.P.—is a country member of one of my clubs. By profession he's an engineer—head of the Barribar Ironworks and Steam Tackle Company.'

'Steam tackle?' I said.

'Steamrollers, steam ploughs, and especially the big, gaudy traction engines, Show engines, that haul and power the merry-go-rounds and switchbacks on the fairgrounds. The yard of the Barribar Iron works, Bunny, is a favourite winter quarters for the carnival folk. They call Squire Barribar "The Showmen's J.P."—because he's the only magistrate in England who has a soft spot for them. He regards them as carrying on the good old tradition of Merrie England. Now, why the devil, Ivor, should that old magistrate want to get in touch with this cocaine-sniffing safebreaker Warren Grapner?'

'Search me,' said Kern.

'I'll see if I can find out,' Raffles said. 'I like the old Squire. I've often played billiards with him at the club he uses when he's in London. I'll drop in at the club tomorrow, see if he's there.'

Three days later, as things turned out, we were in a train bound for Matlock Spa—for not only had Raffles fallen in with the wealthy old ironmaster but also had got us invitations to a house party which Squire Barribar was accustomed to give annually on the occasion of the refurbished carnival outfits leaving winter quarters in his Works yard.

'Springtime, Bunny,' Raffles said, as the train sped northwards with us, 'means different things to different people. The world of the carnival showmen is a world peculiar to itself—as one can see from a study of this newspaper.'

The newspaper, which he had bought at the station, was the showmen's newspaper, *The World's Fair*.

'Did you find out from the Squire,' I asked, 'what he wants this fellow Grapner for?'

'No. All I know is that the squire has a niece called Ruth who acts as his hostess, and two young nephews who're in the Ironworks business with him.'

When we stepped from the train at the attractive little town of Matlock Spa, we found a groom in neat breeches and gaiters and a bowler hat awaiting us with a horse-and-trap.

We were bowling along a winding lane in the springtime sunshine when, all of a sudden, I was startled by a metallic uproar from round a bend ahead. Next minute, an enormous traction engine chugged into view.

Hogging the entire width of the lane, the majestic monster shone green and scarlet with fresh paint. Its elaborately carved wooden canopy, supported by highly polished rods of twisted brass, was a brilliant yellow.

'A Show Engine,' Raffles shouted to me, above the din—'fresh out of our host's Works yard.'

Steady to traction engines, our horse turned calmly into a space before the gate to a field, as the monstrous engine lumbered past, the coal-smudged driver and fireman grinning down at us over the spinning flywheel. The ground shuddered, heat breathed from the engine's firebox. Trundling astern was a long tow of gigantic, tarpaulin-covered amusement contraptions, with carnival roustabouts perched high up on them.

Following the traction engine and its tow came a procession of horse-drawn caravans, some large, some small, but all dazzling with fresh paint, homely wisps of smoke drifting from their chimneys, kids yelling greetings at us as they dangled their bare feet from the rear platforms.

'All very happy to be out of winter quarters and bound once more for the fun of the fairgrounds,' Raffles said, as the din

75

of the procession receded and the horse jingled us briskly on our way again.

Presently the groom looked round at us.

'There be the Works, ahead there, gentlemen,' he said. 'Squire's house, Falloak Grange, be the mansion over yonder, t'other side o' the green there. Squire hisself be at the Works this minute, showin' around some guests as arrived earlier.'

'In that case, groom,' Raffles said, 'please drop us off at the Works, and we'll join the party there.'

Over the Works gateway, alongside the village green dotted with caravans and waddling geese, while ducks quacked from a big pond, arched a wooden noticeboard:

BARRIBAR IRONWORKS & STEAM TACKLE COMPANY

His tweeds immaculate, a pearl in his cravat, Raffles walked into the Works yard, myself at his side.

Several more enormous Show engines, glittering with fresh paint, stood in the yard. From old, rambling engineering sheds sounded the clanging of sledgehammers. Between great sliding doors I glimpsed dim interiors where furnaces glared, sparks flew, bars of white-hot metal were being manhandled with tongs, and roundabouts being tested whirled at great speed, their painted horses, swans, dragons and giraffes rising and falling on twisted brass rods, though no steam-organs were here blaring.

'Mr. Raffles and Mr. Manders?' a voice called.

We looked round.

In a corner of the Works yard was a group of newly-painted caravans, and on the rear platform of one of them a shapely, fair-haired girl stood smiling at us. Another girl, a brunette with hoop-earrings and a vivid Romany beauty, was leaning out from the caravan, her many-bangled arms resting on the half-door.

'Our belated guests, Mr. Raffles and Mr. Manders?' asked the fair-haired girl, as we walked over to the caravan with our tweed hats raised. 'Uncle James told me to watch out for you. Welcome to the Barribar Works. I'm Ruth Barribar and this is my friend Egypta Smith, whose father operates Tinkler Smith's Switchbacks and Wheel-of-Fortune shows—which have the famous motto, "The Lord helps them that helps themselves, but the Lord help anyone caught helping themselves here."'
76

'An admirable motto indeed,' said Raffles. 'And may I say, Miss Barribar, how delightful it is to see the Industrial Revolution grafted on to the English countryside without destroying its rural amenities. But tell me—am I mistaken or is that some kind of safe or *coffre-fort* I see over there?'

Startled, I followed his glance.

From a building marked PAINT SHED, some labourers were lugging out a low-wheeled iron trolley. On the trolley was the most conspicuous safe I had ever seen. Of medium size, it was painted scarlet. On its doors were various brass levers and a monogram in gold leaf: P.S.M.

'It's not our usual kind of work,' said Ruth. 'It's a special order for a showman customer of ours, Mr. Lavengro Plaskett, who operates the famous roundabouts called Plaskett's Scarlet Monsters. Last Easter at the great fair on Hampstead Heath, his caravan was robbed of all his takings. Well, he always has his metal work done at the Works here, so he asked my brother Ronald, who's head of our drawing-office and is a brilliant inventor, to design and build him a burglar-proof safe.'

'And that's the safe?' Raffles asked.

'Yes, indeed. And it's painted scarlet,' Ruth explained, 'because it'll be kept in Mr. Plaskett's caravan, which is scarlet, like all his equipment.'

'I see,' said Raffles, fascinated. 'And the safe's burglar-proof, is it?'

Ruth hesitated. She looked across the yard at the strangely conspicuous safe.

'Well, actually,' she said, and she seemed deeply troubled, 'that's what we have to find out.'

Accustomed as I was to metropolitan society, I found Squire Barribar's provincial house party, when we sat down to dinner that night, some twenty strong, in the fine old dining-room of Falloak Grange, somewhat unusual.

The younger persons among the guests were friends of Ruth and her brothers, Roy and Ronald, and wore conventional evening dress. The older persons seemed to be the Squire's cronies and, from the original and picturesquely colourful attire they seemed to favour for evening wear, I took them to be carnival showmen and their good ladies.

The Squire himself, stocky and rubicund, with grey sideboards and a grey-stubbled bullet head, wore dinner clothes of a kind that had not been seen in London since the youth of William Ewart Gladstone.

When the ladies withdrew, leaving us men to our port and tobacco, the Squire looked around at us.

'All right,' he said, with a hint of belligerence, 'let's get the cards on the table. It's an open secret that me and my nephews—Roy and Ronald here—have been havin' differences of opinion. To put a stop to the rumours flyin' around, the long and short of it is, the boys want to branch into other fields of engineerin' besides steam tackle. Well, it's natural enough that clever, 'varsity-educated boys should feel their oats. Their dad, my late brother, would be proud of 'em. They're my heirs—them an' Ruthie—an' I'm proud of 'em, too.'

'Thank you, Uncle James,' said the nephews, pleasant-looking young chaps both.

'Now, then,' said the Squire, 'the boys want to build new work-shops for a lot o' fancy toolin'-up. Fair enough! I told 'em to go an' build over near Matlock an' leave me an' my foreman Fred Pitts to handle the steam tackle here, same as we've always done. But no, that don't suit the boys' book. They reckon the sound economic policy is to reorganise an' rebuild at the Works here. Now, if that happens, I know very well the boys won't want—an' I say it with some of my showmen friends here at my mahogany—a lot o' caravans clutterin' up the yard all winter, with kids runnin' around underfoot. But showmen have been comin' to Barribar's many a long year—'

'We got no better friend than you, Squire,' croaked an old fellow with a red bandanna choker.

'Any road,' said the Squire, 'me an' the boys was arguin' the toss about it round this very table a week or two back. They were talkin' about manufacturin' some of young Ron's inventions, like a two-tine road scarifier he's patented. An' now there's this safe he's designed an' built for Lavengro Plaskett an' reckons is burglar-proof.

' "Burglar proof, Ron?" I said. "Now, looky here—I'm a magistrate. I know a thing or two about modern safecrackers." An' I told the boys about one I had up in front of me when I was on the Bench. A man come down from Scotland Yard about the case, an' he told me the fellow was a Pittsburgh-trained crook an' there was no safe yet made that he couldn't open, all things
78

bein' equal. You know what these boys here done?'

We all—except for Roy and Ronald, who were looking at the old Squire with a kind of amused affection—shook our heads.

'Quick as a flash,' said the Squire, 'they said they'd lock five hundred pounds apiece of their own money in Ron's safe, an' if I could produce a cracksman who could get at it, he could keep it—an' they'd go an' build their new workshops over near Matlock. But if the crook failed to get the money, I was to agree to their reorganising at the works here. Quick as a flash, bein' a bettin' man an' hot under the collar at the time, I took the young rascals on.'

A thousand pounds! Fleetingly, I met Raffles' eyes.

Ronald laughed. 'Now, look here, Uncle James,' he said, 'Roy and I have told you repeatedly that, if you'd rather wash out the bet—'

'Never done such a thing in my life!' barked the Squire. 'I make a bet, I stand by it. An' by God, I'll give you a run for your money! The crook I had in mind is out of prison now an' I've managed to get hold of him. He's prepared to have a crack at it. Now, here's what's been arranged about this test of Ron's safe. First, the crook's to be given a workin' time of midnight till six a.m. Second, Roy an' Ron bein' married boys with their own houses nearby, we've agreed the test should be on neutral ground, an' Dr. Jackman here—'

'I've agreed to make my house available,' said an amiable. middle-aged man sitting opposite me, 'for this experiment. On the chosen night, I shall be delighted to entertain the Squire's guests.'

'This is Friday,' said the Squire. 'The last o' the carnival outfits'll be pullin' out next Wednesday. So we're holdin' this test on Tuesday night, as kind of a climax to this house party. This crook I'm backin' tells me I shall see nothin' of him till the stroke of midnight, Tuesday, when he'll ring the bell of Dr. Jackman's house. He insists on bein' masked, because crooks don't like their faces becomin' known to every Tom, Dick and Harry. What's more, he don't want his Pittsburgh-made tools and techniques watched. So I've agreed he'll be shown straight into the room where the safe is, an' locked in with it till six a.m.— unless he gets the job done earlier. In any case, if he gets his hooks on the thousand pounds, he walks out with it, umolested. Right, Roy? Ron?'

The nephews nodded. Excited talk broke out around the table.

'Pass the port, gentlemen,' said the Squire. 'We'll drink a toast to the ladies. God bless 'em—then we'll go an' join 'em.'

Later, when those of us who were staying in the house went upstairs with our bedroom candles, which the butler lighted for us in the hall, I put on my dressing-gown in my bedroom, and then—carrying my candle—went into Raffles' room to ask what he thought about the situation.

'My sympathy, Bunny,' he said meditatively untying his white tie before the wardrobe mirror, 'is with the Squire.'

'Mine, too,' I said. 'He's a real old sportsman.'

'I'm afraid, though,' Raffles said, 'that he's overlooked something. Oddly enough, for a magistrate, he's forgotten a certain law.'

'A law, Raffles?'

'The law to which all dope addicts are subject. The law of diminishing returns, Bunny!'

'Oh, dear God!'

'If Warren Grapner's clever professional hands began to tremble like aspens on one occasion we know of,' Raffles said, 'mightn't they do so again on this occasion that means so much to old Squire Barribar?' He gave me a strange look in the candlelit mirror. 'Think it over, Bunny. Good night.'

When I went downstairs next morning, I found about a dozen of my fellow guests at breakfast in the dining-room. They sat far apart from each other at the long table, their heads in newspapers, and made no response to my 'Good morning,' English country house guests never being at their best at breakfast.

Ruth came in as I was helping myself to porridge at the sideboard. I asked her in a whisper, so as not to disturb the breakfasters, if she had seen Raffles this morning.

'No, Mr. Manders. He was up very early, I'm told, and caught the first train to London.'

'To *London*?'

'He left a message,' Ruth said, 'explaining that he'd suddenly remembered he had to attend a committee meeting at Lord's Cricket Ground, and would be back this evening or tomorrow.'

I knew very well that Raffles had no such meeting. And as, in accordance with the custom at country houses, I ate my porridge standing up and my kipper sitting down, my mind was a tumult of surmises. Why had Raffles suddenly taken it into his head to go to London?

I was on tenterhooks until the following afternoon, when I saw him coming up the drive in a four-wheeler from Matlock station. I accompanied him up to his room, where he explained to me why he had gone to London.

'As you know, Bunny,' he said, 'I don't pretend, where knowledge of safes is concerned, to be in the same class as a pro like Grapner. On the other hand, given Grapner's drug addiction, which let him down once and could do so again, which of us is really the better bet to represent the Squire—Grapner or myself? The more I considered the question, Bunny, the more I felt that I had just as good a chance as Grapner of winning that bet for the Squire—and getting the thousand pounds for ourselves.'

'Of course!' I exclaimed, with a sudden thrill of excitement.

'So I went up to London,' Raffles said, 'dropped in on Ivor Kern, explained the situation here, and had him set some of his infamous henchmen to sniff around, find out where Grapner was lodging, kidnap him, and keep him on ice in some place until after Tuesday.'

'Did they find him?'

'No problem at all, Bunny. He'll be quite comfortable. They've seen to it that he has some cocaine to sniff, to help him pass the time. They took his safebreaking tools from him. I have them here in my valise, in a tool-roll. Now, then—here's my plan, Bunny.'

He offered me a Sullivan from his cigarette-case.

'Between now and Tuesday night, when the safe's to be put to the test at Dr. Jackman's house, I must find an opportunity to sprain an ankle—or appear to—so that I can't come with the rest of the party to Dr. Jackman's.' His grey eyes danced. 'You follow my thinking?'

'Vividly so,' I assured him.

On the Tuesday morning, as it happened, a roundabout was to be given its final test for safety, before departing for the fairgrounds, and Squire Barribar inquired genially if we guests would like to ride on the roundabout, as, for testing purposes, twice the normal weight load was required.

Almost all of us, including Raffles and myself, volunteered, and it was with considerable amusement that we joined the

81

engineers, blacksmiths, showmen's children and village hobble-dehoys already on board the roundabout, and found places for ourselves on the painted horses, swans, dragons, ostriches and giraffes.

I found myself astride a giraffe, with Egypta Smith mounted pillion, sidesaddle-wise, behind me, clasping me around the waist.

The roundabout had been set up in the sunshine of the Works yard. The adjacent Show engine, huge and gaudy, began to chug, the belt from its winding-drum setting the roundabout in motion. With its augmented weight load, the roundabout began to increase the speed of its revolutions. My giraffe soared and plunged rhythmically. I gripped the twisted brass rod more tightly, Egypta at the same time more firmly hugging my waist.

Round and round we whirled, at an ever increasing speed, at first in silence except for the chugging of the Show engine and the hiss of steam. Then, suddenly, the steam-organ burst into a blaring rendering of *The Girl I Left Behind Me*, and our pace still further accelerated.

The entire structure of the roundabout began to shudder at the speed of our revolutions. The engineering sheds, the cara-vans, the village green, the pond, the Squire standing in breeches-and-gaiters and a brown bowler hat on *terra firma* as he observed the proceedings with an engineer's eye, became to me just a blur of dizzily spinning colour. Tune after tune blared *prestissimo*, deafeningly, from the steam-organ. Relentlessly, our pace increased, reaching a velocity far in excess of fairground limits, and I clung for dear life to the brass rod, and Egypta clung similarly to me, as our vibrating giraffe plunged down and soared up at such a rate that it seemed actually to be bucking.

Girls began to scream, through the titanic blaring of the steam-organ, as their hats flew off and their hair came down. Just as I began to fear that the roundabout had got out of control and at any second would fly apart, the speed began to diminish, and Egypta's and my giraffe took on a more temperate undula-tion. The steam-organ stopped blaring.

'All right, Fred,' the Squire called to his foreman, 'a little tightening up here and there and the Queen could ride on it as steady as in her own carriage with the Windsor greys.'

The roundabout came to a standstill and we all got off, flushed and breathless, weak at the knees, but stoutly declaring how much we had enjoyed the experience of testing a roundabout for safety. But I noticed that Raffles was hobbling. Ruth, our hostess, noticed it too, and I heard her express her concern.

'I'm afraid I must have come over giddy,' Raffles told her. 'I seem to have sprained my ankle as I stepped off. So silly of me! But, really—it's nothing!'

He forced a brave smile, though his face was etched with the lines of agony.

His ankle did not seem to mend much during the day, so he stayed behind, with cold compresses on it, when, after dinner that night, the rest of we house party guests set off, in evening dress, for Dr. Jackman's house and the great event of the testing of the burglar-proof safe.

Dr. Jackman was standing hospitably at the open front door of his house to receive us. In his large, comfortable hall, his beaming domestics relieved us of our outdoor things.

The hall had a parquetry floor. Drawn curtains of dark-red chenille covered the windows. From a gallery landing four musicians dispensed melody.

'They're the Pumproom Quartet from Matlock Spa,' I heard Dr. Jackman tell the Squire. 'I thought some of your guests might like to dance, to while away the time while your cracksman is locked in with the safe.'

'Excellent, doctor,' said the Squire. 'Where *is* the safe?'

'A gang from the works trundled it over on a trolley this afternoon,' said the doctor. 'I've had it put in a small ante-room off the hall here.'

Soon the Squire and his cronies, mostly showmen, settled down to whist and whisky in Dr. Jackman's dining-room, while the rest of us danced in the hall. Just after eleven, by the grandfather clock, Roy and Ronald and their young wives arrived.

'Hah!' said the Squire, coming out from the dining-room. 'So you haven't got cold feet, then, boys? Let's see the colour of your money.'

Roy opened a baize bank bag he carried. He showed it round, so that we all could see that it was full of currency notes.

'A thousand pounds,' he said. 'Where's the safe, Dr. Jackman?'

Dr. Jackman, opening a door which had a key on the hall side, disclosed a small, windowless room lined with shelves bearing medical books, physic bottles, retorts and pickled organs. On the parquet floor stood the scarlet safe, with three tall candles, in a silver candlestick, unlighted on top of it.

'There's light enough from the hall,' Roy said. 'We'll leave the candles for your safecracker to light, Uncle James. They'll barely last him from midnight till six a.m.'

'Hah!' said the Squire. 'Maybe he'll be out of there—with your thousand pounds—long before six a.m.'

We all crowded round the doorway to watch Roy kneel in front of the safe, open it, put the baize bag of money into it, and secure the safe. Pocketing the key, he came out, closing the door of the ante-room.

Tension grew as the hands of the clock crept towards the hour of midnight.

I was waiting with Ruth, who seemed rather pale and troubled, when the first chime of midnight sounded from the clock. Simultaneously, the front door bell jangled.

The music stopped. We all froze—except for Dr. Jackman, who, as the clock continued mellowly to chime, went to the door and opened it.

A man walked in. He wore a black overcoat and black felt hat. His face was entirely concealed by a black silk scarf in which eyeholes had been cut; the ends of the scarf were tucked into a white muffler at his throat. In his gloved hand he held a tool-roll. His right hand was deep in the pocket of his overcoat, as though he gripped there, distrustfully, a firearm.

In the tense silence, the Squire stumped forward, his face grim.

'This way,' he said. 'The safe's in the ante-room.'

He thought the masked man was the professional cracksman, Warren Grapner. Only I knew that he was the amateur cracksman, A. J. Raffles.

Gazing askance at the enigmatic criminal, the dancers drew back nervously as he followed the Squire into the ante-room, where the old magistrate lighted the candles on the red safe.

'There it is,' the Squire said. 'My nephews claim they've tested it every which way, and they guarantee it's burglar-proof. If you can prove otherwise by six a.m., you can walk out with the thousand pounds that's in it. All right—go to it!'

The Squire closed the ante-room door on the criminal, locked him in with the safe, handed the key to Ruth.

'You keep it, Ruthie,' he said. 'Hey, you fiddlers up there— let's have some music!'

The Pumproom Quartet, with a nice sense of the appropriate, struck up *The Honeysuckle And The Bee*. Ruth was looking worried. She told me she had consulted Egypta Smith, that afternoon, as to the probable outcome of the testing of the safe.

'She's Princess Egypta, of the fairgrounds,' Ruth told me. 'She casts horoscopes, and they nearly always come true. She asked me for the dates and times of birth of Roy and Ronald, and she cast their horoscopes for me in her caravan.'

'Indeed?' I said. 'And how did they come out?'

'They came out very well, Mr. Manders,' Ruth said. 'That's why I'm so worried. Egypta says there's no indication of a money loss in either of their horoscopes.'

I did not like the sound of this, but I tried to make light of it. I felt very restless. I went into the dining-room to get Ruth a glass of lemonade. The Squire and his showmen cronies were laying bets on the outcome of the test.

Time passed very slowly. I danced several dances, but I could not keep my eyes off that locked door of the ante-room. Between dances, everybody stood around listening, trying to hear what was going on in there. Suddenly, some feather-brained girl, looking around at us, put her finger to her lips and, creeping to the door, stooped and peered through the keyhole. She turned back to us with a grimace of disappointment.

'He's hung something over the keyhole,' she said.

Everyone laughed in a high-pitched sort of way, for the tension was growing with every tick of the clock. The Squire came out of the dining-room, took a look at the ante-room door, compared his watch with the grandfather clock, went back into the dining-room.

The clock chimed. One a.m.! I would have given much to be in that room with Raffles, helping him. A thousand pounds at stake! I gnawed my lip. Off in a corner of the hall, Roy and Ronald were murmuring together confidentially.

I went into the dining-room for a drink. The strain was telling on me. I had just poured myself a strong whisky-and-soda when, above the lilt of the music, a woman screamed piercingly. The music stopped. I headed a rush, by the Squire and his showmen cronies, into the hall.

The vapid wench who had tried to see through the keyhole was pointing at the ante-room door.

'I heard something,' she gasped. 'I think he's coming out! Listen!'

We all were still, listening, the musicians peering down over the landing banister-rail. Faint scraping sounds were audible from the lock of the ante-room, then a click as the wards snapped back.

The wench screamed—for, slowly, the door was opening. I felt a trickle of sweat down my face. My heart thumped.

The faceless man emerged from the ante-room.

His right hand was deep in a pocket of his overcoat, as though he held a concealed firearm. In his gloved left hand he held his tool-roll—and the baize bag containing the thousand pounds.

The gaping throng fell back, making a gangway for him, as the masked criminal stalked to the front door, opened it, walked out into the night.

All eyes turned to the ante-room. The three candles had burned down several inches. The red safe stood wide open—empty.

'Five-and-twenty minutes past one,' the Squire said huskily. He walked over to his nephews, stood looking at them with a strange expression. 'Well, boys?'

It was Ronald, the inventor of the burglar-proof safe, who spoke first. He forced a smile, held out his hand.

'Congratulations, Uncle James,' he said.

The old magistrate took Ronald's hand and gripped it hard.

'My boy,' he said, 'I wish it had never happened. I don't know what you're going to tell Lavengro Plaskett about his burglar-proof safe. But, Ron, remember this—trial an' error, trial an' error—that's what makes an engineer.'

'Don't worry, Uncle James,' said Roy. 'Ron'll have another go at designing a safe for Mr. Plaskett.'

'Roy,' said the Squire, 'I ain't worryin' about you boys. Nor about Ruthie, neither. *I* knew what I was doin' when yer dad died an' I took you three under my wing. I'm a good picker. I pick good 'uns. Even that unmitigated scoundrel who just walked out with your money, he's a good 'un—a good 'un gone wrong. Well, there it is, boys—maybe it's a pity we ever got into this, but, any road, you've learned somethin' from it, an' it's cost ye five hundred quid apiece. But bear in mind—the Works'll be yours, to do what you want with, when I'm gone. An' I'm gettin' old— can't stay up skylarkin' all night like I could when I was your age. Now, where's my Ruthie?'

'Here, Uncle James,' she said. She was radiant.

The Squire put a blunt hand on her young shoulder. She was as tall as he was. He looked round at the rest of us.

'Come on,' he said, 'let's all go home now—an' Ruthie'll fry us a platter of eggs an' bacon as big as Show engine's boiler door. Come on, Doc—you, too—*an*' your minstrels!'

As we all returned, chattering, across the village green, I found myself walking beside Egypta Smith. With her hoop-earrings, her bangled arms, her hair in a colourful kerchief, she walked in silence, seeming withdrawn, rapt in some subtle Romany muse. So I resisted the temptation to mention the subject of horoscopes to her; it seemed unsporting, somehow.

Against the sky of stars, the glow above the Works' tall chimney pulsed a dull red. Few of the great, gaudy Show engines now remained. At dawn, they also would depart. But I knew that, from all the fairgrounds of Merrie England, the lumbering carnival engines, the showmen and their families and their horse-drawn caravans would return in due course. They would all—thanks to A. J. Raffles—come back to their favourite winter quarters in Barribar's yard.

When we reached the Squire's house, I nipped upstairs to Raffles' room. Showing no sign of his ankle being sprained, he was pacing up and down, smoking a cigarette.

'Close the door, Bunny,' he said. 'Now, tell me—what happened, what was said, after I walked out with the money?'

I told him. He nodded.

'Bunny,' he said, 'when Ronald Barribar returns presently to his own house, across the green out there, he'll find the baize bag, with the thousand pounds intact in it, stuffed into his letter-box.'

I felt as if Raffles had struck me.

'*Why?*' I said. 'In heaven's name Raffles—*why?* You're *entitled* to the money. It's legitimate!'

'To keep it, Bunny,' he said, 'would be to lose every shred of self-respect. In that locked room, I thought this whole thing out. There's a joker in it, Bunny. It's in the fact that Ruth and Ronald and Roy are the old Squire's heirs. The boys can do as they like with the Works when the Squire's gone, and he's getting pretty old. I realised, of course, when I thought the matter out, that Ruth must have got at her brothers—made them see, at last, that they'd been quite wrong all along the line in their stand against the old man.'

'I don't see what you're driving at,' I said, dismayed.

'Bunny,' said Raffles, 'Roy and Ronald are completely convinced that red safe of theirs is burglar-proof. Whether it is or not, I just don't know. It only took me a couple of seconds to open it  It was the shock of my life, Bunny—and it gave me something to sit down and puzzle out.'

He crushed his cigarette into the ashtray on the candlelit dressing-table.

'They put the thousand pounds into the safe, Bunny, because they'd gone too far to do otherwise. But Ruth must have made them see at last that, even though it cost them five hundred pounds apiece, they *must* ensure that the old man won.'

Raffles looked at me with a wry half-smile.

'So they didn't lock the safe,' he said.


6      CARRIAGES FOR
          BUCKINGHAM PALACE


All of a sudden, as we were approaching Hyde Park Corner in a hansom, Raffles pushed up the trap in the roof.

'Cabbie,' he called, 'pull up near Apsley House.'

We had been visiting Ivor Kern, our receiver of stolen property, to borrow some tideover money from him, none having come our way of late.

The evening was foggy, with few cabs about, so we had been lucky to pick up this hansom as it prowled past Kern's antiques shop in the King's Road, Chelsea.

Raffles had told the cabbie to take us to a club we belonged to in Down Street, where we intended to dine—and Raffles' suddenly changed order to our cabbie filled me with an instant uneasiness, for Apsley House, adjoining the gates to Hyde Park, was the town mansion of the Dukes of Wellington and contained much of the First Duke's Peninsular War plunder, including the

88

unique Salamanca dinner service, to say nothing of paintings by Velasquez, Murillo and El Greco, all of which would be well worth stealing.

'What's this?' I said, with a sinking sensation. 'Raffles, why are we stopping at Apsley House?'

'I want to see what's going on just opposite,' said Raffles.

Peering from the hansom as the horse clopped and jingled us on across Hyde Park Corner, I saw in the dim glow of the street-lamps, abetted by the foggy naphtha-flare of a wheeled coffee-stall, a small crowd of shadowy figures gathered before the arched gateways to the Park.

The crowd seemed to be looking across Hyde Park Corner towards the glimmering lamps of a line of stationary carriages drawn up on the Green Park side of lower Piccadilly.

'Bunny,' Raffles said, 'I've just realised. The Queen's been persuaded to emerge at last from her overlong isolation at Windsor and hold court again at Buckingham Palace.'

'Of course!' I exclaimed. 'This is the night of the first of three Courts she's to hold this season. No wonder there are so few cabs about!'

Our hansom jingled to a standstill just past Apsley House, on our left, and we peered to our right, across the breadth of lower Piccadilly.

It was only the tail-end of the Buckingham Palace carriage line that was visible, drawn up at the kerbside under the leafless tree-branches that overhung the ornate railings of Green Park. Following the curve of the railings, the carriage line looped into Constitution Hill, around the arch, continued all along under the spike-topped wall of Buckingham Palace grounds, and no doubt —though we could not see it—made another looping turn to enter the wide, sentry-boxed gates of the Palace forecourt.

'In effect, Bunny, a giant capital S of carriages,' Raffles murmured, 'carrying debutantes and their chaperones—the quintessence of this country's rank and wealth. And all bedecked with their most valuable heirlooms!'

The line began to move, the carriage lamps mistily reflected in the sleek panels of broughams and the cockaded top hats of liveried coachmen. I glimpsed within the slowly moving carriages silks and satins, ostrich plumes and ermine, the sparkle of tiaras on patrician heads, the glitter of bracelets on elegant, white-gloved wrists.

Escorting policemen, mounted, rode slowly alongside the carriage line. Suddenly one of the policemen turned his horse and started in our direction with peremptory gestures at our cabbie to move on.

'H'm,' said Raffles, offering me a Sullivan from his cigarette-case as we jingled on up Piccadilly. 'That carriage line'll be forming again next Thursday, I believe.'

'And will be equally well guarded,' I reminded him.

'True,' said Raffles.

The hansom turned into Down Street, pulled up before the portals of our club. Raffles handed up a half-sovereign to the cabbie, and I turned to mount the club steps. But Raffles was not with me, and I looked back. He was gazing after the hansom.

'Bunny,' he said, in an odd tone, 'that cabbie's hand—'

'His hand?' I said, mystified.

'A gloved hand,' said Raffles. 'A small hand. A *feminine* hand. Bunny, the cabbie on that hansom is a woman!'

Incredulous, I glimpsed the trim shoulders and grey bowler hat of the cabbie as the hansom was swallowed up in the fog.

Five days later, at an impossibly early hour, the jangling of my bell brought me in a dressing-gown to the door of my Mount Street flat to find an urchin with a note for me.

It was from Raffles. It told me to bestir myself and ride in Rotten Row this very morning, hiring a mount from the Dale Livery Stables, Knightsbridge.

I had an instant presentiment that this must be something to do with the curious incident of the female cabbie, and by eight o'clock, well turned out for riding in the Row, I was stepping from another cab at the entrance to a Knightsbridge mews not far from Tattersall's horse auction yard.

A stone arch over the mews entrance bore the legend: *Dale Livery & Riding Stables—Walter Dale, Prop.*

Flicking my riding-boots with my crop, I strode in under the arch. Early sunshine, gleaming down over slate roofs, filled the mews enclosure with brightness. There was a hissing of ostlers and hoses as shirt-sleeved men in breeches worked on carriages of various kinds standing with upflung shafts.

'Nell!' a voice cried. 'Oh, Nell!'

I looked up. Over wide open stable doors to the right was a small window under the eaves. From the window, which was open,

90

a man who seemed to be propped up in bed or in a chair gave me the impression that he was keeping a supervisory eye on the activity in the mews here. His hair was grey. He had a face of unusual distinction, but fine-drawn and as white as the pillows at his back.

'Oh, Nell!' he called again.

This time, above the clatter of buckets and rattle of spoke-brushes, he was heard—and a young woman came into view from behind a brougham with a discreet crest on its door-panel.

'Yes, Father?' she said, looking up at the window.

She was slender in a skirt of fawn covert and a white shirt-waist, and had a chamois-leather in her hand. The sunshine touched her hair to a warm amber.

From the window, the gesture of a pale hand drew her attention to myself.

'I'm so sorry,' she said, approaching me with a smile. 'I didn't see you come in. Can I help you, sir?'

Could this, I wondered, with an odd thrill of excitement, be the cabbie of the hansom in the fog—this damsel fresh as the morning, clean-cut, with a clear tan, eyes of a dark grey, and a manner composed and pleasant?

I asked, apologising for not making a prior booking, if by any chance I could hire a horse for an hour's ride in the Row, and she told me I certainly could. She was crisp and business-like.

'Magog will give you a good ride,' she said. 'He's in and fresh. I'll have him saddled for you.' She walked across to the stable doorway and called in, 'Herbert, tell Bosworth to leave whatever he's doing and get Magog saddled.'

'Bosworth!' bawled a voice in the stable. 'Miss Nell says to get Magog saddled. Come on now, let's 'ave yer!'

The girl looked up at the window. 'You're sure you're not getting cold there, Father?'

'No, my dear, I'm enjoying this glimpse of sunshine. I was wondering, though—oughtn't John Gilby to be back by now? I'm afraid he'll have to do that eight-thirty job.'

'John'll be back,' said Nell. 'By the way, he took a look at that spring on Lady Mendawe's brougham here. He says he can get it fixed and the brougham'll be perfectly all right for Thursday next.'

'Lady Mendawe,' said the man at the window, 'will no doubt be gratified to hear it.'

A hint of irony in his tone, and something in the look which passed between father and daughter as they spoke of Lady Mendawe, gave me an impression that they shared a certain reservation in respect of the personage in question.

However, as Nell returned to her work with the chamois, the words 'Thursday next' nagged at my mind for some reason. And suddenly I realised why. Thursday next—five days from now— the Queen would be holding her next Court at Buckingham Palace!

I looked with a new interest at the brougham with the crested door-panel.

Hooves rang metallically on the stable cobbles, and a rangy, fifteen-hand chestnut nag, saddled, was led out into the sunshine by an ostler in a battered bowler, breeches, wrinkled gaiters, and braces worn over a ragged red guernsey.

'Here's Magog, sir,' said Miss Nell, returning to me. 'Try a stirrup under your arm for length. Bosworth has put a martingale on him because Magog's inclined to stargaze otherwise and run into things. But, Bosworth,' she added reprovingly, 'please tighten that girth. You've put it on too loose again.'

'Beg pardon, Miss Nell,' rejoined the fellow respectfully.

Wheels clattered in under the arch of the mews entrance, and I saw Nell's face light up.

'Excuse me, sir,' she said, and she hurried to meet a four-wheeler which had pulled into the mews.

The jehu, jumping down from the box, was a tall, lithe, powerful fellow with a rather battered face and a smile that, as he touched his bowler to Nell, was singularly pleasant.

'Oh, John,' she said, 'I'm terribly sorry. You've had no breakfast yet, but I'm afraid there's a job come in for eight-thirty—'

'That's all right, Miss Nell,' he said cheerfully. 'I had a bite at the cabmen's shelter.'

It was easy to see that he would have done anything for the girl. I had a feeling that I had seen his battered face and good grin before and, as he climbed again to the box of his cab, I remembered having seen him more than once in the ring at the National Sporting Club. He was *the* John Gilby, the boxer, The Fighting Cabman, pride and joy of the London cabbies.

I turned to my horse. I took the bridle from the ostler Bosworth, put my foot in the stirrup he held for me. And he spoke to me in a mutter, out of the corner of his mouth.

**92**

'I'll see you at Kern's place, Bunny,' he said, 'at seven o'clock tonight.'

Dumbfounded, I looked into the grey eyes of A. J. Raffles. My face flamed. Impassive, he stepped back, smoothing his grimy hands down his guernsey.

I swung into the saddle, clapped heels to Magog and, infuriated at Raffles' habit of springing surprises on me, rode out under the mews arch.

Curiosity had somewhat assuaged my wrath as I sat drinking Ivor Kern's whisky that night in the cluttered, gaslit sitting-room over his shambles of a Chelsea antique shop.

Shortly after seven o'clock, the doorbell jangled, downstairs. Kern went to answer it. I looked at him inquiringly when he returned. He nodded, his face pale, hollow-cheeked, curiously ageless, his forehead lofty, his dark eyes full of cynical intelligence.

'Bosworth,' he said. 'I've lent him a room here to do his changing in. He'll be with us as soon as he's taken a bath. Believe me, he needs it.'

Presently the door opened and in walked Raffles, debonair in evening dress. He tossed his cape and silk hat on to a chair, rubbed his hands with zest.

'Ah, whisky!' he said. 'To acquire a thirst and an appetite, Bunny, there's nothing like honest work. You should try it some time.' He raised his glass. 'Gentlemen, I give you Miss Ellen Dale—the lady on the box!'

'So she *is* the one,' I said. 'I guessed it. How did you manage to find her?'

'As her hansom picked us up in the King's Road here, Bunny, I thought it likely that she worked out of one of the many stables in the Tattersall's area. So I prowled around them in the guise of an out-of-work ostler. At the fourth stable I tried my luck at, I found this Miss Dale. "This is the one," I thought. I was intrigued, Bunny. I've never known of a woman driving a hansom cab before. I felt there might be something behind it that could be worth finding out. When I saw Nell Dale, I felt sure of it. So I asked her for a job, and she turned me to right away. Mucking out,' said Raffles wryly. 'By the way, Ivor, what luck with the arrangements I asked for?'

Kern, with his cynical smirk, held up four fingers.

'Four?' said Raffles. 'Excellent!' He lighted a cigarette. 'Bunny,

I had two objects in view. In looking for the lady jehu, I was keeping my ears open for certain other stable information.'

'What kind of information?' I asked uneasily.

'Information,' said Raffles, 'as to carriage arrangements for the night of the next Court. And I learned quite a bit about what gentry have carriages standing by at what Knightsbridge livery stables for next Thursday night.'

I was tense. I moistened my lips. 'Lady Mendawe, for one?' I said.

'Lady Mendawe,' said Raffles—'a notorious old battleaxe and conniver. It seems she's kept her brougham at Walter Dale's stables for years, but has no coachman of her own. She uses Dale's drivers—for preference, an old chap called Herbert Light. Bunny, we've stumbled on a situation fraught with possibilities. The debutante whom Lady Mendawe is chaperoning this season, and whom she's to present at Court next Thursday night, is Nell Dale's cousin.'

'I *thought* there was something odd,' I said, 'about the way Nell Dale and her father spoke of Lady Mendawe—and next Thursday night.'

'I gather that the girls have never met,' Raffles said. 'It's a curious story, Bunny. As I've pieced it together, mostly from pumping old Herbert Light and from eavesdropping on Nell and her father, it seems that Walter Dale comes from a family of landed gentry up in Warwickshire. He and his elder brother were in love with the same girl. It was Walter who got her. His brother, a mean hound by the sound of him, never forgot or forgave. When he came into the title and very rich entailed estates, he hit back at Walter by cutting off his allowance.'

Raffles reached for the whisky.

'Walter,' he went on, 'was in the army. Cavalry. With a wife and child—Nell—to support, he couldn't afford to continue in his commission. He sent in his papers and, as horses were the only thing he knew anything about, he got a job as a riding-master in Knightsbridge. He was working at that when his wife died. Not long after that, the jobmaster he was working for offered him a chance to take over the stables. Dale borrowed right and left to do it. He thought his luck had changed, but it hadn't. He was riding in a steeplechase—the Cheltenham Cup—had a bad fall, and has been on his back ever since.'

'Poor devil,' I said, thinking of the pale, gaunt man at the mews window.

'The interest on his loans is high,' said Raffles. 'Bunny, he's a hair's breadth from bankruptcy. It's touch-and-go each week to pay his employees, though they're utterly loyal to him—especially John Gilby.'

'The Fighting Cabman,' I said.

'Yes, that's the chap—one of the best,' said Raffles. 'If it weren't for John, who does about eight men's work, and for Nell pitching in, Walter Dale just couldn't carry on. That's why sometimes, on busy nights, Nell will take out a cab herself. She has, of course, no hackney-driver's licence, but they're shorthanded and, rather than lose badly-needed fares, she takes a chance—without her father's knowledge. Hence our ride in the fog the other night—and I think we may be able to make that a lucky night for Nell. '

'We?' I said, with a deepening disquiet.

'The brother's daughter, the heiress—an arrogant little brat, from all I hear—is in London for her "coming out",' Raffles said. 'When she's presented at Court by Lady Mendawe next Thursday, the girl'll be wearing certain sparklers to which she has no moral right. They belonged to her grandmother, and it seems that the old lady intended that her younger son, Walter, should get at least something, if only her personal jewellery. But apparently the hog of a brother, by some legal chicanery, got his hooks on those gems. Today, Bunny, the cash value of that handful of baubles would make all the difference between life and death for Walter Dale. In his state of health, he simply wouldn't survive a bankruptcy.'

Raffles gave me a strange look.

'In everything but the letter of the law, Bunny, those sparklers belong to Walter Dale. Nell's a girl of spirit. She adores her father. And John Gilby's in love with her. He'd stop at nothing to help her. Surely the thought must have crossed her mind that it would be easy for John to drive Lady Mendawe's brougham into a back street on Thursday night and relieve the debutante of her ill-gotten jewellery?'

'The thought could well have crossed Gilby's mind, too,' said Ivor Kern.

'True,' said Raffles. 'But it's just not feasible, Ivor. It'd make Gilby a hunted man. Nell, however much she might be tempted,

95

would never allow it. They're stymied. But an ostler, now—eh? A stray man, taken on without references, just a few days ago?'

I mopped my brow. The room seemed suddenly to have become very hot.

'All the drivers,' Raffles said, 'are booked solid for the night of the Court. Old Herbert Light is detailed to drive Lady Mendawe's brougham. But Herbert has a little weakness. He takes frequent nips from a bottle he keeps hidden in the harness-room. Now, I think it may happen that Herbert's bottle becomes slightly adulterated by Thursday night, so that he's taken poorly. In which case, who will be left to replace him?'

'Bosworth!' said Kern, with his dry cackle.

'However did you guess?' Raffles said. 'Incidentally, Ivor, it'll be up to you to provide us with an unidentifiable brougham for Thursday night.'

'No problem,' said Kern. 'Who'll be driving it?'

Raffles looked at me. Kern also looked at me. They both sat looking at me. My scalp tingled.

'Oh, dear God!' I said.

So it was that, due to my hopeless infirmity of character, the Thursday night, when Her Majesty was to hold her second Court at Buckingham Palace, found me on the box of a brougham of unknown provenance.

I was bound, by way of devious side streets, for a rendezvous in the vicinity of Brompton Road.

It was just such a raw, foggy night as that on which we had hailed the hansom which had involved us in this adventure. Huddled in an ulster, a grey bowler jammed low over my eyes, my knees berugged, the reins slippery between my gloved fingers, I had a sense of exposure on the unfamiliar elevation of the box.

The narrow street I was traversing turned sharply at its end into a wider space. The wheels of the brougham rumbled on cobbles. The horse's back swayed before me in the pale glimmer of the candlelamps. Its breath was visible on the cold air. I reined the horse down to a walk.

On my left was a high, glass-topped wall which enclosed the back garden of a mansion. On my right was a much lower wall, about knee-high, overhung by trees growing in an old graveyard. It was my rendezvous—the graveyard of Brompton Parish Church.

Leaning down from the box, I blew out the candlelamps. The only light now visible was the misty sheen of a gaslamp high up in an arch of crumbling stone about thirty yards ahead.

Scarcely had I doused the lamps than I heard hoofbeats approaching. A neat brougham passed in under the arch, came on towards me, and was pulled up as it drew level. The coachman was a shadow in cape and silk hat as he leaned over from his box.

'Well done, Bunny,' he said. 'Everything's gone like clockwork so far. Poor old Herbert Light went home holding his stomach. I was put on the job at once. I'm on my way now to Lady Mendawe's house, at the top end of Queen's Gate, to pick up my passengers. If milady asks why I'm taking side streets, I'll tell her the road's up in front of Knightsbridge Barracks, so I'm swinging over to the Brompton Road. I'll be back this way in twenty minutes or so. Keep warm!'

It was a dark, cold and lonely vigil that I kept after Raffles was gone. I thought of the S-shaped carriage line which now, escorted and protected by most of the West End police force, would be starting to form in the vicinity of the Palace. I reflected on my own modest role in Raffles' projected crime. All I was here for was to provide him with a conveyance for a rapid departure from the scene of the robbery.

Suddenly, as I sat brooding there, cursing Raffles and wishing this business was over and done with, I heard a slight sound from the graveyard on my right. I peered down from the box. Faintly in the mist I could make out the leaning, lugubrious shapes of old tombstones. I had an eerie impression that one of them was moving stealthily towards me. Next second, it reared up, became a man. He seemed to pour over the low wall alongside the brougham, and I was looking down at a handkerchief-masked face and into the muzzle of a revolver.

'All right, cully,' a hard, intense voice said. 'Down from that box!'

The rug was snatched from my knees. An iron hand gripped my arm, jerked me down from the box, spun me round to face the brougham. The revolver prodded between my shoulder-blades, a hand slapped my sides, feeling for weapons.

'Right,' the voice rasped. 'Put your hands behind you.'

I had no option but to obey. I felt rope secure my wrists, then wound twice around my chest, pinioning my arms.

'Now, cully, in with you!'

A hand reached past me, yanked open the door of the brougham. I was shoved in, barking my shins, and sprawled on the prickling roughness of the coir mat between the seats. I felt my ankles slapped together and roped, then steely fingers clutched my hair, jerked back my head, what felt like a woollen scarf was jammed across my mouth and knotted tight at the back of my head.

'That'll do you, cully,' the voice said.

The door of the brougham thudded shut on me. I felt the vehicle tilt on its springs as the marauder climbed to my place on the box.

I lay still for a minute, trussed like a turkey, my heart pounding. I began to test my bonds. Breathing stertorously through my nose, I wrestled with them. I could not loosen them. I managed to work myself to my knees and ease myself into a sitting position on the seat facing forward. I had barely done so, my breath whistling in my nostrils, when I heard the trotting sound of approaching hoofbeats.

I knew that this must be the Mendawe brougham coming, with Raffles on the box. He was coming straight into a trap. I was desperate. The window on my left was lowered on its strap. I struggled to heave myself forward so that I could thrust my head out and be seen by Raffles—so warning him. But I was too late. Already the candlelamps of the Mendawe brougham were coming alongside.

As the horse was reined-in, I glimpsed the conventional Court ostrich feathers as a woman stuck her head out from the brougham with the crested door.

'What is it *this* time?' she shrilled at her coachman. 'Why have we stopped, you miserable fellow? What's this other brougham doing here? *Answer* me!'

Peering out obliquely, I saw the gleam of Raffles' silk hat, the swing of his evening-cape, the blackness of the mask he had donned. Springing down from the box of the Mendawe brougham, he opened the door.

'Since you ask, Lady Mendawe,' he said courteously, 'this other brougham is mine. Its coachman is my confederate. I'm afraid you're at a disadvantage. But have no fear. You're in no danger —provided you do as you're told. Now, I must trouble you to step out—and your debutante with you.'

Skirts rustled as the women alighted. In the space between the two broughams, ermine capes palely gleamed, Lady Mendawe's tiara sparkled in the candleshine, the debutante's necklace and earrings glittered.

'In depriving you of your gemmed accessories,' said Raffles, 'let me assure you that Her Majesty will think none the worse of you if you make your curtsies before her with your beauty unembellished by worldly baubles. In any case, I've no doubt you have them fully insured.'

'Sir,' said Lady Mendawe, in a voice that shook with rage, as she handed over her tiara, 'you will pay dearly for this!'

'Sufficient unto the day, milady,' said Raffles. 'A desperate man, brought low by wine, women and cards, lives without thought for the morrow. Young lady—your necklace and earrings, please. No, not the rings on your fingers. Who knows? Rings may have sentimental value.'

'So you have, then,' said Lady Mendawe, 'some shred of sensibility still in your depraved carcase!'

'Lady Mendawe,' said Raffles, with dignity, 'I am as other men are. I have a sister.'

'No doubt, sir,' spat Lady Mendawe, 'you have the poor drab walking the streets for you!'

'For that remark,' Raffles said, 'I'm tempted to make you late at the Palace. But you're overwrought. I make allowances for that. You see the arch ahead there, with the dim gaslamp in it? Just to the right of that arch, a paved footpath skirts this convenient graveyard. The footpath will bring you in a very few minutes to Brompton Road, where you may hope to find a cab. My thanks, ladies, and my regrets—and good night to you.'

'My last word to you,' Lady Mendawe said, 'is this. I am a woman of influence. I shall bring pressure from the highest quarters to bear upon Scotland Yard. I shall see to it that you are hunted down and imprisoned, with frequent floggings, for the term of your unnatural life. Come, Chloe!'

The angry tap of heels receded over the cobbles. I was stupefied by the failure of the man in my place on the box to intervene. Even now, he made no move.

Raffles was standing motionless, apparently watching the dowager and the debutante pass from view. Then he turned, and I saw the smile under the edge of his mask as he looked up at the figure he thought was mine on the box.

The brougham gave a sudden lurch on its springs. Raffles was blotted out, going down under the dark shape that hurtled from the box. I heard the sounds of a brief, violent struggle, then the thud of running feet.

I listened intently. The door of the brougham opened. I saw Raffles' silhouette, heard his hard breathing, felt his hands groping for the knot of the scarf that gagged me. As he freed me from it, I heard him laugh quietly.

'Bad business, this, Bunny,' he said. 'We've been robbed!'

'Who was he?' I gasped.

'If you'd just been on the receiving end of his Sunday punch, as I have,' said Raffles, going to work on my bonds, 'you wouldn't need to ask. He was John Gilby, of course—well named The Fighting Cabman!'

Freeing me, he helped me out of the brougham, handed me my fallen bowler. As he did so, from nearby in the Brompton Road there sounded through the deepening fog the urgent, repeated shrilling of a police whistle.

'Come on!' said Raffles. 'Quick!'

We leaped up on to the box of the brougham. Raffles took the reins, slapped them on the horse's back, and we departed in haste, leaving Lady Mendawe's brougham deserted, with its crested door yawning open.

Not until we were well clear of the scene of the crime, with no sign of pursuit, did we pull up to light our own lamps.

'You understand, of course, Bunny,' Raffles said, as the horse jogged on through the maze of side streets towards the King's Road, Chelsea, 'that the problem was not how to *get* the jewels. That was not only easy, it was almost embarrassingly so. The problem was how to give the jewels to Nell Dale. Had we sent them to her anonymously, she'd have feared some joker in it. So, of course, would John Gilby. They'd have been afraid to *keep* the jewels. No, the only way we could fix things was by giving John an opportunity to get the jewels by, as he imagined, outwitting a crook who actually had stolen them and whose description would be given—as far as possible, since the man was masked—to the police by Lady Mendawe. That way, John will feel reasonably safe. And since the jewels—*recovered* property in the Dales' eyes—will come to Nell from John Gilby's hand, she'll feel reasonably safe, too.'

'Are you telling me,' I said, 'that you *knew* it was Gilby, not me, on the box back there?'

'Of course,' said Raffles. 'As Bosworth, the ostler, I've been deliberately behaving in a suspicious manner, to get them wondering what I was up to. When Herbert went sick tonight, they thought they'd tumbled to my game—that I was out to rob the dowager and the debutante. John then made a plan of his own. When I took the Mendawe brougham out, I knew he was following me on foot. So I deliberately drove at a very moderate pace to our rendezvous. When he saw you waiting there, he thought he spotted our game. So he jumped on you and set his ambush.'

'Why the devil didn't you explain to me?' I demanded.

'Bunny, if you'd known you were going to be jumped on at any second, it would have been agony for you, sitting there on the box. Far better that you should be in ignorance. I knew John'd do you no harm. He's a good fellow. As for you, your part has been vital all the way through. Your visit to the mews to get a horse to ride was the means of arousing the initial suspicion of me. Your face, when Bosworth the ostler whispered to you, would have made the Archangel Gabriel suspicious.'

'But who,' I said, chagrined, 'was there to see me? John Gilby had just driven in, but he and Nell had eyes only for each other.'

'Have you forgotten,' said Raffles, 'the invalid who was keeping a supervisory eye on things from the window over the stables?'

I could have kicked myself. I had, in fact, clean forgotten Walter Dale at the window. But when we had turned the brougham over to one of Ivor Kern's lurking henchmen, and were about to turn in at the doorway of the antique shop, an appalling thought occurred to me.

'Raffles,' I said, 'Nell Dale won't dare to *keep* those jewels, no matter how vital their cash value may be to her father. Surely the police will soon ferret out the family connection between the Dales and the debutante. Suspicion will fall on the Dales. The police will discount the vanished ostler Bosworth as either a red herring or a confederate. When Nell and John get time to think things over calmly, they'll realise that their position's untenable and that the only thing they can do is hand the jewels to the police with some yarn about having recovered them from Bosworth!'

To my surprise, Raffles remained unperturbed.

'We'll see, Bunny,' he said, and he rang Kern's bell.

When Ivor admitted us and led us upstairs with a lighted

candle to the gaslit sitting-room over his shop, he turned to Raffles and held up four fingers.

'All four?' said Raffles. 'Excellent, Ivor! By the way, Bunny here has raised a very shrewd point. I think, if we're patient for a little while, an answer to it may be forthcoming. Suppose, in the meantime, you trot out some of that Napoleon brandy that was stolen from the bonded warehouse. It'll steady our nerves. And you might show us some of your card tricks, Ivor. It'll help pass the time. Have you ever seen Ivor do card tricks, Bunny?'

'No,' I said.

I was mystified, and in no mood for card tricks, but Kern, with his secretive, cynical smile, went into his repertoire, anyway. It was extensive, and at any other time I would have been fascinated by it, but now I could not keep my mind on his long, pale, agile fingers. I knew that Raffles and Kern were waiting for something.

Suddenly, just as Kern was inviting me to choose a card from the pack, preparatory to demonstrating another of his tricks, Raffles held up a hand.

'Listen!' he said.

All three of us were still. From far off along the foggy King's Road sounded the cry of a newsboy. Again the cry sounded, closer. I could not make out what he was shouting about—until the hoarse cry came again, this time from right under the curtained window of the room here.

'Extry! Extry!' bawled the boy. ''Olesale Robbery Court Debertahnts! Great Sensayshun! Extry!'

My heart stopped.

'Bunny,' Raffles said, 'your face is a study. Do forgive me, but I really couldn't resist waiting to see it. You raised a very shrewd point just now. It does you credit. But you realise, now, the answer to it?'

'I'll be damned if I do!' I said.

'My dear chap,' said Raffles, 'the Dales' relationship to a robbed debutante becomes—as I'm sure Nell and John will be quick to realise—a mere coincidence, in no sense specifically incriminating, *provided* that the robbery of that debutante is only one of a series of similar robberies carried out simultaneously.'

'Good God!' I said, throwing myself back in my chair.

'I selected for the purpose,' said Raffles, 'four debutantes of the same type as Nell's cousin—haughty little brats, spiteful to

102

their servants and thoroughly spoiled by rank-proud, purse-proud pappas. I made arrangements with Ivor here, who was able to insinuate four professional but uncreative criminals of his acquaintance into four different livery stables. With minor variations, but with strict instructions to accord the chosen debutantes and their chaperones every courtesy, they were able to work similar coups—on a percentage basis with Ivor and ourselves— to the coup you and I brought off. Ivor, have you our share of the plunder for Bunny to see?'

Kern opened a drawer of the table. He took out the plunder, laid it on the tablecloth. In the white glare from the gas-globe overhead, jewelled baubles leaped to faceted, dazzling radiance.

'I'll now add to the loot,' said Raffles, 'this tiara of Lady Mendawe's—which I took care to place in a secret pocket, *not* the one containing the particular sparklers of which The Fighting Cabman so ruthlessly robbed me.'

He gave me a strange look.

'Normally, as I think you'll agree, Bunny, I'm not a man who allows an insult to rankle. But where one's sister is concerned, I am as other men are. And with all due allowance for Lady Mendawe's overwrought state, I determined that she should never again set eyes on this tiara of hers—after she made that vulgar, shocking, malicious remark about my sister Dinah.'

# 7     DINAH RAFFLES AND OSCAR WILDE

On the night he fell foul of the Mad Marquess, as that brawling nobleman who propounded Rules For The Prize Ring was generally known, Raffles was sitting with me at a table in Willis's Supper Rooms.

A celebrated London after-theatre resort, all red plush, ornate gilding and glittering gasoliers, the place was noisy with the confident voices of people of rank and fashion.

'You know, Bunny,' Raffles said to me, his evening dress impeccable, his dark hair crisp, his keen face tanned from a recent cricket tour abroad, 'no man can choose the name he's born with, and in normal circumstances he goes right through life with it.'

On our way here we had passed a theatre where a brave but doomed attempt was being made to revive a witty comedy by a poet and playwright whose name, due to a scandal not much more than two years before, it was not now prudent to include on the theatre posters.

I thought it was this which had prompted Raffles' remark, but he added, 'For a woman, of course, the matter of names is rather different.'

Warming his brandy-glass between his clever brown hands, he glanced across with meditative grey eyes at the orchestra-dais, to which his only living relative, his sister Dinah, had gone to ask that a piece be played that she particularly wanted to hear.

A graceful, fair-haired girl of twenty-one, with a clean-cut quality and an air of friendly composure akin to her brother's, she stood chatting to the orchestra leader and his melodists in their Hungarian gypsy costume.

Understanding now what had prompted Raffles' remark about names, I said, 'You mean different for a woman in the sense that she changes her name when she marries?'

He nodded, his eyes on Dinah. And a tension began to grow in me—for, oddly enough, I knew more about his sister than he did.

In accordance with the terms of their father's will, Dinah as a child of seven had been placed under the guardianship of an uncle and aunt in Australia, while the residue of the small estate had been earmarked to see Raffles through his father's old school in England.

Dinah had been fond of her uncle and aunt, who had brought her up well and, on their demise within a year of each other, she had decided to leave Australia and come to London. She had arrived, seeking her brother, while he was away on a cricket tour, so I had appointed myself, naturally enough, her brother-by-proxy.

Women being ineligible for residence in The Albany, where Raffles had his chambers, I had obtained accommodation for Dinah adjacent to my own small flat in Mount Street, so that I could keep an eye on her.

In this, I had had no difficulty. On the contrary, my difficulty had been to keep my eyes off her. In fact, I soon had become conscious of aspirations concerning her which were quite incompatible with my role as brother-by-proxy, so it had come as a relief to me to be freed of this hampering status by Raffles' return from the cricket tour.

'Consider, Bunny,' he said now, as he offered me a Sullivan from his cigarette-case, 'my way of life. At any moment, its criminal side may be exposed. My own transgressions are different from those of that poor devil of a playwright—'

'Who was it,' I murmured, 'who said of him, "I don't care what people do, as long as they don't do it in the streets and frighten the horses"?'

'A wise and broadminded remark,' said Raffles. 'I believe it fell from the lips of that enchanting and large-hearted lady of the stage, Mrs. Pat Campbell. It does her credit, Bunny. But, in fact, it's not horses that shy at scandal. It's Society's upper crust. That playwright's transgressions put him where my very different transgressions can put me—'

'In the dock,' I muttered, 'at the Old Bailey.'

Raffles nodded.

'Currently,' he said, 'I'm captain of the England cricket team. I'm received—even welcomed—in some of the best houses in the land. If I were charged at the Old Bailey as a criminal—'

'There'd be a sensational scandal, Raffles,' I said, and my palms moistened at the very thought.

'What effect would such a scandal have on Dinah's prospects,' Raffles said, 'if the disaster happened while her surname still is —Raffles?'

I took a gulp of brandy. My main aspiration concerning Raffles' sister Dinah was that I might be able to persuade her, some happy day, to change her surname to Manders.

'You want to see her married?' I said.

'Yes, Bunny. I want to see her safely, happily married,' Raffles said—'though not, of course, to an Englishman.'

Startled, I put down my glass. 'Why not an Englishman?'

'Because, Bunny,' Raffles said, 'if I come a cropper, I don't want Dinah to be living in this country when it happens. I want her well away from the scandal. Otherwise, I'd like nothing better than to see her married to an Englishman—some sound, loyal chap—yourself, for instance. But that must never be, Bunny, because if some day I stand in the dock at the Old Bailey, I'm

105

afraid it's inevitable—God forgive me for it—that you'll be standing there beside me.'

I felt as if I had been hit by a sledgehammer. Not only did I see his point, he had impaled my heart on it. Fortunately, he did not notice my emotion, for just then an altercation at the doorway of the Supper Rooms attracted his attention.

'It's a small world, Bunny,' he said wryly. 'That playwright's out of gaol now, living in obscurity abroad somewhere. But there's the very man who, because of his titled and fatally attractive son's friendship with the playwright, started the scandal that put the poor devil in prison for two years.'

At the doorway stood the most vindictive man in London, the Mad Marquess. Short, thick-set, choleric, he was slightly bow-legged, for in his youth he had been a fine horseman, a ruthless competitor in the Grand National. Widely unpopular because of his persistent brawling, he was at it again now, beetling his heavy brows and fulminating at the head waiter.

The Marquess's usual cronies were jockeys and pugilists, and he had four of the latter with him now, bullet-headed heavy-weights, lumpy with muscle in their evening dress, and there was also in the party a handsome, orange-haired woman flamboyantly gowned—a notorious courtesan known to dissolute men-about-town, for reasons sufficiently reprehensible, as 'Skittles'.

'It's Skittles,' said Raffles, 'that the head waiter doesn't want to admit.'

'And no wonder,' I said—for as the browbeaten head waiter surrendered and reluctantly led the party towards a table, half the women in the place, followed by their escorts, looking pretty sheepish, swept out with their chins in the air.

The party, with the Marquess guffawing and Skittles wielding her fan with an air of supercilious triumph, passed close by the orchestra-dais—and the Marquess stopped suddenly.

'What, no music?' he said. 'Play *The Beautiful Blue Danube.*'

The orchestra leader, violin and bow in hand, glanced uncertainly at Dinah, with whom he had been talking.

'You heard what I said,' bawled the Marquess. 'Play *The Blue Bloody Danube.*'

Raffles said, 'Excuse me a moment, Bunny,' and he rose and walked over to the orchestra-dais.

'Dinah,' he said, 'is *The Blue Danube* the piece you want to hear?'

'Why, no,' she said. 'I asked for one of Brahms' Hungarian Dances.'

'And did the orchestra leader say he would play it for you?'

'Yes,' Dinah said quietly.

'Then on the principle,' Raffles said, 'of first come, first served, that is what the orchestra will now play. Please go and sit down and enjoy it.'

In the sudden and deathly hush, Dinah came and joined me at our table. Raffles remained looking without expression at the Marquess, who stared back with a dark flush slowly engorging his arrogant face. New shoes squeaked on the red carpet as the four bruisers, massive and scowling, took station to either side of their squat patron.

Tense, my heart pounding, I rose to go to Raffles' side. But the Marquess, just then, flung out a forefinger at him and said thickly, '*I shall remember you!*' Turning, he exploded at the trembling head waiter, 'What are you standing there for?'

The orchestra leader, with a glance at Raffles, tucked his violin under his chin, and the thrall that had held the people in the Supper Rooms immobile was broken by a buzz of voices as the melodists launched into the lilt of a Brahms' Hungarian Dance.

Raffles rejoined us, saying, as he sat down, 'Dinah, I'm sorry that should have happened.'

'I'm not,' she said, a little breathless, her grey eyes shining. 'For I've found my brother.'

True to his intention of putting Dinah in the way of making an advantageous foreign marriage, Raffles in the following week took her to Paris and, at the warm insistence of them both, I accompanied them.

Raffles had with him letters of introduction from people of social consequence in London to people of like consequence in Paris. As a result, the three of us were soon caught up in a whirl of *salons* and dinner-parties, and Raffles received many compliments on the appearance and comportment of his sister.

'Which is all very pleasing, Bunny,' he said to me, privately, 'but keep your eyes open for some grist to the mill. With a foreign marriage my objective for Dinah, I have to bear in mind a custom of well-regulated European families.'

'What custom, Raffles?'

107

'The custom of the dowry, Bunny.'

To give Dinah a change from formal occasions, one free evening we took her over to the Left Bank, and among the places at which we dropped in, looking for amusement, chanced to be a waxworks museum.

The effigies were arranged in groups, each figure having propped at its feet a card bearing a number by which the effigy, with a brief history of its original's claim to notoriety, could be identified in the catalogue—which I was carrying and from which, when asked by Dinah, I read out to her the information relevant to such effigies as attracted her attention.

We came to a group of figures which, in the harsh glare of gaslight, leered out through the iron bars of a cage bearing a placard with the title *Les Ames Damnées*—The Damned Souls.

Some of the figures in the cage wore the striped pyjamas and frayed straw sombreros of felons condemned to Devil's Island, but I noticed, with a shock, one whose ample girth was clad in coarse knickerbockers and tunic stamped all over with the broad arrows of the English prison system.

'Dinah,' Raffles said, at once, 'there's a group over there we mustn't miss.'

He steered her firmly away from the iron cage—for several times, as I knew, he had dined at the tables of London Society people in the company of the poet and playwright whose effigy, with shoulder-length waved hair parted in the centre and a slim volume open in one hand, stood now, branded, among the felons.

I lingered for a moment, fascinated. Stencilled on the breast of the effigy's tunic was the prison number, C.3.3., and on the slim volume which the effigy held open at its title page—*The Ballad of Reading Gaol*, by C.3.3.—lay a shrivelled green carnation.

Chilled, I turned away and, thrusting the catalogue hastily into the side pocket of my suit, joined Dinah and Raffles.

We had a late supper at a lively restaurant in the *quartier* and, much later still, dropped in for a nightcap at a *café* in the Boulevard Saint-Michel. There were half-a-dozen or so men standing in a row at the bar, but at this late hour few of the tables were occupied—and we had only just sat down at one of them and given our order to the waiter when Dinah put a hand on Raffles' sleeve.

'There's a man over there,' she said, 'who seems to know you.'

We followed her glance. And my heart sank like a stone.

In the all too abundant flesh, grown now bloated and debauched, the man looking at Raffles from a table across the *café* was he whose effigy stood, branded with broad arrows, in the cage of *Les Ames Damnées*.

Meeting Raffles' eyes, he turned away his head.

My heart thumped, sultry, as I wondered what, with his sister with him, Raffles would do.

After an instant of hesitation, he excused himself to Dinah and walked across to the table where ex-Convict C.3.3., gross in his rumpled evening dress, sat in the company of a young man in his early twenties who could hardly have made a greater contrast, for his light tweed travelling-suit hung on his painfully lank figure as on a skeleton.

Rich and resonant, with a hint of brogue and a slur of drunkenness in it, the ex-convict's voice reached Dinah and me clearly across the *café*.

'Well, well,' he said, as, still seated, he offered Raffles three fat fingers of a languid hand to shake. 'An Englishman who doesn't cut me dead! But I suppose A. J. Raffles would consider that not quite—*cricket*?'

'Bunny,' Dinah murmured, 'why did the man say that?'

'He's a man, Dinah,' I said guardedly, 'who made a mistake and—has rather fallen in life.'

'What was the man's mistake, Bunny?' Dinah asked.

His mistake, apart from having been too greatly charmed by the Mad Marquess's attractive but capricious son, had been in not getting out of England when he had the chance. Instead, with Irish insouciance and the green carnation of a defiant aesthete in his buttonhole, he had remained to stand alone and meet his ruin in the dock at the Old Bailey.

But I said, 'His mistake, Dinah, was to be born out of his time. He'd have been understood in the Athens of Pericles, but he wasn't understood in our land of the Widow at Windsor, so people don't want to know him any more.'

'*I* want to know him,' said Dinah.

Before I could stop her, she rose and walked over to the table where Raffles stood talking with the two seated men, and I felt obliged to follow.

'You're a fine brother,' she said lightly, to Raffles. 'You desert me.'

The ex-convict, heaving up his bulk from his chair, said quickly,

'Sebastian Melmoth, dear lady. And may I present my gifted young friend Aubrey Beardsley.'

As the wand-thin youth, with his refined face of an almost transparent pallor, bowed to Dinah, the waiter approached with a tray and asked Raffles if the drinks we had ordered were to be served now at this table.

Making the best of a situation I knew he would gladly have avoided, Raffles said, 'If these gentlemen will drink with us—?'

'Absinthe, *garçon*,' said Melmoth, as ex-Convict C.3.3. evidently now called himself—and he explained to Dinah, 'The hue of absinthe is pleasing to the cultivated eye.'

Cultivated as they no doubt were, his own eyes were bloodshot, with bags under them.

He went on, 'Young Beardsley here is only in Paris for one night. He's on his way to convalesce in the mild climate of Mentone, and we ran into each other on the Quai Voltaire.'

'Is it Mr. Melmoth you're sketching, Mr. Beardsley?' Dinah asked—for the frail youth was adding touches, with a stylus pen, to a drawing on a small sketch-block.

He shook his head. 'I'm sketching the backs of those men standing in a row, like a kind of frieze, at the bar over there. D'you like it?'

Tearing it from the block, he handed Dinah the sketch.

'Only their backs,' she said, comparing the sketch with the row of men at the bar, 'yet—somehow—it's caught them perfectly.'

'For that kind remark,' said Beardsley, 'I shall make you a present of it. How are you called, Miss Raffles—by your friends?'

'I'm called Dinah, Mr. Beardsley.'

'Then I shall take the liberty of inscribing this,' said the artist, doing so, ' "For Dinah—*Arte per l'Arte*—Aubrey Beardsley".'

As he presented Dinah with the sketch, the waiter came with a glass of milk for him and the absinthe for Melmoth.

'Your brother, Miss Dinah,' Melmoth said, licking his sensuous lips at sight of the absinthe, 'is instructing you in the ways of the world, I trust?'

'I'm learning something new from him every day, Mr. Melmoth.'

'Raffles, the cricketer,' said Melmoth, 'in the role of Pygmalion. But how bizarre!'

'Bizarre?' said Dinah. 'I don't know what you mean.'

110

'Alas,' sighed Melmoth, 'I so seldom mean what I say!'

He drank his absinthe. But it was clear, as we sat talking, that his wit was gone, quenched by the vindictive persecution, with its dire results, of the Mad Marquess. Melmoth called for more absinthe, grew drunker and maudlin—until young Beardsley, taking a sip of his milk, coughed painfully and a sudden froth of blood appeared on his lips.

He clapped his handkerchief to them—and I saw at once on Melmoth's big, vealy face a look of poignant concern.

'Aubrey,' he said gently, 'it's late, dear boy, for us decadents to be abroad, and you've a train to catch in a few hours. Look there at the window! Day breaks on the Boul' Mich— *And down the silent, sleeping street, The dawn, with silver-sandalled feet, Creeps like a frightened girl.* Come, Aubrey my dear—I'll take you to your hotel.'

Bloated and rumpled, he heaved himself up, took from the table his silk hat and turquoise-knobbed ebony stick.

'Perhaps we shall meet again,' he said to us, as he handed young Beardsley his travelling-cap. 'Aubrey goes to the healing climate of Mentone, and I—who knows whither?' He clapped his silk hat on his straggle of shoulder-length, greying hair, and shrugged, with a twisted smile. 'Melmoth—the Ishmael! Come, Aubrey—'

The bulky, destroyed poet put an arm protectively about the emaciated shoulders of the young artist—and, as they left us, we sat down again, but somehow, for a while, had nothing to say.

It was Raffles who, quite suddenly, broke the silence between us.

'Dinah,' he said, 'let me see that sketch.'

Dinah gave it to him, he glanced at it, then over at the bar, then handed the sketch to me. It portrayed, as a frieze in Indian ink, the backs of half-a-dozen or so men of assorted shapes and sizes standing in a row. I looked over at the men standing at the bar. In the row there, a gap had appeared. I looked again at the sketch, which showed no gap—and I felt the blood rush into my head.

'Come on,' Raffles said curtly, tossing a gold coin on to the marble tabletop.

We hurried Dinah out, and Raffles and I looked quickly each way along the Boulevard Saint-Michel. The breaking day was redolent of roasting coffee and new-baked bread, but there was

111

nobody to be seen except a man with a hose spraying the side-walk trees and the gutters.

'What are you looking for?' Dinah asked us.

'A *fiacre*,' said Raffles. 'It's time you were in bed.'

But what Raffles and I were looking for were two men whose backs appeared side by side in young Beardsley's sketch—a short man with the slight build of a jockey and a tall man with the musclebound build of a pugilist.

We had no idea where the ex-convict who now called himself Sebastian Melmoth was living in Paris.

'In any case, Bunny,' Raffles said to me later, in private, 'the fact that the Mad Marquess's chosen cronies are small jockeys and big bruisers is hardly, by itself, enough reason for warning Melmoth that it's possible he's being watched.'

'Personally,' I said, 'I didn't notice the oddly assorted couple leave the bar. They *may* have been following Melmoth, but they were more probably just a coincidence. After all, Raffles, the Marquess did, more than two years ago, exactly what he set out to do. He wrecked Melmoth's life. What possible motive could the Marquess have now for having the poor devil spied on?'

'I don't know, Bunny. Anyway, confound it,' Raffles said, almost brutally, 'this is none of our business. Forget it! A dowry for Dinah, that's our business now—or mine, anyway.'

He had no suspicion of my own feelings for Dinah and, twisting the hooks in my own absurd Cyrano-de-Bergerac of a heart, I managed to say, 'Your business, Raffles, is my business—as always.'

He smiled then. 'Good old Bunny,' he said.

So it was with a dowry for Dinah in the forefront of his mind—and of my own, however ironically—that we left Paris, some days later, and took Dinah off to Venice, where Raffles had a letter of introduction to present.

On the day when the three of us, Dinah with a pretty parasol raised against the burning sunshine, disembarked from a gondola at a splendid old *palazzo* on the Grand Canal, the major-domo informed us that the Principessa was not in residence, having repaired to her country place in the Tuscan hills.

Raffles said that, in the circumstances, he would post his letter to the Principessa's country place—and leaving our visiting cards with the major-domo, we went back down the steps and Raffles told Salvatore, our gondolier, to take us to the Piazza San Marco, the hour being now hard upon teatime.

At the barber-pole mooring-posts of the Piazza gondola quay, Raffles tipped Salvatore handsomely and, with Dinah arm-in-arm between us and flocks of pigeons waddling away and flapping up before us, we sauntered across the great square, to our left the soaring Campanile, to our right the Doge's Palace and the lofty tessellated porch of St. Mark's Cathedral topped by the equine statuary group once stolen by the greatest burglar in the annals of crime, the Emperor Napoleon.

We passed into the welcome shade of the colonnaded arcade to our left, where, on the sidewalk, the tables of the Caffé Florian were set out.

'Why, look!' Dinah exclaimed. 'There's Mr. Melmoth!'

My spirits sank. The overweight aesthete, in a white alpaca suit that would have been the better for pressing, a boater with a faded ribbon on his straggling locks, sat alone with his absinthe at a table.

'So!' he said resonantly. 'Melmoth the Nomad and Pygmalion the Cricketer, with his malleable maiden, meet again!'

With an opulent but wavering gesture, for he certainly had been looking upon the absinthe at its most alluring, he made us free of chairs at his table.

'I'm here,' he told us, 'in this city of rendezvous, where the mercantile West meets the gorgeous East—with the approval, of course, of Mr. Wordsworth, the Swan of Windermere—to keep a rendezvous myself.'

'A happy one for you, I hope, Mr. Melmoth,' said Dinah.

'As to that, Miss Dinah,' said ex-Convict C.3.3., ' "*King Pandion is dead, All his friends are lapped in lead.*" And yet—and yet, Miss Dinah—"*I have had playmates, I have had companions—*" '

He gazed out with pouched eyes at the Piazza San Marco as though he saw, through the quiver of heat there, English willows in summers gone, and himself, bland with success, idly propelling a punt for the indulgence of a graceful, capricious youth in blazer and straw boater, reclining on the cushions.

Suddenly, to my embarrassment, tears rolled down Melmoth's puffy cheeks.

'It *could* be a happy rendezvous,' he mumbled, 'after so long. It *could* be.' Groping for his turquoise-knobbed stick, he rose

113

with an effort. 'I'm expecting a telegram. I must go to my hotel again and ask if it's come at last. Oh, I *do* hope it's come. Forgive me—Miss Dinah—'

Blindly, he walked out under the arch of the colonnade into the white lightning of the sun. And Dinah, perhaps a little upset by the man's emotion, took up from the table the list of the Caffè Florian's ice-creams and gazed at it unseeingly, biting her lip.

I looked out at Melmoth. Pigeons rose before him as he made his way diagonally across the great square. An opening to the left of St. Mark's Cathedral swallowed him in shade. And I stiffened as I saw two men stroll out from the cathedral porch on the far side of the square—two men in straw hats, a little man like a jockey and a big man like a bruiser. The gap of shade that had engulfed Melmoth swallowed them.

I met Raffles' eyes.

Abruptly, he stood up, saying, 'I'm going to buy some cigarettes. I won't be long.'

But not until I was dressing for dinner that evening did I see him again, when he walked into my room at our hotel looking out upon the twilit tranquillity of the wide lagoon.

'Bunny,' he said, 'they followed Melmoth to his hotel. The jockey's a baby-faced, sly-eyed young Cockney called Titch. He stayed to keep an eye on Melmoth's hotel. The big bruiser's called Josser. I trailed him to a back canal, where he went into a *pensione*. It's evidently where they're lodging. Tonight, when Dinah's retired, you and I'll take a prowl around that *pensione*, see if we can find out what their game is.'

'What d'you think about this—"rendezvous" of Melmoth's?'

'I've an uneasy feeling, Bunny, that it's the one rendezvous in his life he should never keep.'

Venice in the small hours. Moonlight and uncanny stillness. No hoofbeats, no whipcracks, no hansoms, no horses. A city without wheels.

By narrow sidewalks edging devious waterways, Raffles and I reached the *pensione*. The word was visible, in the moonlight, over the iron-studded front door of the tall old building which, with its shuttered windows, stood at the junction of two canals.

'How does one get to it?' I asked, looking at the building across the gap of canal water.

'Plank drawbridge,' said Raffles. 'It was down when I followed Josser here. It's been pulled up now and chained for the night beside the door over there.' He put a hand on my arm. 'Listen!'

A vague mutter of men's voices was coming from the direction of the side of the building. As we listened, a voice unmistakably Cockney rose louder, exclaiming, *'Garn!'*

We moved to our right. The narrow, cobbled sidewalk angled sharply to edge the other canal, at the side of the *pensione.* From the one open window in the tall side of the building, dim lamplight fell across the stagnant water. The window was not much above our own level. High up, moonlight silvered the eaves of the building.

We moved along the sidewalk, against which barges stinking of rotten fruit and vegetables were moored in line, and we came opposite the lamplit window. The voices of the men in the room were now clearly audible to us across the canal:

'Garn, you big baboon, use your loaf, Josser! 'E got 'is bleedin' telegram, didn't 'e? 'Oo else would it be from but young Lord Alf, the Marquess's dandy son? 'E laid low, did 'is young lordship, when the beak at the Old Byeley sent Melmoth down for two years 'ard. Never wrote to 'im in the clink, neither. So Lord Alf's conscience 'as bin givin' 'im socks, bet yer life. An' now 'e reckons it's safe to meet Melmoth again, on the quiet, an' see 'ow 'e's made out.'

"E'll get a bleedin' shock when 'e sees what jyle's done to 'im, Titch!'

Shadows moved on a wall in the room across the canal there. Liquor glugged audibly from a bottle.

'It's like the Marquess told us, Josser. The old ape's suspicious because 'e's 'eard 'is fancy son's rented a villa—Villa Giudice at Posilippo, on the B'y o' Nyples—an' the Marquess reckons Lord Alf may take Melmoth there on the sly. An' you know what the Marquess told you when 'e 'anded you that thahsand pahnds you got in yer baggage there—'

' "Fix Melmoth for me, Josser", the Marquess said, Titch. "I don't care 'ow you do it, or 'oo you 'ave to bribe, or 'ow much, but fix Melmoth for keeps, Josser!" The Marquess an' 'is bloody *Rules o' The Prize Ring*, eh, Titch?'

'Gentry's different, Josser. They makes up their own rules for every perishin' thing as they goes along. No skin off our noses. Tomorrow we fixes Melmoth, an' you an' me can keep most o' that money, 'cos the job won't cost us a blind farthin'. All I does is watch my chance to walk up to Melmoth an' ask 'im the time, an' remark, chatty-like, nice bit o' weather we're 'avin'. Then I walks off to the police stytion where them Venice coppers lolls around in admiral's 'ats an' white gloves. An' I tells 'em, indignant-like, I'm a innocent young 'olidaymaker passin' through which a grown man 'as just made remarks to wot interpretations could be put on.'

'You crafty little baby-faced bastard, Titch!'

'So then I tells 'em, Josser, that I recognises the grown man as an old lag wot was 'ad up for it at the Old Byeley. An' I tells 'em 'is real name. That'll put the fat in the fire, Josser. *They'll* 'ave 'eard of 'im an' 'is scandal. 'Oo 'asn't? An' it'll be a case o' "Give a dog a bad name an' it'll come 'ome to roost"—see, Josser?'

'Blimey, Titch, they'll run 'im in on the spot!'

'What's more, Josser, the British Consul ain't goin' to stir 'imself overmuch for an old lag—bloody Irishman, at that—up to 'is fun an' games again. So Mr. Alias Bloomin' Melmoth'll be in the same fix as them Venice blokes wot got narked on in olden times 'ere. They got frogsmarched across that there Bridge o' Sighs an' flung in the dungeons of the Dodger's Palace—an' that was the last anyone ever 'eard of 'em!'

'Titch, the Marquess'll laugh 'is bleedin' 'ead off! All right, we'll do it tomorrer. Now, go on, get out o' my room an' rest yer intellecks before you gets brain fever. Shove off! I needs my beauty sleep.'

Raffles murmured in my ear, 'While he's settling down to it, Bunny, let's see if we can get a drink to wash a bad taste out of our mouths.'

We found, not far off, a small wineshop that was on the point of closing. The proprietor served us grudgingly with a couple of glasses of *strega*, and Raffles asked for a few toothpicks. Puzzled, I watched him arrange four of them on the tabletop, thus:

———— ———— ———— ————

'What does that signify?' I asked, with a frown.

'It signifies,' Raffles said, 'the position of the barges lying in line, each moored fore and aft, against the sidewalk side of the canal back there. Now, I estimate that if the fore end of the

116

second barge were unmoored, and the barge given a push, it would float out to this position.'

He revised the position of the second toothpick to:

'The barge,' he said, 'would then be aslant across the canal—and its fore end, I fancy, would just about be touching the wall of the *pensione* almost exactly under Josser's window.'

'A bridge!' I exclaimed.

'A Bridge of Sighs for the Mad Marquess,' said Raffles. 'It'll give him something to be mad about, because it's going to cost him the thousand pounds he entrusted to Josser and which is now in Josser's baggage. We'll divert that money from a bad cause, Bunny, to the worthier cause of laying a foundation for Dinah's dowry.'

'Magnificent, Raffles!' I breathed.

When we returned to the canal that flanked the side of the *pensione*, snores were audible from the wide open window and shutters of Josser's room. The lamp there was out, the room was in darkness.

Raffles untied from its mooring-ring the rope at the fore end of the second barge. We stepped down into a slime of rotting vegetable matter on the floorboards of the barge. There we found the heavy, slippery bargepole. With this we thrust hard against the sidewalk parapet. The barge, still secured at its stern, floated out over the stagnant canal and knocked gently against the wall under Josser's window.

Raffles leaped up, gripped the sill, pulled himself higher and, silent as a prowling leopard, vanished into the darkness of the room.

I stood holding the bargepole jammed down into the mud of the canal bottom, to keep the barge in position. The thudding in my chest and the tranquil snores of Josser measured the minutes. Gradually, I became aware of another sound. I strained my ears. The sound grew louder. I realised that it was the throbbing of a *vaporetto*, a steam-launch.

It was approaching.

I peered, in horror, along the dark canal to where, at its further end, about a hundred yards off, it debouched into a cross-canal on which moonlight shone.

The chugging sound began to slow. Now I could hear the water churned by the screws. Would the launch turn into this canal blocked by the barge? My heart pounded. Sweat wilted the collar of my boiled shirt.

Suddenly, Raffles dropped down beside me into the barge.

'Don't move,' I whispered. 'Look there!'

The *vaporetto* had come into view, along there in the moonlight of the cross-canal. It was a police patrol launch. The epaulettes and cocked hats of two policemen were clearly visible as, their launch now scarcely moving, they peered towards us along the dark canal.

We did not move. We did not even breathe.

Clearly, a voice reached us: *'Niente! Vabene, andiamo!'*

Smoke belched from the launch's short stack, the screws churned the water, the launch moved on, its purposeful throbbing died away.

We tied up the barge in its original position and, leaving Josser's undisturbed snores behind us, made our retreat rapidly along the footwalks that edged the jigsaw of waterways.

Not until we came out on the Piazza San Marco did I ask Raffles if he had found the money in Josser's baggage.

'It's in hundred-pound notes, Bunny. He had it hidden in a sock. It's now in my pocket.' Raffles stopped dead. 'There's Melmoth!'

The pigeons had gone to roost. Nothing moved on the moonlit expanse of the great square slanted across by the shadow of the Campanile, but a few figures still sat at the sidewalk tables of the Caffé Florian in the arcade.

Among those sleepless beings, the bloated figure of Melmoth, alone at a table, brooded over his absinthe.

'The folly of the man!' I muttered. 'How can he have brought himself to agree to keep a rendezvous again with the young lordship who wrecked him?'

'Mel*moth*,' Raffles said dryly. 'An apt alias, Bunny. The moth with scorched wings can't help scorching them again—even to death—in the same flame.'

'He's forgotten the lines he himself wrote,' I said, 'in the ballad

**118**

he composed behind prison bars: *"For who can tell To what red hell His immortal soul shall go?"'*

'Bunny,' Raffles said, 'I don't know whether it's possible to help a man who's lost the will to help himself. But one can try. Go on to our hotel. I'll see you when I see you.'

Leaving me there in the moonlight, he walked on, passed under the gas-globes in the arches of the arcade, and joined Melmoth the Outcast.

Broad daylight filled my room at the hotel when Raffles woke me. He had bathed and changed his evening dress for a suit of light grey flannel. His keen face had a slightly haggard look as he offered me a Sullivan from his cigarette-case.

'It's six o'clock, Bunny,' he said. 'Melmoth's gone. I've just seen him off, on the first train out across the causeway. He's not going to keep his rendezvous with the young milord today— or any other day, if he keeps to his present resolve. But that's up to him. Anyway, I gather that Melmoth has just one loyal, wise, compassionate friend—a man called Robbie—who's at Taormina in Sicily. Melmoth has no money except a small allowance from his estranged wife. So I've given him two hundred pounds—all he would accept from me, though he doesn't know it's the Mad Marquess's money—and he's on his way now to Taormina.'

'What about Titch and Josser?'

'No sign of them at the station, Bunny. They're still snoring away confidently in the *pensione*, I imagine. When they wake up to find they've lost the Marquess's thousand pounds, then find they've lost track of Melmoth as well, I doubt if they'll go to the police—who'd want to know how a precious pair like that got their dirty fingernails on a thousand pounds in the first place. No, I'm afraid they haven't much option but to go back to London and report to the Marquess.'

'If I were them,' I said, 'I'd omit the report—and keep well out of his way!'

'In any case,' said Raffles, 'it seems probable that they'll be catching the train for Milan, Paris and London, which leaves at four this afternoon. To see if they *do* go, we'll take Dinah for a gondola ride, and I'll have a quiet word with Salvatore to see to it that we're near the station at about four this afternoon.'

The clocks of Venice were nearing that hour when our gondola, lazily propelled by Salvatore's huge oar, drifted us into view of the broad, water-lapped steps to the arched entrance of the glass-roofed station.

From gondolas and from an awninged *vaporetto,* one of the public steam-launches that plied the Grand Canal, travellers were disembarking and going up the steps to the station. Among them trudged, dejectedly humping their carpet-bags, Titch and Josser.

Evidently a train had just come in, for there also were travellers, obviously newly arrived, emerging from the station.

'Oh, look!' said Dinah idly, as she reclined on our gondola cushions in the shade of her pretty parasol. 'What an attractive young man!'

Following the glance of her cool grey eyes, I saw that the young man in question, accompanied by a porter burdened with expensive luggage, had just come out from the station. Of graceful build, immaculate in white flannels and a pink blazer, a boater jauntily tilted on longish hair almost as fair as Dinah's, he stood at the head of the steps, tapping a malacca cane languidly on his palm as he cast patrician glances over the throng in the obvious expectation that somebody would be eagerly awaiting his arrival.

'He looks like a young Adonis,' said Dinah—'just as, I imagine, Lord Alfred must look.'

It was an instant before, here in the gently rocking gondola fifty yards or so out from the station, the impact of her remark struck me. I stared at her.

Raffles said, very evenly, 'Lord Alfred, Dinah?'

'Mr. Melmoth's—ex-friend,' Dinah said. 'Poor Mr. Melmoth, I know his *real* name—and why he changed it.'

'Indeed?' Raffles said, his tone cold, his expression unfathomable

'But of course,' said Dinah. 'Because when we met Mr. Melmoth with Mr. Beardsley in that Paris *café,* I had a feeling that Mr. Melmoth looked rather like the poor convict, with the broad arrows on him, that I caught a glimpse of in that iron-barred cage at the Waxworks. So I read all about him, and his green carnation, in the catalogue later on.'

'But, Dinah,' I blurted, '*I* had the catalogue.'

'Yes, Bunny,' she said, 'I noticed it in the side pocket of your suit as we were talking to Mr. Melmoth and Mr. Beardsley.'

120

From the shade of her pretty parasol, as she reclined on the gondola cushions, she smiled at us with indulgent composure.

'So I *stole* it,' said Dinah Raffles.

Appalled, I glanced at Raffles. And I knew then, very surely, that, with a view to getting his sister's surname changed by an advantageous foreign marriage, he would not rest until he had amassed her dowry.

For, with a keenly speculative expression I knew only too well, Raffles was looking up at where, high on the roof of the cathedral, which was not far off, the only horses in Venice pranced nobly against the blue of the sky—the priceless golden horses of St. Mark's.

# 8 STEALING THE VENETIAN HORSES

Forwarded from London, a packet of letters reached Raffles in Venice.

'Dinah,' he said, as he shuffled the envelopes, 'here's one for you—addressed in care of myself at Lord's Cricket Ground.'

'There's a French stamp on it,' said Dinah, surprised. 'I don't know anyone in France.'

We were having our morning coffee at the Caffé Florian, in the arcade of the Piazza San Marco.

There was no post for me, so while Dinah and Raffles read their letters I sipped my coffee and watched the pigeons as ceaselessly, in the blazing sunshine, they fluttered up to and down from the famous statutary group, the Golden Horses, which topped the tessellated façade of St. Mark's Cathedral, on the far side of the great square.

Knowing that that pastmaster of the burglarious craft, the Emperor Napoleon, once had made off with the Golden Horses, and knowing also Raffles' resolve to amass a worthy dowry for his sister Dinah and get her married into some European family of consideration, preferably one listed in the *Almanach de Gotha*,

121

I was not altogether at peace in my mind about his motives for keeping us lingering on here in Venice after the assistance he had rendered to poor Oscar Wilde, alias Melmoth.

'This letter,' said Dinah, 'is from Lord Fasterton.'

'And who, may I ask,' Raffles said, 'is Lord Fasterton?'

Though his tone now, as he asked his question, was casual enough, I knew that he was curious about his sister's character, her past—and her acquaintances.

'Lord Fasterton,' said Dinah absently, intent on her letter, 'was Governor of New South Wales when I was a small girl living there with Uncle Fred and Aunt May. They were great friends of the Governor's. We used to spend whole summers at a holiday home he lent to us on an island of the Great Barrier Reef. Oh, it was beautiful! I used to run quite wild there.'

'Indeed?' said Raffles inscrutably.

'When the Governor's term finished,' Dinah said, 'he retired to Shropshire, in England, but it seems he's now taking the waters at Aix-les-Bains. He says here that he's only just learned that my uncle and aunt are no more and that I've come from Australia to be with my brother, the famous cricketer.' She turned a page of her letter. 'Lord Fasterton's rented a villa at Aix-les-Bains for the season and he wants me to go and stay with him for a while—and bring my brother.'

'That's very kind of him, Dinah,' said Raffles.

'He's a dear old man,' said Dinah. 'He's a widower and awfully lonely now that he has no colony to govern. We *must* visit him. He'd be hurt if we didn't. And Bunny must come, too, of course.'

She smiled at me. She had a way, which charmed and touched me, of including me in everything, just as though I belonged to her—as, in my secret heart, I did.

'He used to tell me marvellous tales,' she went on, 'about the bushrangers he had had to have hanged, as Governor. Some of them came from the best families and finest schools in England. They were unspeakable rotters, the Governor said, but their last moments seemed always to bring out the gentleman in them. They just thanked the hangman politely, then gave a reckless laugh as he dropped the trap under them. Oh, the bushrangers have always been my heroes!'

Raffles and I exchanged a speculative glance.

For my part, though Dinah assured me I should be welcomed, I did not consider it decent to impose myself, an uninvited

122

stranger, on the hospitality of the ex-Governor of New South Wales, so I parted company with Raffles and Dinah a few days later at Milan.

Though I could not have said just why that brother and sister meant so much to me in my misspent life, they made a most elegantly attractive couple, standing there on the station platform at Milan as I leaned from the train window to take my leave of them.

'Never mind, Bunny,' said Dinah, for I must have been looking a bit sad at the parting. 'We'll soon be back in London with you.'

And she pulled my head down to her—and kissed me on the lips.

Dinah! I could not sleep from thinking of her, all the way back to London.

Never had my Mount Street flat seemed so desolate to me. But I had been back there only about ten days when the sudden jangling of my doorbell, one afternoon, brought me to my front door. As I opened it a crack, to peer out cautiously, it was pushed wider and in walked Raffles. He was alone.

'I've left Dinah at Aix,' he told me, when I had trotted out the whisky. 'The ex-Governor's a fine, dashing old soldier, Bunny, but terribly lonely. Dinah's found him something to do with his time. She's persuaded him to write his memoirs of the bush-rangers. She's staying on for a while to get  him started, act as his amanuensis.'

'How like Dinah that is!' I exclaimed.

'H'm,' said Raffles. 'I wish I understood her better. You know, it's a strange thing. When you and I were in Australia on that cricket tour a few years ago, you didn't know of Dinah's existence. But I was in hell while we were there, Bunny. I knew I ought to look Dinah up. At the same time, being the damned scoundrel I am, I thought it better not to get involved in her life. Yet, all the while, I was in dread that she'd see my name mentioned in the cricket reports, know I was in Australia, and look *me* up.' He smiled wryly. 'I needn't have worried. She spent the entire summer on that Barrier Reef island—and never set eyes on a newspaper!'

He took a deep drink.

'Dinah worries me, Bunny. I shan't rest until I've got her well and happily married. I need a clear head to plan a campaign to get her a dowry worthy of her. I've years of neglect to make up for. But, for the present, she's safely off my hands—so I'm going to seize the opportunity for a round or two of golf, down in Wiltshire, so that I can think the situation over quietly. Would you care to come along?'

'With pleasure,' I said. 'In fact, I think it's a good idea, Raffles. I've been a bit nervous that this matter of Dinah's dowry might tempt you into something hasty.'

'No fear of that, Bunny,' Raffles assured me. 'Actually, I've a small matter to look into in Wiltshire. Don't worry, it's perfectly innocent. It arises out of one of those letters that reached me in Venice. A man I used to play a lot of golf with thinks I may be able to help him with a little problem. At a time when I was playing off scratch, I gave his young son a bit of coaching. The boy's now at our own old school, and the father's worried about the boy's golf, for some reason.'

I was relieved to see Raffles' attention thus diverted from the potentially dangerous subject of Dinah's dowry to some trifling golf matter. And, three days later, from the window of a train approaching our destination in the Wiltshire countryside, Raffles pointed out to me a flutter of flags that marked the greens of a golf course on a downside dotted here and there with gorse in the mellow sunshine.

'Church Fedden golf course, Bunny.'

'What are those curious figures higher up the slope, Raffles?'

Reaching almost to the rounded summit of the down were two giant, chalk-white, emaciated silhouettes.

'Those are the Long Men of Fedden,' Raffles said. 'They're as famous, in their way, as the golden horses of St. Mark's, but it'd puzzle even so great a burglar as the Emperor Napoleon to make off with the Long Men. They're prehistoric chalk-carvings, Bunny.'

Outlined by the cutting away of the turf from the underlying chalk, the silhouettes were those of a pair of elongated males, facing each other, one taller than the other, each holding some kind of staff before him.

Raffles laughed. 'It took a golfer, of course, Bunny, to conceive the notion that the Long Men of Fedden obviously represent a prehistoric father instructing his son in the correct stance with some Stone Age prototype of baffy or cleek.'

The train whistled, beginning to slow down.

124

'I gather,' said Raffles, 'from the Rector's letter—'

'Rector?' I said, dismayed. 'We're to be guests at a Rectory?'

'Don't worry,' said Raffles. 'The Reverend Walter Matcham's a Church of England clergyman, so his religion hardly shows on him. He's a very sound golfer and archaeologist. I gather that his little golf problem is something to do with a tournament for father-and-son pairs. They're competing for a trophy that's being offered for the first time—a trophy called The Long Golfers. The Reverend Walter seems particularly keen for him and his boy Geoff to win it, but I gather that Geoff's game's gone to pieces, for some reason. Walter seems to think that, because I coached Geoff in the first place, I'm the best bet to pull his game together for this tournament. Ah, there they are—waiting for us,' he added, as the small train steamed to a standstill in the countrified station.

Alighting, we handed our valises and golfbags to a rustic porter—and were greeted cordially by a tall man, tanned and aquiline, wearing pepper-and-salt tweeds, a clerical straw hat and collar, and dusty boots, at his side a slim, good-looking youngster of about seventeen.

'Delighted to see you, Raffles!' exclaimed Mr. Matcham. 'And this is your friend Manders I've so often heard you speak of? Excellent!'

'By Jove, Geoff,' Raffles said to the boy, 'you've shot up quite a bit since I saw you last!'

'Yes, indeed,' said Matcham, 'and so's my daughter Judy, who housekeeps for me these days. You'll hardly recognise her, Raffles.'

Judy, waiting in the Rectory dogcart outside the station, was holding the reins of the frisky cob. She was a year or so older than Geoff, with auburn tints in her pretty hair, and her brown eyes were warmly welcoming.

Geoff took the reins from her and, as the cob jogged off with us along the village street, Raffles said, 'I've been telling Bunny Manders, Walter, about this father-and-son golf tournament.'

'Yes, indeed,' said the clergyman, his tone suddenly grim. 'The trophy's presented by a man, a relative newcomer here, called Maurice Buckley. His son Edward is at school with Geoff. Buckley's house, Fedden Beeches, a considerable mansion he's built for himself, is just the other side of the Long Men Down. Buckley's not a good influence locally. I've had to take issue with him from time to time, with the result that he loathes me. Most unfortunately, this has compromised a Movement in which I'm interested—in common with certain historians and archaeologists. Our ultimate object is an Act of Parliament, setting up a patriotic or, as it were, *national trust* for the preservation of this country's cultural curiosities.'

'An excellent idea,' said Raffles.

'The Long Men of Fedden, a neolithic mystery, are a case in point, Raffles. For years, a few of us here locally have laboured with spade and mattock, in rain and shine, to redeem the strange giants from total obliteration. We've been trying to raise money to purchase the site from its absentee owner. Unfortunately, Buckley—out of personal antipathy for myself—has stepped in and forestalled us. Not only has he bought the site and warned us off, but he's set out to taunt me by putting up this Father-and-Son tournament trophy. It's a miniature, which he chooses to call The Long Golfers, of those prehistoric chalk-carvings.'

'How very unusual!' said Raffles.

'Yes, indeed,' said the Rector. 'Last year, Geoff and I beat the Buckleys, father and son, in the club foursomes. Buckley Senior's a bad loser. Not only has he put up this Long Golfers trophy, but he intends that he and his boy Edward shall be the first to put their names on it.'

'Play for a trophy he's himself presenting?' said Raffles. 'What bad manners!'

'Raffles, he doesn't know the meaning of the word. Naturally, because of the unchristian spirit that prompted this tournament, I had no intention of entering Geoff and myself for it. But a couple of weeks or so ago, I was playing a round with Geoff, just back from school for the holidays. The Buckleys were in the clubhouse. Maurice Buckley demanded, loudly and offensively, if cold feet had prevented my entering Geoff and myself for the tournament. I ignored the man. He has, like many very wealthy people, a cohort of hangers-on and clubhouse boozing cronies. Showing off to them, he bawled a challenge at me. He said that, if Geoff and I entered the tournament and went further in it than Buckley and his boy Edward, he'd deed the Long Men site, gratis, to our movement—'

'Good God!' Raffles said. 'Oh, excuse me, Walter. But—I mean—you took him up on this, of course?'

'I looked him straight in the eye,' said the Rev. Walter

Matcham, 'then I went to the noticeboard and entered our names on the tournament list.'

I noticed Judy frown, biting her lip.

'Of course,' said Matcham, 'this is hard on Geoff. I realise that. Knowing how vital this tournament is to me. I'm afraid he's let over-anxiety affect his game. He's lost confidence, can't seem to do a thing right. But I feel sure, Raffles—a father never being, however sympathetic, a son's best preceptor—that a round or two with you, who's played so often with him in the past, would make *all* the difference.'

The boy said nothing. Pale, tight-lipped, he turned the horse in at the gateway to the Rectory drive.

Raffles glanced up, thoughtfully, at the last of the autumnal sunshine lingering on the emaciated, chalk-white giants, the Long Men of Fedden, a timeless mystery on the green slope of the down.

Early next morning, before other father-and-son pairs were out practising for the tournament, found us up on the golf course. My own golf being erratic, to say the least, it was decided that Raffles should play against the Rector's and Geoff's best ball. I carried Raffles' bag, and Judy carried her father's.

It was glorious, up here on the downs at this hour, with the sun shining on the dew of the gorse-bushes, and the song of larks mingling with the sound of the greenkeeper's lawnmower. But young Geoff Matcham's obvious tension troubled us all. His game went from bad to worse. He was hitting at the ball as though he hated the sight of it. On the eighth tee, he gave the ball a clout that would have been fine if it had not developed a fearful slice that landed it in a gorse-clump alongside the wrong fairway.

'Oh, Geoff, really!' said the Rector, goaded to irritability.

The boy turned sharply, with such a tortured look that I feared he was going to smash his driver over his knee. But Judy moved forward quickly, putting a hand on his arm, in warning and appeal. And the boy gulped.

'I'm sorry, Father,' he muttered.

'Somehow,' Raffles said, in his easy way, 'I think it might pay, Walter, if Geoff and I potter along alone for a few holes and see if we can sort this trouble out.'

So the Rector, Judy and I went off back to the clubhouse, to

127

amuse ourselves on the clock-golf green, and left Raffles and Geoff to it. When they returned for lunch, the boy's manner seemed less taut—and, that night, I went into Raffles' room to ask what had happened.

'Geoff's in bad trouble, Bunny. I guessed it, and I've got the truth out of him. He goes back to school, week after next, for his last term, and he has a good chance of a scholarship at Oxford—or, rather, he *had* a good chance. As it is, he's more likely, when he gets back to school, to find himself expelled.'

Raffles puffed a Sullivan alight over the chimney of the dressing-table lamp.

'There's a racing man, a Major Dodd—at least, he *calls* himself "Major"—who lives near the school. Geoff needed a bit of extra money. He scraped together a stake and got the Major to lay a bet for him. Geoff's horse won, at long odds—sheer manna for him. The dirty dog of a Major didn't pay up. He said he got to the races too late to get the bet on, and handed Geoff his stake money back. Too late at the course, Bunny!'

'An alibi as old as the Turf,' I said. 'He'd pocketed the winnings.'

Raffles nodded. 'Now, here's the real trouble. Geoff found out that one or two other Sixth-Formers had been bunkumed by the Major in the same way. The damned young fools decided to do something about it. They broke bounds, on the last night of term, tied handkerchiefs over their faces and went to the Major's house with the intention of grabbing him, frogsmarching him to a nearby duckpond, and chucking him in.'

'Quite right, too,' I said. 'The damned welsher!'

'Ah, but he was waiting for them, Bunny—with a twelve-bore shotgun. He lined them up, yanked off their handkerchiefs, told them he'd decide in due course what action to take, and let them go. The fact is, he'd been tipped off, Bunny—by a Sixth-Former —young Edward Buckley, in fact. Young Buckley's told Geoff so himself, since they've been back here for the holidays. The betting wouldn't, by itself, get the boys expelled—but the attempt at violent reprisal certainly will, if the Head hears of it. And now, here's the thing. Young Buckley has the Major in his pocket. He'll squeal to the Headmaster if young Buckley tells him to. And young Buckley's price for keeping the Major quiet? Simply this—Geoff's to see to it that he and the Rector don't go further than the Buckleys in the Long Golfers tournament.'

128

'Blackmail!' I said, appalled.

'And Buckley Senior,' Raffles said, 'is privy to it. Otherwise, would he have put those Long Men acres at stake? No, Bunny! Maurice Buckley's a smart City man. When he bets, it's on a sure thing. He's making a fool of a country clergyman who dared to talk back at him, and he's laughing up his sleeve.'

'No wonder young Geoff's game has gone to pieces!'

'And Judy, too,' said Raffles. 'He's told her the truth, and those kids just haven't known what to do. But I've told Geoff now that he's to go flat out to win this tournament—and you and I'll stymie the Buckleys.'

'How?'

'I've pumped Geoff about them, Bunny, and I gather that Buckley Senior has a collection of *objets d'art*, mostly *cloisonné* and rare porcelain. But there's one thing among it, Bunny, which makes me begin to believe that there's such a thing as Fate. Maurice Buckley's prize possession is a statuette, one of the few works of the great goldsmith, Benvenuto Cellini, that's in private ownership. I got the shock of my life when Geoff told me what that statuette represents.'

Raffles crushed out his cigarette in the ashtray on the dressing-table.

'What price Dinah's dowry, Bunny?' He looked at me with a strange smile in the lamplight. 'The Cellini statuette in Maurice Buckley's possession is a miniature representation of a certain famous statuary group at Venice—*the Golden Horses of St. Mark's!*'

Then Raffles gave me his instructions. The Buckley collection, in his mansion Fedden Beeches, was kept in a strongroom built in for him by Hargesson's of Sheffield. Cracking it was out of the question. Finesse was imperative.

As dawn was breaking next morning, I crept out of the sleeping old Rectory, walked to the little station of Church Fedden, caught the five a.m. milk train up to London, leaving Raffles to make my excuses.

From our 'fence' and occasional confederate, Ivor Kern, I obtained an accommodation address I could safely use. I had a few letterheads run off, in the name of *P. D. Lowe, Photographer.* On one of these, I wrote to Maurice Buckley, stating that I, Mr. Lowe, had been commissioned, by a Fine Arts *de*

129

*luxe* magazine shortly to start publication, to photograph exceptional artifacts in private collections; it was hoped to include in this distinguished series his famous Cellini statuette; and I should be in the Church Fedden district, with my photographic equipment, on the afternoon of the following Friday.

'Why Friday?' said Kern, breathing cigar smoke over my shoulder as I wrote the letter in the cluttered living-room over his shop.

'Because Buckley's on the golf club committee, Ivor, and he's fixed it that the draw for the Long Golfers tournament is made in two sections—keeping the Buckley pair apart from the Rectory pair. He's a show-off, you see. He hopes to come up against the Rectory pair in the final, and make a big, grandstand triumph in front of his *claque*. The final will be played over thirty-six holes on Friday. So, with any luck, he won't be at home on Friday afternoon. He'll be out on the golf course.'

'And so?' said Kern, intent.

'And so, Ivor,' I said, 'Buckley, being a show-off, won't want his collection left out of that distinguished magazine series, so Raffles thinks he'll make arrangements for a butler or somebody to receive Mr. Lowe and supervise his photographic activities. Now, what Raffles wants *you* to do is this: Collect Buckley's reply, assuming there *is* one, from the accommodation address. Open the letter to Lowe. If it's as we hope, come down to Wiltshire. Bring photographic equipment, including one of those little "dark rooms" on wheels that some photographers use nowadays.'

'I know the things you mean,' said Kern.

'Right,' I said. 'Put up' at the inn at the nearest village to Church Fedden, send a note to Raffles, at the Rectory, to let us know you've arrived. I don't know exactly what's in Raffles' mind, but if all goes well, you'll then get further instructions. Are you game?'

'The Golden Horses of St. Mark's, by Benvenuto Cellini,' Kern said softly, his dark eyes glittering. 'Cellini did several of those statuettes of the Venetian horses, just as he did several examples of his famous Golden Unicorns. Manders, if Raffles gets his hands on that statuette, I can dispose of it for a small fortune to a millionaire collector client of mine in Philadelphia who'll ask no questions. Tell Raffles he'll be able to retire—and do nothing but play cricket.'

'Raffles,' I said, 'has another purpose for the money.'

But the irony of my situation was a secret that I kept—because I, too, was a criminal, and unworthy of Dinah—locked in my own heart.

And on the Tuesday, after I had returned to Church Fedden Rectory, the competitors for the Long Golfers trophy teed off. The first Father-and-Son team tournament ever held in these parts, it attracted many spectators. The thatched clubhouse on Long Men Down was surrounded with horses, gigs, phaetons, dogcarts. The autumnal weather was perfect. High on the unlit down loomed the mysterious chalk-white figures, the thin giants carved in the ancient turf by neolithic men for some reason now forever unknowable.

The Buckley pair had a gallery of hangers-on trailing them on their rounds. The father was a big, bald, plethoric-looking man in a ginger-hued Harris tweed knickerbocker suit. The son was a handsome youth with a suave manner, a golf swing that spoke of the most expensive coaching, and a slight superior smile.

I kept myself inconspicuous among the spectators, Raffles having warned me that the Buckleys must see neither myself nor him. But when there was no danger of our being seen by the Buckleys, Raffles caddied for Geoff, myself for the Rector, and Judy, hardly able to contain her excitement, provided moral support.

With Raffles' murmured counselling, Geoff's golf was a treat to behold. The boy was a natural. And the Rector, though he did not hit a long ball, kept in exemplary fashion, as might have been expected from one of his cloth, strictly to the straight and narrow.

And it happened as it *had* to happen. They got there. The final was between the Matchams, of the Rectory, and the Buckleys, of Fedden Beeches.

With Judy caddying now for the Rector, and the Rectory bootboy for Geoff, with Raffles and me sweating blood as we kept ourselves inconspicuous among the spectators, the finalists went in to lunch all square after eighteen holes.

The spectators buzzed with talk as they brought out their picnic-baskets and spread cloths on the thymey turf.

To my profound regret, I was not present when the finalists teed off for the last, the vital, eighteen holes on that Friday afternoon.

I was meeting Ivor Kern in an abandoned chalkpit not far

131

from the Buckley house, Fedden Beeches, on the other slope of Long Men Down. Tall and thin in his Londoner's frockcoat and silk hat, with his shrewd, pale face, Kern was waiting for me, as instructed in a note from Raffles.

Kern had with him a large camera on a tripod, and a push-cart rather like a milkman's trolley, with two large wheels, a small wheel in front.

'The portable "dark room," Manders,' said Kern.

The ingenious invention had a cover of thick black cloth in which were the orifices of a kind of pair of tight-fitting sleeves, through which the photographer could thrust his arms and manipulate his plates in developing-fluid. However, on this occasion there was no fluid under the cover. Instead, there was a suit of respectable blue serge, a pair of goldrimmed eyeglasses, and a bowler hat. Donning these articles, which radically changed my appearance, I left my Savile Row tweeds with Kern and, to his fervent 'Good luck, Manders!', I set off, wheeling my perambulator object and carrying my camera and tripod over my shoulder, up the lane to Fedden Beeches.

It proved to be a newly built, considerable mansion in pretentious taste. To my jerk at the bellpull in the Palladian porch, the door was opened to me by a haughty butler, who looked down his nose at the card I handed to him.

'Ah, yes,' he said. 'The master 'appens to be absent, golfing, but 'e's left instructions happertaining to your purpose 'ere, Mr. Lowe. This way with your paraphernalier—and try, if you please, not to mark the polish of the 'all floor with them wheels. 'Arrison?'

'Yes, Mr. 'Icks?' said a burly footman.

'Stand by,' said Mr. Hicks, 'while I open the 'Argesson room for this person.'

Drawing aside an Oriental screen to the left of the large hall, the footman disclosed a door resembling that of a bank vault. It had a brass lever and three separate keyholes. Into these Mr. Hicks inserted three separate keys, turned them in opposed directions, then depressed the lever, drew open the massive door. I followed him, trundling my perambulator, into the dim interior.

I could make out steel shutters over two windows, so I said that I would like these shutters opened, explaining, 'On such a sunny afternoon, Mr. 'Icks, the solar rays will serve the purpose of my sensitive modern camera.'

Harrison, at a gesture of Mr. Hicks' plump hand, clanged open the shutters. And my heart lunged as sunshine flooded in. For there, in pride of place on a pedestal in the centre of the strongroom, was the exquisite Cellini statuette—the Venetian horses, the Golden Horses of St. Mark's.

My hands trembled as I set up my tripod with the big square camera on it. Taking its red rubber bulb in hand, I ducked under the velvet cloth, and held the bulb tightly squeezed until I had counted fifty. I released the bulb then and emerged from under the cloth.

'There'll be no need to expose a further plate, Mr. 'Icks, for a more successful one I never did do, I fancy. Now, I would like all light excluded from this remarkable room while I transfer the plate from my camera to my mobile developer, thus making it possible to send a proof for your master's approval within no more than twenty-four hours.'

Mr. Hicks closed the massive door, Harrison the window-shutters. In the resultant intense darkness, I could hear Mr. Hicks's vinous wheezing. As instructed by Raffles, I did not lay a finger on the golden horses. I merely shuffled my feet and thrust my arms into the sleeves of the developer cover.

'Very well, Mr. 'Icks,' I said then. 'We can now safely admit some light on the scene.'

Mr. Hicks opened the door, Harrison the window-shutters. Sunshine flooded in, to disclose me fastening my cufflinks. The Cellini statuette was naturally, as Mr. Hicks made haste to confirm, intact on its pedestal.

Ushered from the house, I hurried back with my perambulator to the chalkpit. I changed back into my own clothes, left the photographic gear with Kern, and made for the golf course. By the time I got there, the autumn sun was beginning to decline. More time had passed than I realised. It was not until I had covered most of the golf course that I saw the now much augmented crowd of spectators. Tense and silent, they were just moving away from the seventeenth green.

I found Raffles lurking at the back of the crowd. He gave me a quick inquiring look.

'All well, so far,' I told him—'though I don't pretend to know how it advances us. How does the game stand?'

'It's been ding-dong all the way, Bunny. The Rector and Geoff went one down at the thirteenth, halved the next three, and now

133

have just squared the match here at the seventeenth. It's all on the last hole now. And here we go!'

With a shuffling of feet, the gallery formed a semicircle around the eighteenth tee. Nobody spoke a word. I saw that it was the Rector's honour, for he took his driver from the bag Judy held for him. She stooped to take damp sand from the box and tee his ball. Bareheaded, his hair pepper-and-salt, his tanned face fine-drawn with strain above his clerical collar, he looked up at the chalk-white neolithic giants high on the down. All was still. There was no sound but the vesper song of a lark, unseen in the sunset sky.

He turned to Judy. Her brown eyes were wide with anxiety. He gave her a small, tight-lipped smile, and she stepped back and he addressed his ball and he hit it a good hundred and seventy yards as straight as a die down the middle of the fairway. And young Buckley teed up his ball and he clouted it gracefully more than fifty yards beyond the Rector's and right down the middle. His *claque* cheered.

We all moved on, following the players. Judy, carrying the Rector's bag with the breeze of evening fluttering her hair, walked with an arm linked in Geoff's; and Bootboy Bundy, in his billycock hat, trudged faithfully after them with Geoff's bag.

And now it was up to Geoff. I was in agony for him as he studied the lie of his ball. It was his last chance to throw away this game—and perhaps go on to Oxford in due course. On the other hand—

He glanced at his father. Then at young Buckley. And I saw young Buckley's faint warning smile. Geoff turned to Bootboy Bundy, whose face had grown so red with excitement that he looked ready to burst. But Geoff was as white as a sheet as he started to take his mid-iron from his bag.

Here at the back of the crowd, Raffles muttered to me, 'It's a brassie shot for him, Bunny, and he knows it. Damnation, he's losing his nerve!'

For there was a bunker guarding the green, and a mid-iron shot here was a betrayal of tortured indecision, but a brassie shot here could be all or nothing.

But Geoff, still hesitating, glanced up at the thin giants, the Long Men on the down—and, with a sudden resolve, thrust the mid-iron back into the bag held by Bootboy Bundy, took out the brassie, addressed the ball and, with a lovely swing, hit it clean
134

and crisp. And every eye watched it soar over the bank of the bunker, roll on to the green, and come to a standstill within four feet of the pin.

Young Buckley whitened with suppressed rage. Buckley Senior flushed darkly with it. He walked on, followed by the murmuring crowd, to his own ball, took his iron to it, and, in his rage gave it such a welt that it not only carried the bunker but bounced on the green and ran up and over the bank at the back.

And we all surged forward then to the green, to see young Edward Buckley recover brilliantly with a perfect chip shot from behind the green. But it was too late. The Rector's putt was unerring.

A great cheer went up, and Judy, throwing down the Rector's bag, hugged her father and brother, and Bootboy Bundy's billy-cock hat sailed high into the air as he broke into a capering barn dance on the green.

The expressions of the Buckley pair, as they stalked off the green without a word, followed by their deflated *claque* of club-house spongers, were so venomous that I had not a doubt but that a letter would go off tonight to their sycophant, 'Major' Jack Dodd, instructing him to squeal on Geoff and his mis-guided Sixth-Form friends to the Headmaster.

'But as to that, Bunny,' Raffles said—'*now* is the time for all good men and true to rally to the aid of the Rectory. Come on!'

Walking quickly, we made our way to the chalkpit where Ivor Kern awaited us.

'Got the stuff, Ivor?' said Raffles. 'Well done! Now, Bunny, I'm sorry to spoil that excellent tweed suit of yours, but needs must.' With a jerk, he yanked my jacket open so sharply that all the buttons flew off. 'Now the sleeve,' he said, and he cut the shoulder stitches with a razor handed to him by the smirking Kern.

Raffles then ripped down the sleeve with his hands, so that it hung dangling over by knuckles. He made a slash in my trouser leg, exposing my shinbone. He took off my smart corduroy cap, handed it to Ivor Kern in exchange for two small bottles.

'Here's a shiner for you, Bunny,' he said, and with a camel-hair brush delicately decorated the socket area of my right eye. 'Now for the blood,' he said, and he smeared over my face a lot of red stuff, and rubbed it into my hair. 'Now for a gap-toothed appearance,' he said, and blacked out one of my teeth. 'Put your tongue out, Bunny.'

Bewildered, I put it out, and he painted some red stuff on it with the brush.

'Now,' he said, 'you can spit blood into your handkerchief, Bunny.' He stepped back to appraise his handiwork. 'I think he looks enough of a casualty to serve our purpose, Ivor.' Taking off his own corduroy cap, he donned an official-looking Homburg hat and a mackintosh from the perambulator. 'Right! Now, come on, then, both of you.'

I was at a loss to divine his intentions as we walked rapidly to the Buckley mansion, where he plucked the bellpull.

'Groan, Bunny,' he instructed me, 'at appropriate intervals.'

The door was opened by Mr. Hicks, to whom Raffles gave a glimpse of something cupped in his palm.

'My warrant card,' he said curtly. 'I am Inspector Fred Purdy, Fine Arts Section, Criminal Investigation Department. Take us immediately to Mr. Maurice Buckley.'

'The master,' said Mr. Hicks, ' 'as not yet returned from golfing. I expect 'im 'ome in the himminent future.'

'This gentleman,' said Raffles, patting my shoulder, 'has been the victim of a savage assault.'

'The Cottage 'Ospital,' said Mr. Hicks, eyeing me askance, 'is down by the church.'

'My man,' said Raffles, *look* at this gentleman. He's Mr. Lowe, the London photographer. On his way to this house, where he had an appointment, he was attacked. He was left bound and gagged. His camera and mobile developer were stolen from him. Fortunately, this other gentleman and myself, on our way to call on Mr. Buckley, heard groans from a ditch, where we found and released Mr. Lowe. Now, tell me—has any person been admitted to this house this afternoon who looked at all like this unfortunate man?'

I groaned, and spat blood into my handkerchief, with a dismal look at Mr. Hicks, whose aplomb was visibly deserting him.

'Not—not much like 'im,' faltered Mr. Hicks. ' 'Ardly at all, for that matter. But—but I personally admitted a party as represented 'imself as Mr. Lowe, the photographer happertaining to 'oom—'

'Ah! Just as we feared, Professor Neeskens,' said Raffles, exchanging a significant glance with Kern. *'Impersonation!'* To

Mr. Hicks he said, with cold authority, 'Show us to a room where Mr. Lowe, pending the return of your master, can rest awhile. And bring some brandy.'

Mr. Hicks, his dewlaps now quivering with apprehension, led us to a handsomely appointed withdrawing-room, where Raffles and Kern helped me, groaning and wincing, to recline on an ottoman.

Scarcely had Mr. Hicks gone for brandy than Raffles put his finger to his lips. Listening, we heard the front door open. Footsteps sounded in the hall, then the flurried gabbling of Mr. Hicks.

'What?' bawled a voice, undoubtedly Buckley Senior's. 'What the hell d'you mean—C.I.D.? Speak up!'

More gabbling from Mr. Hicks, then again Buckley's bawl: 'Safe? The Venetian horses? How can the statuette be safe if you let an impostor into the Hargesson room? My God, I might have known something like this would happen! Give me those keys! And get a lamp! Bring a lamp here!'

'  'Arrison! 'Arrison! Bring a lamp this hinstant!'

Running footsteps sounded, and cries of female domestics disturbed at tea in the servants' hall.

'Come on,' said Raffles, 'let's see what's happening.'

With a hobbling gait, hugging my ribs as though several were cracked, causing me to list over sideways, I followed Raffles and Kern into the hall, the twilight of which was now relieved by the arrival of Mr. Hicks and Harrison, carrying lamps. Maurice Buckley had unlocked and opened the massive door of the Hargesson room. Seizing a lamp, smoking from its glass chimney, he strode in. And there it was, undisturbed on its pedestal, the Cellini statuette, the Golden Horses.

'Thank God!' said Buckley. 'I feared for a moment—'

'I know well what you feared, Mr. Buckley,' said Raffles, 'and I only wish I could reassure you.'

Buckley turned, staring, lamp in hand. Raffles and Kern strode forward into the Hargesson room, hobbled after by myself, spitting blood into my handkerchief and groaning softly. Raffles turned a stern look on Mr. Hicks.

'Now, you, my man—speak up. Did the bogus photographer at any time demand darkness in this room here?'

'Why—yes, sir,' stammered Mr. Hicks. ' 'E 'ad to 'ave it dark, to transfer the exposed plate from 'is camera to 'is mobile developer. But 'Arrison 'ere, an' myself in person, was in constant attendance, watching 'is hevery move.'

'Ah, you can see in the dark, can you?' said Raffles. 'Then you *saw* him take out the Cellini replica concealed in his mobile developer and exchange it for the genuine Cellini?'

Mr. Hicks's wattles turned ashen. And an explosive sound burst from the lips of Maurice Buckley.

'Why, you frogfaced, blown-up nincompoop!' he roared. 'You—'

'Control yourself, Mr. Buckley,' Raffles said. 'This unhappy simpleton is the victim of an adroit gang of international art thieves. A tip from a stoolpigeon alerted us at the Fine Arts Section, C.I.D., to a possibility that the gang was moving in on a Cellini artifact in your private ownership. I came down immediately from London for a consultation with you, bringing with me Professor Emil Neeskens here, whose name, as the ranking authority on the work of Benvenuto Cellini, will undoubtedly be familiar to you. Unfortunately, we arrived just too late. Mr. Lowe, this unfortunate photographer, had been attacked, left to die in a ditch—and obviously his place had been taken by one of the gang. It was lucky for Mr. Lowe that we heard his groans.'

I swayed a little, spitting blood into my handkerchief, as Raffles turned to Ivor Kern, who, tall and frockcoated, the lamplight shining on his intellectual brow, was examining the Golden Horses closely through a jeweller's glass screwed into his eye.

'What d'you make of it, Professor?' Raffles asked.

'A fake, of course,' Kern said. 'The work, I think, of the Amsterdam craftsman whose brilliant Cellini counterfeits in worthless alloys have been troubling the art world for so long. To be certain, Inspector Purdy, that this particular work is from the mould and furnace of the Amsterdam criminal, I should need to have the artifact in my laboratory for microscopic examination.'

'That, Mr. Buckley,' Raffles said, 'would, I think, be advisable. To establish the exact provenance of this counterfeit without delay would be our best chance of closing in on the gang and recovering your genuine Cellini before they can smuggle it abroad. I'll give you an official receipt, of course, for this—' Raffles gestured contemptuously at the Golden Horses—'this counterfeit which so degrades your well-known collection.'

138

'Take it!' Buckley shouted, his bald head scarlet with rage. 'Get after those blackguards and recover my genuine Cellini. Get that bogus junk out of my house!'

Thus invited, Kern placed the statuette of the Golden Horses, untouched until this moment by any one of us, into the gladstone bag he had brought for the purpose.

'You have made a wise decision, Mr. Buckley,' Raffles said —'one which, I've now every reason to hope, will result in news for you within twenty-four hours. And now, Mr. Lowe,' he added, cupping a hand under my elbow, 'if Mr. Buckley will excuse us, we must get you along to the Cottage Hospital. I don't like the look of that eye of yours.'

I groaned.

In the bat-haunted twilight of the chalkpit, I resumed my normal appearance, donning a spare suit concealed for me in the developer pushcart. Kern then went off with it, the rest of the photographic equipment, and the Golden Horses statuette, to catch the seven p.m. train up to London.

'You did well, Bunny,' Raffles told me, as we lighted a Sullivan apiece and sauntered back to the Rectory. 'Your performance couldn't have been bettered. Remains now only to post an anonymous letter to Maurice Buckley, informing him that, if he wants his Golden Horses back, he has only to keep his mouth shut. Then the statuette will be returned to him on the day after young Geoff honourably matriculates from his last day at school.'

'You intend to *return* the Golden Horses?' I said, incredulous.

'In a way, Bunny,' Raffles said. 'The trouble with many of these wealthy show-off collectors is that, while they know market values, they're not true connoisseurs. They're artistically ignorant about their own possessions. Maurice Buckley's obviously of that type. He probably won't know the difference between the real Golden Horses, *en route* to Philadelphia, and the replica which Ivor Kern, a true connoisseur, will have made for him by the end of the school term.'

I drew in a deep breath of relief. 'Raffles, I thought for a moment—'

'Nonsense, Bunny! The statuette will never again be seen by Maurice Buckley. It lays a firm foundation for Dinah's dowry.' Raffles laughed quietly. 'The Golden Horses of St. Mark's— stolen once before, by the master of our craft, the Emperor

139

Napoleon.' He paused at the Rectory gateway. 'But there's something up there—look, Bunny—that not even *he* could make off with.'

I followed Raffles' glance.

The moon was rising, the golden moon of autumn, the harvest moon—shedding its mellow radiance once more, as it had done through aeons of time, on the two emaciated, chalk-pale, mysterious giants, high on the down: the Long Men of Fedden.

9      THE BAFFLING OF
       OOM PAUL

'*Shh!*' said Raffles. 'Listen, Bunny!'

Tense beside him in the concealment of a thicket of wait-a-bit thorn, I held my breath.

Far off on the veldt, desolate and illimitable in the moonlight, a jackal howled.

Twenty paces or so from us, a water-tank elevated on iron supports cast a shadow across the tracks of a single-line railway.

I heard a faint humming sound from the rails.

'A train,' I murmured.

'At last,' said Raffles.

His grey eyes gleamed, his keen, sunburned face was beard-stubbled.

Any resemblance either of us bore now to gentlemen, in this war which many shrewd military commentators were predicting would be the last war fit for gentlemen to go to, was purely coincidental.

At the outbreak of hostilities, Raffles had temporarily postponed his plans to amass a worthy dowry for his sister Dinah and get her advantageously married before his criminal past caught up with him and damaged her prospects in life.

Leaving her in the care of old Lord Fasterton, who was writing his *Recollections* with Dinah's help as amanuensis, Raffles had pulled strings to wangle duration commissions for himself and me.

Seconded as subalterns to a unit of volunteer Yeomanry, we had trained on Salisbury Plain, then sailed at last with a draft. Just as we were beginning to enjoy our active service, we had been captured in an ambush. But Raffles was a hard man to hold, and we had been scarcely six weeks in the P.O.W. camp when he had contrived our escape.

For many days now, our uniforms in tatters, we had been on the run.

The humming from the rails was growing louder.

'A goods train, probably,' said Raffles.

I swallowed with a parched throat. We still were deep inside Boer territory.

'What if it's a troop train,' I said, 'crammed with Oom Paul's sharpshooters?'

I had seen quite enough campaigning to have developed considerable respect for crafty old President Kruger and his obstinate fighting farmers.

'We'll soon know,' said Raffles. 'There's the locomotive smoke.'

Distant puffs of it, flame-tinted, billowed up against the vast sky limpid with stars. Soon the locomotive itself came into view, the belches from its smokestack becoming less frequent as it approached.

'Slowing down,' said Raffles. 'Yes, they're going to take on water here, Bunny.'

I could make out now the oily gleam of the locomotive's piston-rods. They were beginning to idle. It was a train of a half-dozen goods trucks, tarpaulin-covered, with a guard's small van at the rear.

A jet of exhaust-steam hissed out between the locomotive wheels as it rumbled to a standstill abreast of the water-tower.

From the firelit interior of the cab a man jumped down, evidently the fireman, for his face, overalls and railwayman's cap were black with coal dust. He carried a long rod of iron with a hook on the end, with which he reached up to pull over the loco the cumbersome hose of the water-tower.

The driver, an older, bearded man in overalls and railwayman's cap, clambered down from the cab and began to stuff tobacco into a curved Boer pipe.

'Here comes the guard,' Raffles whispered.

The guard's shadow, in a wide-brimmed sundowner hat, with a bandolier and rifle slung over his shoulder, flickered over the

141

sides of the trucks as he approached from the rear of the train.

Crouching in our concealment, we watched the watering of the locomotive. The driver turned off the small wheel of the water-cock. The fireman, with his rod, started to swing the cumbersome hose back into place.

'Now, Bunny,' Raffles whispered. 'Keep the fireman occupied while I get that guard's rifle. Ready?'

'Ready!'

'Off we go!'

We darted out from the shadow of the thorn-clump, Raffles making for the guard, myself for the fireman who, his back to me, was hooking the hose back into place with his iron rod.

The driver shouted a warning as I raced past him. The fireman turned swiftly. I was almost upon him. He aimed an almighty sideswipe at me with the iron rod. I heard it whistle over my head as I butted him in the belly. We went down together, locked and wrestling, rolling over and over in the dust.

The man was all muscle and sinew, from stoking engines. I never had felt anything like it. I could not hold him. He swarmed over me. His knee drove into my chest, winding me. His hands clamped on my throat. His eyes glared down at me from his mask of coal-dust. I clutched at his arms. They were like iron bars.

Suddenly, just as my senses were leaving me, a solid deluge of water descended upon the pair of us. It was as though the heavens had opened. We rolled apart, gasping and spluttering from the shock of it.

As I staggered to my feet, I saw that in our grapple we had rolled right under the dangling hose-mouth from which the deluge was pouring.

Raffles had started it. He had one hand on the small wheel of the water-cock. In the other he held the rifle, menacing the driver and guard with it. They had their hands up, and the fireman, drenched like myself, his face washed almost white, also put up his hands sullenly.

Raffles turned off the water plunging from the hose.

'Now, then,' he said, in the resultant quiet. 'This train is from Pretoria, of course, and is bound for Beira, in neutral Portuguese territory. It so happens, gentlemen, that my friend and I are going that way ourselves, with all possible dispatch, so we'll be

142

happy to take the train there for you. There's just one small point. When we steam across the frontier, we shall need to look less like a pair of tramps and more like railwaymen in good standing. So we must trouble you for your overalls and caps.'

Mutely glowering, the driver and fireman surrendered the garments, and Raffles and I, taking it in turns to hold the rifle, put them on. Raffles found a clasp-knife in the pocket of his overalls. He told me to cut lengths from the rope that held down the tarpaulin on the nearest of the goods trucks. With the lengths of rope I bound the men's wrists behind them and hobbled their ankles—not too tightly.

'You'll soon be able to free yourselves,' Raffles told them. 'It's a pity trains are so infrequent on this line. You have a long walk ahead of you. But my friend and I have done our share of walking, as you can see from the pitiful state our boots are in. Ah, well—fortune of war! Ready, Bunny? Then come on!'

In overalls and railwaymen's caps—my own overalls soaking wet, though I had wrung them out well—we clambered up into the locomotive cab.

'Can you drive this thing?' I asked anxiously, as Raffles examined the levers and dials.

'I begged many a ride on the footplate when I was a small but active boy, Bunny. I was train mad,' said Raffles. 'This is an old loco of the "Dickens" class, London, Chatham and Dover Railway. I recognised it as soon as I saw it. I think it's the old "*Edwin Drood.*"'

He manipulated various levers. Steam hissed and, with a chugging and rumbling and a clank of couplings from the trucks, the locomotive began to move.

'Turn to with that shovel!' Raffles shouted to me, above the din. 'D'you want to find us back in Pretoria, behind barbed wire again? Stoke up! Give me a head of steam!'

A wild exhilaration filled me as, with the shovel, I opened the door to the red glare and hellish heat of the firebox.

'Steam for the *Edwin Drood*!' I hollered, and went to work shovelling coals from the bunker as the first train we ever had stolen began to gather speed.

The locomotive was steaming across the veldt at a good, steady clip when at last dawn broke over the endless expanse. My overalls had long since dried, my face and hands were black, my muscles ached.

As the crystalline early light gave way to a shimmer of heat-currents, I glimpsed the white buildings of an isolated Boer farm-house or two, and once a distant Cape wagon drawn by a plodding span of yoked oxen. Hunger gnawing as the day wore on, I foraged in the locomotive toolbox, where I found the driver's and fireman's lunch-cans. As we gratefully munched maize-bread and biltong, washed down with Dutch lager, unfortunately luke-warm, the strangeness of our situation induced in me a thoughtful mood.

Watching the vast, lonely landscape speeding by as we ate, I was filled with a sense of the strangeness of our situation.

'You know, Raffles,' I said, 'I can't help wondering if Casualty Returns going back to London have us marked down as "Missing" or—'

'Merely as "Killed"?' Raffles said. 'Who can tell, Bunny? Casualty Returns are always a bit of a lottery.'

'If they've got the facts wrong, back home,' I said, 'I can just imagine the headlines: "England's Cricket Captain Killed In Action—A. J. Raffles' Last Innings." Some imaginative reporter would be apt to make up quite a story about that. It would be the talk of the London clubs.'

Raffles chuckled. 'We're still carrying our bats, Bunny. It *is* odd, though,' he added, his grey eyes meditative, 'to think that at this moment no living soul we know could possibly dream where we are or what we're doing—neither my sister Dinah, nor our friend Ivor Kern, nor that one other man who knows at any rate *what* you and I are.'

'*Other* man?' I said.

'The man,' Raffles said, 'now celebrated throughout the English-speaking world—the man who, years ago, when he was just an obscure medical practitioner in the naval town of Portsmouth, unmasked me, Bunny—bowled me out as clean as a whistle.'

'Oh, dear God!' I said. 'Dr. Conan Doyle!'

'Had you forgotten him, Bunny—and my humiliating mistake, that he spotted, at Portsmouth? *I* never have.' Raffles smiled wryly. 'He's out here, you know.'

'*Doyle*? Here in South Africa?'

'There was a report of it in the *Rand Daily Mail*. Some serving soldier out here, with journalistic ambitions—a medical orderly
144

chap, a Private Edgar Wallace—got an interview with Doyle and wrote it up in an article. I happened to see it. You know, Bunny, I respect Dr. Conan Doyle. I admire him for what he's doing now. At a time when he can command any price he likes for tales of his fictional detective, he's laid down his golden pen, as a matter of duty, and taken up the scalpel again to serve out here as a volunteer, unpaid doctor with the Langman Field Hospital. He's a great man, Bunny.'

Raffles took a swig at the beer bottle, and passed it to me.

'However,' he said, 'the Langman Field Hospital is camped on the cricket ground at Bloemfontein—and *we're* headed in the opposite direction.'

'In a stolen train,' I said uneasily.

Only once, in the great loneliness under the sun, did we see armed men—a group of horsemen, with bandoliers and slung rifles, who were near enough for us to see their stern, heavily bearded faces under the floppy brims of their high-crowned sun-downer hats.

'A Boer *kommando*,' said Raffles.

He pulled the dangling cord of our steam-whistle to give them a courteous salute—but the Boers in general were not much given to saluting, and the *kommando* made no response to us, not so much as a wave.

'Dour chaps,' said Raffles. 'I'm afraid we'll find a lot more of them when we get to the Boer frontier station, Bunny.'

'So we crash through at speed?' I suggested.

'And get a bullet through our heads?' said Raffles. 'No, Bunny. Even if the bullets missed, which Boer bullets seldom do, firing would alert the Portuguese, over on their side. They'd wonder what was wrong, and switch us into a siding, to find out.'

'But the Portuguese are neutral, Raffles.'

'Would they take a neutral view of two men in possession of a stolen train? We can't be sure, Bunny—and I don't much like the idea of internment in Portuguese East for the duration.'

'Oh, dear God!' I said.

Repeatedly, after that, I stopped shovelling coal, wiped sweat from my eyes with a wad of cotton-waste and peered ahead anxiously through one of the two small round windows of the loco-motive cab.

When at last I spotted, far ahead along the rails, a cluster of

145

sheds coming into view, my throat went dry. I saw the small figures of men, some of them on horseback. There seemed to be quite a lot of them—most of them armed, I noted, as Raffles throttled back our rate of approach and pulled the steam-whistle cord, loosing off three short blasts of greeting.

'Behave naturally,' Raffles shouted to me. 'Stick your coal-dusty face out and show your teeth in an affable smile as we pass through.'

'*If* we pass through!' I shouted back.

In a sweat of apprehension, I peered ahead through the round window. There was no barrier across the line. It stretched ahead, between the sheds and the waiting men, into nomansland, as the *Edwin Drood* chugged slowly, hissing exhaust-steam, into the little station—and kept moving.

I leaned out from the footplate, with a smile and a wave to the men as they watched the locomotive steam slowly past them, followed by the clanking trucks. I could see that the men were expecting the train to stop, but it was not until the guard's little van at the rear was gliding past them that I heard shouts of surprised inquiry from some of the men.

'They're shouting,' I called to Raffles.

'Acknowledge,' he called back.

I leaned out, looking back at the men and nodding as though with vigorous understanding, at the same time making gestures of acknowledgement, reassurance—and farewell.

None of them moved. They just seemed surprised. Their figures dwindled as Raffles opened the throttle a little and the *Edwin Drood*'s speed discreetly increased.

'Now for the Portuguese, Bunny!'

Again our speed moderated as we steamed, chugging majestically, towards a cluster of small buildings with whitewashed walls, typically Portuguese. Raffles sounded our whistle, and I saw men emerging from the buildings—short, dark men in dusty green uniforms and shakoes, with white cross-belts and slung rifles.

As we steamed slowly past the soldiers, Raffles and I, from our respective sides of the footplate, protruded our grimy faces, showing our teeth cordially and waving our greetings. One or two of the men waved back, amiably enough. But as the trucks went on clanking slowly past them, and the guard's little van followed, I was taut with dread of a fusillade of shouts—and shots.

Nothing of the kind happened. I could hardly believe my eyes when I looked back at the soldiers gazing after us in mild surprise as they receded behind us. I gave them a final wave and turned to Raffles.

'My God,' I shouted, exultant, 'we're through! We've done it!'

'Now for Beira,' said Raffles, with a grin. 'We'll take no risks of internment. When we get near the town, we'll abandon this train for someone else to find and take in. We'll sneak down to the dock area under cover of night and try to smuggle ourselves on board some ship—outward bound. Come on, now—stoke up! Give me steam!'

'Farewell to Oom Paul!' I yelled, as I seized the shovel again and the *Edwin Drood* began to pound along, with quickening respirations and a triumphant blast of the whistle, on our journey to freedom.

When we finally reached London, after many delays, difficulties and enforced wanderings, we learned that the hostilities in South Africa were approaching a conclusion. Pausing only long enough to report our survival to a Yeomanry adjutant at the Horse Guards, who, though surprised to see us alive and well, sent us on leave pending further orders, Raffles spent a few days with his sister Dinah at the Shropshire home of Lord Fasterton. Finding Dinah well and happy, Raffles rejoined me and, at the invitation of a fellow clubman of ours called Kenneth Mackail, we went up to Argyllshire for a week's fishing.

'Ye bonnie banks and braes,' Raffles remarked, as we leaned on the rail of the little sidewheeler steamer plying from Glasgow to where, up Loch Long, Ken Mackail was to meet us. 'How do they look to you, Bunny?'

'After what we've been through,' I said, 'this mellow sunshine and those high moors in the distance look deliciously peaceful to me.'

'The welkin will be ringing with gunfire soon,' Raffles reminded me. 'It'll be the Twelfth of August in a few days, when fashionable London stampedes into Scotland for the grouse-shooting.'

'I'm glad Ken doesn't own a moor,' I said. 'My warworn nerves are only equal to a little quiet fishing.'

On the jetty at our destination, Ken Mackail was waiting to

meet us. A slightly-built, wiry chap with sandy hair, he wore the kilt, with a dirk in his stocking. He had brought his dogcart to meet us, and the horse trotted off with us sturdily on the long, jolting ride to Mackail Lodge, which was up among the moors.

Presently, as we clattered along, Ken touched on a subject about which from his tone he seemed to feel some diffidence.

'There's one thing, Raffles, Manders,' he said slowly, 'which I feel I should mention. You chaps are just back from active service in South Africa, whereas I was out there—as you know—as correspondent for a newspaper with a strongly anti-war policy.'

'Different people, different views, Ken,' Raffles said. 'In the main, Bunny Manders and I go through shot and shell with judiciously open minds.'

'Absolutely,' I said.

'I'm relieved to hear that,' Ken said, in his rather serious-minded way. 'The fact is, I'm involved in a by-election in Glasgow. Broadly speaking, I share the views publicly expressed by Dr. Conan Doyle, who's just back from service in South Africa with the Langman Field Hospital. Although the war's not quite finished yet, I hear that he's writing a history of it. He advocates generous peace terms for the Boers—which is my own platform in this Parliamentary by-election.'

'Good luck to you, Ken,' Raffles said.

'Polling will be on the fourteenth, in Glasgow,' Ken told us. 'So I'm afraid I shall be busy on the hustings down there during most of your visit. But my ghillie Macpherson and his wife, my housekeeper, will look after you very well.'

'We have no fears on that score, Ken,' said Raffles.

'Absolutely not,' I said.

The road, a rutted track winding and undulating up over the moors, was traversing now the edge of a gorge where, deep down on our left, a stream tumbled merrily over falls, foamed among boulders, and broadened out here and there into fishworthy pools.

I was mentally reviewing the salmon and trout lures in my fly-case when an exclamation from Ken jolted me out of my abstraction.

'Quick!' he said. 'We shall have to get out!'

I saw then that another dogcart was bowling down the narrow track towards us with the horse at a rapid trot and showing not the slightest sign of being reined in.

148

We jumped out of our dogcart, and Ken, going to his horse's head, backed the cart up, precariously tilting, on the heather slope to the right—just in time for the oncoming dogcart to get by.

A ramrod, hawk-nosed man in tweeds, with a highland bonnet, held the reins. At his side was an attractive girl in a tartan skirt and velvet doublet, a blackcock's feather in her tam-o'-shanter.

As they clattered past with a wheel of their cart about an inch from the gorge-edge, we all three stood with our hats raised— but, for all the acknowledgement we got, we might just as well have kept them on.

'My opponent,' Ken said with a hint of bitterness, as we resumed our places in his dogcart. 'General Finlayson and his daughter Janet. The General's another who's not long back from South Africa. He's been put on the Retired List, and he's standing against me in this Glasgow by-election on a platform of punitive peace terms to be imposed in Pretoria.'

'Bunny and I heard of him, out there,' Raffles said. 'A real fire-eater, by all accounts.'

'He owns the Castle Crissaig grouse moor, up above my place,' Ken told us. 'He's on his way now to catch the steamer to Glasgow, with Janet to see him off and bring the dogcart back. The General's due to harangue the Clydeside shipyard workers tomorrow. What did you think of Janet?'

'Conspicuously bonnie,' said Raffles.

'I was practically engaged to her once,' Ken said gloomily, 'but the damned war ruined my chances. I wrote critically, in dispatches to the newspaper I represented, about General Finlayson's harsh methods in the field. The result is, he regards me as a knock-kneed pacifist traitor, and it's ruined me with Janet. But damn it, a man must stand by his principles—or what is he?'

'He's certainly not a Scotsman,' Raffles said, 'fit to wear the trousers—or, rather, the kilt—in his own house.'

Ken Mackail's house was a fine, old, though rather dilapidated place, hard by the brawling stream—which Raffles and I, next day when Ken had gone off early to catch the steamer to Glasgow and the hustings, fished in the company of Ken's ghillie, Macpherson, a man lean as a whipcord, with an old retriever called Shoona perpetually at his heel.

All the morning we caught nothing but a couple of small brown trout.

149

'Well, Macpherson,' said Raffles, as the three of us sat in the heather, eating the sandwiches and drinking the whisky put up for us by Mrs. Macpherson, 'I'm afraid Mr. Manders and I seem a bit out of practice.'

'Ye canna tak' fish, sir,' said Macpherson, 'if there's ower few fish in the watter.'

'So the fault's not entirely ours?' said Raffles. 'You set our minds at rest. But tell us, Macpherson—how d'you fancy Mr. Mackail's chances in this by-election?'

' 'Deed, sir,' said Macpherson gloomily, 'wi'out the London gentleman coming up to support him on the hustings makes awfu' persuasive speeches to yon Glasga folk, I wouldnae gie a bawbee for Mr. Mackail's chances. General Finlayson's a dour opponent—an' a gleg one, forbye, which is why there's nae muckle fish in our watter.'

Raffles asked what General Finlayson's glegness, a term unfamiliar to me, had to do with the paucity of fish, and Macpherson said grimly that, if we were so minded, he would show us—after dark.

As it turned out, the night was far from dark. In fact, when we reached the higher moor after a long, rough, uphill trudge alongside the tumbling stream, the moon was almost as bright as we had seen it over the veldt.

We were now, it seemed, on the Castle Crissaig grouse moor, General Finlayson's property, and Macpherson, with Shoona slinking at his heel, warned us to watch out for the General's gamekeeper, James Fraser, who, with the Glorious Twelfth not far off, was apt to be on the prowl.

'Wi' a whup for trespassers,' said Macpherson. 'Bluidy James Fraser!'

Near a small corrie of rowan trees, a little old stone bridge cast a humpbacked shadow over the stream, which here flowed deep and fishworthy. Macpherson led us furtively on to the bridge and showed us a small iron wheel secured by a chain and a massive padlock. He explained that the wheel was used to raise and lower a fine-mesh metal grille. When the grille was lowered, as it was now, all the fine fish in the upper waters of the stream were unable to return downstream, through Ken's water, to the loch.

'And this is General Finlayson's little pleasantry?' Raffles asked. 'Well, now, I happen to have in my pocket a small imple-ment that might, just possibly—'

'Hist!' said Macpherson. 'Somebody coming—bluidy James Fraser! Quick—mak' for yon rowans!'

The three of us, with the wise old Shoona at Macpherson's heel, darted off the bridge and into the tree-shadowed corrie. Peering out, I saw in the moonlight a figure on a bicycle, lamp-less, approaching along the rough track through the heather.

'Och!' whispered Macpherson, incredulous. ''Tis the young leddy from Castle Crissaig!'

Reaching the bridge, the girl in the tam-o'-shanter laid down her bicycle, looked searchingly around over the moor, then ran on to the bridge. Taking from her skirt-pocket what must have been a key, she unfastened the padlock. Through the chortling of the stream as it flowed fast under the bridge, I heard the jingle of the padlock-chain, then a grinding sound as she began, exert-ing considerable effort, to turn the iron wheel.

'She's raising the grille,' I whispered.

'Letting many a fine fish through into Ken's water,' Raffles murmured.

'Goad help the lassie,' Macpherson whispered, 'if bluidy James Fraser comes roarin' on her like a bogle an' tells her feyther!'

For an hour or more Janet Finlayson remained on the bridge, glancing continually about her over the moonlit moor; then she wound the grille down again into the water, refastened the chain and padlock, and pedalled off on her bicycle.

'Now we know where her heart is,' said Raffles. 'This'll be good news for Ken.'

As we stepped out, elated, into the moonlight, we were all three of us grinning, and I fancied that even Shoona was baring her canines with sly amusement.

Our fishing next day, on Ken's water, was unbelievable. Mac-pherson was bandy-legged under the weight of our creels. And in the evening, just in time for dinner, Ken turned up on a quick visit to see if we were being looked after well. As buxom Mrs. Macpherson set a superb dish of salmon on the table, Raffles and I were waiting for Ken to comment on it, so that we could tell him to whose midnight intervention we owed the noble repast.

But Ken seemed scarcely aware of what he was eating. He looked preoccupied, worried, and Raffles asked him if the election was not going well.

'A spectre's arisen to haunt me,' Ken admitted, 'but I'm not going to depress you chaps with it—you're here to enjoy yourselves.'

'We might enjoy a romp with a spectre,' said Raffles. 'Tell us about it.'

It turned out to be the spectre of the written word. In one of his dispatches from South Africa to the anti-war newspaper he had represented, Ken had accused General Finlayson of ordering an entire Boer family, caught sniping from a farmhouse, to be severely flogged with a rhino-hide whip, a *sjambok*.

'I'd sent off the dispatch, written in my own hand,' Ken told us, 'by a route that bypassed the Censor, when I found out that the story was untrue. By the fortune of heaven, I was able to stop my dispatch from being published.'

'Then what's the trouble?' Raffles asked.

The trouble, Ken explained, was that his manuscript on the *sjambok* atrocity had not been destroyed by his newspaper, but filed; and he had now received a warning from a colleague on the newspaper that the manuscript had vanished from the files and fallen into the hands of a newspaper that supported General Finlayson's candidature.

'According to my colleague,' Ken said, 'that newspaper's sending one of its staff men up to Glasgow with the manuscript to confer with General Finlayson's election agent. That agent's as crafty as Lang Sim o' the Glens. I wouldn't put it past him to have my story printed in pamphlets that seem to emanate from my own Election H.Q., and flood Glasgow with them.'

'And plant people at your meetings,' Raffles said, 'to ask you why, if the story were true, you suppressed it at the time?'

'Exactly! I couldn't deny I'd written the story,' Ken said. 'But it could be made to look as if *I'd* raked it up now—a story I knew to be false—to defame my political opponent. It could ruin my chances. Lesser things than this, just before a poll, have swung many an election.'

'And polling's on the fourteenth?' Raffles asked. 'H'm! What's this journalist chap's name and when is he expected in Glasgow?'

'I don't know his name,' Ken said, 'but my colleague's pretty sure the chap'll be coming up tomorrow on the London-Glasgow express.'

'The Cock-O'-The-North,' Raffles said thoughtfully. 'And tomorrow being the tenth, a lot of important Londoners'll be on that train, bound for the grouse moors. As I recall, the Cock-O'-The-North gets into Glasgow at eleven p.m., and most of the visitors put up for the night at that huge hotel right alongside the station.'

Frowning, he lighted a Sullivan, saying no more on the matter.

Next morning, when I went down to breakfast, Ken already had left to catch the steamer back to Glasgow and the hustings, and I heard Raffles' voice from the kitchen. I was buttering an oven-fresh bannock when he came into the breakfast-room.

'What were you talking to Mrs. Macpherson about?' I asked.

'I was taking a look at her game larder, Bunny.'

'Grouse-shooting doesn't start till day after tomorrow, Raffles. There can't be anything in the larder yet.'

'Only ground game,' Raffles said, unfolding his napkin. 'After you with the teapot, Bunny.'

I had no idea what was in his mind when we arrived that evening in Glasgow and booked in at the hotel adjoining the station. The hotel, which Raffles told me was familiar to every dedicated grouse-shooter, was a huge warren of a place. It seemed virtually deserted. We had the echoing cavern of a dining-room almost to ourselves. But at eleven p.m., when we heard the Cock-O'-The-North express, dead on time, steam ponderously, rumbling and hissing, into the station next door, what a change came over the scene!

We were sitting, with our coffee and liqueur whisky, in saddle-bag chairs loomed over by a castor-oil plant in the vast, gaslit mausoleum of a lobby, when suddenly the Glorious Twelfth brigade of London's rank and fashion came streaming in, all talking in loud but cultured voices, all tweed-clad, the ladies looking about them through their lorgnettes in search of old friends in the throng, the men with their guncases and shooting-sticks and their setters, pointers, retrievers and spaniels, all of which looked as if they had pedigrees at least as long as those of their owners.

'Keep an eye open for anyone who looks like a journalist,' Raffles instructed me, through the din that was going on, the barking of dogs, the shrill yapping of a solitary Pekinese, the cries of well-bred delight as ladies kissed each other through their travelling-veils, while men with bluff shouts shook one another by the hand.

153

'As a social occasion,' Raffles remarked, 'only a Buckingham Palace *levée* can compare with the annual invasion of Scotland by the grouse-shooters, Bunny.'

With trains or steamers to catch at an early hour, bound for the castles and moors further north and the sacred rites of the Glorious Twelfth on the day after, the eminent Londoners soon started going upstairs in loud converse to their rooms, while venerable, sidewhiskered pageboys, each with the leashes of half-a-dozen dogs in either hand, hobbled downstairs with them to the basement kennels.

'I didn't notice anyone who looked particularly like a journalist,' I said, as the retirement of the ruling class restored peace to the lobby.

'I'll see what I can find out at the reception desk, Bunny,' said Raffles. 'Order us a couple of nightcaps.'

When he returned to me, there was in his eyes a gleam that I knew well.

'He's here, Bunny! I'm told there's a journalist in Room Three-o-one. That'll be our man. He's probably arranged to meet with General Finlayson's election agent first thing in the morning.'

With a sudden flash of enlightenment, I exclaimed, 'But he's going to lose Ken Mackail's compromising manuscript during the night?'

'*Shh!*' said Raffles. 'Come on, we'll take these drinks up to my room.'

In his room, when he turned up the gaslight there, I saw that his valise had been unpacked by the chambermaid, his night-shirt laid out neatly on the bed, a box of Sullivans and his favourite bedtime reading, *The Adventures Of Baron Munchausen*, placed conveniently to hand.

'These doors have bolts, Bunny,' he said. 'People in hotels are apt to bolt their doors before disrobing, and bolts can be awkward things to deal with. So, as conspirators seem to have started a hare in this election, I thought we might as well take a leaf out of their book.'

He unlocked a small grip he had brought from Mackail Lodge.

'This is from Mrs. Macpherson's game larder,' he said—and he held up, dangling by its ears, a fine moorland hare.

'It's been paunched,' he said, 'and very well hung. Now, while we finish these drinks, the hotel'll be settling down for the night. I'll leave you then for a short while. Wait for me here.'

154

He was gone for about fifteen minutes, returning then so suddenly that, with my nerves still ragged from the hardships of our South African campaigning, I sprang to my feet with a racing heart.

'Now, then, Bunny,' said Raffles. 'I've gently tried the door of Room Three-o-one, and it's bolted, as I thought it would be. So I've laid a good scent of hare on the carpets of all the stairs, landings and corridors. There's only the night porter on duty, down in the lobby, and he's asleep already. Here's my dressing-gown. Put it on over your clothes, slip down to the basement kennels and release the dogs to pick up the scent. When turmoil ensues, as may be reasonably anticipated, and people come out of their rooms to find out what's going on, I shall be watching for my chance to slip into Room Three-o-one. Off you go, and I'll see you at breakfast—all being well.'

'Oh, dear God!' I faltered.

On the stairs and in the broad corridors only an occasional gaslight had been left burning, dimly blue in its globe, as I stole down to the lobby. Most of the lights there had been turned off. The night porter was indeed sound asleep in one of the saddlebag chairs. He did not stir as I tiptoed past him, across the lobby, and down stone stairs to the basement.

I opened the kennels door.

Dimly I made out, in faint light filtering down from the lobby, the aristocratic heads of setters, pointers, retrievers and spaniels as they thrust them out between the bars of their cages to sniff at me in friendly inquiry.

'Good dogs, clever dogs,' I whispered to them, as I opened cage after cage. 'Go find the hare, dogs! Push him out! Hie on! Go seek!'

The Pekinese, waking with a startled snuffle, started hurling scandalised yaps at me—and when I released him, immediately attacked my socks with needle-sharp teeth and bloodcurdling snarls. But then he spotted the procession of shooting dogs, led by a fine Gordon setter, streaming up the stairs to the lobby, and immediately the dauntless little warrior rushed with outraged yelps to take his rightful place, as oriental royalty, at the head of the exodus.

Normally mute when on business, the well-trained shooting dogs, excited by their unfamiliar surroundings and the hysterical yapping of the Pekinese, so far forgot themselves, when they picked up the delicious scent of hare, as to give tongue—especially the spaniels—with a fearful clamour. Through the din I heard the wild shouting of the night porter.

When I reached the lobby, I saw the porter chasing the pack up the main staircase and whacking vainly at the tail-end dogs with what looked like a rolled-up copy of the *Glasgow Evening News.*

I followed unobtrusively.

In the dimlit corridors, bedroom doors were opening on all sides. People were coming out in disarray and alarm, some carrying candlesticks, and all shouting at each other to know what was happening.

'Keep calm!' I called to them, as I hurried along the corridor. 'There's nothing to fear, ladies. You'll be taken care of. Arrangements are being made.'

'What kind of arrangements?' demanded a man wearing a nightcap and Turkish slippers and carrying a candlestick.

'Adequate ones, m'lud, adequate ones,' I assured him, recognising his splendid judicial features as those of a notorious hanging judge often seen at the Old Bailey. 'Pray calm the ladies, m'lud!'

I hurried on up to the next floor, where my own room was situated. On this floor, too, though the shouting and barking of the main chase seemed now to be coming from the floor above, was a swarm of people clad in the motley of Morpheus, bearing candles and shouting inquiries.

Twisting and turning through the throng, I gained the refuge of my own room. Closing and bolting the door, I stood panting, listening to the uproar going on all over the hotel, but particularly, it seemed to me, on the floor above—the third floor.

Shaken and appalled, I wondered if Raffles could have been trapped, red-handed, in Room 301.

Not until long after the disturbance died down did I collapse on my bed and fall into an exhausted slumber. My nervous debilitation caused me to sleep so heavily that, when I went apprehensively down to breakfast, the grouse-shooting brigade had left with their guns and dogs to catch trains and steamers northward to the various moors, and the vast dining-room seemed abandoned to a few cataleptic waiters.

My heart sank. I feared the worst. But then I saw him. His

156

dark hair crisp, his tweeds immaculate, a pearl in his cravat, Raffles was breakfasting at a corner table—in the company, to my surprise, of Ken Mackail, who was wearing the kilt and a fresh morning smile.

Approaching the table, I wondered uneasily what Ken's presence portended.

'Ah, here's Bunny Manders,' Ken said. ''Morning, Bunny. I'm here at the hotel to meet the man who's coming up from London to speak in my support on the hustings today. I ran into Raffles in the lobby here. He tells me you chaps decided to come down from Mackail Lodge yesterday evening to see young Harry Lauder at the theatre. How was he?'

'Harry Lauder?' I said, momentarily confused. 'He—he seemed quite well. I mean—he was most diverting—pawky, I believe is the word.'

'I've just been telling Raffles,' Ken said—'I've got great news. General Finlayson called on me last night at the place I'm lodging at during the election campaign. He came to see me in case I'd heard any rumour of a conspiracy to make use against me of a certain war dispatch of mine—a dispatch which, as the General put it, he understood I'd had the decency to suppress when I realised it was untrue. He wanted me to know that, the moment he himself got wind of the conspiracy, he told his election agent that, unless he stopped the journalist who'd got hold of my manuscript from coming to Glasgow, and made him destroy the unfortunate dispatch, the General would publicly take a horse-whip to the pair of them.'

'The journalist—never *came*?' I said.

Stunned, I looked at Raffles. Meditatively peppering a finnan haddie, he did not meet my eyes.

Ken laughed.

'The damned man didn't *dare* come,' he said. 'You know, General Finlayson's a fine old sportsman, at heart. He's so ashamed of his election agent's plotting that he's suggested we call a truce to the election campaign just for tomorrow, the Glorious Twelfth, and shoot grouse together on his Castle Crissaig moor. He's invited me to bring my guests, too—meaning you chaps. You'll come, of course—*and* stay on at Mackail Lodge until after the declaration of the poll, on the fourteenth. I insist!'

'We'll be delighted, Ken,' Raffles said. 'Now, Bunny, you'd better get on with your breakfast if we're to catch the next

157

steamer back to Mackail Lodge and cast a fly or two today—'

'Go ahead,' said Ken. 'Enjoy yourselves. I must wait here. This chap who's coming up from London to speak in support of my policy of generous peace terms for the Boers seems to be sleeping late. He's in Room Three-o-one, but—'

'Room Three-o-one?' I said.

'Yes,' said Ken, 'but I don't like to have him called. He may not have slept well, as the Hall Porter here tells me there was some trouble with dogs during the night.'

'They often howl, in unfamiliar kennels,' said Raffles. 'Eat your breakfast, Bunny.'

Not until we were in a cab together, bowling along to the steamer wharf, did I demand of Raffles what the devil had happened in Room 301.

'Something extremely odd, Bunny,' he said. 'I'll tell you about it when I've had time to think over its significant ramifications.'

I knew from his introspective manner that I should get no more out of him until he chose to impart it. I felt very uneasy. Even so, and despite the fact that we had not anticipated doing any shooting when we came to Scotland, the following day, the Glorious Twelfth, which I was experiencing for the first time, lived wholly up to its reputation.

The sky was cloudless over the high moor of Castle Crissaig, and the grouse coveys were plentiful and strong on the wing. As a host, General Finlayson turned out to be surprisingly genial, and I noticed that his daughter Janet, bewitching in her tam-o'-shanter, made a point of acting as gun-loader for Ken Mackail. With Macpherson performing a like office for Raffles, and bluidy James Fraser for myself, while Shoona retrieved faultlessly to hand, I added my quota of bangs to the volleys of gunfire resounding on this great day all over Scotland, wild and beautiful.

With the thaw that had set in between Mackail Lodge and Castle Crissaig bidding fair to prove permanent, and Janet as good as his, Ken Mackail was not noticeably depressed when, on the declaration of the poll on the fourteenth, a third candidate—standing on a platform of reduced Excise duty on whisky—was elected to Westminster over the heads of both Ken himself and General Finlayson.

In fact, it was as happy a chap as ever wore the kilt whom Raffles and I left waving to us from the jetty when we went off

158

on the steamer to Glasgow to catch the Cock-O'-The-North express back to London.

'So, in any case,' I remarked to Raffles, as we paced the deck of the little steamer, 'that man who came up from London to speak for Ken made no great difference to the election result.'

'Obviously not,' said Raffles. 'But by heaven, Bunny, he gave me something to think about!'

Raffles offered me a cigarette and, lighting up, we leaned with our arms on the rail, alongside the starboard paddle-wheel, rumbling and splashing in its housing.

'As you know, Bunny,' Raffles went on, 'they told me at the hotel desk that the man in Room Three-o-one was reputed to be a journalist. Well, sure enough, when you released the dogs in your clever way, the man came out of his room, in his nightshirt and dressing-gown, and walked along the corridor to a linen cupboard the dogs were jumping up at because I'd hidden the hare in it under a pile of sheets and towels. I was able to slip into the man's room quite easily. There were various documents littered on the bedside table. Ken's manuscript was not among them, but a newspaper with an article ringed round in blue pencil caught my eye. I skimmed through it hastily, and realised at once that it referred to the occupant of the room himself.'

'The occupant?' I said.

Raffles nodded.

'He was a journalist, right enough, Bunny. The article said he'd been a war correspondent in South Africa, was captured by the Boers and put in the P.O.W. camp at Pretoria. It must have been the same camp you and I were in, with several hundred others, and he evidently escaped a few days after us. The article said he hid among empty coal-sacks in the tarpaulin-covered goods truck of a train bound for Beira. He was in dread that the train would be stopped and searched at the Boer frontier station —but as he peered from his hiding-place, he saw that the train was passing slowly through, first the Boer station, then the Portuguese station, *without stopping!*'

'The stolen train!' My heart gave a great lurch. 'The *Edwin Drood!*'

'The evidence, I think, is conclusive,' Raffles said. 'We had a passenger on board, Bunny, when we stole that train. Evidently he didn't see what happened at the water-tower on the veldt, but when the train steamed through both frontier stations without stopping, he thought—according to the newspaper article—that his star was watching over him, especially as the Boer High Command had offered a reward of twenty-five pounds for his recapture—dead or alive.'

'Only twenty-five pounds?' I exclaimed. 'He can't have been very important!'

'As to that, Bunny, the newspaper article referred to him as a brilliant young journalist who might well turn out to have a promising political future before him. Of course, one never knows about the future. It's on the knees of the gods.'

Raffles looked thoughtfully across the tranquil waters of Loch Long at the banks and braes gliding by, bonnie in the northern sunshine.

'Who knows, Bunny? Life is strange. Perhaps we may live to learn, some day, that you and I were the sport of the gods,' said A. J. Raffles thoughtfully, 'when we stole, you stoked, and I drove the train that carried young Mr. Winston Spencer Churchill to safety.'


# 10    RAFFLES AND THE
#        AUTOMOBILE GANG


Through the glades of the New Forest, early on a winter morning not long after the turn of the century, sounded the note of a hunting-horn and the belling clamour of an eager pack.

'King Rufus's Foxhounds, Bunny,' said Raffles. 'We're late for the Meet.'

We quickened our hired horses to a canter through the oak wood and found ourselves in a clearing where a timeworn monolith reared shoulder-high from a drift of dead, damp leaves.

Nearby, on a small grey mare, sat a man with a small grey beard. Wearing, like ourselves, a tailcoat of the hunting hue named in memory of the great sporting tailor, Mr. Pink, the lone horseman stood up in his stirrups and raised to us the rather faded velvet riding-cap which marked him as a Hunt official.

'Good morning, gentlemen,' he said, and we reined in, raising our well-burnished toppers. 'The Hunt's moved off, but I saw you hacking across the heath, so I waited for you. I'm Habbakuk Hooper, the Hunt Secretary. I fancy you're the visiting Londoners, Mr. Raffles of The Albany, and Mr. Manders, who're lodging for the nonce at Abel Emms's cottage.'

'We saw the accommodation advertised in *Horn And Hound*,' said Raffles, 'with a date list of the Meets in this neighbourhood.'

'We of the Hunt are always pleased to welcome a contribution from visitors for a day with the hounds. Ah, thank you,' said Mr. Habbakuk Hooper, as we produced a couple of sovereigns apiece from the pockets of our white cord riding-breeches. 'This, you will be pleased to know, is a special day. It's the twenty-first birthday of our Master of Foxhounds' daughter, Miss Philippa Morton, and your contributions make you welcome guests at the Hunt Ball this evening at the seat of the Darsey-Mortons. Meantime, behold the Rufus Stone, where the Hunt met just now.'

Waving his riding-crop at the venerable monolith, he read aloud in a high, pedantic voice its partially defaced inscription:

' "On this spot stood the Oak Tree from which an Arrow, aimed by Sir Walter Tyrrel at a Stag, glanced and struck King William Rufus in the Breast, whereof he Instantly Died, on the Second Day of August, A.D. 1100." '

Through the brooding glades sounded again the note of the horn, more distant.

'I observe, gentlemen,' said Mr. Hooper, as the three of us rode on our way, 'that you favour the cavalry seat.'

'We're but lately posted to the Reserve,' Raffles explained, 'from service with the Piccadilly Yeomanry.'

'A volunteer unit which, I'm told,' said Mr. Hooper, 'gave as good an account of itself in South Africa as Skinner's Light Horse in another theatre of operations. Soon, let us hope, the Boer generals, Botha and De Wet, will be finally pacified and peace descend once more upon our farflung dominions, from "Afric's sunny fountains" to "India's coral strand", as has been so well said in *Hymns Ancient and Modern*. I should perhaps tell you, by the by, that our M.F.H. is of Norman stock. His fore-bears were the Counts D'Arzac-de-Mortain—their name ren-

161

dered into our bluff English tongue as Darsey-Morton. You'll have heard, perhaps, of the D'Arzac Coronet?'

'Coronet?' said Raffles, interested.

'The last Count of the D'Arzac line in Normandy,' said Habbakuk Hooper, 'bequeathed the Coronet to the English branch of the family, with the proviso that a custom of the Counts D'Arzac be perpetuated—namely, that on the eldest daughter in each generation reaching her majority, the Coronet be presented to her, to be held in trust. So tonight at The Moot Hall, seat of the family, you'll see our M.F.H., Sir Darsey Darsey-Morton, place the Coronet on the head of his daughter Philippa—to her secret dread.'

'Dread?' Raffles and I said, together.

'The Coronet,' explained Mr. Hooper, 'has brought only misfortune and catastrophe to the daughters of the house who in turn have inherited it. Gentlemen, take note of Miss Philippa today. Watch her take her fences. You'll see a girl of courage. She dreads this evening's ceremony, but she'll not evade it.'

'If her father knows how she feels about it,' Raffles said, 'why doesn't he spare her this experience?'

'De Quincey, author of *The Confessions Of An Opium-Eater*, remarks in that work,' said Mr. Hooper, 'that a man who has no superstition in him lacks charity of mind. That could not be said of Sir Darsey. Nevertheless, he claims to despise superstition. I say "claims to"—because in fact he loves his daughter dearly. And, gentlemen, I've often thought it significant that, despite the intrinsic value of the Coronet, Sir Darsey keeps it in a mere glass-fronted Chippendale bureau in his study. Doesn't such a lack of elementary precaution betray an urge to tempt providence—a secret hope, subtle and unadmitted to himself, in the paternal heart of our M.F.H., that the Coronet might one day *disappear*? As a student of human nature, I fancy so.'

My scalp tingled. In all my life I never had heard, innocently given, so open an invitation to A. J. Raffles, gentleman of prey. I dared not look at him as we rode out now from the woodland ride on to open heath.

Under heavy clouds bespoke by the rays of a sullen sunrise, undulations of wine-dark heather, dotted here and there by free-roving Forest ponies, rolled away to the swell of the distant downs, and before us a grit road sloped down to the roofs,

162

mostly thatched, of a village that straggled widely about a steepled church.

'Brackenbourne,' said Mr. Habbakuk Hooper—'and there's the Hunt, gentlemen, taking the first of its five stirrup-cups.'

'Five, Mr. Hooper?'

'When the Meet's at The Rufus Stone, Mr. Raffles, it's a Hunt tradition to pass through this nearby village of Brackenbourne and take a stirrup-cup at each of its five inns. I may add that I'm by way of being the local artist. I designed and painted the inn signs myself, and their modest size and consistent style have been favourably commented upon by no less a newspaper than the *Southern Daily Messenger*.'

As we tailed on to the Hunt and I glanced up at the inn sign—The Hawk and Heron—which depended on hooks from a beam protruding from the inn's low, thatched eaves, I could not help thinking that Mr. Hooper was perhaps a more accomplished Hunt Secretary than artist, though obviously he painted from a lavish palette.

We were too late for a stirrup-cup at The Hawk and Heron, for the Hunt was moving on—the pack of tan-and-white eager hounds; the male riders mostly in the coats of Mr. Pink; the ladies black-habited and tophatted, graceful in their sidesaddles; a group of smocked and gaitered rustics looking on excitedly, while the village dolts and hobbledehoys whooped and pranced on the outskirts.

'A great turn-out for this Birthday Hunt,' said Habbakuk Hooper. 'There rides our M.F.H., gentlemen—the tall, grey-moustached man on the chestnut, with his Huntsman, Jack Goodridge, riding beside him. And there, Mr. Raffles, Mr. Manders, is our birthday girl! Ah-hah, see how that great roan stallion of hers kicks and dances! Quite a handful for a girl, Javelin's feeling his oats this morning. Miss Philippa's three suitors had best keep their distance. Not that they will, of course —they'd ride through fire and brimstone to keep at her side.'

I saw that the three fine-looking fellows so hazardously attendant on the slender, dark-haired girl in the side-saddle of the temperamental roan were in Army uniform.

'Officers,' Habbakuk Hooper explained to us, 'from the garrison at Winchester. The one in scarlet is Major Hector Barron, of the Lancers. The one in artilleryman's dark-blue and gold is Captain Hugh Archibald. And the handsome chap in Rifle

163

Brigade bottle-green with black buttons is Captain the Marquess of Stoneycross. They bring their own chargers and batman-grooms with them and spend the night here at Brackenbourne—in different inns, I may say, for they're at daggers drawn over Miss Philippa.' He chuckled dryly. 'Today may be the last chance any one of them has to get her, for they're all three on stand-by orders to embark for India.'

On the road that curved like a strung bow through the village the Hunt paused at another thatched inn. Over the low doorway dangled a sign depicting a white-bearded old salt in a brass-buttoned peajacket.

'The Masterman Ready,' said Mr. Habbakuk Hooper—'named, don't you know, for the splendid romance written by Captain Marryat. He used to live nearby. I painted him from the life for this sign—which is not, as it purports to be, Masterman Ready writing up his logbook, but is actually dear old Marryat himself in the act of composing his novel *Children of The New Forest.*'

'You give us a rare literary insight, Mr. Hooper,' said Raffles, as, from the tray proffered to us by the beaming landlord of The Masterman Ready, we accepted a stirrup-cup apiece.

This proved to be sherry, a passable *amontillado*. And, the Hunt moving on to The Bellringers Inn, near the church and the green in the village centre, we got sherry again, a sound *manzanilla*. Clip-clopping on around the curve in the village street, followed by the marvelling rustics, some of the more clownish walking on their hands, we came to the next inn, The Laughing Cavalier.

'The sign for which,' said Mr. Hooper, indicating it with a modest gesture of his riding-crop, 'I painted after—rather a long way after, I fear—the famous portrait by my great predecessor with the brush, the incomparable Franz Hals.'

Under the thatched eaves of The Laughing Cavalier, we drank sherry once more, a nutty *oloroso*. And, thus refreshed, the Hunt moved on to the fifth inn.

'The Bugle Boys,' said Mr. Hooper. 'The sign depicts two fifteen-year-old brothers from our neighbouring village of Cadnam. They were killed simultaneously by a Spanish bullet, a single bullet which passed through both their heads as they were sounding the "Stand To" call on the casemates during the last Siege of Gibraltar. In the Trafalgar Cemetery there, where their remains now lie, I have personally seen the memorial that records their unusual fate.'

'You render their heroic likenesses very powerfully, Mr. Hooper,' said Raffles.

Here at The Bugle Boys, the whole Hunt raised their glasses in a toast to the noble youngsters depicted on the inn sign. And, this stirrup-cup proving to be rum punch, I felt the hunting blood coursing hotly through my veins as, to the cheers of the local worthies, and with the excited dolts and hobbledehoys loping, whooping and somersaulting after us, hounds and riders began to stream on out of the village.

'I fancy, Mr. Raffles, Mr. Manders,' said Habbakuk Hooper, 'that Sir Darsey will draw the Driftway copse first. An artful dog fox often lurks there, licking his cynical whiskers at us from the coverts. Ah-hah, yes! Excellent! Sir Darsey's heading for the Driftway!'

To the note of the horn, the birthday Hunt broke into a canter over the heathland, the hounds with their sterns well up and their noses well down, in quest of the Driftway fox.

Unfortunately, we found him. And so gruelling was the run which he gave us, before hounds lost his scent in a chalkpit on the all too remote downs, that I ached in every muscle and, that evening, did my utmost to get out of attending the Hunt Ball, birthday or no birthday.

But Raffles insisted, with the result that, in the fine old ball-room of The Moot Hall, seat of the Darsey-Morton family, I had to grit my teeth and, notwithstanding my muscular twinges and fundamental tenderness, dance with a succession of ladies.

I had just escorted one of them back to her chair when I found Mr. Hooper, in vintage evening-dress, at my side.

'Ah-hah, Mr. Manders! An animated scene, is it not? Did you notice the way Miss Philippa put her horse Javelin at that nasty gate to the Driftway covert?'

'I did indeed, Mr. Hooper. My own hireling refused it—so emphatically that I fell off.'

'Yes, I saw you cut a voluntary there. Yet how boldly Miss Philippa sailed over it! You know, Mr. Manders, in this life the most precious of gifts is that of *confidence*. A little sad, therefore, is it not, that from the moment her birthday heirloom is placed upon her brow Miss Philippa will no longer face her fences in the field, as in life itself, with her whilom carefree spirit.'

Thus reminded of the D'Arzac Coronet, I glanced nervously around the ballroom for a glimpse of Raffles amid the revels. To the lilt of the orchestra in the minstrels' gallery above the double doors standing wide open to the panelled hall, the dancers wove their vivid kaleidoscope.

Misgiving stirred in me. Raffles was conspicuous—to me—by his absence.

'Miss Philippa this evening,' said Habbakuk Hooper, 'is as beautiful as some raven-haired damsel at the Love Court of Margaret of Navarre. It's the blood, you know, Mr. Manders—the Norman blood. Yet is she not a little pale, a little tense, as she dances there in the arms of the dashing Lancer, jealously watched by her other two chevaliers *sans peur et sans reproche* —the gallant Gunner and the noble Rifleman? Poor girl, I fancy so! The fateful ceremony now looms close.'

His tone changed.

'Ah-hah, I see Sir Darsey talking to the Chief Constable of the County—an honoured guest and firm supporter of the Hunt, Mr. Manders. I must go and shake him by the hand. Pray excuse me.'

Left alone, I took my handkerchief from my cuff to mop my palms, grown suddenly damp at this mention of Chief Constables. And I saw Raffles. He appeared from the hall. Keen of face, his dark hair crisp, his evening-dress immaculate, he paused in the wide doorway.

I started towards him, to demand where the devil he had been, but his grey eyes, surveying the scene, noted a neglected lady and, approaching her with a bow, he whirled her gracefully into the maze of the schottische.

As I stood troubled by uneasy thoughts, a tinkling sound from the hall caught my attention. It was the tinkling, faintly audible through the music, of champagne glasses on supper-trolleys wheeled by a bevy of wholesome-faced parlourmaids. Marshalled by the butler, the trolleys bore a sumptuous collation of viands. Alone in its glory on one of the trolleys was a splendid birthday cake topped by twenty-one unlighted candles.

The butler came into the ballroom for a quiet word with Sir Darsey. The tall, grey-moustached M.F.H., in his hunting-pink dinner coat, accompanied the butler into the hall. Standing as I was at an angle to the doorway, I saw Sir Darsey cross the hall, open a door, close it behind him.

I guessed that the ceremony must indeed be imminent and that he had gone into his study to get the D'Arzac Coronet from the glass-doored Chippendale bureau.

My heart began to thump as a strange feeling of premonition came over me.

The study door opened. Sir Darsey came out, his expression unfathomable. The butler handed him a lighted taper. Sir Darsey touched the flame to each of the twenty-one birthday cake candles. Returning the taper to the butler, Sir Darsey came into the ballroom and, looking up at the minstrels' gallery, raised an arresting hand.

The violins fell abruptly silent. Expectant, the dancers made way for the M.F.H. to walk to the centre of the floor.

He stood looking around at us all.

'My friends,' he said quietly, 'I know you're all anticipating an ancient custom of this house, The Moot Hall, to be observed here tonight. That ceremony will not take place. I have to tell you that the D'Arzac Coronet, of the Counts of Mortain, has disappeared.'

Dead silence. Then a voice said harshly, 'Sir Darsey, I suggest that the outer doors be immediately locked and a search organised of every person present.'

'My dear Chief Constable,' replied Sir Darsey, 'whatever unknown hand has been at work here tonight, I cannot and will not believe that it was the hand of any guest under my roof. What has happened—has happened. It must not be allowed to spoil what remains to be celebrated—for it comes but once in a lifetime.'

He beckoned towards the doorway. And the butler entered, proudly wheeling the trolley of honour which bore the birthday cake with its lighted candles. He was followed in single file by his harem of jolly parlourmaids, each wheeling a trolley of viands.

Voices buzzed, corks popped, the bubbly fizzed. Philippa, radiant now that the brooding shadow of the Coronet was lifted from her life, blew out the candles very ably, and cut the cake. Her father kissed her—and, raising our glasses to her, we chorused, one and all of us:

'Many happy returns!'

Even as we drank, spurred boots stamped in the doorway. We all turned. There stood, stiffly at attention, a man in mud-spattered uniform, forage cap clamped under his arm, on his sleeves the gold chevrons of a sergeant and the crossed flags of a regimental signals section. His voice rang loud in the sudden hush:

'Dispatches from Garrison H.Q. for Major Barron, Captain Archibald, and Captain the Marquess of Stoneycross.'

The three officers, resplendent in the mess-kit of their respective regiments, went to him, he handed each of them an envelope from the pouch on his belt, they tore open the envelopes.

'India,' said Major Barron, the Lancer. 'Sir Darsey—Philippa —I'm so sorry. It's immediate embarkation for us at Southampton.'

Father and daughter accompanied the three officers into the hall, to make their farewells. And as a hubbub of voices broke out, one spoke softly into my ear.

'And when he got there,' the voice murmured, 'the cupboard was bare—and so the poor dog had none.'

It was Raffles. Startled, I met his eyes. Vivacity danced in them.

'Which of them was it, Bunny?' he whispered. 'Which of them, undoubtedly with the same motive as myself, got to the D'Arzac Coronet before me—the dashing Lancer, the gallant Gunner, or the noble Rifleman?'

Summer came. And we returned to the New Forest, where the deep glades were now in full leaf and the pony-trails which meandered over the heaths were dust-white under a shimmer of heat-currents, at the invitation of Mr. Habbakuk Hooper.

Besides being the Hunt Secretary, Mr. Hooper also was Secretary of a New Forest cricket club, The Rufus Stonemen, and he wrote inviting Raffles and myself—though, of course, the one he really wanted was A. J. Raffles—to turn out for the Stonemen team against the regular Hampshire XI in a charity match on behalf of inmates of the County Workhouse.

It was a Sunday match played, after Divine Service, on the village green alongside Brackenbourne Church. Raffles, going in first, scored 82, I myself, going in last, contributed a useful 3 off a ball which hit the edge of my bat, and the game was

168

followed by cider-drenched convivialities at The Bellringers Inn.

The night was dark when we all were thrown out of the inn at closing time. Raffles and I were putting up again at the Emms's cottage—and, still in our blazers, white flannels and cricket boots, we mounted the bicycles we had borrowed from Mr. Abel Emms and his son Matthew.

There were no lamps on the bikes and, as we pedalled swiftly round a bend in the dark lane through the woods, an ambling pony and her spindle-legged foal suddenly loomed up before us. I swerved skilfully to avoid the foal, but my night sight was perhaps a shade impaired by cider, with the result that my front wheel ran between the legs of a pedestrian and precipitated him abruptly forward, with a shout of surprise, into the ditch.

The fellow seemed to be some kind of tramp and, though the ditch was quite dry and we quickly retrieved him from it and dusted him off, he did not take the trifling mishap in a sporting spirit.

'No bloody lamps or bells on your bikes,' he snarled. 'Sky-larkin' bleedin' cricketers!'

'Never mind,' said Raffles. 'You shall have a sovereign to steady you and a whisky to brace you up. Come on—we're lodging at that cottage you can see through the trees there.'

In the parlour of the Emms's cottage, when Raffles turned up the wick of the lamp, the spirit-tantalus and a plate of chutney sandwiches set out for us by Mrs. Hester Emms, the family having retired, as I could tell from the snores coming from above the low ceiling, awaited us on the table.

Seeing the sandwiches, the tramp made no pretence of ceremony but started cramming them into his mouth with both hands. He had no cap. His bullet head was close-cropped, his stubbled face had a cadaverous pallor—which led Raffles, as he poured three stiff whiskies, to surmise in a casual tone, 'Just out of quod, aren't you?'

The tramp's munching jaws froze.

'Don't let it embarrass you,' Raffles said, with an understanding smile. 'A spell as the nation's guest can happen to the best of us.'

The tramp's jaws unfroze and resumed munching.

'All I done, guv'nor,' he said, his accent Cockney, 'was to fetch me wife a love-tap over the ear'ole, to stop 'er tongue

**169**

everlastin' waggin'. Would you *believe* it, she made out I'd concussed 'er brains, such as they is, an' she 'ad me up for assault. The beak give me three months in Wormwood Scrubs. I got out just last Wednesday. I seen 'er waitin' to get my five bob ticket-o'-leave money off me, so I give 'er a sock on 'er other ear'ole an' took to me 'eels. I bin trampin' down from London to find this 'ere Brackenbourne place.'

'Why Brackenbourne?' said Raffles. 'Got a job to go to in the village?'

The tramp's eyes, beadily appraising, flickered from one to the other of us as he munched. He took a swig of whisky.

'I'm on probation, gents. Wherever I go, I'm supposed to report to the perishin' police. The bleedin' peelers'll tell my old woman where I'm at, and she'll come yar-yar-yarin' after me an' run me in again—for non-support. An' they call this a free country! No, I don't want no job in England. The country's done for itself, as far as I'm concerned. All I want is to get aht of it—on a ship from Southampton, just over yonder.'

'Getting a ship could be a bit awkward, couldn't it,' Raffles said—'for a ticket-of-leave man?'

'Money could fix it, guv'nor—palm oil, see, for some bleedin' bosun. I ain't got no money, due to misfortunes which if I was to tell you of would be more than your flesh and blood could stand. 'Owsomever, it so 'appens I got information what's worth money. I'm lookin' for a family o' gentry 'ereabouts, which I don't know their name, but a little bird told me they 'ad a valuable stole off 'em a while back—an' if I can find the family, I got news for 'em.'

I felt a sudden excitement. I looked at Raffles with a wild surmise. He sipped his drink, his eyes on the tramp.

'If the stolen valuable is by any chance a Coronet,' Raffles said, 'I'm afraid I must warn you—your news will *not* be welcome to the family concerned. For superstitious reasons, they never want to hear of it again.'

The tramp's jaws clamped, in obvious shock.

'So it *is* a Coronet,' said Raffles. 'I see. H'm! Well, now—as it happens, you're talking to friends of the family. We have their interests at heart.'

'Absolutely,' I concurred.

'So if your information's useful,' Raffles said to the tramp,

'*we* might help you get a ship outward bound from Southampton
—with a modest stake in your pocket.'

'Stone the crows,' the tramp said slowly, 'me luck's changed!'

'We'll see,' said Raffles. 'Now, what d'you know about that
Coronet?'

'Guv'nor,' the tramp blurted, 'it's 'id in the inn at Brackenbourne.'

'Which inn?' said Raffles. 'There are five of them—The Hawk
and Heron, The Masterman Ready, The Bellringers, The Laughing Cavalier, and The Bugle Boys.'

'*Five* inns?' said the tramp, dismayed.

'It's a thirsty village,' said Raffles. 'H'm! So you don't know
the name of the inn? That's a bit awkward. Well, now—I think
you'd better have another whisky and tell us just what you
*do* know.'

Stimulated by another whisky and our obvious sympathy, the
tramp confided to us that at Wormwood Scrubs Prison, which
was overcrowded, he had been put in a cell already occupied
by two lodgers. One of them, a man called Garner, was serving
six months. The other, a denizen of Limehouse, London's
Chinatown, was called Sing and was serving three months.

A letter had been smuggled in to Garner, who had bragged
to his cellmates that it was a letter which would make a rich
man of him when he got out, as it was from his brother, an
Army officer's batman-groom stationed in India, and the letter
told Garner where a stolen Coronet of great value was hidden.

'From what Garner told me an' Sing,' said the tramp, 'it
seems what 'appened was that Garner's brother an' 'is officer
was spendin' the night at an inn. Garner's brother 'ad to drive
'is officer in a 'ired pony-trap to a 'Unt Ball, see? Well, Garner's
brother were lollin' around outside, a-listenin' to the music,
like the rest o' the gentry's coachmen, when 'e 'appens to notice
a window open stealthy-like. 'E glimpses summat green an' a
kind o' sparklin' object throwed out into the laurel shrubbery.
The window shuts, and Garner's brother goes an' moseys
around in the shrubbery—an' lo an' be'old, what does 'e find
but a Coronet in the damp leaves. So Garner's brother fathoms
it out in 'is 'ead that the valuable's bin stole, see, an' the thief
reckons to pick it up after the Ball, when the gentry's all gone.
So Garner's brother pockets the Coronet, thinkin' it'll maybe
pay 'im to await developments, as you might say.'

171

'Sound thinking,' said Raffles.

'But then,' said the tramp, 'it seems a bleedin' Army sergeant comes a-gallopin' up the drive wiv dispatches. Turns out it's immediate embarkation orders for three officers at the Ball, an' Garner's brother 'as to drive 'is officer back lickety-split to the inn to get 'is kit packed. Well, Garner's brother knows 'is own kit'll get inspected, for embarkation, an' 'e can't think what to do wiv the Coronet, so 'e 'ides the ruddy thing right there in the bleedin' inn.'

'And on arrival in India,' Raffles said, 'writes and asks his brother to collect the Coronet and "fence" it for him?'

'Right,' said the tramp. 'On shares, fifty-fifty, an' no bloody 'alf larks. Garner reads out bits o' the letter to me an' Sing, but 'e don't mention the name o' the place nor o' the inn neither. An' when I inquires of 'im, innocent-like, know what the bleeder done, guv'nor? Would you *believe* it—'e stuffs the letter in 'is bloody great mouth an' eats it!'

'So how, then,' Raffles asked, 'did you get on to the name of Brackenbourne?'

'Ar, I were one too many for 'im there,' said the tramp, with malicious satisfaction. 'You gets allowed two books a week out o' the Scrubs library—one what they calls Devotional type, one what they calls General Knowledge type, meant to expand blokes' minds, see. Well, Garner 'ad a book out, an' it 'appens I see 'im *mark* summat in it. So when 'im an' Sing's got their 'eads down asleep, one time, I takes a dekko through the book, which it's about this 'ere New Forest an' some bloody Rufus Stone, reckoned to be 'istorical, an' there's a map of the Forest, an' what Garner's marked wiv a circle round is a village—Brackenbourne.'

'So you put two and two together,' Raffles said. 'And now, for once in a way, it's added up to five. Five inns!' Thoughtfully, he puffed a cigarette alight over the lamp-chimney. 'Is this fellow Garner still in the Scrubs?'

''E is, guv'nor. Sing got 'is release about two weeks ago. I got out Wednesday. Garner—let's see, now—' The tramp looked suddenly startled. 'Stone the crows, 'e's due out tomorrer.'

'*Is* he now,' said Raffles. 'H'm! Well, my friend, tomorrow I'll take you over to Southampton and see if I can subvert a venal ship's captain for you.'

'God bless yer, guv',' said the tramp. 'It'll make all the difference me bein' under a gentleman's wing.'

'As to that, palm-oil speaks louder than breeding,' Raffles said. 'Thank you, however. Now, for tonight, you can eject the cat from that wicker chair and curl up in it. I'll pin a note to the door here, to let our landlady know there's an unexpected guest in the parlour. I daresay she'll wake you with a cup of early morning tea.'

'I takes sugar in it—two lumps.'

'I'll inform her in the note. Meantime, help yourself to the whisky, make yourself at home—and goodnight to you. Come, Bunny,' Raffles added, to me, 'I have some instructions for you.'

Outside the grim portals of Wormwood Scrubs Prison, in the warm July sunshine of the following morning, a London bobby with his thumbs in his belt paced slowly to and fro, making at each turn the knee-bending movement distinctive to his calling.

At a discreet distance along this Hammersmith street, I was sitting in a hansom with Ivor Kern.

Before dawn, I had cycled from the Emms's cottage to Lyndhurst Road Halt, the little New Forest station that served the Rufus Stone area, and caught the London & South-Western Railway milk train up to the capital. Raffles had taken the wife-beating tramp to Southampton, while I myself, on reaching London, had collected Kern from Chelsea, and we had proceeded here at once to Wormwood Scrubs.

Kern consulted his half-hunter.

'It's close on ten a.m., Manders,' he said. 'What if this Garner fellow's already been released?'

'That would be unfortunate,' I said, 'because Raffles' instructions were that I was to collect you, watch for Garner's release, follow him, find out where he lives. In the event of his catching a train down to the Forest, I'm to wire Raffles at the Emms's cottage and go down on the same train as Garner.'

As I was speaking, a hoof-clop and harness-jingle were growing louder from behind our hansom. A closed carriage, too glossily black to be a hackney cab, rolled by—and I caught a glimpse of the driver's face. It was a bony, impassive, slant-eyed face, saffron-hued under a bowler hat. My breath caught in my throat. The man was Chinese.

'The Limehouse man!' I exclaimed. 'Garner's and the tramp's

173

recent cell-mate! Ivor, as sure as fate, that's Sing!'

A short distance ahead and nearer the prison, the four-wheeler came to a standstill. Lean and wiry in a blue serge suit, the driver leaned down sidewise from his box and seemed to be speaking to some person or persons unseen in the carriage. Then he straightened up and, his back to us, the horse's reins in his hands, sat waiting.

'Manders,' Kern said softly, 'the Tongs hang out in Limehouse, and that chap looks to me like a Tong hatchetman!'

Almost as Ivor Kern spoke, I saw that a wicket door in the ponderous portals of the prison was opening. A man stepped out. I recognised him at once, from the tramp's description, as the letter-eater, Garner. Of brutal appearance, he carried his belongings in a brown-paper parcel under his arm. As the wicket door closed, the patrolling bobby looked Garner over and, bending his knees officiously at him, made some remark. In reply, the released prisoner hawked insultingly and spat on the cobbles. Then he noticed the waiting four-wheeler. He stared at it for a moment, then approached it.

'Well, chase me up a gum tree,' he said, 'if it ain't the unscrewable Oriental! What's this, then? Think it 'ard on a bloke not to be met what's bin a victim of a cryin' injustice? Borrowed yer employer's kerridge, Sing, to meet an old chum an' drive 'im 'ome in the style 'e'd be accustomed to if 'e 'ad 'is rights?'

Sing was nodding, all smiles.

'Why, Sing,' said Garner, 'such loyalty is what I likes to see. Me palatial residence is midway between Wapping Old Stairs an' Execution Dock, an' me neighbours' peepers'll bug out when they sees me lollin' in me personal equipage, a-puffin' lordly at me Flor-de-Dindigal cigar. Right you are, Sing—'ome, me lad —an' you shall 'ave a cut off the fatty calf when we gets there.'

With a dignified gesture, he opened the carriage door—and disappeared into the vehicle with a sudden jerk, as though emphatically assisted from within. The door was pulled shut, Sing whipped his horse into a turn, the carriage came clattering back past our hansom.

Thrusting up the trap in the roof, I told our cabbie to follow the carriage.

'Fatted calf, eh?' said Kern cynically. 'There'll be funeral baked meals for Mr. Garner if he doesn't trot out the information his captors want. Typical brainless crook! No sooner out of quod than the Tongs nab him. Manders, I want nothing to do with Limehouse highbinders. You can let me off at the corner of Ducane Road here.'

'Nonsense,' I said. 'Raffles' instructions were to follow Garner.'

To my surprise, our quarry led us, not towards the East End and the opium dens of Limehouse, but, presently, down Exhibition Road into the irreproachable Brompton Road, where the soundless electric broughams of the wealthy glided eerily to and fro, scornful of horse traffic. Here the highbinders' carriage ahead turned off suddenly to the left, then to the right, then rounded a corner into what I knew to be a *cul-de-sac*. I called to our cabbie to drive on past the corner, then I stopped him, paid him, tipped him an extra half-bar for his skilful driving, and, with Kern, hurried back to the corner.

This *cul-de-sac* was one of those that abound not far from Montpellier Square. Taking a cautious look round the corner, I saw that, to either side, were sunny little back gardens. Across the dead end were green-painted double doors. Before these, the highbinders' glossy carriage stood stationary. Sing had alighted and was unlocking the doors.

As he opened them, I glimpsed the small yard of the kind of private coach-house which abounded in this pleasant district. Sing, afoot, led horse and carriage into the yard, then ran to shut the doors; I heard bolts drop, rattling, into their sockets.

'Come on, Ivor,' I said.

We hurried along the *cul-de-sac*, opened the gate of the little garden just to the right of the doors, slipped through the gate, and crouched down behind a big fuchsia bush in purplish-crimson bloom.

'What d'you plan to do?' Kern muttered.

'We know Garner's in there,' I said. 'We'd better watch those doors.'

From the street at the open end of the *cul-de-sac* sounded an occasional clip-clop of hoofs as a vehicle passed. Bees bumbled in the flowers around us. It was hot. Suddenly I heard again a rattle of bolts. The coach-yard doors opened. Two men appeared on the threshold.

To my surprise, they were not orientals. Big men, solidly built, they wore tweed caps and long white dustcoats. The slightly shorter but bulkier man took off his cap to mop beads of sweat

175

from a large, pink, hairless head. Replacing his cap, he beamed genially at his harder-featured companion.

'Sing's a good lad, squire,' I heard the pink man say. 'He keeps his ears open for his employers—even when he's in quod. I'll raise his wages one of these days.'

'If he'd been quicker in the uptake, a few months back,' growled the hard-featured man, 'we'd have made a good haul, Flood, and he wouldn't have been caught and landed himself in quod.'

Kern's fingers bit into my shoulder, as he breathed in my ear, 'I know these men!'

Peering through the fuchsia blossom, I saw the pink man produce a leather cigar-case from his dustcoat pocket.

'That fiasco was just the rub o' the green, squire,' he said. 'You know your trouble? You brood over the past. It gives you indigestion and makes you surly. You want to be like me —calm and collected at all times, with my head well down and my eye on the ball. Right now, we got one all tee'd up for us. We got the name of the inn out of this Garner fellow, and just where this D'Arzac Coronet's hidden there.'

Kern breathed in my ear, 'Five years ago, I fenced a haul of Georgian silver for the pink fellow.'

I put a warning finger to my lips. Through the fuchsia, the fragrance of good Havana cigar-smoke floated to us, and from the coach-yard came sounds that puzzled me—a kind of metallic cranking followed by popping and gasping noises.

'No need to hurry ourselves,' said the pink man. 'We don't want to reach that village, Brackenbourne, till about midnight, when the yokels there are asleep and all's quiet. We'll take our time on the road down, lunch at some good pub, dine at Winchester. There's a hotel there famous for its lobster mayonnaise and Traminer Riesling. Garner can stay tied up in the coach-house here. If we collect the Coronet from where he claims it is, he gets five per cent of the proceeds—as introduction money.'

'Two-and-half,' growled the surly man.

'We'll call it three,' said his companion—'to make up for the way you knocked him about when we had him in the carriage. You don't realise your own strength at times, squire. You want to be more like me—smooth but firm. Anyway, Balm can stand guard over Garner here till we get back tomorrow.

Balm's a bladder of lard, not fully trained to buttle for us yet, but he's got a gun and knows how to use one. And so do we, if need arises—eh, squire?' beamed the pink man genially, patting a bulge in his dustcoat pocket.

A sudden clattering uproar broke out in the coach-yard. I heard a grinding sound. A vehicle nosed out through the coach-yard doorway. It was an automobile, virtually the first I had seen at such close quarters.

It had high mudguards over its metal-studded anti-flint tyres. The brass rims of its huge carbide headlamps glittered in the sunshine. Sing, who had changed his coachman's bowler hat for the vizored cap of a chauffeur, sat at the vertical column of the steering-wheel. He tugged at the brake-lever on the step of the tonneau. The automobile halted, throbbing with eager but hidden horsepower.

Sing donned goggles as his employers pulled shut and locked the coach-yard doors. The two hefty scoundrels in their travelling dustcoats reversed their caps, so that the peaks were at the back. Adjusting goggles over their eyes, the motorists mounted into their machine, the pink man taking the seat beside Sing, the surly man climbing into the rear of the four-seater tonneau.

Sing released the brake and, with a roar of power, the automobile rolled off along the *cul-de-sac* and turned out of it to the right, causing the horse of a passing milk-float to shy violently, with a clang of falling churns.

As the backfiring of the automobile receded into the distance, bound for the dusty turnpike to Winchester and the New Forest beyond, Kern and I stepped out from our hiding-place into a cloud of acrid vapour.

'Modern crooks, Manders,' Kern said grimly. 'Progress. You can't stop it. We've entered the century of the internal congestion engine.'

I was more shaken by these developments than I cared to show.

'Ivor,' I said, 'I'll wire Raffles, at the Emms's cottage, a full account of the situation, in the private code we use. Then I'll take the first train I can get back to the Forest. You say you know those men?'

'I certainly do,' Kern said. 'Man alive, the pink fellow's come up in the world! Five years ago, he wasn't much more than a "dip"—picking pockets with a big, innocent smile. "Smiler" Bunn, they called him. He's lost his hair but put on flesh, with his hock and lobsters, and a man being trained to buttle for him, and a motor with a chauffeur to drive him about to do the jobs he pulls. And as for the ugly-tempered partner he calls "squire"—he was a fraudulent company promoter. He used to call himself Lord Fortworth, Chairman, on his bucket-shop prospectuses. There was a scandal, his picture was in the papers, he had to disappear for a while.'

Kern gave me a grim look.

'The amazing Mr. Bunn and ex-Lord Fortworth—Easy Street Experts, that combine. Manders—tell Raffles to watch his step!'

When I stepped off the train at Lyndhurst Road Halt that night, Raffles was waiting to greet me.

'So I gather, Bunny,' he said, 'that you've had a disturbing day?'

Clean-cut, hatless, his tweeds impeccable, a pearl in his cravat, he was standing under the dim oil-lamps of the little station in the Rufus Stone area of the New Forest.

'The earliest train I could get out of London,' I said, 'was the six-thirty to Southampton, and I had a maddeningly long wait there for the local to Lyndhurst Road.'

'It's now close on eleven-thirty,' Raffles said. 'Come on! Your borrowed bike's where you left it here with the Stationmaster this morning, and I came on the other bike to meet you.'

'What about the tramp?' I asked, as we pedalled off on the Emms's lampless bikes along the lane through the woodlands.

The quiet here among the ancient trees, darkly brooding under a sickle of horned moon, made the glitter and tumult of London seem strangely unreal. I had a sense of disorientation.

'The tramp was no problem,' said Raffles. 'I got him on to a ship bound for the River Plate. Your coded telegram was waiting for me when I got back to the Emms's cottage.'

'Where are we headed for now?'

'Brackenbourne, of course. Where else?'

'Raffles, there are three of them in this motorist gang, one of them a Tong hatchetman, and they're armed—as we never are. They know the name of the inn. They know where the Coronet's hidden there. They'll get it. Now, I ask you—what earthly chance have we got of wresting it from them?'
178

'There's a principle, Bunny, which I've found to be sound in practice.'

'What principle?'

'Just to take things as they come,' said Raffles. 'By the way, did you get a newspaper to read in the train?'

'I had other things on my mind.'

'Then you missed something—an announcement, Bunny— the engagement of Philippa Morton to Major Hector Barron.'

'Then it was probably *he* who stole the Coronet!'

'No, Bunny. He's a Lancer.'

'What difference does that make?'

'A significant difference, Bunny. Garner's brother, the batman-groom, glimpsed "something green" at the moment a "sparkling object" was thrown from a window of The Moot Hall. What he glimpsed, almost certainly, was the sleeve of the thrower. But, Bunny, a Lancer's mess-jacket, like his uniform, is scarlet. The only man wearing green at the Hunt Ball was Captain the Marquess of Stoneycross—in the bottle-green mess-jacket of the Rifle Brigade.'

'Good God!' I exclaimed.

'The D'Arzac Coronet,' said Raffles, 'is reputed to bring misfortune. It certainly hasn't brought the noble Marquess much luck. His chivalrous theft has done him no good. It's the Lancer who's won the lady.'

'Then be warned, Raffles, be warned! The Coronet can prove as unlucky for us as for the Marquess.'

'Surely you aren't superstitious, Bunny?'

'As Habbakuk Hooper told us, Raffles—De Quincey says a man with no superstition in him lacks charity of mind.'

'De Quincey's thinking was befogged by opium, Bunny.'

From the dark coverts, a roosting cock pheasant sounded its startled, panic-stricken alarm note as we swept round a bend on our bicycles.

We emerged from the woods. The glimmer of the horned moon sailing on its back among drifting clouds faintly illumined the wide, rolling heaths. Before us, down the slope of the grit road, lay the thatched roofs of Brackenbourne. Not a light was visible in the sprawling village.

'The place has been dark since just after ten tonight,' Raffles said. 'Country folk retire early, Bunny.'

Freewheeling, silent as our shadows speeding along at our

179

side, we raced down the slope. Nocturnal coots piped and splashed restlessly in a pond to the right. We reached the village. Along the road that curved like a strung bow between the squat, thatched dwellings, we pedalled to the church on its small knoll in the village centre beside the green, on which dark lumps faintly visible here and there were recumbent cows chewing their cuds.

I was at a loss to divine Raffles' intentions as he dismounted at the churchyard gate. I followed his example.

'The rude forefathers of the hamlet sleep,' he said, as he opened the gate and wheeled his bicycle in among the lichened tombstones. 'Lean your bicycle against a convenient tomb, Bunny—not that winged angel, because her marble pallor suggests she's still fresh from the mason's chisel. Choose an older tomb whose inmate is too far gone to care. Now, then—from here in the churchyard, among these rather lugubrious yews, we can see each way along the village street. As we aren't actually *in* the church, I think we might steady our nerves with a Sullivan apiece.'

He gave me a cigarette, held a match-flame in cupped hands to it. His hands were steady. Not so were mine. Lighting his own cigarette, he held the match-flame to a mossy tomb-slab on which lay a short ladder.

'We can sit on this slab,' he said. 'But no—on second thoughts, we'd better not. We'd be sitting on our friend Habbakuk's ancestors. It says here "To the memory of Ebenezer Hooper, died 1803, Huntsman to King Rufus's Foxhounds, and his Spouse, Abigail, died 1812. *For the race is not to the swift, nor the battle to the strong.*" H'm, maybe that's a good omen for you, Bunny—as you're so superstitious.'

'Shh!' I said. 'Look!'

The match went out. Far off beyond the green where the cows munched with occasional ruminative lowings, a light moved. Surmounting a swell in the road away off there, the light became the sudden, lilac glare of carbide headlamps lancing out over the heaths. Almost simultaneously, the clock of the steeple soaring above us began mellowly to chime.

'The witching hour,' said Raffles. 'Punctual, aren't they—the amazing Mr. Bunn and Company. Here they come, armed to the teeth—the strong, travelling fleetly in their swift chariot.'

The midnight chimes, vibrating above our heads, drowned

180

for us the throbbing of the approaching automobile. Its headlamp-glare swept round like a scythe on to the road which dipped down to the village—and vanished. And the last chime struck. Now all was still.

'They've pulled up on the slope,' said Raffles. 'They evidently intend to come into the village on foot, so as to make no noise.'

I strained my eyes along the village street. Clouds, slow drifting, obscured the sickle moon. A pony whickered in the distance and was answered from nearby. Unshod hoofs came tapping briskly along the village street. Shadowy, three Forest ponies trotted past the churchyard gate and vanished on to the green, where a cow lowed a soft inquiry to them.

Moonlight began to return, spectral. Cloud shadows stole over the low roofs. We trod out our cigarettes—and my heart jumped as I saw, far along the sleeping street, a pencil of light ray upward and, almost instantly, vanish.

'Can you make them out?' I whispered.

'Very faintly,' said Raffles—'three figures. There's their light again.'

I saw it, too—directed upward for an instant, then gone again. Vaguely then, as the moonlight strengthened a little, I discerned them—two bulky figures in pale dustcoats, and a dark-garbed, more slender figure.

'The Chinese chauffeur,' I whispered.

'He seems to be unfolding something, Bunny. I think it's an extendable ladder. Yes, he's propping it against the inn there—at the angle of the thatched eaves. He's going up the ladder.'

'To enter through one of those little casement windows under the eaves, while his employers stand guard—London crooks, Raffles, goggled men with guns!'

'No, I see what's happening,' said Raffles. 'Come on!'

Mystified, I saw Raffles pick up the short ladder which lay on the Hooper tomb-slab. Carrying the ladder in one hand, wheeling his bicycle with the other, he moved away between the yews, the grassy mounds, the sepulchral monuments, ancient and recent. I followed, wheeling my bike.

We emerged from the churchyard by another gate, on the side away from the motorist marauders. The bend in the village street hid them from our view. We mounted, riding away from the Bunn Gang. About a couple of hundred yards on, Raffles dismounted. So did I.

'Hold my bike, Bunny!'

While I held the bikes, Raffles propped the ladder against the eave-angle of the inn here. Clouds obscured the moon as he mounted the ladder. He seemed to be thrusting something up into the thatch. A sound of steady snoring was audible from a small window, latched open on this warm night, close under the eaves. Something fell, soundless, from the thatch. Peering down, I made out a last year's bird's-nest.

Raffles came down the ladder.

'Now, Bunny—we'll detour round over the green and regain the road about halfway up the slope.'

It was bumpy pedalling, Raffles carrying the ladder, lamp-lighter style, on his shoulder, but we reached the road at a point about fifty yards above the pond where the restless coots piped and splashed.

As we pedalled on strenuously up the slope of the grit road, we came upon the Smiler Bunn gang's automobile, drawn up with its lights off at the roadside. Raffles dismounted from his bicycle, gave it to me to hold, and laid down the ladder.

He climbed on to the step of the automobile, gripped the steering-wheel, turned the front wheels to a slight angle. Stepping down, he released the brake-lever on the step of the tonneau. He gave the automobile a push that set it moving slowly down the slope.

'These things,' he said, 'make this new century a menace to every pony, deer, pheasant, rabbit and hedgehog wandering free in this Forest—and the creatures were here first.'

The automobile, jolting over the potholes and beginning to gather speed, was travelling at a shallow angle aslant across the road. Raffles picked up the ladder and, remounting our bicycles, we pedalled on up the slope.

All of a sudden, from behind us, sounded a considerable splash, followed by scandalised ejaculations from the coots.

We gained the woodland at the top of the slope and within ten minutes stole quietly into the parlour of the Emms's cottage. Raffles turned up the lamp-wick. The cat purred at us from the wicker chair. The spirit-tantalus and a plate of sandwiches awaited us on the table. The casement window was latched wide open to the fragrance of flowers from the garden.

'What the devil,' I burst out, still breathing hard from our ride, 'was the idea of planting something in the thatch of an

182

inn the Bunn gang has no reason to go to?'

Raffles, taking the whisky-decanter from the tantalus, looked at me in surprise.

'Why, Bunny,' he said, 'at about half-past ten tonight, when Brackenbourne had bedded down, I cycled quietly through the village with Mr. Emms's ladder on my shoulder. As Habbakuk Hooper remarked to us, the inn signs he painted with his talented brush are of modest and uniform size. I found it quite easy to lift them from their hooks and deal the pack afresh.'

'Deal it *afresh*?'

'No problem at all, Bunny. So, naturally, as the motorist gang was judging by the inn signs, whichever inn they went to was bound to be the wrong one. Then I only had to watch what they did at the wrong one—and I knew what to do at the right one. I left the ladder in the churchyard, in case it might come in useful again, then cycled over to Lyndhurst Road to meet you.'

I stared at him.

'The Bunn gang put up their ladder at what they thought, from the sign, was The Laughing Cavalier,' said Raffles, 'but actually it was The Masterman Ready. Mr. Bunn, the motorist, may be called "Smiler", but the real smile is still, as it's been for centuries, on the features of Mynheer Franz Hals's immortal Cavalier.'

'Good God, Raffles!' I said.

'Planting?' said Raffles. 'Why, no, Bunny. Emulating the action of the motorist gang's chauffeur at the wrong inn, I wasn't planting something, I was groping in the thatched eaves of the right inn for something already planted—by Garner's batman-groom brother on the night of the Hunt Ball, as he hastily packed his own and his officer's kit in the inn bedroom just to the left of the eave-angle. Plant, Bunny? You and I don't plant. We reap.'

He took from his pocket a red bandanna handkerchief, unfolded it on the table. And there it was—the Norman coronet, a circlet of heavy gold crusted with precious stones. They dazzled my eyes.

'Oh, dear God!' I breathed, my feelings strangely mixed.

The decanter glugged as Raffles poured whisky.

'An exhilarating hunt, Bunny,' he said—'from stirrup-cup to nightcap. Of course, this Forest called New is very old. And

183

when it's found that the five inns of Brackenbourne have changed names in the night, and a newfangled menace to man and beast is discovered mysteriously bogged in the coots' pond, no doubt there'll be loose talk among the rustics about the Forest's guardian spirits being at work on a night when a horned moon rose over the Rufus Stone.'

Raffles laughed.

'But you and I,' he said, 'are Londoners. Whatever De Quincey may say under the influence of opium, superstitions and omens and legends of misfortune have no meaning for the likes of *us*, Bunny. So why are you looking at the D'Arzac Coronet with such a peculiar expression?'

I was about to answer when, silently, ghost-pale out of the night, an apparition materialised at the open window.

The words froze in my throat.

For an instant, from the sill, a great white owl with a field-mouse struggling feebly in its beak stared in at us with huge eyes glowing green, enigmatic and blind in the lamplight.

Then the wide wings spread. The owl floated away, soundless.

Neither Raffles nor I moved.

A breeze rustled, stealthily, through the glades of the Forest.

## 11    THE *BASKERVILLE* MATCH

'I wonder if by any chance, Mr. Raffles, you're one of that now world-wide fraternity of perceptive persons who devote admiring scholarship to the unique cycle of detective tales created by Dr. A. Conan Doyle?'

The question was tossed at A. J. Raffles by Mr. Greenhough Smith, the brilliant Editor who, thanks principally to the detective tales mentioned, had made *The Strand Magazine* England's most successful monthly periodical.

On this morning in early Spring, a watery sun cast its anaemic beams through the two large windows of Mr. Smith's editorial sanctum in Southampton Street, just off the Strand, the busy London thoroughfare from which the magazine derived its name.

Mr. Smith had invited Raffles, who was generally expected to be appointed captain of the England cricket team for the coming season, to contribute an article on aspects of leadership at the game, and Raffles, dropping in on Mr. Smith to discuss the article, had brought me along with him.

Remembering how, a decade or more ago, when Dr. Doyle had been just an obscure general practitioner in the naval town of Portsmouth, Raffles and I had had an encounter with Dr. Doyle, and nearly gone to prison as a result, I considered a visit to *The Strand Magazine* office the height of imprudence. For, in the intervening years, Dr. Doyle had become the magazine's most famous contributor, and, considering what he had found out about us at Portsmouth, my mind boggled at the mere possibility of our coming face to face with him in the office of the magazine.

But Raffles had dismissed my misgivings.

'It's not every cricketer, Bunny, who's invited to write about the game for the country's best magazine,' he had said, 'so I think it's worth the risk.'

For my part, when Mr. Greenhough Smith, after agreeing terms with Raffles for the cricket article, asked his sudden question, I felt extremely uncomfortable—though Raffles himself, at ease in a saddlebag chair, coolly replied, 'Why, yes, Mr. Smith— my friend Manders here and I can claim, I think, to be students of the saga from its earliest days.'

'You may be interested, then,' Mr. Smith said, 'to note this big basketful of letters on my desk. They're just a small part of the mail that's been flooding in from readers of Dr. Doyle's latest tale, *The Hound Of The Baskervilles*. It's the twenty-sixth published adventure of Dr. Doyle's great fictional creation.'

'Whom, so very surprisingly,' Raffles said, 'Dr. Doyle, for reasons best known to himself, hurled to his death, some years ago, in an Alpine maelstrom.'

'A most unhappy decision of Dr. Doyle's!' exclaimed Mr. Smith. 'And unfortunately, this new tale he's given us doesn't signify that he's repented of his decision and somehow explained away the reported death of his great detective. No, this new tale, *The Hound Of The Baskervilles*, pre-dates the melancholy event in Switzerland. However, this new tale is fresh from Dr. Doyle's

185

pen—and the response, from readers, has been quite overwhelming.'

'So I see,' said Raffles, glancing at the basketful of letters.

'The first instalment of the *Baskerville* tale,' Mr. Smith said, 'appeared last year in our issue of *The Strand Magazine* for August 1901. Its eighth and final instalment is in our current issue—practically vanished already from the bookstalls. Have you been following the tale?'

'Who hasn't?' said Raffles. 'Manders and I consider it quite the most enthralling of Dr. Doyle's great detective series.'

'An opinion, to judge from these letters,' Mr. Smith said, 'concurred in by most readers—with one extraordinary exception.'

The hoof-clop and jingle of traffic was faintly audible from the bustling Strand, nearby, as Mr. Smith, a rather pale, moustached man of intellectual appearance, polished his glasses and frowned at a letter which lay open before him on his blotting-pad.

'You know, gentlemen,' he said, 'Dr. Doyle was asked once if he'd based his incomparable detective on any real-life original. He replied that he had had in mind a preceptor of his days as a medical student at Edinburgh, a certain Dr. Joseph Bell. On being told of Dr. Doyle's remark, Dr. Bell smiled. He said that Dr. Doyle's kind remembrance of his old teacher had made much of very little—and that in fact the *real-life* counterpart of Dr. Doyle's famous fictional detective is, of course, Dr. Conan Doyle himself.'

Raffles and I had known this great truth long before Dr. Bell. It had been revealed to us, to our peril, at the time of our encounter with Dr. Doyle at Portsmouth, when he had published only one tale, *A Study In Scarlet*, of the unique detective saga which subsequently had become popular from pole to pole.

And here now, in Mr. Greenhough Smith's editorial sanctum, twenty-five of Dr. Doyle's detective tales later, the conversation was taking a turn that made my palms moisten with embarrassment.

I found it increasingly disquieting.

'Of late,' Mr. Smith was saying, 'Dr. Doyle's own quite exceptional investigative ability has been concentrated on an urgent real-life problem—a problem of slander—in this new century in which we find ourselves. As you may know, on the success of his detective tales, Dr. Doyle abandoned medicine for literature.

186

But when this wretched war with the Boers broke out, he temporarily forsook literature to return to medicine—in order to serve in South Africa with the Langman Field Hospital. That photograph of him was taken at the time.'

Among the framed drawings and signed photographs on the walls of Mr. Smith's sanctum was the original, I saw now, of a Sidney Paget illustration for *The Hound Of The Baskervilles.* The illustration depicted Dr. Doyle's great detective, in deerstalker cap and Inverness cape, firing his revolver at the apparition of a gigantic hound charging with lambent eyes and slavering, phosphorescent jaws out of the fog of a Dartmoor night.

Beside this illustration of the fictional detective hung a photograph of his creator, who had unmasked Raffles at Portsmouth so long ago. There he was again, Dr. A. Conan Doyle, in the photograph—a big, burly, bushy-moustached man, wearing khaki fatigues and a sun-helmet and smoking a Boer curved pipe as he stood, a stalwart, uncompromising figure, against a background of hospital bell-tents on the parched South African veldt.

'That hospital camp was at Bloemfontein,' said Mr. Smith. 'I believe Mr. Raffles, you saw active service in South Africa yourself. You may have met Dr. Doyle out there?'

'Manders and I,' Raffles said, 'served in a different sector.'

'Bar some continuing guerilla activity here and there,' said Mr. Smith, 'an armistice prevails. A full peace treaty is expected to be announced any day. Meantime, Dr. Doyle has felt it his duty to investigate foreign allegations that the British used dumdum bullets and committed other transgressions. As a doctor who saw a good deal of what went on out there, Dr. Doyle found no evidence to support these allegations. Nor did his researches for the history he's been writing of the war reveal any such evidence. On the contrary, he has good reason to believe that the allegations emanate from tainted sources in Europe with a vested interest in maintaining discord among nations.'

'The traffickers in armaments,' said Raffles.

'Exactly! And as our government,' said Mr. Smith, 'apparently considers it beneath its dignity to take official note of such foreign allegations, Dr. Doyle has undertaken the task of investigation and refutation himself, at great personal expense of time and money. He has, nowadays, a world-wide audience. He feels a duty to it, for he knows that when he speaks it's with a voice to which people have become attuned to listen.'

'He's a great man,' Raffles said quietly.

'He's gathered his documented evidence, in rebuttal of the malicious allegations,' said Mr. Smith, 'in what he calls a "brochure"—in fact, it's almost a full-length book—which he calls *The South African War: Its Cause and Conduct*. Written without fee and printed far below cost by a sympathetic publisher, the volume was issued in this country in January of this year. With the object of financing the translation of the book into many languages and its printing and world-wide distribution at a merely nominal price, a Fund has been opened for the receipt of contributions—'

'A Fund?' Raffles said, his grey eyes alert.

'A Fund,' said Mr. Smith, 'administered by Dr. Doyle's own bank—which is also, you may recall, the bank of his fictional detective: the Capital and Counties Bank, Oxford Street branch. Of course, this great task Dr. Doyle has taken upon his broad shoulders leaves him scant time for fiction. In fact, he tells me that he intends *The Hound Of The Baskervilles* to be, quite definitely, the last tale of his detective cycle. This is bad news, inevitably, for the writers of this basketful of letters. Strange as it may seem to you, I dare not bother Dr. Doyle with them in his present grave frame of mind—which is a pity, because there's one here that—'

A knock sounded on the door, and Mr. Smith called, 'Come in!'

The door opened to admit a tall young man, meticulously frockcoated, with a high, starched collar and clean-cut features.

'My Assistant Editor,' said Mr. Smith, effecting introductions—and he handed the newcomer a set of page proofs. 'You want these for Mr. W. W. Jacobs, no doubt. Very well, they can go off to him now. We mustn't keep humorists waiting. By the way, I was on the point of getting Mr. Raffles' impression of this curious letter from Dartmoor.'

'It's a hoax, Mr. Smith,' the Assistant Editor said firmly. 'It's another humorist at work—an unlicensed one with a warped mind. It'd be a great mistake to bother Dr. Doyle with it in his present mood. A hoax would only irritate him and probably put the seal on his determination to write no more detective tales for us. Gentlemen, if you'll excuse me—'

With a brisk nod to Raffles and myself, the Assistant Editor, obviously under a press of business, left us.

188

'It's likely that he's right about this letter,' said Mr. Smith, as the door closed. 'It came in this morning in an envelope postmarked Bovey Tracey. That's a small town—the "Coombe Tracey" of *The Hound Of The Baskervilles*—on the edge of Dartmoor. No harm in getting a fresh eye cast on this letter. As a man of the world, Mr. Raffles, what d'you make of this screed?'

Over Raffles' shoulder, I read the letter, which had been amateurishly typewritten on a machine with a faded purple ribbon:

Dartmoor,
Devonshire.
27th March 1902

The Editor,
The Strand Magazine,
London.
Sir,

As a resident in the Dartmoor area, scene of *The Hound Of The Baskervilles*, now concluded in the current issue of your magazine, I have read the narrative with particular interest.

Your author, A. Conan Doyle, has based his tale on the case, which occurred in this area in 1677, of Sir Richard Cabell, Lord of the Manor of Brooke, in the parish of Buckfastleigh. This evil-living baronet, notorious for profligacy, had his throat torn out by an enraged hound, which then, according to legend, took on phantom form, to range evermore upon Dartmoor.

Your author has adapted the legend to his own purpose, making the Phantom Hound 'the curse of the Baskervilles' and skilfully using the topography and certain phenomena of Dartmoor to lend his Gothic tale verisimilitude. Among such phenomena mentioned by him are strange nocturnal howlings sometimes heard, as indeed of some hellhound baying the moon. Sceptics attribute these sounds to natural causes—the wind in the rocks of the moorland tors, or the slow upwelling and escape of vegetable gases from the depths of the notorious Dartmoor morasses, such as the one which your author, with dramatic effect, calls 'the great Grimpen Mire', which I take to be in reality the Fox Tor bog.

These sounds and other phenomena mentioned in his tale have never really been satisfactorily explained, and I had hoped, in reading his tale, that your author might advance some interesting theory to account for them. But not so! Instead, I now find that he is content to end his narrative with his fictional detective destroying the 'phantom hound' with five shots from a revolver and proving the beast to be mortal and doctored with phosphorescent paste by an evildoer whose motive is to acquire an inheritance by chicanery and murder.

Now, Sir, I must reluctantly confess to a slight sense of disappointment—which constrains me to narrate a recent experience of my own.

As something of a folklorist, I have cultivated the acquaintance, for the sake of profiting from his unique knowledge of the moor, of a certain local deer-poacher, sheep-stealer, all-around ne'er-do-well. I am, frankly, ashamed of my furtive association with this scoundrel. However, one night not long ago, he came skulking to my back door to tell me that his poacher's sawed-off shotgun had been confiscated, and he begged the loan of my double-barrelled twelve-bore and a handful of cartridges.

I gathered from him that a lurcher-like bitch he owned, a gaunt, rangy, grizzly-grey beast he called Skaur, had for some considerable time been wild on the moor. Trouble was now brewing over slaughtered sheep found half eaten, and other depredations. The police were on the look-out for the culprit. That it was Skaur, under some pressure of particular hunger, my degraded acquaintance was certain, though he had long ago given it out that the bitch was dead and buried. If the police now downed her and proved his ownership, it would certainly mean goal for him, as he could not pay the fines and damages.

He was in such a panic to down Skaur before any policeman or farmer did so that I lent him my gun. About a week later, he appeared at my door again, a profoundly shaken man. He had sighted Skaur, shot at her, crippled her. Following her blood trail, he found her laired among the rocks. She lay panting, bloodstained, with three grizzly-grey whelps so savagely at her dugs that she was like to be eaten while still alive.

As the man crouched, peering into the lair in the failing daylight and howling wind, some instinct made him look round. He swears that, stealing towards him, was a creature, big as a pony, shadowy—some species of diabolical hound.

190

He shot at it, wildly—and the apparition was gone.

The fellow was in such an overwrought state on the night he came to me that it was all I could do to get him, the following day, to take me on the long, rough trudge across some of the worst parts of Dartmoor to the alleged lair.

It exists. Skaur lay there dead, stiff and cold, ripped and torn by her own whelps. Sir, I never have seen on canine pelts such uncanny markings as those on these savage creatures.

I have penned them into the lair and, at great inconvenience to myself, kept them alive. Curious as to their sire, I have maintained long vigils at the lair by day and by night, but have caught no glimpse of the creature described by my disreputable acquaintance, though I have heard on two occasions a distant, grievous, hound-like howling—but no conclusion, of course, can be drawn from that nocturnal phenomenon.

I can devote no further time to this matter. I intend to shoot the whelps. As you will appreciate, I have no desire for my association with my ruffian acquaintance to become known. I must guard my local good repute and, hence, maintain anonymity in this matter.

Nevertheless, I will make this much concession: If your author should wish to view these weird whelps, he should insert forthwith in the Personal column of the daily *Devon & Cornwall Gazette* an announcement to this effect: 'Sirius. Instructions awaited.' There will then be mailed to your office a map of Dartmoor with, clearly marked upon it, the precise location of the lair of the strange whelps. What your author may then choose to do about them, should he look into the matter, will be his responsibility, not mine.

In the event of no announcement appearing, as specified above, by 7th April, I shall carry out the intention I have expressed in this notification.

Meantime, I have the honour to be, Sir,

Yours truly,<br>SIRIUS

'Well, Mr. Raffles?' Mr. Greenhough Smith asked, as Raffles handed the extraordinary communication back to him.

'A hoax, obviously,' said Raffles. 'Eh, Bunny?'

'Undoubtedly, Raffles,' I said.

'How well, Mr. Smith,' Raffles asked, glancing thoughtfully at the wall where hung the illustration of the fictional Consulting Detective and the photograph of his creator and real-life counterpart, 'is Dr. Doyle actually acquainted with Dartmoor?'

'He spent a few days there, researching for *The Hound Of The Baskervilles*,' said Mr. Smith, 'at just about this time last year. He was with his friend, Mr. Fletcher Robinson, of Ipplepen, Devonshire, who knows Dartmoor well. It was Mr. Robinson who, by telling Dr. Doyle of the legend of the Phantom Hound, prompted the writing of *The Hound Of The Baskervilles*—a fact which, as you will see when the tale is published soon in book form, Dr. Doyle gratefully acknowledges in a dedicatory letter to Mr. Robinson.'

Mr. Smith frowned at the letter in his hand.

'You know, I'm sorry, in a way, that you add your vote, Mr. Raffles, to the consensus in the office here that this letter is a hoax. Personally, I must confess to a slight hope that, if I were to let Dr. Doyle see it, it might kindle a spark in his creative mind and result—who knows?—in a sequel to *The Hound Of The Baskervilles*. Editors have such dreams at times. But common sense inclines me to agree with the consensus that votes this letter a hoax. Ah, well!'

With a rueful smile, Mr. Greenhough Smith put the letter reluctantly into a drawer of his desk—and became businesslike.

'Now, Mr. Raffles,' he said. 'About a delivery date for your cricket article—'

A date readily agreed upon by Raffles, we took our leave.

'I suppose that, as usual when you get an invitation to write about cricket, Raffles,' I said, as we sauntered down Southampton Street, 'you expect me, as an occasional journalist, to ghost-write this article for you?'

'Why else, except for you to hear Mr. Smith's briefing for it, would I have brought you with me this morning, Bunny? Innocent appearances in print are useful cover for—less innocent activities. But literary toil's more your cup of tea than mine—though, of course, it'd have been impolitic to mention your spectral function to Mr. Smith.'

'I appreciate that,' I said. 'I'm not complaining. I just feel, seeing that the throes of composition fall on me, that you might have held out for a later delivery date.'

'You'll manage, Bunny,' Raffles said absently. 'Dartmoor air will stimulate your muse.'

192

'Dartmoor air?' I stopped dead. 'Why should we go to Dartmoor?'

Raffles gave me such a grim look as I never had had from him before.

'I think our chance may have come at last to settle an old account,' he said—'by muzzling a dangerous hound.'

Not until next day, when we had a first-class smoking compartment to ourselves in a train bound for Devonshire, did Raffles explain his reasoning to me.

'Dr. Conan Doyle,' he said, 'is a man it's impossible not to respect. I respected him when we had that humiliating encounter with him at Portsmouth so long ago. There's been a sore on my self-respect ever since, and everything I've subsequently heard or read about or by him has increased my esteem for the man, and made that sore fester. Every cubit he's added to his stature has diminished me in my own eyes. I've asked myself a thousand times how I could square my reckoning with him, and forget what happened at Portsmouth—and turn the page. I had an odd feeling, Bunny, that some opportunity might arise out of this invitation to write for the magazine with which he's so prominently associated. And I think it's happened! I think our chance has come to do that great man a service. If we can, and even if he should never know of it, I'd feel—in my own mind—that I'd done something to balance my score with him.'

A heavy shower lashed the windows of the speeding train. I did not like this mission we were on. I had a premonition of disaster.

'Surely, Raffles,' I said, 'in this *Baskerville* matter, we'd do better to let sleeping dogs lie.'

'Bunny, I feel pretty sure that the dog behind that "Sirius" letter is not sleeping. He's very wide awake. I think that that letter's an attempt to set a trap. I think "Sirius" is a running dog of those "tainted sources" who'd like to stop the translations and world-wide distribution of Dr. Doyle's book disproving their mischief-making slanders.'

'Oh, dear God!' I said.

'Dr. Conan Doyle, Bunny, carries that entire project on his own shoulders. Remove him, in some way that would appear mere accident, and the project would die on the vine—and, incidentally, there would indeed be no more tales of—'

193

'But, Raffles,' I said quickly, 'surely Dr. Doyle, with his great investigative ability, would be as quick as you are to scent a trap in that "Sirius" letter.'

'Of course he would, Bunny. And precisely because Dr. Doyle is the man he is, would he not do what his fictional *alter ego* would do—that is, investigate this "Sirius" in order to establish and expose the identity of his paymasters?'

I could not deny it. I swallowed with a dry throat.

' "Sirius" thought, of course,' Raffles said, 'that his baited letter would be passed on immediately to Dr. Doyle. "Sirius" couldn't know what *we* know, Bunny, which is that Mr. Greenhough Smith would be in two minds about it—a not infrequent editorial predicament. That's why I added my vote, such as it is, to the office consensus that the letter's just a hoax. *We* don't want Dr. Doyle to be shown that letter—because it may give us a chance at last to square our reckoning with him *by trapping his would-be murderer.*'

My scalp tingled. The train rat-tatted along, vibrating, through the wind-blown rain of a day that was growing increasingly inclement the further we went westward.

Raffles offered me a cigarette from his case.

'Consider,' he said, 'what's probably happened. Assume we're right and that "Sirius" is a man briefed for a mission to silence the authoritative voice of Dr. A. Conan Doyle. Seeking ways and means to get at him, "Sirius" studies Dr. Conan Doyle's detective tales—as I have, from a quite different motive. "Sirius" reads *The Hound Of The Baskervilles*—with its vivid descriptions of the bogs, fogs and other natural hazards of Dartmoor. Where more likely, thinks this murderous running dog, for Dr. Doyle to meet with a fatal accident than amid the scenes of his own tale —if only, somehow, he could be lured there?'

'I see your point, Raffles,' I had to admit.

'It seems likely, Bunny, that the idea of a Dartmoor trap began to shape in the mind of "Sirius" as he finished his reading of *The Hound Of The Baskervilles*—the end of which, he had the impudence to say, "disappointed" him. Now, it's highly improbable that the man is, in fact, a Dartmoor resident. So what would he do?'

'Presumably,' I said, 'he'd reconnoitre the area himself, to decide just where and how he could best contrive a trap there.'

'Sound thinking, Bunny. What's more, old boy, he'd want to

194

find out just how familiar Dr. Doyle really is with the area. "Sirius" would probably make discreet inquiries in the neighbourhood, to find out if Dr. Doyle had personally explored Dartmoor and, if so, how extensively. So, then—what are you and I to look for?'

'An inquisitive stranger!'

'Asking questions in a sparsely populated area—within, probably, not much more than the past week or two, because the current issue of *The Strand* containing the last instalment of the *Baskerville* tale only became available about then. No, Bunny,' Raffles said, ' "Sirius" shouldn't be hard to find.'

He tapped ash from his cigarette.

'As Mr. Greenhough Smith told us, Bunny, Dr. Doyle did in fact visit Dartmoor almost exactly a year ago. So if we can find out who's been sniffing, just recently, to pick up that year-old scent, we'll have discovered the real-life "diabolical hound" of Conan Doyle—*"Sirius"*. And here, by the look of it,' Raffles added, 'is our first glimpse of the moor coming up.'

The daylight was fading. Bleak hills swept by wind and rain loomed in the distance—the outlying bastions of Dartmoor with its sombre tors and insidious quagmires, its neolithic hut circles and notorious prison.

As I peered through the rain-running window at those brooding sentinel hills, an eerie foreboding possessed me.

After changing to a local train, Raffles and I arrived that night at Lydford Station and put up at an inn near Black Down on the edge of the moor.

'Dr. Conan Doyle?' said the landlady, in reply to Raffles' inquiry. 'In these parts about this time last year? No, sir, I don't recolleck any Dr. Doyle.'

'Have you had any visitors during the last couple of weeks?' Raffles asked.

'No, sir, you're the first for many a month. It's early in the year yet. Dartmoor gets visitors in the summer, more. Mostly they likes to see The Sepulchre—which is the tomb of Sir Richard Cabell, 'im as was Lord of the Manor, wenchin' an' carryin' on something dreadful in 'is prime, over Buckfastleigh way. Ended up with 'is throat tore out by the 'Ound that turned diabolical, as is well known in these parts.'

Raffles and I exchanged a glance.

'There's a key'ole in the door of Sir Richard's tomb,' the landlady informed us, 'an' to this day, if you pokes yer finger through, 'is skeleton'll up an' gnaw at it.'

'There are mysteries on Dartmoor, Missus,' Raffles concurred, with a wise look, 'and you'll join us in a nightcap to steady us. What'll you take?'

'Just a small port-and-peppermint,' said Missus graciously.

All next day Raffles was out on the moor on a hired hunter, seeking word of Dr. Conan Doyle's visit to these parts a year ago.

The weather, howling in from the Atlantic, was vile. I was not altogether sorry that my assignment as Raffles' 'ghost' kept me indoors by a cheerful fire in the inn snuggery, working on his cricket article while the equinoctial gale wuthered in the thatched and dripping eaves.

As the wan daylight died and Missus brought the lamp in, lighted it, and drew closed the snuggery curtains against the blustering dark, there still was no sign of Raffles. It was such a night as made it almost possible to believe in the Phantom Hound, a night for it to be abroad, ranging the desolate moor for human prey.

I began to grow anxious.

At last, I heard a ring of hoofs on cobbles and, holding aside the curtain to peer out, saw the gleam of the stable bumpkin's lantern on the puddles of the yard, and Raffles, soaked to the skin, dismounting from his horse.

I heard him, as he came in, shouting to Missus for a sponge-bath and hotwater cans to be carried up to his room.

When he appeared, his tweeds immaculate, Missus set before us on the snuggery table a great sirloin of beef, done to a turn, with floury boiled potatoes, perfectly cooked turnip-tops, rich gravy, and a foaming jug of nutbrown ale drawn from the wood.

Sharpset from his tussle with the weather, Raffles honed the carving-knife briskly on the steel, and, Missus having left us, I asked him how he had got on.

'Not badly, Bunny,' he said, as he began to carve the sirloin, oozing luscious red-brown juice. 'I made a start at Bovey Tracey, where the "Sirius" letter was postmarked, and I struck what we're seeking—the trail behind the tale of *The Hound Of The Baskervilles*. I found that Dr. Doyle's remembered at Bovey Tracey and so's his friend Mr. Fletcher Robinson. Two big, genial, moustached gentlemen exploring Dartmoor for Dr. Doyle's tale of

196

the Hound. They went from place to place in a dogcart driven by a groom.'

'What about "Sirius"?'

'Not a sniff, as yet. I'll get his scent tomorrow, with luck. After you with the horseradish, Bunny.'

Actually, it was not until our fourth night at the Black Down inn that Raffles returned from his explorations with, in his eyes, a glint I knew of old.

'Got him, Bunny! I picked up his scent today at Widecombe-in-the-Moor. I had the luck to fall into conversation with the Vicar there—elderly man, a great admirer of Dr. Doyle's fictional treatment of the local legend of the Phantom Hound and Sir Richard Cabell. The old Vicar told me about a man who'd called at the Vicarage just over a week ago—a tall, lean, mean-eyed individual in black. The Vicar said there was something about the look of the stranger that made him think of some lines the poet Shelley once wrote. The Vicar quoted them to me:

> I met Murder on the way.
> He had a mask like Castlereagh.
> Very grey he looked and grim.
> Seven bloodhounds followed him.

'My God, Raffles!' I breathed.

'Apparently,' Raffles said, 'he told the Vicar he was a book-dealer visiting country houses and would give a good price for any first editions the owners might care to part with—particularly first editions of books by A. Conan Doyle. A pretty good gambit, Bunny, to find out if Dr. Doyle was known to have visited this area.'

'He's "Sirius", for a certainty!'

'But with only *two* bloodhounds following him—you and me, Bunny. And the scent's now hot and rank, because the old Vicar told me he recognised the horse the grey-faced stranger was riding—a hack hired from an inn called Rowe's Duchy Hotel at Princetown.'

'That's where that damnable prison is, Raffles!'

'Yes, the highest point on Dartmoor—Princetown. And we'll shift our base there tomorrow, Bunny, and see if there's room at the inn there.'

In the night, the wind dropped, the weather changed. We hired a dogcart from Missus. Raffles took the horse's reins and, under a leaden sky, we clattered along the lonely, potholed road to Princetown.

An uneasy stillness brooded over the wide moor, with here and there, in its desolation, smooth great patches of green among the rock outcrops and the heather—the deceptive, inviting green of the deadly quagmires. Distant tors loomed up, eccentrically jagged shapes in the distance, out of a growing hint of mist.

Suddenly, on that road, we came upon a dreary procession—a shuffling file of convicts in knickerbockers and tunics and round caps stamped with broad arrows. Under a strong escort of blue-uniformed Civil Guards armed with carbines, the country's born losers in life trudged along with shovels over their shoulders, their heads shaven, their sullen chins sunk on their chests.

'There, Bunny,' Raffles muttered, 'but for the grace of God—'

I touched the wood of the dogcart, devoutly, as we clattered past the dismal platoon. And, coming on lunchtime, there loomed up ahead of us their cheerless abode—the place of a thousand hatreds and revenges, the most notorious of penitentiaries, its great, gaunt complex of buildings towering starkly over the squat little cluster of dwellings, Princetown, isolated in the moor under the gunmetal sky.

'Caution's our watchword, Bunny,' Raffles said, as he reined-in our horse before the long, low, stone-built inn that faced the prison across a plunging dip in the moorland. 'We'll feel out the ground.'

We found the landlord behind his counter in the Bar Parlour. A stout man in his shirtsleeves, with an oiled cowlick of hair, he was polishing the shove-ha'penny board. He gave us good day, and Raffles ordered whiskies-and-soda.

'See any lags on the road?' a voice asked.

We turned from the bar. There was one other customer present, sitting on a settle by the small, diamond-paned window which had potted hyacinths on its sill. Tall, with a look of great physical power, his face bony, with a tight mouth under a small, wax-pointed, drill-sergeant type of moustache, he wore a buttoned-up frockcoat, a bowler hat set square on his head.

'Yes,' Raffles said, 'we saw a group.'

'Being marched in from the stone quarries—at this hour? That means there's fog coming.'

The man drained his tankard, mopped his moustache with a red bandanna handkerchief, stood up and, with a curt nod to the landlord, went out.

Fleetingly, I met Raffles' eyes. He turned to the landlord, invited him to take a drink.

'Thank 'ee, sir—just a small nip o' gin, then, to give me an appetite. You gentlemen on holiday?'

'Snatching a few days from the treadmill,' said Raffles—'like that gentleman, perhaps, who just went out?'

'Well, no, sir, not exactly. That's Sergeant—but I'd better not mention his name, he likes to keep it quiet.' The landlord glanced around, lowered his voice. 'Between ourselves, gents—he's the Man With The Cat.'

I stared. We had come to Dartmoor to see a man about a dog.

'The Man With The Cat?' Raffles said.

The landlord nodded.

'It's not like the bad old days,' he said, 'when it was done 'ap'azard, catch-as-catch-can. We're in a new century now. When a lag's sentenced to corporal punishment nowadays, he has to be flogged as laid down in regulations of Parliament. So the official flogger comes down from the Prison Authorities in London to do it. He brings the Cat-o'-Nine-Tails sealed up proper in hygienic wrappings.'

I gulped my whisky.

'What's more,' said the landlord, 'the Man With The Cat has to do the job within a prescribed time of the lag bein' sentenced, an' lash the skin off the lag's back in the scientific way laid down by Parliament.'

'Progress, landlord,' Raffles said dryly.

'Yes, sir, you see it everywhere nowadays—horseless carriages, and these new germs that are being found for us. We never had them before. We died natural. This Man With The Cat now—he lodges with me for a night or two when he comes down on 'is official business. If he lodges in the prison across the way, the lags seem to smell he's arrived. They catcalls all night. They keeps yowlin' *Miaouw-Miaouw* like a thousand randy toms on the roof.'

'I've heard,' said Raffles, 'that strange nocturnal howlings are sometimes audible on Dartmoor.'

'Yes, sir, you can hear 'em for miles when the lags kick up a shindy to stop the Man With The Cat from gettin' is sleep so as

**199**

to sap his strength. I gets a lodging allowance for him, but I can't say I like the man's personality. He relishes his work too much, for my taste.'

'Landlord,' said Raffles, 'I think we could do with another drink. Is the—Man With The Cat your only guest just now?'

'No, sir, we've one other here. Book-dealer gent. Rides round to country houses, trying to buy old books. Asked me, he did, when he arrived a week or so ago, if I'd 'appened to read the tale about our Phantom 'Ound that's come out in a magazine. Well, I don't get the time for reading, but it so happens we had the writer of it lodgin' here about a year ago—a Dr. Doyle, a big, hearty gentleman who had a Mr. Robinson an' Mr. Baskerville with him.'

*'Mr. Baskerville?'* Raffles and I exclaimed, together.

The landlord chuckled. 'I showed the book-dealer gent our Guest Book, to prove it.' He produced a leather-covered volume from under his counter, moistened his thumb to turn the pages, then showed an entry to us. 'See for yourselves, gents!'

Under the date 2nd April 1901 were two signatures, the first neat and firm and clear, the second a bold scrawl:

A. Conan Doyle, Norwood, London.

Fletcher Robinson, Ipplepen, Devon (and coachman, Harry M. Baskerville)

'How it was, see,' explained the landlord, 'Mr. Robinson brought his own dogcart and coachman. Mr. Baskerville'd drive the two gentlemen here and there on the moor, then wait with the dogcart when they went trampin' off to points they could only get to afoot. Mr. Baskerville took his meals in the kitchen with me an' my family an' staff. He was tickled pink because Dr. Doyle'd asked him if he'd mind bein' raised to the baronetcy and put in a tale as Sir 'Enery Baskerville. We pulled Mr. Basker-ville's leg about it no end, but he had a great sense of 'umour. Act like Sir 'Enery, he would, in the kitchen, an' call us "you peasants"—kept us in stitches, he did!'

'Well, well,' said Raffles. 'This would be of interest to the fraternity of scholars who study Dr. Doyle's great detective tales. Is your book-dealer guest in the house just now?'

'No, he's out. He's out all day, most days, on a horse I hires him. If he ain't back well before dark, by the look of it, he'll get caught in the fog. It comes on awful quick here an' Dartmoor's dangerous in fog.'

'Then perhaps we'd be wise to spend the night here ourselves,' said Raffles. 'Got a couple of rooms?'

'Certainly, sir.'

As soon as we had been shown to our rooms, I joined Raffles in his.

'There's no doubt of it, Bunny,' he said. 'The book-dealer's "Sirius". I want to find his room, take a look through his belongings while he's out.'

Raffles opened the door slightly, listened at the crack, then turned to me.

'Mealtime sounds from downstairs, Bunny. The inn folk are in the kitchen, eating. Now's my chance. Keep watch from that window. If a grey-faced man on a horse rides up, stick your head out of this door and whistle *Drink, Puppy, Drink*.'

He was gone.

As I kept watch through the diamond-paned little window, I thought of the 'Sirius' letter with its stealthy insinuation that some such uncanny creature as had inspired *The Hound Of The Baskervilles* had now sired whelps—and the old hunting ditty of G. J. Whyte-Melville ran weirdly through my mind:

> 'Drink, puppy, drink, and let every puppy drink
>   That's old enough to lap and swallow,
>   *For he'll grow into a Hound—*'

I swallowed with a dry throat. Outside, a creeping mist was beginning to grope its way around the grim complex of prison buildings across the dip in the moorland. In front of the inn our dogcart still stood, the horse brooding morosely into its nosebag. No grey-faced stranger in black had come riding enigmatic out of the mist when, so suddenly that my nerves jumped, Raffles was back in the room.

'It's him, Bunny. I knew his room because it's the only one with a few books in it. There's also a locked portmanteau. I picked the lock with the little gadget I carry. I found in the portmanteau a small Blick typewriter with a faded purple ribbon.'

'That settles it!'

'Yes. What's more, there's also in the portmanteau an envelope containing five sheafs of currency notes, each sheaf a hundred pounds. I dared not take it, of course, for fear of alerting him. There's an Ordnance Survey map of Dartmoor in the portmanteau. I took a look at the map. I could faintly make out the pressure marks left by a pencil when a tracing had been made over the map—and an X marked on it.'

'My God! Could that be the lair of the alleged—"Baskerville Whelps," Raffles?'

'Almost certainly *yes*, Bunny. Because there's also in the portmanteau a copy of the daily *Devon and Cornwall Gazette*—with a small announcement in the Personal column ringed round in pencil: "SIRIUS. Instructions awaited." '

My scalp tingled. 'But that would mean—'

'It can only mean, Bunny,' Raffles said, his eyes hard, 'that the one thing we didn't want to happen has happened. Mr. Greenhough Smith must have been unable to resist showing the "Sirius" letter to Dr. Doyle. Knowing what *we* know of him, I think Dr. Doyle would be *bound* to smell the trap in it. So if he's inserted that announcement, it can only be because he's decided, as we surmised he might, to track down "Sirius" himself, to find out what "tainted sources" are behind him. *But*—that copy of the newspaper is four days old. I checked the date on it.'

Raffles, as he spoke, was searching through his own valise.

'You see the point, Bunny? If the map tracing showing the alleged lair of the whelps was posted to the *Strand Magazine* office on the same day that the announcement appeared in the Devonshire newspaper, the tracing can have reached Dr. Doyle yesterday, or even the day before, assuming normal mail. So he may be on the moor *now*—Dr. Doyle himself—investigating! He may already have trapped "Sirius." '

'Or—been trapped himself?'

'From our encounter with him at Portsmouth, Bunny, I think Dr. Conan Doyle would be a damned hard man to trap!'

Raffles was studying his own Ordnance map, dug out from his valise. Borrowing my pencil, he marked an X on the map.

'There it is, out on the moor, at a spot marked "Neolithic Site", which I take to be akin to Neolithic Hut Circles described by Dr. Doyle in *The Hound Of The Baskervilles*. But this spot seems to be north of the Hut Circles and near what's marked here as Higher White Tor. There's where "Sirius" must have set his trap, Bunny, and where he's probably been keeping vigil over it for at least the past two or three days.'

'Then that's probably where he is at this moment!'

'Bunny, it's where they *both* may be at this moment—stalking each other in this fog that's closing in. There may be *just* a chance that we can take a hand—and settle a reckoning long outstanding to our own self-respect. The dogcart's outside. The map shows Higher White Tor to lie almost due north from Princetown here.'

I hesitated, my heart pounding. 'Raffles, this could bring us face to face with—the Doctor!'

'A return match with him has been steadily on the cards for a good many years now. If it happens at last,' Raffles said grimly—'it happens. Come on!'

With Raffles at the reins, Missus's horse clopped along, now at a trot, now at a canter, along a rough track through the heather, the wheels of the dogcart jolting in ruts and grinding on flint patches.

Mist, slowly deepening over the moor, was taking on the grey tinge that presaged the menace of a Dartmoor blindfolder.

The track, after a while, became impassable for the cart. We left it, trudged on afoot. Loose flints, underfoot among the sparse tough heather, became more plentiful as we went on.

'Debris, probably,' Raffles said, 'of prehistoric flint-knappers— our skin-clad ancestors with the gorilla brows and prominent canines. We must be getting near their settlement.'

Almost as he spoke, from somewhere ahead came a cry that stopped us in our tracks. Again came the pitiful, neighing cry, soared to a despairing screech—and ceased.

'A pony,' said Raffles—'bogged and gone under in some morass and not far off.'

I felt the fumble of blinding vapour dankly chill on my face as we trudged on, peering ahead, up ground, scattered with flint chippings, that rose in a steady slope before us.

Suddenly, Raffles gripped my arm, pulling me down flat beside him.

'Listen,' he breathed.

Listening intently, I peered ahead up the slope, where I could vaguely discern a thickening in the mist—a thickening that I judged to be the remains of an ancient stone wall. We probably had reached the Neolithic site with its ruined evidences, up there on a small tumulus or plateau, of the life of our remote

203

forebears. And I heard a slight crunching sound, as of booted feet.

There was somebody up there—somebody walking around among the ruins.

Crouching, Raffles moved higher up the slope, which grew steeper, like a glacis. I moved with him. Again he gripped my arm, pulling me down flat beside him. Peering up, I could make out now in the mist the rock-edge of the plateau—and the vague form of a man materialised up there, a man in black. His thinness and his height were accentuated by our low-angle viewpoint, so that, with the addition of the stovepipe hat he wore, he had the spidery look of an elongated funeral mute.

'The "book-dealer",' Raffles breathed in my ear—"Sirius".' The lurker wore a cutaway tailcoat, and his long legs encased in riding-boots moved like calipers as he stalked slowly to and fro between the plateau-edge and a ruined hut-wall dimly discernible in the mist. Flints crunched under his boots. A strange figure, this gaunt assassin who had been ranging Dartmoor on a hired horse, sniffing at the year-old trail of the author of *The Hound Of The Baskervilles*.

Patiently, interminably, the man paced to and fro. At last, he moved on, passing out of view around the angle of the hut wall. Careful not to dislodge loose flints or boulders lying among the sparse heather-tussocks of the glacis, we seized our chance to clamber higher—then froze again, flat on our fronts, as Sirius reappeared.

He resumed his slow patrol, to and fro between the hut wall and the plateau edge. We kept low, unmoving, peering up. I could feel the thump of my heart against the ground. Hours seemed to me to pass. Deadly patient, this Sirius, this implacable stalker, who must thus for two, perhaps three days now, have been keeping vigil here over his trap, baited with whelps that never were.

Even as the thought crossed my mind, as I lay here beside Raffles on the glacis in this mist-muffled solitude, utterly silent but for the crunch of the stalker's slow pacing, he stood suddenly still.

For a moment, his head cocked, he seemed to be intently listening. Then he did a thing that sent a chill along my spine.

He threw back his head and howled like a mournful hound.

The weird ululation died away in the mist. All was still, the

204

lurker a macabre figure up there, motionless, listening. And now, faintly, as from the further slope of this tumulus, sounded the hoof-thud and bit-jingle of a horse approaching slowly, at a walk. The sounds ceased. I sensed that the horse's rider had dismounted, was coming on afoot. But I could hear nothing, though I saw the lurking Sirius draw out something from his coat. It was a long-barrelled revolver, and he reversed it, holding it clubbed.

A sudden yelp sounded, a ky-yi-ing as of pain, a sharp bark, snarls and growling. My hair stirred on my scalp. The whelps! I was certain, in that instant, that the sounds emanated from whelps contending, biting fiercely at each other, in a lair among the ruins, but in the next instant I saw that the source of the sounds was not canine, it was the gaunt, eccentric, stovepipe-hatted figure dimly visible there above on the ledge. It was Sirius.

'Bait,' Raffles breathed in my ear—'to draw his man on to look for the lair. As he comes around the hut wall, he'll be clubbed senseless and dragged down for disposal in that mire we heard the pony scream from as it was sucked under.'

'Who comes?' I whispered, through the whelp sounds from above. 'Doyle?'

No answer—for just then, out of the mist-dim ruins of the Dawn Age dwellings, a voice rang, calling:

'Is there anybody here?'

Silence. Then sudden barks, shrill, on a note of challenge and interrogation, as from the hidden lair of the 'Baskerville Whelps.'

Before I sensed his intention, Raffles moved.

He lunged upward at the rock-ledge. He seized the barking man by the ankles, jerked his feet out from under him. The man toppled backward against the hut wall, recovered his balance, tore his ankles free, aimed a vicious kick at Raffles' face, then made a tremendous bound and, revolver in hand, his coat-tails flying, soared clean over the pair of us.

He landed on the glacis, went slithering down it in a cascade of loose flints, and vanished into the mist—as the voice from above rang out again, peremptory:

'Who's there?'

We looked up.

'Who are you?' demanded the man who stood now on the

rock-ledge above us. 'I require an answer.'

The figure looming up, there above in the dank mist, was not the big burly, unmistakable figure of Dr. A. Conan Doyle, but one even better known, a lean, tall figure in Inverness cape and deerstalker cap, a figure whose name I never could bring myself to utter, a figure celebrated throughout the world—and addressing us now with icy authority:

'You see with whom you have to deal. *Speak up!*'

I seemed to feel the frail foundations of human reason crumbling around us as Raffles and I, struck to immobility, crouched there on the glacis, staring up, unbelieving, at that materialised apparition—that hawk-featured figure sprung now to living, breathing reality out of the pages of *The Hound Of The Baskervilles.*

'Incredible,' I heard Raffles whisper, beside me—and he drew in his breath, deeply, as though released from a thrall.

He clambered up on to the ledge and stood erect there.

'Yes, we *have* met,' he said. 'You're the Assistant Editor of *The Strand Magazine.*'

The spell broke. My paralysis left me. My reason restored, with reservations regarding the newcomer's choice of outdoor attire, I clambered up on to the ledge.

Already, Raffles was smoothly explaining that, prompted by our interested reading of *The Hound Of The Baskervilles*, we had decided to spend a few days on Dartmoor while he worked on his cricket article. Visiting this Neolithic site, we had noticed a man here who seemed to be behaving irrationally. We had kept him under observation—and, quite suddenly, he had begun to foam at the mouth and emit canine sounds. Thinking that the poor devil had been seized by a fit of hydrophobia, we had advanced up the glacis to restrain him before he bit himself to the bone, but with the agility of demoniac possession he had sprung clean over our heads.

'Like a veritable stag,' said Raffles. 'Listen!'

We listened. From the mist and somewhere below us sounded the thudding hoofbeats of a horse receding at a gallop.

'There he goes,' said Raffles. 'He must have had that horse tethered down there somewhere.'

'Good God, Mr. Raffles,' said the tall young Assistant Editor, with his cleanly-chiselled features, 'don't you remember that
206

"Sirius" letter Mr. Greenhough Smith showed you? *That's* who the fellow undoubtedly is—"Sirius"! He's no more suffering from hydrophobia than I am—he was *hoaxing*, with his hound howls and whelp-like barkings and whisperings. He's the individual with the warped, elaborate sense of humour that conceived that letter. My God, I wish you could have held him! Dr. Doyle's detective tales have prompted various hoaxes, and it might well have been rewarding to plumb the mentality of a conspicuous example of such hoaxers.'

'Damnation,' said Raffles. 'Bunny, if only we'd realised—eh?'

'*Ah!*' I said, shaking my head.

The Assistant Editor, not best pleased with us, explained that he had judged from the first that the "Sirius" letter was a hoax. In order to prove it to Mr. Greenhough Smith, who still had been in two minds as to whether or not to show Dr. Doyle the letter, the Assistant Editor had persuaded Mr. Smith to let him insert the reply—'Sirius. Instructions awaited'—in the *Devon & Cornwall Gazette*. On receipt by mail of a map tracing marked with the lair of the alleged whelps, the Assistant Editor had come down from London by train, spent the night at an inn, then hired a horse and set out across the moor to locate the marked spot.

'Lucky to find it, with this mist thickening,' he said.

Alert and able as he obviously was, he had not the faintest suspicion that he had come very close indeed to having his skull fractured, in mistake for Dr. Conan Doyle's, and of ending a promising editorial career in the morass that had swallowed the pony.

'I borrowed this deerstalker and cape,' he told us, 'from our famous artist, Sidney Paget, who illustrates Dr. Doyle's detective tales for us. Sidney's brother, Walter, who's also an artist, usually models the chief figure for Sidney. But occasionally, as Sidney says I'm more or less the right build and facial type, he calls on me. It's exciting, in a way, to have a small part in the development of a unique detective saga—just a very *small* part, of course.'

' "They also serve," ' Raffles assured him, ' "who only stand and wait." '

'It's kind of you to say that,' said the Assistant Editor, with a modest laugh. 'Actually, though, it was what gave me the idea of wearing this deerstalker and cape today. I thought that, if the

207

hoaxer should dare to show himself, I'd frighten him out of his wits by suddenly appearing before him as—*the world's Greatest Detective!*'

'Brilliant,' said Raffles. 'But it was Manders and I you scared the wits out of—eh, Bunny?'

Before I could corroborate, in all sincerity, Raffles' remark, the Assistant Editor held up an arresting hand.

'Listen,' he said. 'D'you hear a strange sound?'

We listened. From somewhere remote in the fog still deepening over the wide and desolate moor sounded a weird howl—a prolonged, uncanny ululation. The Assistant Editor's clean-cut face tightened. He looked at us with a haunted surmise.

'Strange sounds,' said Raffles, 'are indeed reported to be heard sometimes on Dartmoor. But if you listen carefully, you may detect that the one we're hearing now is not canine. It's feline. It's coming from the direction of Dartmoor Prison. I think the convicts must just have found out that a visitor has arrived—and they're chanting him their anthem of greeting.'

The anthem, a banshee yowling and catcalling, was hideously audible to me in bed that night at the Princetown inn, where the Assistant Editor, because of the fog, also put up for the night.

At first light next morning, however, the great grim complex of prison buildings was a dark, silent, shadowy tomb of the undead, as Raffles and I set off in Missus's dogcart, to return it to her at the Black Down inn and catch a train from Lydford up to London.

The Assistant Editor, who was to go up to London in the same train with us, was astride his hired horse, trotting along steadily a couple of hundred yards ahead of us. In the bleak, misty daybreak, that mounted figure ahead, lean and tall in Inverness cape and deerstalker cap, fascinated me in the strangest way. I found it hard to keep my eyes off it.

'By the by,' said Raffles, the reins in his hands as we clattered along in the dogcart, 'the yowling from the prison didn't keep the Man With The Cat awake, Bunny. He was certainly building up his strength, snoring like a grampus, when I visited his room in the night.'

'You visited his room?' I said, startled.

'Have a look in my valise, Bunny.'

Mystified, I unstrapped his valise—and took out, in its hygienic

208

wrappings bearing the official seal of the Prison Authority, the Cat-o'-Nine-Tails.

'Good God, Raffles!' I said.

He smiled grimly.

'If sentence must be carried out within a prescribed time of its order, Bunny, and with the specific scourge brought down from London for the purpose, we may have saved some poor sinner a tiresome experience this morning. He's undoubtedly suffered enough, in anticipation. Incidentally, this is the reason I insisted we leave the inn at crack of dawn—before the Cat-fancier wakes up and misses his nine-tailed pet. And there, just ahead on the left,' Raffles added, 'I think I see a small but succulent quagmire. *Whoa*, boy!'

Reining-in Missus's horse, Raffles took a quick look each way along the road, then took the Cat from me and, standing up in the cart, heaved the instrument of chastisement from him, overarm. It arched high through the air, plopped into the quag, remained briefly erect there before, dragged down by its heavy stock, it sank slowly like some sordid Excalibur and, to the accompaniment of a lugubrious gulp, vanished under the green scum.

'So now, Bunny,' said Raffles, as we clattered again on our way, 'having drowned the Cat, we have nothing incriminating on us if there should be a hue and cry. All we have is five hundred pounds in currency notes that, I fancy, will never be missed.'

'What the devil,' I said, 'are you talking about?'

'The five hundred pounds from the portmanteau of "Sirius", Bunny. I visited his room also in the night. He didn't return to the inn. His bed was untouched. We gave him a shock at the Neolithic site. He probably took us for plainclothes men—and decided not to risk going back to the inn but to leave Dartmoor without delay. So I have his five hundred pounds in my pocket.'

But 'Sirius,' it turned out, had not in fact left Dartmoor—as I learned when, three days after we got back to London, I finished at my Mount Street flat the ghost-writing of Raffles' cricket article and took the manuscript round to his chambers in The Albany.

He showed me a brief newspaper item. It stated that, a guest being missing from Rowe's Duchy Hotel, Princetown, a search had been made on the moor. A saddled horse had been found straying. It evidently had had a fall, for further search had led to the finding of the body of its rider, whose identity had not as yet been satisfactorily established. He had a fractured skull.

'That's what comes of galloping a horse in a Dartmoor fog,' Raffles said. 'Not really a clever man, Bunny—certainly not clever enough to have caught Dr. Conan Doyle in a trap, even if he *had* been shown the "Sirius" letter, which he wasn't, and no doubt will never know about. Still, the five hundred pounds exists, Bunny—and, tainted as its source is, we'll use it by way of settling at last a reckoning that has long been owing to Dr. Doyle. True, we haven't directly saved Dr. Doyle's life, but we've certainly been instrumental in removing his would-be murderer —and with five hundred pounds as a material token of the fact, if ever we encounter Dr. Doyle again we can feel that, morally, it's on level terms.'

Myself admittedly a moral lightweight, I marvelled, as often before, at the subtlety of Raffles' personal code, compared with my own simple instinct of self-preservation.

'It's now half-past two,' said Raffles, consulting his gold half-hunter as a hansom carried us, in the Springtime sunshine, to the bank mentioned to us by Mr. Greenhough Smith. 'At two-forty-five, my sister Dinah will be arriving at Paddington Station, from Shropshire.'

'Dinah's coming?' My heart gave a bound of delighted anticipation.

'Yes. I'm taking her to the Continent this evening. Would you care to come with us, Bunny?'

The struggle between my instinct of self-preservation and my secret love for Dinah, to say nothing of my devotion to Raffles himself, was merely momentary—due to my innate weakness of character.

'I should love to come, Raffles,' I said.

'Good,' said Raffles, as the hansom pulled up. 'Then let's get this Conan Doyle matter off our minds, and we'll be free to give serious thought to plans for amassing a worthy dowry for my sister Dinah.'

He told the cabbie to wait, and we walked into the dignified premises of the Capital & Counties bank.

'There is here,' Raffles said to the cashier at the counter, 'the sum of five hundred pounds in currency notes—a contribution to the Fund to finance the translation into many languages, and

210

world-wide distribution virtually gratis, of Dr. A. Conan Doyle's book exposing the evil of slander between nations.'

'Very good, sir,' said the cashier, counting the notes with deft fingers. 'This is, if I may say so, a very handsome contribution indeed.' He glanced up at the wall-clock. 'As it happens, Dr. Doyle himself has an appointment with the manager, in connection with the Fund, and will be arriving very shortly. If you don't know him personally, you might appreciate an introduction to him?'

I felt the marble floor rock under my feet.

'There is no privilege,' Raffles said, his voice seeming far off to me, 'that my friend here and I would appreciate more. Unfortunately, we're on our way to meet a train due in very soon at Paddington Station.'

'What a pity!' said the cashier. 'Ah, well! To whom do you wish this generous contribution attributed?'

'As sincere admirers of Dr. Conan Doyle,' Raffles replied, 'and in the hope that we may one day see a sequel to *The Hound Of The Baskervilles,* my friend here and I would like to honour the gentleman who originally inspired Dr. Doyle to pen that matchless tale.'

I was itching to get out of the bank.

'So attribute this contribution, please, to Sir Richard Cabell, and post the formal acknowledgment,' said Raffles gravely, 'to his country seat—The Sepulchre, Parish of Buckfastleigh, Dartmoor, Devon.'

Having thus arranged for the bank's acknowledgment to be sent to a baronet who had been dead since 1677 and whose skeleton, if legend held good, was liable to up and gnaw the delivering postman's finger, Raffles took a courteous leave of the cashier and, much to my relief, we walked out into Oxford Street.

Just as we took our seats in the waiting hansom, another cab drew up.

Dr. Conan Doyle stepped out.

Tall, burly, bushy-moustached, wearing frockcoat and silk hat, a gold watch-chain looped across his white waistcoat, his manner preoccupied, he tossed pipe-smoke vigorously back over his shoulder as he strode into the Capital & Counties Bank—without a glance in our direction.

A strange notion occurred to me.

211

'Raffles,' I said, 'I wonder if he's *really* given us a single thought since—what happened at Portsmouth?'

Raffles' expression was meditative.

'Your guess is as good as mine, Bunny. Our reckoning with him, which we've now squared, dates back to twenty-five of his detective tales ago—twenty-five permanent milestones to mark, so far, his road through life. We've had to do with some interesting men in that time—John L. Sullivan, Robert Louis Stevenson, poor Oscar Wilde, promising young Winston Churchill. All of them Men Who Count—or may do. But there can be no question about Dr. Arthur Conan Doyle—a great man, a Man Who Counts, and always will—a greater man, Bunny, than you and I can ever be. And who can tell? He may decide to resurrect, from the maelstrom of that Swiss ravine, his unforgettable Other Self—some day, perhaps,' said A. J. Raffles.

But today was today.

And this day, for me, this day as ever was, held now no cloud, for we were jingling off in the hansom along busy, sunny Oxford Street to join Raffles' sister Dinah—the thief with grey eyes, who, the very first time that I met her, had stolen my heart.

# INQUEST FOR UMPIRES

In estimating what degree of credibility may reasonably be accorded to the clandestine Manders Papers, recently discovered, a selection from which is included in the present volume, the following points may be of possible relevance:

*The* Victory *Match:*
H.M.S. *Victory*, fully restored at the instigation of Sir James Caird, and now preserved in dry dock, can still be visited at Portsmouth, and the uniform stained with the lifeblood of Admiral Lord Nelson may be viewed today in the National Maritime Museum, Greenwich.

Due, presumably, to the official ban of silence referred to in Mr. Manders' narrative, no biography of Conan Doyle makes mention of the *Victory* crime, but the handwriting and signature of Dr. Doyle's friend, Mr. Watson, Secretary of the Portsmouth & Southsea Literary & Scientific Society, exist to this day in the Minute Book of that Society.

*Tusitala And The Money-Belt:*
Although, in Mr. R. L. Stevenson's letters to *The Times* from Vailima, protesting against the provisions of the Berlin Convention of 1890, brief mention is made of unexplained dynamite found under the old Apia Jailhouse during the incarceration of four village Chiefs at the height of the Samoan Crisis, not until Mr. Manders' narrative became available has some measure of light been thrown upon this mystery of a bygone Age of Imperialism. In later years, the Tattooed Man became a familiar, though always bizarre and mysterious figure on the waterfront of Tai-o-Hae, the capital and port of entry of the Marquesas Islands.

*Dinah Raffles And Oscar Wilde:*
Subsequent to the events described by Mr. Manders in his narrative, Oscar Wilde does in fact appear to have sojourned briefly at the Villa Giudice, Posilippo, where he revised *The Ballad of Reading Gaol* for an edition published later under his own name.

Aubrey Beardsley, who illustrated so much of Wilde's work, died at the age of 24, shortly after the meeting described by Mr Manders.

In the Père Lachaise cemetery, Paris, on the memorial carved for Wilde by Jacob Epstein, which caused yet another scandal, appears Wilde's self-composed epitaph containing the line: 'And alien tears will fill for him Pity's long-broken urn.'

*The* Baskerville *Match:*

In general there is a paucity of dates in the Manders Papers. One of the few specified is that of Dr. Doyle's sojourn with Mr. Fletcher Robinson at Rowe's Duchy Hotel, Princetown. This date, as it happens, is corroborated by Mr. John Dickson Carr in his superb *Life of Sir Arthur Conan Doyle.* As for Conan Doyle's use of the name of Mr. Fletcher Robinson's coachman, Harry M. Baskerville, this is corroborated by the eminent scholar of Dr. Doyle's great detective stories, the late Mr. William S. Baring-Gould.

Research in the files of *The Strand Magazine,* of revered memory, has failed to disclose an article attributed to A. J. Raffles on the subject of Cricket Captaincy. No doubt this article, which Mr. Manders claims to have ghost-written, ended up in the wastepaper basket of *The Strand*'s highly discriminating Editor, the late Mr. H. Greenhough Smith, for the reason that A. J. Raffles did *not* in fact captain the England XI during the 1902 season.

He seems to have played in no first-class cricket at all in 1902, for his name is absent from cricket journals of the time. Ironically enough, Dr. A. Conan Doyle himself is recorded as having played a notable innings at Lord's that year for a strong M.C.C. side.

On the evidence available, it seems reasonable to suppose that A. J. Raffles, in company with his sister Dinah and the irretrievably involved Mr. Manders, must have spent most of the year in question frequenting distinguished European social circles in furtherance of his plans for amassing Dinah's dowry.